THE SHEPHERD OF THE STARS

THE STAR OF ATLANTIS SERIES
BOOK 3

TRICIA D. WAGNER

LYRIDAE BOOKS

PRAISE FOR TRICIA D. WAGNER

"*With its juxtaposition of supernatural intrigue, mystery, and personal evolution, The Shepherd of the Stars represents a heavy draw for readers. Tricia D. Wagner creates a fine young adult read that builds on Swift Kingsley's story in the Star of Atlantis series, yet proves accessible to newcomers. Libraries that choose this story for its powerful adventure components will find so much more in a tale that spins off additional insights into friendships, trust, healing, and self-empowerment.*"
- D. Donovan, Senior Reviewer, *Midwest Book Review*

"*The Shepherd of the Stars is a must read, a thoughtful and immersive coming-of-age story that will resonate with young adult readers and adults alike. Readers of all ages will appreciate the intensity of the feelings observed in Swift as he struggles to make sense of the new world in which he has emerged.*"
- Mary R. Lanni, MLIS, *Reedsy Discovery*

READ THE STAR OF ATLANTIS SERIES!

The Strider and the Regulus, The Star of Atlantis & The Shepherd of the Stars

A starry-eyed boy.
A cryptic map. A mythical treasure.
What perils await in the chasing of dreams?

"Wagner has a beautiful and poetic writing style which serves to enhance the descriptive detail she provides to her novels. This gives her books a whimsical and otherworldly quality that supports the fantastical elements within them. Readers who appreciate thoughtful narratives that focus on the human condition within the context of charming and memorable stories will quickly fall for this series and its immersive quality. The medical and scientific elements found within this book help readers puzzle out the question of what is true in Swift's world alongside the legend and lore. This is a satisfying series that will speak to young adult readers and adults alike."
- Mary R. Lanni, MLIS, *Reedsy Discovery*

"As Swift lives up to his name and his family legacy, young adults receive a fast-paced fantasy that will appeal not just on the adventure or fantasy levels, but in matters of the heart as the young struggle for independence and action in the face of parental restrictions. Tricia D. Wagner's attention to pairing psychological struggle with the adventure of finding a promised treasure creates a story that pulls on the emotions of young readers as it satisfies their desire for action and adventure."
- D. Donovan, Senior Reviewer, *Midwest Book Review*

This book I offer to the muse
in all its forms.
But mostly to Swift and those to come—
these shadows fully fleshed in mind—
I and they like family
torn asunder,
then brought home.
Thank you for the moments close
of whispering your legends.

*Their shapes,
their burrs and branch stumps and rootstocks
are a living record of what has happened to them historically.
In their maturity, trees are so etched with experience
that they become recognizable
not just as species, but as individuals.
And then yet another kind of grain begins to develop—
the accumulating layers of myth and affection that gather round
ancient trees.*

\- Richard Mabey

1

Swift struck a match, brightening the face of his best friend. Feeling Ash by his side—imagining Ash was actually on his side—it was even more thrilling than the idea of reclaiming the book Caius, Swift's older brother, had unjustly taken from them.

Swift hushed the match's flame inside an old oil lantern, keeping the wick barely simmering. He glanced at Ash.

Ash's expression formed into the cunning look of adventure Swift always had loved.

It seemed, at this moment, that Ash could be trusted. That finally they were salvaging what they'd lost. What they'd broken.

"Where could Caius have hidden your book?" Ash whispered.

The Pembrokeshire beach house wasn't large, but it kept plenty of great places to conceal the book of sea histories and legends Caius had confiscated—*The Shepherd of the Stars*. Swift's only hope lay in the possibility that Caius hadn't tried very hard to hide it. Perhaps, though, he hadn't.

When Caius had stumbled through the front door in the wee hours, his face bright and cheered by his wine, his hand clasping Brooke's, they'd spent just a minute downstairs before stumbling up to the master bedroom.

Swift and Ash, both awake on their cots in the den, had kept stone still. But neither of them had seen precisely where, in the dark room, Caius had walked.

"I bet he stuffed it someplace by the front door." Swift picked up the lantern and led Ash toward the entryway.

At the base of the stairs, he paused.

Caius and Brooke, up there, behind the closed door, were speaking softly. Laughing quietly.

"What if they took it up with them?" asked Ash.

Caius and Brooke's laughter changed. Into something... else.

Swift snatched Ash's arm and pulled him away from the stairs.

As gently as he could, Swift opened the coat closet in the entryway, while Ash rifled through a cabinet, drawer by drawer. Both came up empty-handed.

A storage trunk, its old blue wood silvered by light shafting in from the cold autumn moon, caught Swift's eye.

Swift whispered, "He wouldn't have."

It was just a plain trunk for blankets, but to Swift it was magical. When he was small, Caius had commandeered it as a makeshift treasure chest in their play.

Swift opened the trunk.

The blue moon streaming in through the beach house's windows tumbled across the silver print on the cover of his aged book, *The Shepherd of the Stars*.

"Nice work!" Ash lifted the book from among the woolen folds.

Caius had taken *The Shepherd of the Stars* from Swift in a fury, accusing accused him flat out of lying, which had been unfair.

It was true, Swift had kept the book from Caius, Brooke, and Ash, and even from the museum curator to whom he'd formally agreed to show all his finds. But he was planning on telling everyone about it—just not yet.

Swift and Ash together startled at the floorboards above them creaking. Rhythmically.

"We have to get out of here." Swift hurried to the front door.

Ash, staring up the flight of steps, stalled. "Don't you sort of wonder what they're doing?"

"God, no."

From growing up with three older brothers—Caius the closest at twenty-four—these noises weren't new. And Swift had heard plenty of talk to let him understand exactly what Caius and Brooke were doing. Swift quietly lifted the lantern.

Ash crept back to the trunk.

"What are you doing?" Swift whispered. "We don't have much time."

"Getting blankets," said Ash. "If your fever spikes again, we won't be able to get to the museum tomorrow."

Ash was right. They had to be cautious. Swift was at the tail end of a recurring fever disease—born from a blood infection he'd landed after the boating accident with Caius.

And tomorrow was the day he'd find out whether he could keep the relics he'd discovered—his Sunstone, the Star of Atlantis; the book that'd led him to it; and its ancient map.

"Warmth and quiet," whispered Ash, handing Swift a blanket. "That's what Brooke said you need to stay well."

But more than warmth and quiet, Swift needed to understand what secrets this book of legends told. He had to know what insights it might keep about the Star of Atlantis. And his place in its mystery.

Swift softly opened the front door and slipped out, Ash following.

They together broke into a run, racing each other beneath Pembrokeshire's blazing constellations, Draco the starry black dragon and Cygnus the blue swan bright in flight straight above.

Swift ran so fast, so hard, he felt he was charging along the Milky Way. The sense of sea wind bathing his face, the elation of straining over packed sand, bright white and sparkling like stars in the ocean of black overhead, was ecstasy.

Just a week ago, he wouldn't have been able to run like this.

The fever disease had dropped him into a coma for nine days, and coming out of that, he couldn't do much of anything without dropping into fits of exhaustion.

He couldn't even read like he used to—sailing through one of Caius' medical texts in a week.

They tore to the campsite on the beach, its kindling cold now, where they'd been reading *The Shepherd of the Stars* before Caius confiscated it. Before Brooke slipped it into her satchel, keeping it. Damn Brooke.

Ash won their race, reaching the charred firewood an instant before Swift. He hollered.

"Hey, quiet." Swift, needing to catch his breath, knelt in the cold sand.

"We don't have to be quiet anymore," said Ash. "I mean, Brooke and Caius couldn't hear us from all the way out here."

"Caius seems to have a sixth sense when it comes to what I'm up to." Swift swelled the flame inside the lantern. "I'd rather not tempt fate."

Ash checked the dark house behind them. "Any chance they'll see our light?"

"Their bedroom doesn't look out this way. They won't see us unless they come downstairs."

A wave of exhaustion washed from the sprint. Swift dropped back to sitting in the sand.

Ash knelt before him. "Well, open the book to where we left off."

Swift studied the worn cover of *The Shepherd of the Stars*.

Looking at it, a pang of regret struck. Maybe he shouldn't have kept this a secret.

But he'd done so for very good reasons. And despite how much fun this was, sneaking out to the beach with Ash to read it, deep down, he wished Ash hadn't found out about it. Now, Swift would have to report it to the museum curator—Octavian Krakau.

Octavian wasn't just untrustworthy, as Ash could be. Octavian felt dangerous.

He'd been cordial with Ash, like they were old friends. But

the way he'd watched Swift—the finder of the Star of Atlantis, it seemed he'd been harboring a temper kept barely under control.

And he'd been so possessive of it, along with Swift's other relics—the *Star of Atlantis* book and its map.

Ash inched closer. "Let's find out if it talks about those old Welsh clans—whether they're still around. What secrets they might've kept."

A noise sounded—far off, from the north. From the great ancient forest—the Wentletrap Forest.

It was like a dog's howl, but more savage.

Like something hungry or in pain.

It was the very same sound Swift had heard earlier tonight when he slipped into the Wentletrap Forest.

Swift stared at the forest's deep shadow looming up the coast, delivering to the wind a smell of wildness, of leaf litter, of pine.

He'd heard something very like it, too, on the night of the boating accident, while searching the wilds for help and stumbling across the fisherman. It was the sound the fisherman had called "a summons."

The noise struck louder—its shrillness, its ferocity sending a chill through him.

"Have you ever heard a noise like that?" asked Swift.

"Probably." Ash shrugged. "It's just a night noise. Only someone's dog."

The howl—the creaturely scream—rang again.

That was no dog. And there were no people around here to have dogs. But Ash seemed unafraid. He seemed hardly to have noticed.

"Go on," said Ash. "Try to read more from your book. Like you said, we don't have much time."

Swift flipped through the stiff pages of *The Shepherd of the Stars* to where he and Ash had left off—to a section entitled, *The People of the Stones.*

This told about the mysterious, mage-like Welsh clan thought to have originated from Nordic countries.

They were treasure finders. Mystics who kept secrets and

wisdom and claimed to have visions. People of the sea who hid and guarded treasures. People who still might stand guard over treasures.

Swift turned the page.

There lay a woodblock illustration of an ancient oak tree, sharp points of starlight descending in the background. A man was drawn at the base of the tree, holding a streaming lantern.

Looking at this picture brought Swift a strong sense of what he'd seen not two hours ago, when, in the Wentletrap, he'd spied a ghostly person moving by low lamplight.

But he couldn't really say it was the same. The fevers made him second guess his perception, and even now he was struggling through a fit of chills that signaled the onset of an intense one.

Swift's doctor—Dr. Keats—thought the impairment of the fevers, his challenges with reading, might be temporary.

But who knew? The eerie person in the forest with his lantern could've been a hallucination. And the glowing eyes Swift had sighted—that'd sighted him—what if they'd been nothing more than a waking dream?

Swift laid the book in the sand. Closed it.

"What's the matter?" asked Ash, a tint of frustration in his voice. "We have to keep reading."

But Ash looked more than frustrated. Was he angry?

It was upsetting anytime Ash's demeanor changed like this. Mostly, he displayed kindness. But when he shifted into agitation, Swift worried that he'd been foolish to bring Ash here with him.

Even at the best of times, depending on Ash felt like riding a bike blindfolded, reflexively fearing that something destructive was coming.

But Ash, too, was trying to heal. And it seemed their reborn, discordant friendship was making that happen.

Swift watched Ash, waiting to see which side might get the better of him.

Ash asked more softly, "Don't you want to keep reading?"

He was trying to recover his patience. And of course Swift should give him the space to check himself.

Ash was here, right before him, reflecting the loyalty and support Swift badly needed.

Swift often told himself that all his setbacks were temporary. That he just needed some time, some practice, before diving into the difficult medical books, readying for the trials that could win him a seat in a medical practicum program.

Every sea legend book Swift had tried to read with Ash, he found he could blaze through. Reading these books—especially *The Shepherd of the Stars*—seemed the best way, if not the only way, to gain back his bearings for reading medicine.

"I know you can do this," said Ash, more gently still.

By persevering through their five years of separation—a mixture of silent persistence, unrequited reaching, and strife, Swift finally had Ash's confidence. He might really be earning back his best friend.

"What if Caius is right, though?" asked Swift.

Caius, who seemed to be losing confidence in Swift. Caius, who believed Swift's legend books were detracting from his capacity to read biochemistry and anatomy.

"What if I'm only creating distractions by exploring this? Caius wants me to set aside all these fantasies."

Ash crouched closer. "Think about what you saw in the Wentletrap."

If Swift had hallucinated that man in the forest, those glowing eyes—that could mean Caius was right.

"What if what I saw wasn't real?" Swift asked.

"Look." Ash shifted to sitting by him. "You have to keep your brother out of your head. He means well, I'm sure, but he's bloody controlling." He pulled the book back onto Swift's lap. "And besides, he doesn't understand these books like we do." He caught Swift's glance. "They aren't fantasies. They're histories."

Ash had a handsome, muscular face, and the expression he was casting was puckish. By it Swift felt he was slipping straight back to his childhood, to the company of the old Ash; to when he and Ash were each other's first and best friends; to when they could get lost in each other's adventures and spend whole days in the magical worlds they made up.

Swift glanced back at the beach house, where Caius and Brooke were certainly knotted up together in the sheets.

Brooke was the first girl Caius had ever brought home. Since he had, he'd grown distant and seemed less himself. The Caius Swift knew never would've chosen a girl over him.

It suddenly seemed not to matter whether *The Shepherd of the Stars* was history or fantasy, whether it was a distraction or a support. There seemed to be enough truth in the fact of himself and his best friend venturing through it together, entranced.

Swift shifted to kneeling in the cold sand. By the light of his lantern, he opened *The Shepherd of the Stars*.

Ash settled in front of him, beside the cold embers. "Read it to me like you were doing before they caught us. It's okay if you have to go slowly."

Swift smoothed the page. "This bit mentions Cynfael Maddox."

"That's incredible," said Ash. "What's it say?"

Swift read—

"Cynfael Maddox came to be known as 'The Shepherd of the Stars' by his peculiar fondness for wandering along starry beaches, through ancient oak forests by night, speaking wisdom to the ocean, to the trees. Some say he cast spells on the people he happened upon."

"Whoa," said Ash. "That's precisely what you described seeing tonight. Do you think that man you saw cast a spell on you?"

"I don't know—he didn't come near me," said Swift. "Or, I don't think he did." He wiped at his eyes, tearing from the wind and from a heat welling in his chest.

The lighthearted expression faded from Ash. "That fisherman you saw the night you and Caius wrecked—if he's some sort of descendant from Maddox's clan, maybe he didn't just land that knife cut on your chest, but actually did cast a spell on you. The Shepherd of the Stars clan—if they do have mystical powers and foresight, maybe your struggle to read, to focus, is because of a spell. What if your whole fever disease is some sort of curse?"

Swift laid aside the book.

"We have to keep going." Ash glanced toward the beach house.

"I want to." Swift shivered. "It's just—I'm getting so cold."

Ash threw one of the blankets around Swift's shoulders. "Should we light the campfire?"

"No way. We can re-hide the book well enough, but when Caius wakes up, the first thing he'll do is come out here and make sure the embers are dowsed." Swift pulled the blanket tightly around him. "He'd definitely notice if more wood were burned."

"Can't you read any more?" Ash tucked the second blanket around Swift. "Try. Or let me."

Swift handed him the book.

Ash rifled through. "I'll see if I can find anything more about Maddox's spells."

Swift pulled the blankets up around his neck and ears.

They were woolen blankets and very thick—where they enclosed him, heat blazed. But the cold wind drifting from the ocean, trickling through the gaps, felt like a drenching of seawater.

Ash bent low to the lantern and studied a page. "You said this handwriting is like the penmanship in *The Star of Atlantis*?"

"I think it's the very same. But I'll need to get that book back from Octavian to be sure."

"What if that book is cursed too?" asked Ash. "What if the bloody Sunstone is cursed? What if all this is the reason you and Caius almost drowned when you led him into that deathtrap of Sterncastle Cove?"

At hearing Ash speak the truth of the accident, Swift's chest seared. It might've just been the cut, still raw and flaring a bit at the heat of what had to be a rising fever.

But this agony felt deeper. He'd led Caius into a deathtrap.

"Oh! Here's something." Ash laid the book on the sand before them.

"Those encountering Cynfael Maddox often reported leaving his presence dazed."

Ash pulled closer the lantern. "You had to be dazed as you sailed off from that fisherman into those deadly night waters." He glanced up at Swift. "Weren't you dazed?"

"I guess, but that was the fever disease starting," said Swift. "Not a curse."

"And I'd say you're looking a bit dazed now," said Ash. "You might be lucky the man you saw tonight didn't cut you."

"If Cynfael Maddox and his clan cut everyone stumbling onto their path, wouldn't the book talk of them as villains more than heroes? And wouldn't it speak plainly of his violence if people left his presence cut and blood-poisoned rather than 'dazed?'"

"Cut and blood-poisoned." Ash held up the lantern. "Are you all right? I mean, even in this poor light, I can tell the color's gone out of your face. That's one of the signs Brooke told me to look out for—it might mean a fever's starting."

Swift was unable to control the shivering now.

This was definitely the fever relapsing, but it wasn't just starting. The truth was, he'd felt its slow simmering since a few hours ago, when he refused to take the medicine Brooke offered. Now it seemed to have its claws in him.

"We should go in," said Swift.

"One more second." Ash flipped through more pages. "Whoa—listen to this—

"The so-called 'spells' Cynfael Maddox used—some believe these to be bits of great thoughts and wisdom. Insights about the Celtic seven-pointed star, about seafaring, astronomy, and mathematics."

Ash thumbed back a few pages. "That would explain why there are so many maths formulas and chemistry looking things and such rubbish scrawled all over the place in this book. These might somehow be Cynfael's pieces of wisdom. Or somehow his curses."

"Ash," Swift whispered.

The fever was definitely spiking. Swift's skin and muscles were quaking with the sensation of ice touching him, but inside his chest and belly, it seemed lava was boiling.

"Listen," said Ash—

"People encountering the spirit of Cynfael Maddox, over centuries have reported that they felt a sense of destiny, a great wisdom imparted. Many think of him as a true renaissance man—a magnificent teacher with endless ideas and knowledge. And some in his company were known to be gifted with foresight."

Swift tried to catch Ash's glance. "I need..."
Ash read on—

"And their lives, after meeting Maddox, often were changed."

Ash finally looked at Swift.
"Your life certainly did change. But do you think the fisherman imparted any wisdom?"
Swift lost all strength and fell to his side.
"Swift?"
Ash knelt over him.
Swift couldn't speak. Couldn't breathe.
The trembling from the fever seemed more than just chills.
His body was spasming.
Seizing.
Dr. Keats had said seizures were possible. And Swift was losing all control of his body.
"Get Caius," Swift said, or tried to.
In what seemed like seconds later, Caius was kneeling over

him, pushing back the blankets, clearing away the kindling pile Swift's wild hands were hitting.

"You're okay." Caius held on to Swift's shoulder. "I have you."

Brooke knelt at Swift's head and gently guarded his face from the sand he was kicking up.

"From the porch, I saw him tip," Caius said to Ash. "Was he seizing before then, or did this just begin?"

Ash's face was tear-streaked. "I don't know."

Brooke filled a syringe. Caius held down Swift's arm as she injected it.

The shot incited a pleasurable buzz that took Swift's mind off the fact that he hardly could move.

After a moment, his body calmed, and he dropped into a state of complete exhaustion.

"Is he not breathing?" asked Ash. "What's happening?"

"This is a febrile seizure," said Brooke, calmly. "It looks scary, I know. But he'll be all right."

Caius, seeming to catch Brooke's half-lie, glanced at her.

Swift knew exactly what Caius was thinking. It was a bad sign that a fever had stricken so hard as to spur this.

Caius carefully dusted sand from Swift's face. "If we hadn't happened to come down just then..."

Ash bent closely over Swift.

"Is he through it?"

Caius moved Ash back. "What were you two even doing out here?"

"My fault," Swift whispered.

Ash, clever as always in a tight place, slid their contraband book beneath a discarded blanket.

"No, the fault was mine," said Ash. "Swift said he was hot. I thought coming outside would help."

Caius pinned Ash with a glare. "Next time, check with us."

"We were going to"—Ash glanced from Caius to Brooke—"but..."

Caius' look sharpened. "Understand, lad. If you can't help

us care for Swift—if you interfere with the rest he needs—then you're gone."

Ash, gone.

Ash—the only help Swift really had, with Caius well-claimed by Brooke. Ash—Swift's only link to feeling that he was in any sort of control.

"I'm sorry," said Ash. "I can't tell you how sorry. Of course I want to care for Swift. Please, let me stay. I've tried to help him. I'll keep trying."

"You can save your begging," said Caius. "I really don't buy it. You're proving more distracting to him than any legend book."

The words seemed to sink Swift.

Brooke offered Caius a gentling look. "This may have happened to Swift whether they came out here or not. You know that, right?"

"This shouldn't have happened." Caius glanced at Ash. "Trusting him seems to have been a mistake."

Darkness encased Swift. Whether he was losing some consciousness, or whether another fit of seizing was coming on, he couldn't tell. All he knew was that he couldn't feel whether he was breathing.

"I truly am sorry," said Ash.

"One more false move out of you," said Caius, "and I'm sending you straight back to Devon. Got it?"

"Can't"—Swift snatched Brooke's hand—"can't breathe."

2

TWO MONTHS EARLIER

*D*arkness, Swift never had feared. But this darkness pressing him seemed to divide him from everything. He couldn't decipher his thoughts from his dreams, and his body—senseless—felt out of reach.

He worked to comprehend this medium of nothingness, black as a starless night shifting over the deep Celtic Sea. He felt numb. Floating. Falling.

This was the same sense of slipping as what he'd felt under the water in Sterncastle Cove, the icy sea taking him, waves ripping him from the *Strider*. From Caius.

After a moment, though—he could feel something. A chill wind troubled him.

The longboat.

He was in the longboat. How could he have forgotten? He'd reached the shore and left Caius on the beach. He'd run to find help.

Yes, the fisherman had given him a longboat.

Was it night, still? There didn't seem to be stars.

Perhaps the stars were there, only shrouded by bleak cruising clouds.

Swift felt around his thigh for the sharp points, the cool rims of the Sunstone—the Star of Atlantis.

His fingers found nothing.

How striking its box had been, the box with its silver Celtic star, perched high on its pinnacle in the center of the cove's islet cavern. How terrible had been the feat of climbing the treacherous rocks into the cave. How marvelous was his triumph in taking the Star of Atlantis. How destined he'd felt. For the Star of Atlantis was said to come to the hands of one destined.

THE SEA ALL BLACK, the stars all drowned –
I strike the bloody colors down!
The rain-rent sea – a cursed realm –
Cthulhu calls – I take the helm.
Yo Ho, Yo Ho – Fight the waves and keel the foe!
Yo Ho, Yo Ho – Over the waves we go.

SWIFT COULDN'T TELL whether he'd spoken or merely thought the words, the verse from his book—*The Star of Atlantis*—that'd led him to his treasure, his Sunstone.

His mind traveled back to a moment, before the accident, of Caius speaking to him about Star of Atlantis myths.

"I've always wondered whether sea monsters and pirate ghosts weren't conjured by sailors, truly in danger, deathly afraid," Caius had said. *"I wonder if they're not an imaginative mind's manifestations of the actual terrors of the sea."*

Swift had asked him, *"What terrors of the sea could be more horrifying than bloodthirsty mermaids, or the Cthulhu, or the bone-crushing Kraken?"*

"What about actual drowning?" Caius had asked. *"Drowning people certainly would feel like they were slipping into the belly of a beast. Or how about running out of food or water on the sea? Just imagine the terror of knowing you're about to die, in the worst way, and yet being unable to do a thing about it. Wouldn't you feel like you were inside the jaws of the Cthulhu?"*

The Cthulhu.

Swift pictured it.

Tentacled. Raging.

A creaturely manifestation of the tempestuous sea.

"But the Cthulhu isn't the same as the sea," Swift heard himself saying. "It isn't even real."

H.P. Lovecraft had dreamed up the Cthulhu more than a hundred years ago, in *The Thing on the Doorstep and Other Weird Stories*.

But Caius had been right about sea monsters.

In the desolation of Sterncastle Cove, the Cthulhu had all but been on their doorstep. Being in the water with Caius, terrified that they both might drown, was a slipping into the metaphorical belly of a beast.

"It was so long ago," Swift heard himself saying, "that thing on the doorstep."

A pressure laid heavy on his hand. It seemed someone was tightening their hold on his fingers.

"But a hundred years isn't so long, is it?" Swift asked the darkness.

Something cool touched his face, bringing him a greater sense of wakefulness.

He used the rousing to follow a surfacing thought that was drawing up nausea.

If the Cthulhu had been invented by Lovecraft a mere hundred years ago, how could it appear in *The Star of Atlantis?* Its myth was many hundreds of years old. As was the hiding of the Sunstone.

If his cherished book—*The Star of Atlantis*—included a creature so recently devised, would that mean it was forged? And the map with its beautiful drawing of the Cthulhu—could it be a fake?

Swift jolted at the thought—the Cthulhu, this young monster incriminating the treasure he'd worked for, the treasure he'd nearly died for; the treasure he believed he'd been destined to find.

If the timeframe didn't make sense, then the Star of Atlantis

—his Sunstone—was it counterfeit? Did his chase after it add up to a terrible nothing?

God—who else might've noticed this dreadful inconsistency? And who might find out? Who might discover that Swift had taken Caius into treacherous waters for nothing?

"Caius." The word, as it left him, felt screamed.

And then came a sense of rocking. And then—a sweet sound of whistling.

Whistling, melodious—full of the sense of the old, old pirate verse written in *The Star of Atlantis.*

How solid it felt. How full of truth. How it carried the spirit of the sea.

With the dashing, old melody, he spoke—

THE MORNING BREAKS – I look to sea,
  to where the storm has ferried me.
  Mine eyes deceive! But no – there be:
  Atlantis' Star heaved from the deeps!
  Yo Ho, Yo Ho – Swab the deck and lash the tow!
  Yo Ho, Yo Ho – To Brandy Brook we go!

THE STAR OF ATLANTIS—HIS Sunstone—couldn't be counterfeit. It would keep him true to west. Norse sailors had forged the Sunstone to trace stars lost behind clouds, behind storms. He had to stay true to west.

But where was the Sunstone? He tried to move, to straighten, to push up far enough to feel for it, to see over the edge of the longboat—to search the horizon for a ship. But his muscles wouldn't respond.

How long had he slept? The sun must be still underneath the dark waters. He couldn't have been out long.

His chest ached horribly, the cut's searing keeping him from peace.

And Caius. How could Swift have let himself fall asleep while Caius was alone on the beach beyond Sterncastle Cove?

Swift struggled to grip the bench of the longboat, but something kept him restrained.

This emptiness, this cold—it must be a mist coming off the water and washing toward the coast, weaving into the edge of the dangerous Wentletrap Forest.

Or was this chill the water itself?

Was he breathing? Had he tipped the longboat? Was he in the sea, drowning?

He jerked to free his arms—kicked—reached for the longboat's bench, for the *Strider*, for the sharp edge of the islet, for Caius, for Ash.

He tried to cry out but could no longer make any sound.

But—he was breathing.

Not in the water, then.

And not even inside pure darkness. Rather, lights were flickering.

Starlight, it seemed, was twinkling through a black forest canopy, heavy with leaves.

He forced his eyelids, hot and tight, open to slits.

A voice whispered from no place. The words, unintelligible, somehow felt aimed at him.

A cool hand touched his head. The rim of a cup came to his lips.

Swift swallowed a mouthful of icy freshwater. He worked his eyes open more.

He found himself resting against a leather-jacketed shoulder, spicy-smelling of pipe tobacco. Around him, lights smeared and winked.

"There are the stars," Swift whispered.

No, not stars.

Electric lights—small and hazy.

"Don't try to speak, lad." It was Justus. It was his father, Justus, holding him.

They seemed to be not in a longboat, but in a bed with rails.

The cut on Swift's chest, smarting, felt drug-distant, floating more around him than touching him. He tried to push free, to give the cut space.

But moving only brought Justus' arms wrapping him more snuggly. "There, lad. You're all right."

Justus was not a father one presumed to hug, and the intimacy felt outlandish. It dredged up flashes of being held as a child at the dinner table. Of sitting with Justus in the big study chair, training his eyes on his father's and listening to him whisper Norse myths and Welsh legends.

But the memories were mere flashes. Recollections of closeness to Justus were subconscious. Rare.

Memories of being a small boy in Caius' arms, Swift could concretely remember. Caius had often carried him, and it was Caius who'd nightly shuttled him to bed.

The stinging in his cut shifted to itching. He had to move. He pushed away from his father.

But once he loosed himself enough to sit up on his own, he realized he couldn't.

This maddening chilly heat had to be a fever, and it was a drain. Every muscle felt made of water.

"It hurts," Swift heard himself say.

Justus adjusted Swift's shoulders in the cradle of his arms.

Swift tried to speak more, to explain that he was awake and could lie back on his own.

"It's fine if you want to go," were the words he intended, but they came out garbled.

"Not to worry. I have you." Justus' hands fussed over the bandage a moment.

The itching, the stinging, cooled.

"You've a fever, lad," said Justus. "It's keeping you quite low. It has for some days."

He had a fever. He had a cut.

But Caius had a bone sticking out of his leg. Caius was alone on the beach beyond Sterncastle Cove.

Did Justus know?

Had anyone helped Caius?

Swift held his eyes open. Fought to work out one clear phrase—"Caius is bleeding."

Justus bundled a blanket around Swift's shoulders. "Caius had surgery a few days ago."

"A few days?" asked Swift.

"It's been almost a week since you and Caius wrecked in the *Strider*, since your dauntless chase after your ancient crystal."

A week since their dauntless chase. Or perhaps their foolish chase after a crystal that might not be ancient, but faked.

Tears crept into his eyes from nausea welling. "Caius is broken."

"Caius will have quite a recovery—a year, perhaps. But he shall recover."

That couldn't be right.

A year was too long. A year was, well—a year. Caius had to do med school.

"He doesn't have a year," Swift managed.

"The break was complex to begin with, but an infection set in to worsen matters," said Justus. "However, Dr. Keats believes he'll make a near-full recovery."

Swift felt himself growing hotter. Whether because of the fever, or from thinking of Caius damaged so badly, or from the fright of realizing the Star of Atlantis might be counterfeit, or because of the odd way Justus was looking at him, he couldn't tell.

"Here you are, your mettle shown," said Justus. "You've finished your work, and now you may rest."

The infection in Caius' leg—had that happened because Swift swam Caius through the death-ridden waters of Stern-castle Cove?

He might've used the tourniquet wrong. Or cleaned Caius' leg poorly.

A memory surfaced of seeing Caius lying on the medic's ship.

Caius' leg had been wrapped.

On the beach, he himself should've wrapped it. Why hadn't he thought to do that?

Swift found the gaze of his father. "I wrecked the *Strider*. I did that."

"Forget the *Strider*," said Justus. "You're here—that's all that matters."

Justus ought to be furious Swift had wrecked their dinghy.

And he would be furious once he learned it'd been Swift who talked Caius into scaling up into that cavern; Swift who'd drawn Caius, bleeding, into the water. Swift who'd done everything wrong in trying to tend Caius' broken leg.

"If Caius can't rest, I can't rest." Waves of heat flashed like tides, dragging more nausea with them.

"Are you managing to get him talking?" another voice, unfamiliar, asked.

A metallic taste came into his mouth as something cool streamed into his wrist.

"He's wakeful," said Justus. "But barely."

"Swift," said the new voice, "I'm Brooke. I'm here to help you. Your waking up more is a good sign."

He did feel more wakeful with whatever she'd given him now flashing through.

"The water was cold," Swift told her. "The sailors will come, but they'll be a while." His mouth felt dry, like a fire was roaring too close, his lips cracking. "The *Strider*—she's swamped in Sterncastle Cove. And the knife—it was very sharp. Mermaid on the hilt. Bright like a bone. I should've heeded that."

"There was a mermaid on the hilt of a knife?" asked the nurse—Brooke.

"The stars are sharp, aren't they?" Swift asked her. "So bright, without any shine. The mermaid had diamonds for eyes. But does the Sunstone shine? It might mean nothing. The fisherman—he'd know. I've got to ask him."

Swift wasn't cognizant that he'd been talking aloud until the words stopped flowing.

"Hold on, Swift," said Brooke. "Just a bit more medicine, and you'll be quite comfortable."

The nausea faded, and so did his impression of Justus' arms around him, leaving him alone in the black.

When he was in the fisherman's longboat, Swift never had felt so alone.

And now, it was like his body was remembering the feel of the longboat as he'd sat in a shocked and despairing contemplation of how he was ever to find rescue for Caius.

It was like a void had been punched into his chest that dark night—pain and loneliness pouring in like molten metal, and he himself hardening in that vessel, morphing in his chrysalis into a creature altogether different.

There'd been no ship in sight for so long, and he'd had so little hope of finding help. Now, even though he knew he must still be lying in Justus' arms, it was as though a sea yet divided them.

Justus was someplace steady, whereas Swift could feel nothing but a hard current and waves.

Justus had once warned him not to let a small moment of boyhood triumph define him. But the question of whether his life would be defined by a moment of boyhood tragedy was a more difficult quandary. If Caius couldn't recover, if the treasure they'd fought to discover proved fake, how could Swift's life not be labeled a failure?

Swift tried to rouse, to talk more—but speaking was impossible. Breathing, even, was proving difficult.

Because he was in the water, dodging rough waves.

He could take breaths between them but couldn't let out any air.

"Lie him flat," said Brooke.

"You're all right, lad." Justus' voice. "You're panicking some. But you're fine. We're here with you."

Swift grew aware of Justus' hand on his chest, carefully placed to one side of the cut.

The pressure seemed to make air easier to let go of.

"Are we in the water?" Swift's lids batted open.

"We're in Bristol," said Justus.

"The islet's rocks were too slick," Swift told him. "I should've taken him swimming before the bone came out. Always, I should swim first, or at least try. That bone—it was glaring as the moon."

"Swift, be still."

"If he'd bled one drop more, Caius might've gone out." Hot tears were sliding down Swift's temples, though he didn't feel he was crying. "I should've listened to the *Strider* screaming."

Swift took air in a gasp.

"He might've drowned with that shark. I might've watched him sink."

He gulped another breath.

"His head was white with concussion. That beach looked on fire, but it was freezing."

"Hush, lad."

Softness brushed darkness off Swift's cheeks—his father blotting his face with the sheet. It felt like the wingtips of gulls fluttering over a carcass.

Swift waited until the birds crept up into the sky and vanished.

"Caius might die."

He drew a strained breath.

"I can't stop it."

Light sliced into the room with the door opening. Someone pulled back the sheets.

"Caius says he knew," said Justus. "The whole time he was on that beach, he knew you'd come through for him."

There were several hands on him now—someone touching his neck and chest. Someone pushing cold fluid into his wrist.

Justus gently held on to Swift's shoulder as someone fussed with his bandage. "Caius is alive because of how smart you were. How fast. How brave. Are you hearing me?"

Swift had clearly heard his father's words, and they were coaxing more nausea.

It was a flattering narrative—Swift as a rescuer. But it was pretense. As false as the Sunstone might be.

"The steps you took," said Justus, "how you got Caius to safety. How you found him help."

Swift managed to again open his eyes. Justus was gazing at him the way he looked at Caius when they talked medicine.

"And your care of Caius," said Justus. "Dr. Keats says you saved both his leg and his life."

Justus' expression went contemplative. It seemed he was envisioning something—maybe Swift in the medical Practicum they'd planned.

"Caius is so proud of you," he said. "As am I."

On the beach, faced with all that trauma, Swift had found himself able to at least try to handle the medical interventions, the fright, though he had little idea what he was doing. But how could he dream of going after something like the Practicum now, with Caius stalled?

Caius' eyes—at points when rationality visited—had been lightless, void of hope. His assurances to Swift had been so calm. A ship would come in the morning. Swift should keep himself warm and wait.

Swift could see now what Caius was doing. Caius knew he wasn't likely to survive. He was coaching Swift on how to get rescued, after he himself died.

Swift tightened his hands into fists.

His fingers clenched a cool, prismatic crystal resting beside him.

The Sunstone.

The Star of Atlantis.

Genuine or not, he clung to it like it was keeping his face at the top of the sea.

"Caius is so anxious to see you," Justus told him. "Dr. Keats has had to sedate him to help him sleep."

At the thought of Caius, warm and at rest, a clarity struck— a resolve to reach Caius, to see him all right. To say he was sorry.

"Can you take me to him?" Swift asked.

Justus turned aside. "Could that be arranged."

"In this condition, certainly not," said Brooke, typing at a computer. "Perhaps you could snap a video of Caius to show Swift when he next wakes."

"But Swift is awake now." Justus cast her a look that seemed pleading.

"It isn't a good idea," said Brooke.

Justus' face darkened as with sorrow. But the expression on him seemed deeper than sorrow. More, it was grief.

It was like he was imagining Swift and Caius never again seeing each other.

He seemed to want to press the issue—but he looked lost as to how.

Justus, a doctor himself, had once told Swift how scattered, how helpless he felt when his own lads were hurt or unwell. And the sense of decisiveness, of determination that he usually carried was indeed missing.

Justus sat taller, as though gathering resolve. "Seeing Caius —could it not be helpful to Swift's recovery?"

Brooke stopped what she was doing and faced him.

"I daresay," said Justus, "the meeting would be just as medicinal for Caius."

"I can tell you right now," said Brooke, "Dr. Keats wouldn't even consider signing off. Rest is the priority for Swift."

Justus eased back.

Brooke smiled sweetly at Swift. "You'll see Caius soon enough. You'll see that he's well, and that he's still quite decided that you're his favorite brother."

Swift watched his father. "When will Caius get back to med school?"

"Brooke is right." Justus seemed to force a smile. "You'll soon see for yourself that Caius is well."

Swift didn't release his father's gaze, although focusing was growing difficult. "When?"

Justus glanced off, his expression gone grim.

In the stillness of the room, in the closeness of his father's presence, Swift knew it without Justus having to say more.

Med school was probably out of reach, now, for Caius.

On his feet for procedures that lasted all day; keeping pace handling emergency after emergency—there was no way his damaged leg would supply that kind of stamina.

And by the time his leg took its year to mend, Caius would be too far behind, too swept off course to manage enough momentum to pick up his training. And med schools were fussy about imperfection. It was possible they wouldn't even want him back.

"We shouldn't be speaking of this." Justus took Swift's hand and held it strongly. "Why don't we talk about what you found? It's extraordinary."

With his free hand, Swift gripped the Sunstone.

Might Justus suspect it was fake? Justus was the sharpest person Swift knew. And he'd read *The Star of Atlantis* with Swift several times. If he hadn't noticed the anachronism of the Cthulhu, he might yet.

Swift covered the Star of Atlantis well with his hand, lest Justus think on it too long and come to suspect it as some terrible joke.

The Sunstone felt heavy and cool. Solid. But where it jagged at the edges, it felt like a bone. A horrible, blood-shiny bone.

On that desolate beach, part of what moved Swift to feel he could help Caius, that he could find rescue, was the idea that he himself—the finder of the Star of Atlantis—was one destined. If he were destined, he'd thought, how could he not be rescued? If he were destined, how could his brother die?

Swift felt glad, looking back, that he'd bought into that foolishness. It'd helped him muster some courage as he searched the coast, as he set out to sea with no assurance of finding a ship.

But now, with the sense of being "destined" fading, so, too, was his hopefulness—hopefulness that Caius would be all right; that he himself would be all right.

"The bone wasn't right outside of his body like that," said Swift. "I wanted to put it back in him and stop all that blood."

A small smile visited Justus as he gently placed his hand over Swift's, gripping the Star of Atlantis. "You're as much of a trauma medic as your brother, for all your doubt. For all your fourteen years."

3

Swift's room cycled between daylight and darkness more quickly than he could track.

He levitated in a sense of impermanence—wakefulness striking in mere flashes, like flying fish breaking the sea. No matter how he tried, he couldn't reach the awareness he'd won when he'd woken in Justus' arms.

Sometimes when he roused, nurses would be near, straightening the bedding, tampering with the IV and monitors. Turning out the light. There was always a heat hanging over him, sweltering his face. A low ache stirred in his bones, and it sometimes felt he had ice in his chest, making him shiver, keeping all comfort at bay.

He was aware of the cut, constantly sharp beneath a bulky bandage.

At times, its pain pierced so strongly, he'd cry out.

Sometimes, it seemed remote, like a storm kept off the coast by strong winds. Anytime someone drew close, he'd flinch with the terror of them touching it.

When someone did touch it, the stinging would rouse him enough to know he was holding his breath, to feel tears sliding down.

Now and then, upon opening his eyes, he found Mum beside him, holding his hand.

Once he was aware of her bathing him, changing his clothes. Sometimes he awoke to her voice—but the meaning of her words felt beyond reach. They seemed to be about Caius.

Often when he managed to open his eyes, he found himself starkly alone in the dark.

In would rush the feeling of the jolt—the *Strider* striking the reef; of ice water taking him, of pain paralyzing him in the fisherman's longboat.

But the sense of strangers handling his limp body was almost worse. Their tries at soothing were robotic—just checkmarks, it seemed, for their charts. And it'd been sheer frustration that he couldn't speak, couldn't ask anyone about Caius.

Swift drifted into a half-wakefulness once, to Trystan reading to him out of *The Star of Atlantis*. But trying to comprehend the words felt like listening to an unstudied language.

All he'd caught was the verse Trystan softly chanted—

THE SEA ALL BLACK, *the stars all drowned –*
I strike the bloody colors down!
The rain-rent sea – a cursed realm –
Cthulhu calls – I take the helm.
Yo Ho, Yo Ho – Fight the waves and keel the foe!
Yo Ho, Yo Ho – Over the waves we go.

THE CTHULHU, even whispered, was a wretched fright, a reminder of the terror lying beside Swift's thigh—the Sunstone, maybe forged.

The first time Swift felt he managed a complete though short-lived consciousness, was at hearing Edric's voice.

Edric had leaned over, his big fists pressing the mattress and said, "You did good, Little Brother."

Even with his family close—his family who knew instinctively how to soothe him—there'd been a sense of dismemberment. A chasm forged of delirium, of pain, of fever, of seawater, of cold sand.

Many times, he grew sensible to his own voice reciting the names of his favorite stars. In those moments, he seemed to be drifting again in the *Strider* while saltwater streamed through her hull, encasing him.

And among all the impressions of what'd happened since he'd arrived in Bristol, he couldn't recall a single moment of seeing Caius or hearing his voice.

Finally, an awareness of bright light brought a strong sense of wakefulness.

Swift opened his eyes and found himself lying on his back, beneath a cool sheet. He rubbed his face—gritty with dried sweat. The fever felt less. His cut was sore, but not unbearable. It felt dry and tight.

He was alone in the hospital room.

Sunlight, dappled with an aspen tree's fluttering, splashed a patchwork of gentle whites and grays across his blue sheets. Beside him stood a flickering monitor to which he was tied with a dozen small wires.

He glanced around, looking for Justus, for Mum, for Caius.

The room stood empty and still, its door closed. The only sound was the soft hum of the IV regulator.

He touched the Sunstone, resting in the pocket of his pajama bottoms.

He pulled it out. Felt of its edges and planes, cold and sleeping now. Shrouded from all stars.

How could this be counterfeit?

Awake as he was, for the moment at least, the notion of having found a fraudulent relic felt impossible.

Holding the Star of Atlantis felt like handling a mythical creature, unearthed from its secretive nest, still cold from the wet of its egg.

That it existed, that it might be genuine, was marvelous. And that it was his—this was more unbelievable yet.

Perhaps that mention of the Cthulhu in *The Star of Atlantis* had a feasible explanation.

Swift startled at the door's opening.

He twisted toward the door. "Caius?"

It was not Caius. It was a nurse.

She bustled in, tossing him a sly smile like she understood him very well.

"I just knew you'd wake on my shift," she said. "Do you remember me? I'm called Brooke. I've been with you most often at night."

The memory of her voice dawned. She was the nurse who'd argued with Justus. The nurse who'd refused to let him see Caius.

"My brother—"

She took a gentle hold of his cheek and held a thermometer to his face.

Swift glanced around the room, finding two whiteboards scrawled with notes. On them, nine days were represented.

Nine whole days.

For nine days had Odin presented himself to the Norns and their magical runes, that he might be gifted with fearful insights and abilities.

Beside the whiteboards stretched a counter that held a computer. On the seat of a chair by his bed rested a stack of magazines and a couple of books—Mum's it seemed, warped as they were from the way she tended to roll a book's pages as she read.

Brooke set aside the thermometer. "Fever-free on my watch. A double win." She made a note. "Any pain?"

"My brother," said Swift, his voice raspy. "Where's Caius?"

Brooke didn't look up. "I'll contact him to say you've woken."

Swift dropped back to lying on the pillow.

Caius was contactable. Caius was alive.

He held his Sunstone closely to his chest, situating its coolness along the edge of the cut's irritation.

Its weight there felt so good, like Caius' hand resting on him.

Brooke leaned over him. "Mind if I set that crystal aside, where it'll be safe?"

"Isn't it safe with me holding it?" asked Swift.

"Maybe," said Brooke. "But I promised your father I'd look after it, and I have—as carefully as I've looked after you. Now that you're moving around more, you'd possibly forget it's by you, and it could fall."

Swift could never let fall a treasure that'd cost him so dearly.

"There's no way I'd let that happen."

"And yet—let's set it aside, right here in this box on your bedside table," said Brooke.

Swift tightened his fingers around the Sunstone.

"Your father rested it in your hand from time to time as you slept—darling to watch, that was," said Brooke. "He hoped, by its touch, you'd feel some sense of joy in the middle of all this discomfort." She held open her hand for the Sunstone. "With you awake, your father would prefer that crystal stowed."

Though Brooke's voice was sweet, though her large, pretty eyes held gentleness, she carried a determined air, like she was accustomed to getting whatever she wanted.

Swift carefully handed her "that crystal." His Star of Atlantis.

"I'd like to see Caius."

"He'll be proud that the first thing out of your mouth was to ask for him." Brooke tucked the Sunstone inside the box.

The Sunstone looked extraordinary, lying inside the square of simple wood. More than a stone, it seemed a creature of light, deposited carelessly into an ill-fitting cage.

"Can you take me to him?" asked Swift.

"You're stuck in this room for at least another day." She went to a monitor and studied its readings. "Twenty-four hours fever-free, and Dr. Keats will clear you to walk around. Possibly, he'll let you go home."

"Where are my father and mum?"

"I'll call them. I expect they'll come right over." She focused on making notes. "You've a lovely family. Caius, of course, is wonderful. And your other two brothers are so sweet. They've been in and out. Came as often as they could." She looked up. "Can you describe your pain for me?"

Swift glanced down at the bandage on his chest. "I feel bruised."

Brooke pulled over a duffle bag. "Your mum brought a change or two for you. You can dress in real clothes if you'd like. You're probably tired of hospital jammies."

"When can I see Caius?"

She held up her mobile and showed him a text. "I just invited him up."

This nurse texting Caius—that seemed a bit unprofessional. Wouldn't most nurses have called?

"He's been camped in the coffee shop downstairs all afternoon, studying," said Brooke.

"Why isn't he in a hospital room?"

"He was released three days ago." Brooke checked her chart. "You've been with us nine days. Tomorrow will make an even ten."

Nine days. And Swift had no memory of Caius with him.

Maybe Caius hadn't wanted to see him.

"Has Caius not been here at all?"

"Oh—he has," said Brooke. "We noticed something quite odd. Whenever he came near, you dropped more deeply into sleep. Seems you could rest better with him close." Brooke pointed at a folded-up cot in the corner. "For the last few days, he's been my buddy on the night shift, looking after you." She glanced at the clock. "I've got to get on. Do press your button, should you need anything." She lifted the duffle bag onto the foot of his bed. "Don't try to do too much. If you feel dizzy or tired or nauseated, or any strain of unwell, can I count on you to lie back and rest?"

He nodded as she left, closing the door.

Swift opened the duffle bag. From it he drew a pair of athletic shorts and a long-sleeved T-shirt.

Working himself into them proved a struggle. Navigating around the IV, the wires and leads, was a trick, and moving even a little bit made him feel winded.

But finally he managed it, carefully sticking leads back to his skin where a fine ring of adhesive told him each belonged.

Wearing his own clothes went some distance in helping him feel more like himself.

Once dressed, he sat up on the edge of the bed. He lifted his Sunstone from the wooden box and cradled it.

Its coolness felt like ocean air, trapped. Its white wisps of crystal seemed to hold stratospheric ice.

Looking at the Star of Atlantis in the bright light of day, it seemed even more magnificent than he remembered. Its heaviness made it seem strange and extraordinary—more like a transparent metal than crystal. It lent the stone a sense of authenticity.

Studying it, he tried to conjure the sense of destiny he imagined that finding the Star of Atlantis would bring.

But he felt nothing.

It struck him how nebulous was the concept of destiny. None of the legends in *The Star of Atlantis* promised what "destiny" this might deliver to its finder.

He'd imagined, though, that finding the lost Star of Atlantis would make anything possible. That studying medicine, that making the Practicum, would come easy.

He'd imagined that, by it, he'd find true friends and keep them. He'd entertained the idea that this would earn him the respect of his brothers and parents, of all Devonshire, of the United Kingdom, of the wide world, maybe.

But holding the Star of Atlantis, it seemed not even to belong to him.

And he couldn't shake the dread that it might possibly turn out to be fake.

Even if it was the real thing, though, it certainly didn't seem likely to deliver what he'd dreamed.

If the Star of Atlantis belonged to anyone, it seemed it should belong to the fisherman—the man on the coast who'd figured out Swift had taken it; the man who'd given Swift his longboat and let him sail off with the Sunstone in his pocket.

The fisherman had seemed strangely glad that Swift had taken the Sunstone.

But why would he be?

Maybe the fisherman had let him have it because he knew it to be phony.

But the fisherman's words—how fantastic they were. How bizarre.

Despite all Swift had been through, despite the knife cut, despite the frenzy he'd felt to reach the open ocean, Swift could recall the man's words perfectly:

"Understand that by claiming the Star, you're pinned with a role in this magnificent mess. We both are."

The strangeness of those words seemed to match the extraordinary nature of the fisherman himself. And of the Star of Atlantis.

For he couldn't look at the Sunstone without thinking of its myths—legends of Icelandic nomads, like Arthurian Mages but real, living in secrecy in the Welsh wilderness; descendants, possibly, of Cynfael Maddox' clan.

Sightings had been recorded over centuries, and lore had it that they—the Shepherds of the Stars—were protectors of treasure. Teachers of wisdom living in harmony with nature.

Despite that it was all rather mythical, it didn't seem too far-fetched to imagine the fisherman as one of them.

Swift wrapped his fingers around the Sunstone's edges, finding the places they'd hardly let go of for these last nine days —when Brooke had allowed it.

He tried viewing it as a gemstone—something valuable. Precious. Something that might've been protected by Maddox's Star Shepherds. Something the anomaly of the Cthulhu couldn't touch. Something he ought to be proud of possessing— something that ought to bring him the joy Justus had wanted him to feel.

He discovered that, with just a small shift in perspective, his perception of the Sunstone could change.

As light might advance above the horizon, showing a way

through a forest, Swift found he could believe that the Sunstone was truly authentic.

If it were, was Brooke right? Perhaps it was something he shouldn't be touching—a piece of history far bigger than himself.

But even perceiving it as glorious, he couldn't press back a twinge of repulsion. How could he ever look at the Star of Atlantis without remembering how it'd glared, lying by Caius' leg on the blood-stained sand?

But how beautiful the starlight had glittered through its facets.

Swift held it up to the window. Though the sky shone bright blue, though laced with thin clouds, inside the Star of Atlantis, fine points of light gleamed.

Stars secreted. Stars that'd guided him. Stars he had named, one by one, as he slept. Stars that seemed to belong just to him as they presented themselves meekly, but for all that in profound beauty, for his eyes alone, through his crystal.

The Sunstone's capacity to capture the stars—this, more than anything, lent Swift a sure hope that it might yet be genuine. That it still might deliver him to a great destiny.

When he'd spoken to Ash on the phone, on the rescue boat, Ash said he knew where Swift could have the Sunstone appraised. Ash seemed to think it was worth some money.

And if it were authentic, it would carry a price.

Swift couldn't imagine accepting money for it.

For all its wonder, for all the sweat he'd invested into learning to sail on the Welsh North Atlantic, for all his research, for all he and Caius, not to mention the *Strider*, had been through—nothing, not even an ancient Norse Sunstone, was worth facing the deadly sea like they had.

And the mere idea of assigning the value of a coin to something so extraordinary, so tied to myths and to histories, to stars —it seemed vile.

Swift held the Sunstone to the lights on the hospital monitoring screens and watched its facets glint.

How strong his ambition had been, his competitiveness.

How resolutely he'd argued with Caius, how bullheaded he'd been about chasing this.

And how kind Caius had been to receive all that and still take him sailing—to suffer, so Swift could realize this dream. So he could claim his so-called destiny.

If Swift had known, though, that this would cost the *Strider* a gashed hull, that it would cost Caius a broken leg and the death of his own dream of studying medicine, he never would've touched a sail.

At a sharp knock, Swift glanced up.

The door opened.

Brooke was there, holding the door as Caius, leaning on crutches, limped through.

"Caius!" Swift wanted to jump up but felt too unsteady. He eased the Sunstone back into its cage.

4

"Hey, you."

Caius, shimmying in through the doorway, seemed unable to take his eyes off Swift.

Unchecked delight shone on his face despite that he was having to wedge himself through the small opening Brooke—holding the door—was allowing.

Why wasn't that nurse moving out of his way? Why wasn't she helping him? Caius was on crutches, and his whole leg was strapped into a brace. It even seemed she was making him squeeze by her on purpose.

As Caius eased in, something passed between him and Brooke that Swift had no part in. It made him turn away.

Brooke smiled sweetly at Caius, then at Swift. "I'll leave you two to catch up." She slipped out.

"What a relief." Caius limped to the bed. "I can't tell you how badly I've needed to see you awake." He stopped before Swift. "You still look very pale. I hoped you'd have more color when you fully woke."

He leaned his crutches against a chair and hopped to sitting next to Swift on the bed.

"You look"—the words hitched in Swift's throat as images

rushed of Caius white as the moon; Caius lying unconscious on the cold sand—"alive."

Swift's gaze traveled his brother's body down to his shin, which was bandaged neatly beneath the brace.

"I thought—"

"You thought I might not have the decency to be right in when you woke?" Caius felt Swift's cheeks. "Why don't you lie back? If you wear out, that nurse of yours will make me leave."

"I bet she would." Swift rested against his pillow. "All I've wanted, all this time, was to see you. I remember waking up once, even, asking for you." He was patient for Caius to adjust a sheet over him. "But she hasn't let me. She seems very bossy."

"Bossy." Caius, half-smiling, fidgeted with his phone, read a text, then slid it inside his pocket. "Brooke's actually great. She's the best nurse here if you ask me. Your doctor, Dr. Keats, would say the same. Anyone in this place probably would. She took care of me, and I asked that she care for you, too. She even worked overtime when I was in bad shape—as many hours as she could."

"Well, I'm thankful to her for that," said Swift. "But she should've let me see you."

"Can I take a look at your cut?"

Swift lifted his shirt.

Caius loosened the bandage.

"The swelling is sure down, but you're still a mess of bruises."

He lightly pressed the skin around the scab.

"Still. This is looking loads better. Every day."

"Every day—for nine days. It feels like barely any time has passed since we were in Sterncastle Cove."

"I can imagine it seems so to you," said Caius. "This about did you in."

"Did me in?"

"It was touch-and-go with you for the first several days," said Caius. "You were flat out in a coma. I couldn't rest at all until I was told you'd turned a corner."

He pressed on a rash of red dots spraying across Swift's ribs.

"What could you possibly have rambled into to win a wound like this?"

"I was so worried about you," said Swift. "A bone sticking out of somebody is way more terrible than a cut. Every time I came around the slightest bit, you were all I could think about. You, and the *Strider*."

He caught Caius' glance.

"Is the *Strider* gone?"

"She's patched," said Caius. "Tied up by our dock in Pembrokeshire."

"Is Justus meaning to fix her?" asked Swift.

"The hull suffered a gouge—"

Swift winced at that.

"—but she might sail again."

"With your leg"—Swift glanced down at it—"with what the *Strider's* been through, it's difficult to believe I escaped with only a cut."

Caius gently replaced the bandage. "This is some serious trouble—a blood infection. You suffered a pretty dangerous fever with it. Dr. Keats thinks you were bitten by a tick you picked up in the rough, and a relapsing fever disease set in. Delirious, you might've stumbled on some scrap metal on the beach to manage this cut. Or you may've slipped on sharp rocks, like I did. Do you remember a fall?"

Swift pushed to his elbows. "When I left you to find help, I stumbled on a fisherman, sleeping. I startled him awake, and he cut me with a dagger. It was a long dagger. It sliced right through my clothes. Its hilt was silver and shaped like the twisting tail of a mermaid."

"I understand that's what you reported to the medics on our rescue boat," said Caius. "But you were far gone with fever, even then. Do you remember nothing besides those hallucinations?"

"I didn't hallucinate," said Swift. "I did find a man on the beach. He really cut me with his dagger."

Caius felt Swift's forehead.

Swift ducked back. "I'm not making this up. I remember it all, clear as starlight."

"What else do you remember?"

Swift recounted his journey, from leaving Caius in their makeshift camp, to stumbling his way through the brambles edging the Wentletrap Forest, to happening upon the sleeping fisherman.

He described how the man had complained of the poor fishing and uncovered the boat's rope, concealed with sand and seaweed; how he'd drawn the longboat out from behind a cluster of rocks; how he'd been sorry for cutting Swift; how he'd vanished.

Swift held up the Star of Atlantis as he relived for Caius the wonder of using it—a Sunstone forged by ancient seafarers. He told Caius about oaring the fisherman's longboat until he couldn't oar; how he'd kept true to west by spying veiled stars and constellations through the Sunstone; how he'd spotted a ship by peering at the shape of its sails against the shine of the stars through his crystal; how he'd sent up a rocket flare to hail it; how he'd dreamed of seeing Caius appear in his boat and felt, at long last, some relief.

After Swift finished, Caius remained quiet.

"You don't believe me, do you?" asked Swift.

Caius gently took the Sunstone from Swift.

He turned it over in a familiar way, as though he'd held it, too, over these last nine days.

"While we were making for the beach," said Caius, "I roused from time to time. There were moments when it seemed your face was underwater."

He glanced off.

"I actually believed you'd drowned. If you did fall unconscious in the water, the cut could've happened without you realizing it."

The memory of the knife was so vivid—Swift could precisely recall how it'd flashed in the moonlight.

"It's not that I mistrust you," said Caius. "It's just...why in the world would a fisherman be sleeping on a cold beach so treacherous, beside waters so dangerous? Why would he have cut you, then been sorry for it, then just disappeared?"

That last point was sound.

Swift, even, couldn't account for the fisherman's disappearance. A strange cry had pealed from the Wentletrap Forest—a sound the man had said was "a summons." Then he was just gone.

"Once on shore, I put us in dry clothes," said Swift. "I dressed in my hoodie and windbreaker. When the fisherman cut me, blood got everywhere. Those clothes have to be around, someplace."

"What sort of person, upon seeing a boy in profound distress, would offer no help, other than a heavy boat, and then vanish?" asked Caius. "You must admit how extraordinary that seems, that he'd let a boy—a boy he just cut with a dagger—go out on the North Atlantic alone."

"He was extraordinary," said Swift. "Maybe even a little disturbed. But there's nothing wrong with camping on wild Welsh coasts. I mean—we've done that. And besides, it seemed the fisherman was there for some purpose other than fishing. He somehow guessed I'd taken the Star of Atlantis, and he wanted me to keep it. The way he spoke—he made me feel I was destined to find it."

"To be honest, that bit of your story is mostly what's making me skeptical," said Caius. "You and I were the only ones who knew you took the Star of Atlantis. So doesn't it make sense that, if you imagined talking to a fisherman, he'd know what you know?"

A stinging in his chest made Swift sit up more. Although the pain didn't seem to be coming just from the cut. Caius' doubt was churning up not a small measure of anxiety.

"Maybe the fisherman saw us climbing that islet," said Swift. "Or he might've guessed I was after the Star of Atlantis, being so near to Sterncastle Cove."

Caius had always given him the credence of being a good thinker. The idea of Caius discrediting him was unbearable.

"Because he knew"—Swift drew a sharp breath—"all about it."

"Take it easy," said Caius.

A great deal of Swift's confidence was founded on how confident Caius was in him.

"He told me things I'd never read about."

"Swift, slow down."

Was Caius withdrawing his trust? Would he do that?

"How could he know things I didn't"—Swift managed, with the little air he could hang on to—"if I made him up?"

Caius rested his hand on Swift's chest, just above the cut.

The weight of it made breathing easier.

"Look, you have a great imagination," said Caius. "Maybe what you recall was all part of a vivid dream."

"The fisherman was real. He knew I had the Star of Atlantis. And he knew all about it." Swift took the Sunstone from Caius. "He seemed like some sort of—I don't know. Sentry."

"Oh, boy." Caius rubbed his eyes. "Please don't tell me you think you saw Cynfael Maddox. A ghost."

"That isn't what I'm saying, exactly. It's just—"

Caius glanced off.

"—Cynfael Maddox was a historical person," said Swift. "Do you not remember the accounts I've found about a Welsh clan living in secrecy—the Shepherds of the Stars? I can't help wondering if the fisherman was one of them."

"You're an outstanding researcher, no doubt," said Caius. "So tell me—don't you find the idea of running across some vagrant connected to an obscure, centuries-old-pirate-turned-good-guy story you dredged up, unlikely?"

"The way you're saying it out loud, with your eyebrows all up and everything"—Swift rested the Sunstone beside his thigh—"of course it sounds ridiculous. But Maddox captained a ship called the *Checkered Whelk*. I found the fisherman mumbling in his sleep, and he said, 'Checkered Whelk.' A descendant or follower of the Shepherds of the Stars would've known about that ship. What I can't figure out is why he would've let me sail off with the Star of Atlantis? I wish I could find him. Ask him."

Caius straightened the sheet over Swift. "We'd do well to leave this for a bit."

"Leave it with you not believing me?" Swift blinked back a sudden flash of tears. "With you thinking I'm crazy?"

"I don't think you're crazy. It's just—"

Swift forced himself to sit up all the way. "Let's assume everything I've told you is true." He struggled to recover from a windedness from moving. "If so, what would you make of it?"

"If it's true, I'd like to find that mad fisherman and give him what for, for cutting my brother."

"The things the fisherman said to me were absolutely nowhere in any research I've read." He paused to draw breath. "Doesn't a person having such rare knowledge seem more purposed than mad?" Another quick breath that was hard to let go of. "And I was rescued in his longboat. That's not something dreamed. It's evidence."

The door swung open, and in came Brooke. "Swift?"

At the sight of her, he deflated. Despite that he was losing some control, he'd just started feeling he was getting somewhere with Caius.

"You okay?" She hurried to a monitor and divided her attention between studying it and studying him.

Caius glanced at the monitor. "I'm sorry. I shouldn't have pressed him to talk over his memories just now."

"Don't apologize," said Swift. "With you here, I'm feeling better and better." Though he couldn't garner enough strength in his voice to make the claim sound believable.

"I don't at all like what I'm seeing," said Brooke.

"What are those screens telling you?" asked Swift.

"That you're quite agitated and need to rest." Glancing at Caius, she tipped her head toward the door.

"Please don't make Caius go," said Swift. "We only were talking."

"I'm afraid, then," said Brooke, "even talking might be too much activity."

It wasn't. It most certainly wasn't. Working this out seemed critical.

With all that gravity on Brooke's face, though, with how Caius was watching her in a trusting way—it seemed Brooke carried as much power over Caius as what she wielded over Justus.

Swift laid down flat. "I'll stay just like this. Please—let Caius stay."

Caius glanced at Brooke, then dipped a rag in a cup of ice water. He scooted closer to Swift.

"I'll be right at the station if you need me," said Brooke. "And I'll be watching your monitor from there. If I see another spike in your heart rate like that, I'll have to administer a sedative."

Caius watched her close the door, then touched the cool cloth for a moment to each side of Swift's neck.

"The longboat," said Swift, concentrating on the feel of his heart slowing beneath Caius' hand.

"The longboat was covered in hundreds of fingerprints," said Caius, gently. "The Coast Guard thinks that it's probably a community fishing boat, used by the rare local over a very long span of time. That's the truth of the matter."

"But the fact of the longboat even existing," said Swift, "does that not hint that the truth in all this might be strange?"

A small bit of wonder crossed Caius' features.

Caius might be finding his story intriguing, if unbelievable. He might be wanting to believe it.

"I'll concede that stories," said Caius, "like the one you're conjuring, are compelling. Stories of spirits haunting desolate coasts. Stories of people who lived on the water, died on the water, centuries ago, who can't walk away from the sea."

"I'm not conjuring anything." Swift rubbed the edge of his bandage, where the cut's stinging was sharpening.

"We probably could even find stories where daggers are the implement of choice for Norse pirates."

Swift relaxed some.

What if—just what if—that were the case? Who knew but

that the dagger was a relic belonging to Cynfael Maddox, passed down through generations of Star Shepherds?

"But to help you heal," said Caius, "Dr. Keats needs fewer stories and more of the truth."

The ease that'd settled vanished, leaving Swift feeling wasted.

"Aren't stories sometimes the closest we can get to the truth?" Swift rested his hand on his Sunstone. "Without that fisherman telling me how to use this, I never would've kept my heading out to open water. The current would've dragged me way south." He winced at an ache striking the center of the cut. "Without his teaching, I never would've spotted that ship, or known when to send up the rocket flare."

"You're feeling some pain, aren't you?" Caius reached for the nurse's button.

"Don't." Swift glanced at the monitor.

Every reading was lighting up "normal."

Caius pressed the button.

"Do you need something urgently?" asked a voice over the speaker. "Brooke stepped out, but she'll be back in a moment."

"Nothing urgent," said Caius. "Please send her in when she's back. Swift could use something for a bit of pain. I'll get him some ice water."

He eased to standing.

Swift snagged Caius' shirt.

It was reflexive—the same impulse that'd made him grip Caius as he leaned over the bludgeoning waves to try and right the *Strider*.

Caius gazed at Swift's fingers, hooked in his sweater's hem.

"It was the memory of how cold you looked," said Caius, sitting back down. "That's what's kept me from rest. Every time I close my eyes, I see you trying to climb, numb handed, out of the water. And you were a heartbeat from slipping off those chancy rocks." He pulled a blanket up across Swift's chest. "I'm told I even talked in my sleep about you, about being afraid you weren't warm."

Swift held Caius' hand against his chest, beside the cut.

Whether the Sunstone had granted him a destiny or not, having Caius here with him—it seemed like they both might be all right.

"Will you answer me something honestly?" asked Swift.

"Ask me anything," said Caius.

"Do you blame me for what happened?"

"Blame you—"

"Justus told me." Swift couldn't look at Caius as he spoke the sorrowful words. "You might not keep on with med school. That's my fault." He shifted the Sunstone away from his thigh.

"Understand this." Caius held Swift's gaze. "We wrecked, yes. But our tale is this—I pulled you out of the water to save your life. And you pulled me into the water to save mine. Neither of us has anything to regret."

"Is it true—now you can't be a trauma surgeon?" asked Swift.

"Some people are saying that." Caius lent a small smile. "But I hope they're wrong."

Swift glanced at his brother's leg, purple at the rim of the bandage.

"And along that score, there's something else we need to speak about." Caius gathered the Sunstone into his hands. "If you're up for some brother-to-brother honesty, that is. Because I'd like you to hear this first from me."

Swift glanced at the Sunstone in Caius' hands. Did he know it might be counterfeit? He met Caius' gaze.

"There's talk that you, likewise, have little chance of keeping on," said Caius. "The toll a coma takes is significant. And we don't know how long you may suffer with recurring fevers. To get into the medical Practicum—if you're still wanting it—your entrance exam scores would have to be perfect."

They would have to be perfect, it was true. They would be perfect.

"After what we've been through," said Swift, "I know I have what it takes. And I'm not talking about mastering chemistry and biology and maths and managing difficult projects. I was desperate to help you. And I found I could—or at least I could try. In that moment, I saw what it was to be wholly with someone, helping them. It was pure medicine I dealt in. Not medicine damaged by ego and politics and power struggles like what you and Justus talk about. It was sheer empathy. And I loved it."

"Just—be prepared." Caius, wincing, adjusted the position of his leg. "You might hear doubts from others. Like Dr. Keats."

"How could he have any opinion?" asked Swift. "He doesn't know me."

"But he knows the body, its limits. And, as one of its teaching doctors, he knows the Practicum. He's not wrong that we both might be in for a challenging recovery."

"But I'm healing." Swift glanced at his chest, aching, yes, but as a mending bruise aches.

"Even sitting upright might prove fatiguing for you," said Caius, "for a while."

"Then I'll study lying down."

Caius cast him a half-smile. "If you decide not to go for the Practicum—that's fine. But don't let anyone tell you that you can't. All right?"

Swift held his hand out for the Star of Atlantis. "This won't be the first time I've forged a path through dark waters."

Caius placed the Sunstone in Swift's hand.

5

Caius stood from Swift's bed at their mum and father opening the hospital room door. Mum hurried in and took Caius' place. Justus followed and shrugged off his coat.

"Are you in pain, Love?" Mum cradled Swift's cheek. "Any at all?"

Swift was patient for her to gather him into a gentle hug. "I'm fine." He pulled away at a twinge of stinging from the cut.

Justus held him by the shoulders and looked him over.

He pulled up Swift's shirt and glanced beneath the bandage. "Hand me that ointment, Adara, from the counter. We'll see him more comfortable."

Justus seemed not so much the tender father Swift remembered from when he first woke. Justus now was all business, his fingers—easing the sting of the cut, prodding at its edges— doctor's fingers.

This was the Justus Swift knew. Distant. Though warm at that distance. And it was some comfort.

Brooke, holding a lunch tray, shouldered open the door.

Caius pulled the door wide for her.

Brooke was a pretty girl. Too pretty.

Her large eyes were dark, and they shone. Her hair seemed

51

as glossed as the North Sea beneath a moonlit night. She wore it in a perfect twist, like what Mum wore only for formal events.

Brooke was slender, but not slender everywhere, which Caius seemed to be appreciating.

"Want to try and eat?" Brooke asked Swift.

Swift could imagine he might grow hungry soon, but he wanted the snacks, the cooking they kept at home. Not whatever was under that lid on Brooke's tray.

"It's worth a try, yes?" Brooke placed the tray on Swift's bedside table. "Caius loved the dishes I served."

Caius smiled at her in a simpering way.

Swift met Justus' eyes. "Any chance you could get them to let me go home?"

If they'd let him go home, he could have Caius to himself, and they could work up a study plan for the Practicum entrance exams. If they'd let him go home, Caius couldn't whisper whatever he was whispering to Brooke, making her widen her too-pretty smile.

"They'll likely release you in a day or two." Justus glanced at the tray. "They'll want to see you can eat."

"If you aren't hungry now, I bet you soon will be." Brooke lifted the lid off the tray. "You've not had anything for a week that didn't come from a tube."

Swift examined the tray and its scant blandness.

"But do go easy," said Brooke. "You eat too much too soon, it'll all come right back up."

She lifted a syringe and took his hand.

Swift held back.

She smiled pleasantly at him. "This won't make you fall asleep—it's a light pain medicine." She injected it. "You're not yet due for the strong one."

She moved to the counter and flicked on a laptop.

Caius, staring at Brooke, leaned close to Swift. "Isn't she something? Not too bossy, right?"

Swift just stared at her, her hair gleaming darkly in a gorgeous way even beneath the severity of the fluorescent exam lights.

Justus approached Brooke. "Is there word on Swift's biopsy?"

"I haven't seen any reports come through today," she said. "But let me check."

"What biopsy?" Swift pushed away a bowl of gelatin that had seemed passible until he removed the plastic and discovered it runny.

"Doctor Keats ordered a biopsy of your cut, and it's due back today," said Caius. "Traces of metals or chemicals can sometimes linger, which can clue us in as to what did that to you."

"I know what did this to me."

Caius and Justus exchanged glances.

Mum gathered Swift's fingers inside her soft hand and held them gingerly, careful to avoid any pressure on his IV. "Could you try telling us about it?"

"Of course I can tell you—I remember it perfectly," said Swift. "I ran along the coast and found a fisherman. I startled him awake. He was holding a knife, and he cut me. He didn't mean to, though."

"Let's think harder, lad," said Justus. "Putting aside your fisherman, let's see if we can remember a fall."

Swift sat taller. "I didn't fall."

"Perhaps think back to being in the water," said Mum. "Do you remember the swim?"

"Of course I do."

"All of it?"

"Yes, but—well—what happened there sort of runs together."

Swift held Mum's hand tighter.

"There were spans of just darkness. I might've passed out. I don't know. But I'm certain I came fully to myself when I felt the sandbar under my feet."

"So—it could've happened in the water." Mum glanced at Justus. "That must be."

"But in the water, I didn't feel this pain. And wouldn't my sailing suit have been torn? But it wasn't." Swift gently touched the edge of the bandage. "Once on shore, I would've seen that I was cut."

"The biopsy report—it's arrived," said Brooke. "It was entered a half-hour ago. Looks like Dr. Keats already signed off that he's seen it."

Caius hobbled to standing behind her.

"How odd," said Brooke.

Justus slipped on his glasses and leaned in. *"Traces of metal,"* he read.

"That's standard enough," said Caius, "if he stumbled into some beach rubbish."

Swift pressed his temple. "I didn't stumble into any rubbish."

"Finding traces of metal is common." Brooke pointed at the screen. "But this isn't."

"Nickel ore," read Justus.

Brooke faced him. "I've never seen nickel appear in a wound biopsy."

"Is that a poison or something?" asked Mum, unsteadily.

"No, nothing like that," said Brooke. "It's just unusual. It means he was cut by something out of the ordinary."

"It means he was cut by a weapon."

Everyone spun toward the doorway, where a tall doctor stood, his badge reading: *Dr. Jairo Keats.*

Dr. Jairo Keats seemed only a few years older than Caius, yet he carried a dignity rivaling Justus. Striding in, he was the advance of a thunderhead.

From the stories Justus and Caius had told Swift, Dr. Keats had grown into almost a myth.

Being in his care brought his patients a strong sense of peace, they said. Dr. Keats tended not just to the disease, but to the person. He kept in close tune with his patients, with their pain. No one in his charge unnecessarily suffered.

And the doctor's gaze—it held Swift, keeping his attention hard fixed. Dr. Keats' eyes weren't at all common—they were a shade of hazel tending golden. Lion eyes.

Being unconscious in a coma for these last nine days struck

Swift as quite a shame. He'd been Dr. Keats' patient, but not consciously.

Caius backed off from the computer, from Brooke, in an obsequious way.

Justus removed his glasses and reached his hand. "Keats."

Dr. Keats took Justus' hand. "How's your lad?"

He advanced toward the bed and laid Swift flat. In a split second, he had Swift's shirt off, his bandage removed, and was pressing carefully at the wound. Swift was so surprised at being handled, he had no chance to fear the pain that might erupt with the prodding. But none came. The doctor's tuned hands seemed to know how to avoid inciting any.

Brooke read off a list of status points.

"And his pain?" Dr. Keats felt along the red seam of the healing cut.

Swift held his breath. But the doctor's hands remained easy, their intelligence and sensitivity winning, and they left the wound in peace.

Caius had mentioned that Dr. Keats was a teacher in the Practicum program. It was he from whom Swift would be learning—possibly mentoring with—should he manage to test in.

Watching the doctor's intelligent eyes, his hands keen and fleet in his work, Swift wanted nothing more than to be his student.

"Has he any nausea? Difficulty moving?" Dr. Keats asked Brooke.

It seemed odd he wasn't talking to Swift—lying right here, fully awake.

Dr. Keats probably wasn't used to him awake, though. Swift had been his unconscious object of study for nine days—little more than a damaged machine.

Dr. Keats quickly felt Swift's forehead, his neck, his belly.

Swift tried to come up with something to say, but the doctor never slowed long enough in his work to let Swift think.

And the gold in his eyes, when they did meet Swift's, lent a weight that kept him stone still.

"He's in a little pain, now," said Brooke. "I've just tended that. He's getting some strength back. He dressed on his own. Not much appetite, though."

Swift glanced at the liquidy gelatin. "If you'd eat that, so would I."

Dr. Keats cast an amused look at Swift—at the oddity, it seemed, that his damaged machine had spoken.

"Doctor." Mum touched his arm. "What did you mean—he was cut by a weapon?"

Dr. Keats went to the computer and analyzed it with the same intensity he'd used to read Swift's body.

"We never see nickel in an acute cut like this. Even if you look at large samplings of trauma wounds, beyond this hospital —beyond this country—it's not to be found."

Swift pushed his way to sitting.

Dr. Keats returned and deftly laid him back down.

He studied the two tips of the wound. "This looks like a classic knife slash. I thought so when I first saw it. And with nickel showing up in the biopsy, it undoubtedly was a knife. It's likely that the infection came from a bacteria carried on a blade rather than from an insect bite, as we theorized early on."

"But if nickel's so rare," asked Mum, "how can you be certain that it came from a weapon? Surely, a beach might have scrap metals of all kinds among what might wash up."

"Nickel is uncommon in metal manufacturing," said Dr. Keats. "If we'd seen other alloys, I'd maintain suspicion that the cut came from beach waste. Nickel, in this concentration, doesn't come from sheet metal, wire, cans, or other such goods. It actually doesn't even come from the Earth."

"Not from the Earth." Justus rested his hand on Swift's knee. "Then, where?"

"Meteorites," said Dr. Keats. "There isn't all that much nickel to be found in Earth's mines. The Earth's core is dense with it, but most of what once threaded through the crust has drifted inward. Meteorites, though, are chock full of nickel. And there are accounts of ancient peoples fashioning weapons from meteorite ore, strong as it is. Meteorites are so rarely discovered now that you couldn't count on finding knives made of nickel today. Though you can see them in museums."

"Was there no sediment in the cut?" asked Justus, rubbing his beard. "No granite? No feldspar?"

Brooke looked again at the report. "Not a trace."

"Then—Swift's story of the fisherman," said Caius. "Is it even possible? If knives like this are scarce, could some coastal wanderer manage to get one?"

"Who can say?" asked Dr. Keats.

Swift relaxed a touch at the fact that the doctor wasn't doubting his claim, nor reaching to find some more palatable explanation.

His family, holding silence, seemed struggling to let go of their doubt of his story. But they did seem to be letting it go.

"So, it actually was a knife." Mum's purse slipped off her shoulder. "Someone cut him."

A tinge of defensiveness for the fisherman rose in Swift. Not only were his memories of the man founded on gratitude for giving him the boat that led to their rescue—they were also colored with a touch of tenderness for the way he'd reminded Swift of a disturbed soldier.

And how mystical his words had been. In them, Swift had sensed knowledge. Cleverness. Gentleness. Greatness.

"The fisherman wasn't aggressive," said Swift. "He was troubled a little, I think. Maybe not quite all there, at first. But he was wholly present once he fully woke."

How much he'd known about Sunstones, about the Star of Atlantis. And how insightfully he'd spoken of its legends, even if some of the talk had been cryptic.

Swift couldn't guess what the fisherman had meant, saying Swift was pinned with a role in the tale of the Star of Atlantis— what he called "a magnificent mess."

But that remark felt like the opening of a complicated riddle —it hinted at a great depth of insight resting just under the surface.

And it instilled in Swift a sense of destiny—though perhaps of a dark nature.

"I wish I could find the fisherman," said Swift.

He could show the man his *Star of Atlantis* book and map and see what he knew of the Cthulhu myth.

If anyone could reconcile the anachronism with the wonder, it seemed the fisherman could. And the craving Swift felt to connect with a teacher, like Dr. Keats—to learn insights by which he could accomplish great things—extended to the fisherman. He felt desperate to ask the man what he knew about the Star of Atlantis—what he hadn't revealed.

Mum shifted her gaze from the doctor onto Swift. "Why ever would you want to find him?"

Swift glanced at his Sunstone. "It was extraordinary talking to him. And it's possible he needs help. He has to be missing his longboat."

"A dagger-wielding vagrant isn't anyone you should be worrying about." Mum touched the corner of her eye. "These findings in his biopsy—will they be given to the police?"

"Yes, they must be," said Brooke, "seeing as this might be a knife crime."

"It isn't any sort of crime," said Swift.

"Let's leave that for the police," said Mum. "I, for one, think it quite obviously is."

"Mum—he gave me his boat," said Swift. "If it weren't for him, Caius and I might not have survived. I ought to at least try and return his boat."

Dr. Keats looked up from the computer. Looked straight at Swift.

At the sight of those golden eyes—intelligent, compassionate —Swift stilled. Dr. Keats understood the cut, yes, and was healing it. But more importantly, he seemed to grasp what was going on beneath the cut.

In this second of connection, Swift felt he was this doctor's student.

"I'd urge you not to bother with that notion," said Dr. Keats. "It seems your memory of what happened is pretty accurate. But I'd guess your fisherman is mentally ill. Likely a drifter. Difficult to track."

"If weapons made from meteorite metals are ancient"—Swift sat up as much as he could—"maybe Icelandic pirates had weapons like that."

"Swift," said Caius. "Don't badger Dr. Keats with that manner of thought."

Doctor Keats came away from the computer and sat at the foot of Swift's bed.

Caius and Brooke's eyes together widened. They exchanged glances.

"Who's really to say?" Dr. Keats folded his arms. "It's consistent with tradition, I guess, that Icelandic seafarers kept rarities. A meteorite-fashioned knife is no scarcer than the Sunstone you found, seated in Icelandic legends."

The room lay in a dead silence, everyone seeming to be waiting for more from Dr. Keats. Or perhaps they didn't want to sully the effect of the sound of his voice.

Though Swift felt the charm of it as much as anyone seemed to, he couldn't resist the sense of invitation now waiting in those golden eyes.

"Do you want to see it?" Swift presented the Star of Atlantis.

Dr. Keats took the crystal as though he were receiving a bird who'd broken a delicate wing. He eased it over. Studied its edges. Held it up to the window.

Swift held himself in a desperate fit of quiet, waiting for Dr. Keats to talk about the accident. About meteorites and ancient weapons. About his Practicum. About medicine. About anything.

"Astonishing." Dr. Keats handed it back to Swift. "Not unlike the boy who found it."

"Is it true you're a teacher in the youth Practicum program?" asked Swift.

Dr. Keats watched Swift in a keen way.

Maybe he could sense how profoundly Swift wanted to be in his company.

Maybe he could tell Swift was craving to be with a teacher —a great one.

"I'm the lead lecturer for our youth interns." Dr. Keats stood. "Your father tells me the Practicum's something you might like to do."

Here, in the presence of Dr. Jairo Keats, the flame in Swift, simmering for the study of medicine, roared. "More than anything."

Dr. Keats glanced at Justus and Mum with an expression reflective of their pride in their lad. But the look also seemed to carry a shared sorrow.

"Astrochemistry appears quite to your liking." Dr. Keats, moved again to the computer. "I learned a bit of astronomy from you, as you rested. Your mind is full of the names and positions of stars. Their chemistry and composition. Their physics. And you're clearly adept at languages. Some of your speaking, Caius identified for me as Old Norse and Celtic Akkadian."

Dr. Keats didn't seem put off by the fact that Swift had been rambling while asleep. Rather, he seemed to be admiring Swift for it.

Swift wanted to hop up and follow him, just to watch him at whatever work he had. "Would you teach me medicine?"

The words came blurted, surfacing wholly from a deep, pure desire.

Dr. Keats, his eyes on the screen, his fingers rapidly typing, seemed to be smiling to himself. "If you make your way into my Practicum—yes."

Of course Dr. Keats would want nothing to do with Swift now. Swift had hardly proven to possess anything he might want in a student. Even though he'd tried to take care of Caius, he'd botched the job. Swift's best accomplishment was seeing to completion the discovery of the Star of Atlantis.

But Caius had stressed—before they even sailed into Stern-castle Cove—that a discovery of a treasure, even one so remarkable, would get Swift nowhere in medicine.

Dr. Keats watched Swift, his expression betraying a close understanding. "It's important that you realize how brilliant you were on the night that this happened."

Dr. Keats—so empathetic—seemed to grasp how painful it'd

been for Swift to see Caius so terribly injured; how frightening had been the isolation of that desolate beach; how shocking the realization that he might not save Caius. Or himself.

"The way you handled your brother was marvelous." Dr. Keats' eyes on Swift no longer seemed like the gaze of a physician on a patient.

It was as though he were a war-seasoned general regarding a small act of bravery on a fresh recruit.

Caius seemed to notice the esteem in the doctor's expression. He flashed a smile Swift's way.

Swift lay back, not for any fever or exhaustion—it was more a swoon. A disbelief that magnificent Dr. Keats was speaking like this to him; Dr. Keats, who dealt in the horrors of medicine. And its wonders.

Swift could imagine Dr. Keats like himself—loathe just to function within a medical system. Dr. Keats seemed like a maestro musician, a technical wizard—someone who innovated, improvising strategies to drive back death and pain.

"You kept your brother warm and managed to control the bleeding to an extent," said Dr. Keats. "When I was briefed that Caius was on his way, my heart broke. I was sure I'd find him beyond help. But looking him over, it was like I was receiving him from another physician who'd been on location."

Swift lowered his gaze from the doctor. Despite those generous words, he couldn't bring himself to believe he'd had much to do with Caius' survival. Much of the credit was due to the medics on their rescue boat.

And Dr. Keats was the ultimate champion who'd brought Caius back to the world of the living.

Swift's own survival, too, was owed to Dr. Keats.

Dr. Keats felt Swift's forehead, his wrist. "I must get on." He didn't look at Swift again. Just at Brooke. "Keep me posted, should there be any change." He glanced at Mum, at Justus. "Brooke will educate you on how to treat recurring fevers, and on the risk of febrile seizures."

"Seizures," said Mum.

"The chances are slight but concerning." Doctor Keats

glanced at Swift. "I expect that the fevers aren't finished with him."

"Must he stay here much longer?" asked Justus.

"He's out of the worst of it." Dr. Keats set to scrubbing his hands at a sink by the door. "I expect he'll grow stronger by the day. If he remains fever-free for us, he may go home in the morning."

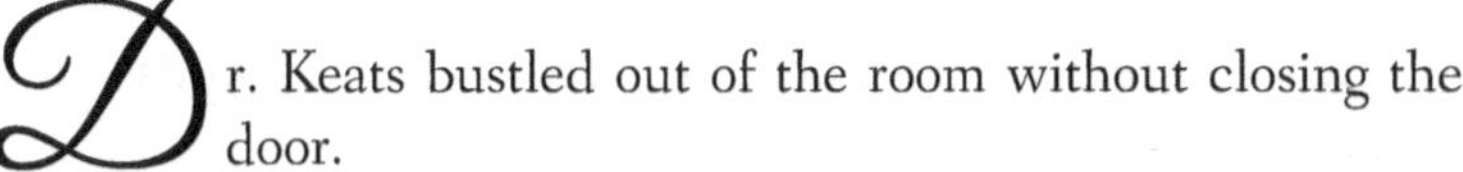

6

*D*r. Keats bustled out of the room without closing the door.

His departure felt like the dying down of wind, like a storm had moved in, making everyone tense and bracing—and now the clouds were slipping away, pressure lifting by degrees.

Everyone kept their eyes on the doorway, the sense of something deific passing hanging in a silence they all kept.

It wasn't just that Dr. Keats was a great physician. Justus himself, an anesthesiologist, had been in medicine a long time and had earned a great deal of acclaim. Dr. Keats was known, worldwide, for his laser-sharp insight. He could diagnose quickly and with precision, setting critically ill patients on the way to healing at unheard of rates. And his skill with performing complex operations was unmatched.

As young as Dr. Keats was, he also seemed ancient—the way an oak, merely decades old, carries the density, the deepness, the scars, that will serve to anchor it on the dawn of its five hundredth year.

Swift lifted his Sunstone and, through it, watched the doctor recede. Veiled by the crystal, his lab coat looked like a mainsail billowing. Or a full moon flying west and vanishing in a mist.

Finally, Justus closed the door. It fell with reverent finality—a curtain draping a holy place.

"Ever seen him sit on a patient's bed?" Caius asked Brooke.

She was staring at Swift. "Not once."

Justus took a seat. "Among our colleagues, Dr. Keats is known as 'Emperor Vespasian.' *Miracle Worker.*"

"That's not his only name," said Brooke. "His students call him *the Thresher.*"

"That sounds awfully threatening," said Mum. "Why would they?"

"He's good at dividing the wheat from the chaff," said Brooke. "From the outset, he seems to know who's going to succeed and who's bound to struggle."

"He's good at everything," said Caius. "He's in a league of his own for his skill with lost cases."

Swift's stomach dropped at hearing those words—"lost cases."

"Do you think you'd want to intern with him—perhaps mentor with him?" asked Justus, watching Swift with an appraising stare. "Were it to be."

Swift rested his gaze on the Star of Atlantis, the tendrils in the crystal gleaming white.

The victorious moment of claiming the Star of Atlantis felt morbid and gaudy from where he now sat, having almost lost Caius, having wrecked the *Star Strider*. Having set himself down in a touch-and-go coma.

But interning with Dr. Keats, investigating his approach to healing—this felt like the ultimate prize.

And there was no risk of, in the end, discovering Dr. Keats to be fake.

"I'd love for him to teach me." Swift laid his Sunstone aside.

Mum smiled gently at Swift. At his stone.

"Have you thought about what you might do with your discovery?"

Swift glanced at the stone, its corners sharp, sculpted by some ancient tool. Maybe a blade forged from a meteorite.

"You could situate it in a museum," said Mum. "I'm sure lots of people would love to see it."

A museum sounded like something he ought to consider—if the Sunstone were authentic. And perhaps getting rid of it would lessen the ache of the suffering he'd caused.

But a stronger part of him felt connected by the suffering, by the accident itself, to the Sunstone. Bound to it as the fisherman said that Swift was, and after gripping it for nine days and nights, it felt as essential to his body as a bone.

And what if it were truly the stone the myths described? What if by claiming it, he really had unlocked a destiny?

Even now, lying dully on a hospital blanket, the crystal seemed to carry the memory, the promise of starlight.

It'd delivered him to rescue. And perhaps it had yet more places to take him.

"You might have the option to keep the Sunstone," said Justus, leaning back in his chair. "Though, Wales will have laws governing the proper proceedings for discovered artifacts."

"When I spoke to Ash from the rescue boat," said Swift, "he told me of the museum that's keeping the relic he found."

"I shall reach out to Ash's father, then," said Justus. "The museum they used could likely appraise the Sunstone and lay out options should you chose to donate it."

"I don't want you to donate it." Caius limped away from Brooke and stood before Swift.

Swift glanced at Caius' leg. "Why wouldn't you want us to be rid of it?"

Caius picked up the Sunstone. "In the long run, you'll be glad you kept this. And I want it to get to be yours. I want a picture of you in the Metro, holding this—your conquest, your gallant discovery."

"Would it not make you ill, looking at that?" asked Swift. "Wouldn't it remind you that you almost—"

"—it would make me pleased and proud." Caius placed the Sunstone in Swift's hand.

Swift shivered at the chill of it.

Mum, her eyes still bearing tears, whispered, "A knife wound—"

"I'm up for a break in a minute," said Brooke, to Mum. "Why don't we go downstairs for some tea?"

"Oh"—Mum glanced at Swift—"I couldn't leave him."

"Mum, go," said Swift. "I'm all right."

"Go ahead with Brooke, Adara." Justus smiled at Brooke. "Great nurses have a sense of what we—all of us—need, to heal."

Mum kissed Swift on both cheeks, staining them with her tears.

Swift wrapped his arms around her. "I'm okay. Dr. Keats took good care of me." He glanced at Caius. "He took good care of both of us."

Caius, though, wasn't looking at Swift. He was looking at Brooke. Gazing at Brooke.

Mum, smiling gratefully at Brooke, eased away from Swift.

"Leave the lad to us." Justus stood and supported Caius to sitting on Swift's bed, taking the pressure off that leg. "We'll see that he eats some, then rests."

Mum followed Brooke from the room.

When the door closed, Swift pushed himself to sitting higher.

"Not too quickly." Justus eased him back. "I need you taking it very easy today."

Swift moved his father's hands off him and sat all the way up. "Can we talk straight? I'd like to make something very clear."

Justus pulled the chair closer to Swift's bed and sat.

Swift glanced at Caius. At Justus. "I want to go for the Practicum. I want it more than I ever have."

"I see," said Justus. "Can you articulate where this fresh resolve is coming from?"

"It's been strengthening for a while," said Swift. "But on that beach, with Caius, I felt something new. I didn't just think I could study the practice of medicine. I practiced medicine. Or— sort of. I saw it for all its terror and found I could face it anyway.

I saw what knowledge and skilled hands could do for someone. I wanted to be the rescue Caius needed."

"You were that rescue," said Caius.

"I was desperate to take away your pain," said Swift. "To fix what I'd done."

Caius leaned in. "I thought we'd established—you did nothing wrong."

Swift didn't meet his eyes.

"I must be frank with you, lad," said Justus. "The odds of testing into that Practicum are slim, as you know. With what you've been through—I suppose one might call this a setback. I don't mean to imply that you couldn't study well enough to prepare for the trials and possibly test in. But you might not manage to grasp the material as quickly as we imagined."

"Are you saying I can't do it?" asked Swift. "That you won't let me even try?"

"That's not at all what he's saying," said Caius.

"If you were to try," said Justus, "you'd need to acknowledge that it would be perfectly acceptable—were you to find it too strenuous—to bow out."

"I'm not going to bow out," said Swift.

Justus glanced at Caius. "We must be direct with you, lad." He eased forward in the chair. "As direct as you're wishing to be with us."

"I get what you're wanting me to hear," said Swift. "You're saying that I could quit. And I'm telling you that I won't. What more is there to talk about?"

Justus cast a prompting glance toward Caius.

"Following a trauma," said Caius, "one that set you down in a coma—it's possible you might have some longer lasting impairments."

"Impairments." Swift leaned back. "Like what?"

Justus rested his hand on Swift's bedrail. "Dr. Keats believes it's unlikely you suffered any brain damage, but—"

"You think my brain is damaged?"

"It's just," said Caius, "you might discover, over the coming days and weeks, that with some tasks—physical or cognitive—

you might need a bit more time, more effort, to perform at the levels you're used to."

"Look—I know comas are serious," said Swift. "But I'm fine. I could go home right now if they'd let me."

"And that fact delights us," said Justus. "But—"

"—but going at difficult tasks," said Caius, "such as running" —he cleared his throat—"or reading, might summon frustration."

"Okay—running, I might not be great at, right away," said Swift. "But reading? That won't be an issue."

"Indeed, you might have no struggle," said Justus. "But—assure me that you'll be honest with yourself, and with us, if you do. There's no shame in allowing oneself time to heal."

"Getting back on track might be a challenge, sure," said Swift. "But all I need is a chance to try." He glanced at his Sunstone, still seeming to hold the brightness of Dr. Keats' coat. "All I need is a teacher."

And for now, Caius could be that teacher. Caius was a great teacher. And he'd offered, many times, to help Swift prep for the Practicum exams.

Swift glanced at Caius' rucksack. "You have some texts in there?"

"I thought you'd never ask." Caius drew out a biochemistry textbook.

The look Caius cast him was electrifying.

Caius was wanting to teach him. It seemed Caius was enjoying the thought of how great it would be for them both to move forward, together.

Justus stared at Caius. "I don't believe you've taken that level of biochemistry."

"No." Caius handed Swift the book. "This is what Swift was most recently exploring. I brought it along in case I found him with an appetite for it."

Swift opened the book.

Justus leaned back. "Very well." He crossed his arms.

Swift turned a touch away from his father and those crossed arms, the sight of which was proving more painful than the cut, which was starting to sting again. He rubbed at the edge of his bandage.

"The pain's getting to you, isn't it?" Caius pressed the nurse's call button.

Knowing that Brooke was on break was a comfort.

Another nurse could come and see about his pain. Another nurse, maybe, wouldn't capture Caius' focus the way Brooke did.

Swift flipped through the biochemistry text to where he'd left off. He studied the section headings.

"Think you could read through that chapter and do the quiz for me at the end?" asked Caius.

Swift turned a few pages in.

This section included technical words. Not to mention a few challenging diagrams. The basics of the chapter outline were familiar—but there were too many new concepts for him to recall everything he'd studied.

Surmising the list of chapter objectives was like gazing up a mountain's height; like looking up a steep islet, a treacherous islet; an islet shaped like the sterncastle on a ship; an islet harboring treasure, yes, but lashed by deadly waves; an islet studded with jetting rocks—sharp—to break bone.

Swift could no longer see the words on the page but could only see blood on the sand. Blood beneath Caius' leg, the bone jagged, the purple skin cold.

Justus eased the book from Swift's hands.

It wasn't until he was free of it that Swift realized he was hyperventilating.

Caius unbuttoned his own flannel overshirt and drew it off. He wrapped it around Swift.

The gesture was as habitual and old as their brotherhood. When Swift used to wake from nightmares as a tiny child, Caius would swathe him in his shirts, wrapping their long sleeves snuggly around him. Bundled like that, Swift could usually find his way back to sleep.

Justus eased Swift to lying back. He settled his hand gently on Swift's chest, alongside the cut, the way he'd done when Swift first had roused from the coma, panicking.

With the smell of Caius' flannel, and beneath the weight of Justus' steady hand, Swift no longer felt he was struggling to reach the islet. The sense of drowning faded as breathing grew easier.

"You must feel like you're spinning quite out of control," said Justus. "But we've got you."

Out of control.

That was precisely the gist of this sinking feeling, the emotion of it a throwback to the waters of Sterncastle Cove swallowing him.

There was nothing he could do to stop those memories from encroaching. The accident had happened. It was as much a part of him as was the Sunstone.

Odin had surfaced from his nine-day torment—peering down from a branch of Yggdrasil—victorious, receiving the giftedness of reading, of wielding magical runes. What if Swift, coming out of his own ordeal, had lost his giftedness?

But it was difficult to consider such dark possibilities with Caius and Justus right here—Justus, feeling for the pulse in Swift's neck; Caius, looking down at him gently, admiringly, as though he were proud of Swift for trying to read that text.

With Caius and Justus beside him, he felt he had a shot at gaining control.

"That was just my first try," said Swift. "I can do it."

"Yes, lad, I know." Justus rested his hand on Swift's forehead.

The door flashed open. "You rang?"

In an instant, Brooke was hovering over Swift.

Caius drew his gaze away from Swift and laid it on Brooke.

Caius withdrawing—it brought back the moment of being in the cave, calling for Caius and seeing nothing but the dark sky.

Swift clenched the Sunstone.

"Feeling a bit of pain?" asked Brooke. "Any nausea?"

"Lots of nausea," whispered Swift.

"Not to worry, I'll have you comfortable again in a flash."

"Is your break over already?" Caius asked.

It felt good to hear Caius ask her that. Maybe Swift was misreading Caius. Maybe he, too, was getting tired of her. It was, after all, pushy of her to insist on handling things, even when she was on break.

Brooke flashed Caius a look that seemed to carry some sort of thrill. "No—I still have a few minutes."

Caius stood from Swift's bed.

Swift snagged Caius' belt loop.

Caius stared down at him.

The expression on Caius was compassion. No—heartbreak.

He knew Swift wanted him close.

Caius limped nearer to Swift. He tightened his flannel across Swift's chest. He checked and straightened the bandage beneath it.

And then he untangled Swift's fingers from his clothes.

"I'll just be gone a short while."

Something inside Swift's chest broke.

Caius knew Swift needed him. And yet Caius was leaving. He was choosing Brooke.

Swift rested his fingers—cold, almost stinging with the sense of rejection—back on his Sunstone.

Brooke stared at Swift as she adjusted his IV. "Is your fever coming back?"

Justus felt Swift's cheeks. "He's quite cool."

"He looks flush," said Brooke.

Caius seemed unwilling to look at Swift.

Because Caius certainly knew what Swift was feeling—that he got flush like this when he was upset.

And yet Caius was standing behind Brooke now—one hand wrapping her slender waist.

"Swift needs a bit of rest, I think." Justus eased the biochemistry book away from him.

Swift clung to it.

Drew it back tightly against his side.

"I should say so."

Brooke fed a syringe of medicine into his IV.

"He's been up quite long enough for his first stint."

Justus patted Swift's shoulder. "We'll let you sleep." He glanced at Brooke. "I'll join Adara. Call us when Swift needs us."

Swift, holding back tears, couldn't manage his voice to say that he needed them now.

Brooke smoothed the tape on Swift's IV. "When I stopped at the station, I saw we'd just received a visitor's request." She glanced at Justus. "How do you feel about non-family visitors at this point?"

"Who?" asked Justus.

"Swift's friend—the boy who's been here on and off," said Brooke. "Ash Emberly."

"Ash has been here?" Swift whispered.

"I allowed him to stop in a few times to see you," said Justus. "The poor lad was quite upset, and I thought visiting you might help him. I hope the fact that I permitted him in doesn't upset you. From now on, of course, it'll be up to you whether you feel like seeing anyone."

"It isn't a question of whether Swift feels like it," said Caius. "I've never understood what business Ash could have, hanging around here. And with Swift needing rest, he shouldn't be let near this room."

Why would Caius be so irritated at the thought of Ash here? Ash was the only familiar person Swift had spoken to on the day they were rescued. It'd taken the medics hours to find Mum and Justus, and by then Swift was far gone in the coma. It was Ash who'd offered a brotherly comfort when no one else could.

And Ash had cried as the nurse on the rescue boat hinted about the severity of Swift's situation.

Swift swallowed back a pressure of tears. "When I spoke to Ash from the boat, I asked him to come."

"Should I say you'll see him?" asked Brooke.

The thought of Ash here—it seemed to lessen the sting of Caius and Justus moving toward the door.

"You can tell him Swift's awake," said Caius, "but please say he isn't up for a visit."

Caius was probably thinking of Ash in terms of what a menace he'd been, provoking and competing with Swift in the chase to the Star of Atlantis.

Caius had always been agitated with how Ash messed with Swift's confidence; how he could manipulate Swift.

But Caius didn't know the side of Ash Swift had glimpsed after the rescue.

"I want to see Ash," said Swift.

"Are you sure?" asked Caius. "I mean—why?"

"He was caring towards me," said Swift. "I want to honor that."

Caius advanced to argue, but Brooke squeezed his arm. "I'll see that Swift gets some rest first."

"I'd like to see Ash now," said Swift.

Justus studied Swift as though reading the desperation on him. And yet Justus was opening the door, with Caius right there behind him, leaving with Brooke.

Ash, on the other hand, was asking to be here. Justus said Ash had been upset during Swift's coma; that seeing Swift had brought comfort to him.

"Tell him to come," said Swift, straight to Brooke. "Please—tell Ash, the moment I open my eyes again, I want to see him."

7

Swift grew aware of a voice, speaking softly.

"Hey, are you awake?" Ash's voice. "Is he awake?"

"He's waking," said another voice—Brooke's. "He wanted you with him the instant he opened his eyes."

Swift struggled to move and found he couldn't.

Despite that he'd asked for this, how vulnerable it felt to be incapacitated while knowing Ash and Brooke were looking at him.

Brooke tugged at the biochemistry text.

Swift clung to it.

Brooke let go. "Looks like he fell asleep reading, the dear."

After Caius and Justus left, Swift had tried to read the textbook again. He'd assumed it was only a matter of effort to connect with the challenging biochemistry concepts; just a bit of mental sweat needed to attach those to what he already knew.

But the harder he tried to read, the more his focus slipped, and the heme synthesis—a process he was already familiar with—took on a horrific new meaning, the heme being produced in bone marrow, and hemes as components of hemoglobin—the chemical redness of blood.

Passing out wasn't exactly the feeling of consciousness

leaving as he tried to press on—but he'd found himself unable to remain sitting and had fallen back against the pillow.

And even then, holding the book open beside him, his eyes drilling the text, he could visualize nothing but Caius on the beach, his bone marrow exposed, the chemical redness of him staining Swift's fingers.

Swift half-slept in a state of panic until he heard Brooke asking him to breathe slowly; until he tasted the tang of something medicinal pushed in his IV.

The medicine had helped him get a grip on himself.

But what really diminished the panic was the feel of the Star of Atlantis resting on the sheets by his thigh.

For it called up flashes of the fisherman speaking to him.

The fisherman had said that the Star of Atlantis was fabled to deliver insights not just to the course of the ship, but to the course of the man. He'd said that Sunstones had come from other worlds; that they'd been stewarded by ancient seafarers and starfarers.

A shock of cold air—

Brooke pulling the sheet off him.

A sense of nakedness struck, and with the mortification came an uncomfortable heat. It sounded like Brooke was opening a fresh dressing. And all the while, Ash was whispering with her.

Swift found himself able to grip the covers and drew them up again, close to his chest.

Brooke chased back his hands. "Just a quick look."

Brooke, leaning over him. Brooke, widening Caius' flannel at the chest. Brooke removing the dressing.

The cold of the room seared the cut.

The agony was rousing, and finally Swift could open his eyes.

Beside Brooke, staring at Swift's chest—inflamed, stitched, and stinging—stood Ash.

At seeing Ash standing over him, a torrent of painful memories flooded.

Ash stealing his book collection. Ash driving him to a state of frantic competition. Ash controlling him, manipulating him. Ash unable to tolerate Swift surpassing him in any arena.

"That's what the fisherman did to you?" asked Ash. "Whoa."

It was what the fisherman had done to him. The fisherman who, it seemed, may have been guarding the Star of Atlantis. The Star of Atlantis—the Sunstone, for which many had killed.

"There, now." Brooke set the new bandage. "All finished." She closed the flannel around Swift.

Swift tried to sit up but couldn't find the strength.

Brooke helped him, propping him a bit higher with a pillow.

Ash sat in the chair by his bed. "I could hardly believe it when they told me you'd woken. I wanted to come hours ago, but they made me wait. Said you first needed rest."

"You have a real friend here, Swift," said Brooke. "Ash never wants to leave you. We've even had to shuffle him out a time or two. I wish I had a best friend like that."

A best friend.

Did Swift have a best friend again in Ash?

"I've been so worried about you." Ash eased his chair closer. "Isn't that right, Brookey?"

Brookey.

"I've come every day," said Ash. "And I'd have spent the nights, too, if they'd let me."

Ash coming every day—was this kindness?

Or was this the Ash Swift was used to, commandeering someone else's ordeal so he could place himself at the center of something?

Swift rested his hand by the cut, searing still from the exposure.

Maybe Ash's gestures of friendliness were false—just his way of getting something he wanted from Swift. Some petty triumph. Or something he craved so desperately he'd be willing to steal.

"It's been difficult watching you in a coma." Ash's expression was pained.

Swift focused on just breathing a minute. All this reflexive distrust rearing toward Ash suddenly didn't seem fair.

Ash looked sincere. Kind.

His expression was bringing back the very old sense of being together on some high adventure, when they were just eight years old—true best friends.

Those years ago, when Ash declared their friendship over—Ash himself had been going through some unspeakable pain. His mum had just abandoned him and his father.

Swift rested deeper into the pillow. Rested his eyes on Ash —on his clever, muscular face, with its animated expression.

"How are you feeling?" asked Ash.

Swift started to speak, to tell Ash about the pain, the sense of spinning out of control—but with the words came a thickening of tears. He couldn't speak without risking that they might slip out.

There was a clever look to Ash—the corner of his mouth turned up, as though he were enjoying some idea or plan.

The childhood Ash always had a joke waiting like that. Some adventure up his sleeve.

Ash being here, almost every day since Swift had arrived—that had to mean something about the way their friendship was changing.

Swift blinked back the tears. He used the moment of forced silence to let himself finally believe the old Ash—his best friend —had returned to him.

"But don't even feel you need to speak," said Ash. "Just take it easy."

Brooke, hanging fresh fluid on the IV stand, smiled adoringly at Ash.

Caius and Justus had both wanted to leave, despite that Swift clearly needed them.

Ash, though, was wanting to be here. Begging, even, to get to Swift's bedside. Wishing he could stay all through the night.

Caius had spent the nights here, watching over Swift. But he'd also been Brooke's "buddy." Clearly, Caius had more than one motivation.

Swift couldn't even glance at the cot Caius had slept on without wondering if anything had happened there.

God, if it had.

Brooke squeezed Ash around the shoulders. "You'll take care of Swift for me by not wearing him out, yes? When Swift tires, can I count on you to excuse yourself?"

Ash smiled handsomely at her. "Of course."

She checked Swift's IV a final time. "Do you need anything?"

"Just," Swift managed, "some privacy."

That'd probably sounded rude, but she'd asked, and what Swift needed was for her to go.

"I understand." She smiled sweetly at him.

Too sweetly.

When she left, when the door closed behind her, when the room felt vacant enough again to breathe easily, when Swift could finally take in the sight of Ash sitting peacefully before him, applying no pressure, not fussing over him but just letting him rest—he found enough strength to sit up more.

"Brooke said it would take you a bit to fully wake." Ash rested his ankle upon his knee.

It was the way Caius often sat. A brother's way.

"While you wake, do you want to hear something amazing?"

"Let's hear it," Swift whispered.

"Do you remember me telling you that I placed the box I found—my incredible treasure—in a Welsh museum? Well, the curator is sure it's connected to the Star of Atlantis myth! Can you believe that? We suspected it, as the seven-pointed star of the myth is inlaid in the box. It's great that you found the Star of Atlantis—but how cool is it that I found something connected as well?"

"That's very cool," said Swift. "What's the connection?"

"Do you remember, when you were on your rescue boat, I told you my box held a bunch of old papers? Well—you'll like this—they're written in Old Norse and Celtic Akkadian. It turns out they're records of a people from hundreds of years ago —probably seafaring nomads from Iceland. They're about farming and fishing, although a few lines reference battles and conflicts."

"Any poetry?" asked Swift.

"Poetry? No. It's all pretty ordinary. I hope the curator's missing something—that the papers will turn out to hold more interesting than historical records."

"Historical records are interesting," said Swift. "Especially if the culture is old or scarcely known. And poetry shows up in a lot of Old Norse documents. Maybe that's what we can hope for."

"I've found a reason to hope for more." Ash pulled from his satchel a book.

Swift recognized it.

It was a part of his original collection—one of the books Ash had stolen.

He looked carefully at Ash. "When I was on the rescue boat —didn't you tell me you gave Edric back all my books?"

"I did. Oh!" Ash straightened. "Please, don't worry. I gave Edric back everything except this one."

So, Ash had lied to him. A small lie. But still a lie.

"I know what you must be thinking," said Ash. "Let me explain. I kept this one book so I could study it, then talk it over with you. See, I followed the research you did on the Star of Atlantis. Your librarian guided me through what you pulled. I really grew to appreciate how brilliant you are as a strategist."

Okay, that was different.

Ash had never, in recent years, been capable of showing Swift any approval, much less admiration.

Still. Seeing that Ash had kept back one of Swift's books brought the same sting of exposure as when Brooke had pulled back his sheet. It was like Ash had just lifted the shroud off a wound from their past.

"I know all about Cynfael Maddox stealing the Star of Atlantis from a treacherous king," said Ash. "I know Maddox was a good guy who used the treasures he swiped to help people." He held up the book. "This includes an account of that ancient Welsh clan from your research—the Star Shepherds.

According to Octavian—he's the museum curator—it was that very clan who hid my box."

At that, Swift's stomach dropped.

If true, this was a marvelous connection.

To have actual written records of the people who hid the Star of Atlantis—the mage-like clan from whom the fisherman might be descended—it was wonderful.

And what if Ash's hope panned out, that there was even more to the papers?

"Do you think the curator could really be missing something?" asked Swift.

"The renowned historian, Octavian Krakau," said Ash. "Probably not. He's a great, great man who owns a little dive of a museum up in Pembrokeshire. I never would've found him, but when he saw me on the news, he reached out to me. He knows incredible things about legendary treasures—although, he's joked that he might know less than we do about the Star of Atlantis."

But probably no one knew as much about the Star of Atlantis as the fisherman did.

What would the fisherman have to say about Ash's box and its records, connected, as they seemed to be, to the Star of Atlantis.

If only he might find the fisherman and learn from him.

"May I see the book?" asked Swift.

"Do you remember what's in it?" Ash handed it to him.

The antique feel of the book, its musty smell, seemed to be working on Swift like pain medicine, rousing him to greater energy.

"It's been years since I read this." Swift opened it. "I remember that it's old—not as old as *The Star of Atlantis*, I think, but written not long after."

And it was written long before Lovecraft invented the Cthulhu.

Maybe the Cthulhu myth was actually ancient. Maybe Lovecraft had poached it from someplace archaic.

Who knew but this book might hold some mythology on

that score? If the Cthulhu were mentioned here, that would stand as evidence that Lovecraft's monster was old.

Such a finding would cast the authenticity of the Star of Atlantis in a much more favorable light.

Swift flipped to the table of contents, which he discovered he could read. That was thrilling. But nothing referenced the Cthulhu.

"What are you looking for?" asked Ash.

Swift glanced at him but kept silent.

If Ash found out that the Star of Atlantis might be fake—that its book and map might've been fabricated hundreds of years after they claimed to have been written—his competitiveness might rouse. For that would suggest that the Star of Atlantis—the real Star of Atlantis—was still out there.

"I was just trying to recall," said Swift, "whether this references the Star of Atlantis." He flipped to its section about Welsh coastal clans. "It seems not to."

Ash stood. "It doesn't, but this is exactly what I wanted to look at with you."

Swift focused on the weathered page.

Here, words didn't seem elusive as they had when he'd tried to read the biochemistry text. And having Ash quietly standing by his side felt empowering.

Swift read the first paragraph. The second. The rest of the page. And the next page.

It seemed that Ash, staring expectantly, was lending a force for reading that Swift had been missing. He felt allowed a permission—one Ash long ago had denied him—to explore these myths. Ash really was seeming changed, like he'd found himself again, his kindness winning out over his greed.

Swift read on.

The book described the Shepherds of the Stars as a wise and generous people, successful in their endeavors of farming and fishing and herding and trade—so prosperous, they seemed almost magical. And with this brilliance, they developed a small renaissance age of their own.

They innovated, creating solutions for the challenges cast by hard living, by tyrannical monarchs. And they centered their focus on enlightenment, on learning and sharing arts and sciences, on writing poetry and stories. And venturing.

And the book spoke of their end as abrupt and a great loss. It was believed that a king they'd pillaged wiped out the clan.

But the Shepherds of the Stars hadn't been entirely vanquished, the book told.

Whispers of sightings were apparently still happening when this book was written, which was a good hundred years after the dismemberment of Maddox's clan.

Wanderers, known to be associated with the Shepherds of the Stars, were thought to maintain access to some treasures, preserving their renaissance, their micro-society, their wealth, for the ages.

Every word of the book felt delicious on Swift's eyes. The thought of reading it through—a history of Welsh legends, a context of its ancient clans—how thrilling.

And it felt electrifying to know Ash's discovered box and its contents were undergoing analysis within reach, just in Wales.

Swift, glancing at Ash, felt like he'd stumbled upon a sunlit pathway in the deeps of a treacherous wood.

"Is there any chance you'd let me have a look at that box you found?" Swift asked him.

An expression of relief crossed Ash's face.

"I'm so glad you asked." He again sat. "I'd like nothing better. But I wasn't sure if you'd want to. I mean, it's generous of you and your family to let me visit you. But I'm not entirely sure where we stand."

"I guess we do have to take that sort of head on." Swift laid aside the old book. "The thing is, though we haven't seen eye to eye in the past, it's feeling really right having you here."

"In the past, I was a mess," said Ash. "When my mum left, it all but ruined me."

"I've always wanted to tell you how sorry I am," said Swift. "It's awful, you having to deal with all that."

"I never felt I could deal with it," said Ash. "After she left, I got sort of reckless. I wanted to tear down everything, so I trashed most of my friendships—including the one most important. And after breaking something—almost a brotherhood, like what we had—I've never quite known how to fix it."

At seeing Ash ready to be friends again—deep friends—tension slipped out of Swift's muscles like a poison drawn. "Consider it fixed."

Ash cast him his most clever, most dapper expression. "It's definitely feeling right, being here with you."

Swift lowered his gaze to the biochemistry text. "Then, I think I'd like to let you in on you something."

"You can tell me anything."

Swift rested his gaze on Ash. "I'm having a difficult time reading."

"No, you're not." Ash glanced at the old book. "You just read that whole piece."

"Yeah"—Swift handed Ash the biochemistry text—"but I can't get through a single sentence of this. Before the coma, I could read a full chapter from a medical text in under an hour— and recall everything perfectly. That skill feels now locked away. Or gone."

"Don't you need to give yourself time? I mean, it's no surprise if you can't study such difficult material today, just waking up as you are, right after causing an accident that almost killed your brother."

Swift felt his face blanch, adrenaline prickling his cheeks at the shock of hearing, in Ash's direct way, precisely what Swift had done.

"Maybe," said Swift. "But the coma might've wrecked my body. Dr. Keats told my father that any debilitations probably won't last. But he doesn't really know. He expects fevers to recur."

"I'm sure you'll bounce back." Ash opened the biochemistry text and stared at a page, his brow crossed. "You certainly shouldn't use this as your standard." He slid the book back onto

Swift's lap. "All that science jargon—it's like it's written in a different language. But you—you're great at strange languages."

A smile, so genuine, lit Ash's face, making him look exactly like the boy he'd been at eight.

"Caius even once had me believing you'd sipped from Odin's mead as a baby. Remember?"

Swift, warming at the memory, set the old book of Welsh cultures on top of his biochemistry text.

Ash again opened the old book before Swift. "Try reading a bit more."

Swift rattled off a whole page with no problem.

"See—your reading isn't impaired," said Ash. "You're really gifted at understanding all these complex histories and legends, at locating connections. I mean—that intelligence led you to discover the Star of Atlantis. I can't wait to see what you might make of my incredible treasure, its papers."

Swift lowered his eyes in relief, the sense of companionship between them strengthening.

"Maybe it's because you're here that I did well with this old book." Swift met Ash's gaze. "It's really great that you're here. I sort of needed a friend today."

"Well, you've got one," said Ash. "When you're better, we'll find a way for you to see my treasure box. Though, it's not technically mine anymore since I sold it."

"Would the curator allow us a close look?" asked Swift.

"Sure he would," said Ash. "And who knows—maybe you'll end up placing your relics there, alongside mine. You could get a ton of money for them. He says navigational Sunstones are priceless."

Priceless, if authentic.

"Octavian and I have talked over your book—*The Star of Atlantis*," said Ash, "along with the map that helped lead you to Sterncastle Cove. They've got to be worth a fortune!"

"This Octavian guy knows my whole story?" asked Swift. "He knows about my book and map?"

"While you slept, your father told me all about your adventure. It's so marvelous—I couldn't help but talk it over with Octavian."

Swift went quiet.

"I hope that's all right."

Ash sat forward.

"My God—is it not all right?"

Swift didn't respond.

The problem wasn't that Ash had told someone about the *Star of Atlantis* book and map, and how they'd led to the Sunstone. The problem was that Ash had told a "renowned historian."

If there was any fraudulence about the book and map, marred as they were by the Cthulhu, a historian would see it.

"I didn't think twice about telling Octavian," said Ash. "Because you yourself once said that there's worth in sharing with the world a great find. I guess I took that to heart. I mean— you were right about that."

Swift glanced at Ash, leaning in, his expression sincere.

The fact was, Swift would have to show his relics to a historian. But it would've been nice to explore the inconsistency of the Cthulhu himself, to try to resolve it before anyone else's suspicions were raised.

"I guess I assumed, too, that you'd consider selling them to Octavian," said Ash.

"I haven't decided what to do," said Swift.

"You aren't angry are you?" asked Ash. "Say you aren't angry."

Despite the tinge of betrayal in this, it was nice to see Ash understanding Swift's value of sharing discoveries.

And Ash didn't know of Swift's concern about the Cthulhu. The betrayal was unfortunate, but not purposeful.

"I'm not angry," said Swift.

"Well, thank God." Ash relaxed back.

"In fact," said Swift, "do you want to see the Star of Atlantis?"

Ash's expression shifted from anxious to brightly enthusiastic.

Swift felt around the sheets.

His Sunstone wasn't there.

Had it slipped off the bed? He leaned to check the floor but found nothing. Had Caius taken it?

Swift sat up more and glanced about the room.

Or Justus? Dr. Keats hadn't. Dr. Keats had put it right into Swift's hand.

He checked the box on the bedside table that Brooke had designated for its safekeeping. Empty.

Had they changed his sheets while he slept? God—had the nurses crumpled up his priceless relic in a bundle of dirty laundry and discarded it?

He felt around the bed again, lower, reaching as far as he could.

The movement incited a strong pain in his chest that made him let out a stifled cry.

What if the Sunstone was lost? What if he'd gone through the entire ordeal of finding the Star of Atlantis—authentic or not —only to stupidly lose it in a hospital?

The air seemed to thicken.

If the Star of Atlantis was lost, Swift was lost.

Ash cast a clever grin as he reached into his jacket pocket.

He pulled out the Sunstone.

"Swift," he said, laughing, "the look on your face!"

Swift, through a film of tears sheening his eyes, could do nothing but stare.

Did Ash not get that the Sunstone was no joke? That messing with it was equivalent to messing with Swift.

Swift blinked back the tears.

And like a veil lifted, Swift saw in Ash's expression a keen pleasure at seeing his distress.

Of course Ash knew he was inciting this pain.

So, Ash didn't mean well.

The Ash who'd blamed him for their rocky past, the Ash who'd manipulated and controlled, who'd provoked Swift and Caius to chase the Star of Atlantis—who'd driven them to the deadly waters of Sterncastle Cove—that Ash was right here.

"Legends say that the finder of the Star of Atlantis is destined." Ash gazed at the Sunstone, resting in his own hand.

The Sunstone which pirates, seafarers, mariners, shamans, and kings had coveted.

The Sunstone that the fisherman had indeed said aided in the destinies of fortunes and kings. Of commoners. Of worlds.

The Sunstone that many had bled for and killed to possess.

"I've held this sometimes as you slept," said Ash. "I wonder —could its destiny have extended to me?"

That told Swift everything he needed to know.

Ash, who'd made a habit of stealing Swift's things, wasn't finished with him.

He wanted the Star of Atlantis.

Ash had said, after his mum left, he'd aimed to tear down everything. And it seemed he wasn't out of that rage. For here he was, offering a counterfeit friendship for the sake of making a personal gain.

He'd draw Swift in, just like always. And like always, he'd cast Swift away.

Looking at the Sunstone—which was possibly fake, looking at Ash's friendly smile, which certainly was fake—Swift felt unmoored.

The only thought that brought any relief was a pale hope that he might be wrong on both scores.

The Star of Atlantis might very well be authentic.

And Ash—clearly still a wreck—might yet change.

Perhaps the contrived kindness Ash was showing was a glimmer of what could yet be.

Ash was giving Swift access to him. This, he'd always refused, though Swift had been frantic for reconciliation, for years.

What if Ash, deep down, was feeling lost in those dark waters of separation?

Swift had rescued him once. Could it be that Ash, in his heart, was desperate for Swift to do it again?

Swift, himself having been drawn from dark waters, first by

Caius, then by the Scottish sailors who'd found him—he felt redeemed. He couldn't repay that by denying Ash.

Swift held out his hand for the Sunstone. For Ash's hand.

Ash's gaze remained on the Star of Atlantis.

"Give it to me, Ash."

A moment of distance, of darkness seemed to slide between them—some shadow cast by the Sunstone, empty of light, gripped inside Ash's hand.

"I've kept in mind the last thing you said to me," said Ash, "on the medic's ship, as they took the mobile from you. You were in such pain you couldn't speak. But it felt like you were going to ask me—if something bad happened to you—to take care of the Star of Atlantis."

Ash placed the Sunstone in Swift's waiting palm.

The feel of it was cool relief.

The panic in Swift drained away, letting his heart finally slow.

Swift held the stone closely. He studied its edges, its translucent interior, displaying what seemed to be still, seaborne clouds.

On the rescue boat, when Swift recognized he might not survive his ordeal, he had wanted to see the Star of Atlantis into good hands.

In that moment, thinking of it in Ash's hands had brought comfort.

Swift rested his gaze on Ash. "I was going to ask you to take care of it."

Ash smiled. "But of course you don't need me to now." He settled back. "What I can do, if you'll let me, is be here for you." His eyes drifted to the bandage crossing Swift's chest.

"It's horrific, I know." Swift closed Caius' flannel higher over his chest.

"I wouldn't call it horrific," said Ash. "It's kind of fascinating. I mean—someone cut you."

Swift studied the Sunstone, its smart rhombus shape. "The fisherman—talking to him was so wild."

Ash moved to the edge of his seat. "Was he mad, do you think?"

"No—he looked clean. Well-dressed. Though very strange, he was captivating. And he saved me and Caius."

"On the medic's ship, you said no one believed you about the fisherman. Are they believing you now?"

"Dr. Keats did a test that proved this cut came from a knife," said Swift. "My family is starting to trust my story—though, it's difficult for them."

"When you described the fisherman," said Ash, "all I could think about was that old book you're holding. I've entertained the idea that he might be somehow connected to those Star Shepherds. What if he's a descendant from that Welsh clan—a ghostly Icelandic wanderer?"

Despite the distrust Swift carried for Ash, Ash's confidence felt assuring.

It was like when Dr. Keats had taken the time to listen—really listen—to Swift's questions, his thoughts.

"The Coast Guard still has the fisherman's boat," said Swift. "I think I should return it. Don't you think so? He's got to want it back. No one seems to be thinking of him, though."

"If you want to find him, then I want to help you," said Ash.

"The thing is, the chase is probably hopeless," said Swift. "Dr. Keats believes he's likely long gone."

"We both want more insights about the Star of Atlantis and its myths," said Ash, "about treasures that might still be out there for the claiming. So if you're game, here's what we're going to do."

A thrill shot through Swift. Ash was donning an impish expression, just the way he had back when they were little—Ash plotting their games, leading Swift in their fun.

The thought of Ash's companionship was intoxicating. And there seemed little risk to indulging in some connection with him, finally.

As much as Ash might covet the Sunstone, it seemed impossible he could actually steal it. If he'd wanted to, he would've already tried.

It was very clear Ash was untrustworthy. But, surely, he wasn't dangerous.

Even Caius, at one time, had coaxed Swift to understand he could partner with Ash while protecting himself from getting hurt. If he opened himself to Ash's encouragement, his leadership, Swift felt he might truly right himself.

And the two of them teaming up—it seemed a medicine that might deliver Ash from the dark waters, too.

"I'm listening," said Swift.

"Tell your father about Octavian Krakau, and how he's helped me document my incredible treasure. Tell him that's where you want yours documented, too. When you're strong enough, we can go to Wales. You can examine my box and its papers, and you can show Octavian your finds."

As much as Swift hated the idea of Octavian seeing his finds, he probably needed—more than anything—a historian.

And if Octavian assessed the book and map as fraudulent, maybe he'd be discreet.

Maybe Ash would be, too. If Ash could grow to become a true friend—the friend he was pretending to be, having him close for so agonizing a moment might be helpful.

Few people, besides Ash, would understand such a particular pain.

"My father would love for me to spend time with you," said Ash. "He's always wanted me to try fixing things between us. And in Pembrokeshire, maybe I could help you get on with reading those medical texts. Would you parents let us go, do you think?"

Ash had wreaked so much damage in the past—the chances seemed grim.

But. Mum and Justus had invited Ash into Swift's room, to see him in a most vulnerable state.

Maybe Caius or Justus would take Swift and Ash to their beach house in Pembrokeshire, away from distractions—so Swift could heal and really take on the medical texts. As full as those wilds were of legends, for all practical purposes there waited just an empty coast, an old forest, and a plain beach house.

"I think I know how we can approach this," said Swift.

Ash leaned in.

"I've told my father flat out that I've decided to go for the Practicum," said Swift. "I know he'll help me, despite that he seems full of doubt. I'll say I want to get away, to relearn how to focus, to heal. Our beach house isn't all that far from Sterncastle Cove. We could return the fisherman's longboat to the place I set out from. I'll say I want you to come, to help me get back on track."

Ash grinned. "The thought of being at your beach house, where we were together as lads—your beach house, where we..."

He let a cold silence hang.

Swift waited to see if Ash would reference "the Tumble," the accident that'd happened when they were eight, when they both nearly drowned. The accident that'd ended their friendship.

Ash said nothing more. He only leaned back, stretching his legs out in front of him, casually crossing his ankles, a look of enthusiasm brightening his face.

Ash would pretend to support Swift, to suit his own motives. And Swift would let him, all the while patiently waiting for the friendship to turn real.

This would mean Swift would have to manage some deception, too, keeping Ash at arm's length while feigning trust.

The thought of keeping up a pretense didn't feel quite right, and it was possible Ash would see through him. Ash had always been able to read him.

But if a little pretense was all it took for him to safely be near Ash, then so be it. The longing he felt to restore their friendship was striking almost viscerally. If he could truly bring Ash back to a deep friendship, that achievement felt more worthwhile than claiming any legendary treasure.

Swift rested back.

This was perfect. Maybe Caius would be the one to come with them to Wales. Maybe Caius really would be the teacher Swift longed for. If Caius came, he could buckle down with his own studies, alongside Swift. They could together get back on their feet.

And all the while, Swift and Ash could delve more deeply into Ash's discovery, into the whereabouts of the mystical fisherman, into the legends surrounding the Star of Atlantis.

Swift held the Sunstone up to the window, brightening now with the sun's golden fall. "I think you and I are going to make quite a team."

Ash leaned in and peered with him through the stone at the sun—seeming to spark like a star ready to go supernova.

8

Swift, sitting at his dining room table, held the Star of Atlantis—cradled in a black cloth.

The quartz fissures twisting inside the stone looked like swirling campfire smoke, frozen beneath the skin of a crystal ball.

If only it were some oracle that could grant a wish—or at least lend a hint of how he could get his family on board with what he and Ash wanted to do.

Around the table with him sat Justus, Edric, and Caius—all wearing grim expressions, all chock full of opinions on what was to be done with the Star of Atlantis. On what was to be done with Swift.

Anxiety was simmering in Swift's chest—fright over being denied what he felt he truly needed. Keeping his breathing steady and slow was becoming an act of deliberate will.

The way they were all looking at him, though, with consideration—they did at least seem willing to hear him out. If they would truly listen, they'd see that his next steps were clear.

Ash's idea for the two of them to go to Wales—though wrongly motivated—had been insightful. Swift did need to get someplace where he could focus on his med texts, and the beach house was perfect.

95

He needed to be again in the company of the Celtic Sea. He needed to make peace with the sea.

"Going to Pembrokeshire with Ash," said Swift, "Would it not be the perfect place to study? Ash's father thinks this is a winning plan."

He glanced at Justus.

"What do you think?"

Justus studied Swift.

This was not the admiring, proud Justus. This was the doubtful Justus.

This was the Justus who seemed to see straight through Swift's skin, to the anxiety percolating inside him.

"We have some time before school starts," said Swift, "and Ash wants to spend it together."

He cradled his chest to manage a feeling of tightening.

"The museum that bought Ash's treasure box is very near to our beach house, which is perfect."

Setting aside the question of Ash joining him, they'd all agreed that Swift's relics needed to be examined at the Pembrokeshire museum.

Despite the revulsion that still bubbled up when Swift envisioned a historian condemning the Sunstone, its book, and its map as fakes, he equally hated that he might be clinging to a lie.

After researching the Cthulhu, Swift was left with almost no hope that the *Star of Atlantis* book and map were genuine. Lovecraft did seem to be the originator of the Cthulhu, and he'd created that monster hardly more than a hundred years ago.

Even if *The Star of Atlantis* book were that old, a century was meager compared to the age of the Star of Atlantis myth. Cynfael Maddox died a full 300 years before the Cthulhu crept into the stories of Lovecraft.

But. Perhaps another explanation was possible—one Swift hadn't thought up.

Showing the relics to the museum curator—Octavian Krakau—might be very positive, delivering answers.

And if the Sunstone and other relics turned out to be real—Swift ached to explore the questions that would follow.

Questions about destiny, about who the fisherman was and the meaning of his wondrous words.

"I've seen you trying to go at your textbooks," said Justus. "I know it's been a struggle."

"Yes," said Swift, metering his breathing. "But being at the beach house while I try would really help."

Justus, his look somber, glanced at Caius. "Your thoughts?"

Despite how difficult this conversation was bound to be, it was relieving to be sitting with just his father and brothers. Brooke had been at their house every day in the month since Swift had come home.

But tonight, Mum had kindly taken Brooke out for a spa date and tea, which seemed more a favor for Swift than for Brooke.

"We don't fully understand what's triggering Swift's anxiety," said Caius. "Brooke has said often how we shouldn't introduce any unhealthy stress or unhelpful complications. And I agree."

"What complications or stress could possibly happen at our beach house?" asked Swift. "It's the coziest place I can imagine."

"It was also the last place you and Ash were on friendly terms," said Caius. "You haven't been there with him since the day of the Tumble when he shrugged you off. We can't ignore that it was Ash's cruelty all those years ago that set you to panicking in the first place."

"So I've had panic attacks since the Tumble," said Swift. "That isn't necessarily Ash's fault."

Caius tossed Justus a doubtful glance.

Yes, Ash had been cruel, back when they were little kids. Yes, he'd heaped blame onto Swift and tended to be controlling and manipulative. Yes, he once even struck Swift in the face with a stone.

But Caius' grudge still wasn't fair. Ash was damaged and could use some slack.

"We're way past the Tumble and all that," said Swift.

And whatever Ash's capability was for true friendship, his

attentiveness since Swift had come home was like salve on an old wound.

The book Ash had brought to Swift in the hospital, they'd together read almost all the way through. Swift still had to take it slowly, and he couldn't make it through even a chapter on his own before falling asleep.

But when he read the book to Ash, he could make it through two, or sometimes three chapters. Ash's companionship seemed to be leading Swift out of the murk of the trauma and onto clear waters.

"And the beach house," said Swift, "it might be the perfect place for me and Ash to rebuild what we lost. I've wanted to fix our friendship for so long, and he's finally letting me. He's showing me that he truly can change."

Caius crossed his arms. "I don't buy that."

Swift dropped against the back of his chair.

"Hang on, let's leave off with Ash for a minute," said Edric. "The beach house, if nothing else, is a great place for reading." He met Swift's glance. "You've been giving your medical texts a solid try. The beach house would be a wonderful place to keep at that."

Swift lent Edric a grateful look.

"Do you honestly think the beach house would help him that much?" asked Caius. "Since he's come home, Swift hasn't made it through even one chapter of his med texts."

"I just need a chance to get back on my feet," said Swift. "And I'm telling you how I can."

"I think it's a rather good idea."

Edric glanced at Justus, at Caius.

"Swift is right that he'd have quiet and solitude at the beach house. He'd have the ocean. His stars. He's bound to make strong progress if he retreats to such a place, free from distractions."

"He wouldn't have solitude, and he wouldn't be free from distractions," said Caius.

"Ash wouldn't get in my way if that's what you're implying," said Swift. "At the beach house, you and I both could be free from distractions. Don't you see? We could study together."

Justus and Edric glanced at one another.

It was clear Caius wanted to get back on track with medical school—but Swift was in the minority in thinking he would. From time to time, even Caius caved to Justus' reasoning. To Brooke's.

There was plenty Caius could do with the education he had, Brooke often said; Caius didn't have to pile on four more years, Justus said; there was no shame in changing course, they both said.

The course everyone seemed to think most favorable was for Caius to go for nurse practitioner training.

Edric, his expression soft, watched Swift. "Caius might be on a new heading. If he wants to get on with that nursing business that's caught his eye, it'll mean intensively studying with Brooke."

The subtle smile blooming on Caius was sickening.

"Brooke wouldn't be able to teach you that much, probably," said Swift.

Edric, smirking, leaned back. "I bet she could teach him a thing or two."

Caius focused on Swift. "Ease up on Brooke, all right?"

This distractedness in Caius didn't seem caused by the accident.

It was like he'd willingly taken his eyes off his goal and placed them on Brooke.

And the more time Caius spent with her, the less interested he seemed—not just in medicine, but in Swift.

Caius and Brooke couldn't seem to keep their hands off each other, which was revolting. And their conversations were nothing but inside jokes and talk about people they knew from the University, and Brooke's work, in which Swift couldn't partake at all.

And if Caius needed anything, no one was to help him but Brooke.

Every time Swift tried to make Caius more comfortable or

get him something he wanted when his leg hurt, Brooke was there, saying, "Swift, please don't trouble yourself," or, "keep in mind—you're in need of rest, too."

And worse—when Caius tried to offer any care to Swift, Brooke was right there to intervene, directing Caius to take it easy while Brooke herself did whatever was needed. Or she'd solicit Mum or Justus for the job while focusing her attention more closely on Caius.

What Brooke didn't understand, what Justus and Mum seemed to have forgotten, was that the love Caius had for trauma medicine was old and true to himself. Caius needed a strong wind to blow him back to where he was before the accident.

Time with Swift in Pembrokeshire could be the bluster that would wake Caius up and help him remember who he was and what he loved.

"When we spoke in the hospital," said Swift, to Caius, "you said I should compete for the Practicum. But now it's like you think I can't do it. What's changed? Do you not want to help me anymore?"

"Of course I think you can do it," said Caius. "And of course I'll help you. But you don't need Ash hanging around."

Edric cast Caius a confident look. "After the accident, I put that Emberly lad well in his place. Ash is certainly motivated to make amends."

Justus gave Edric a nod. "Ash's father believes, as Swift does, that this would be very good for him."

"You two can't seriously say you trust Ash," said Caius.

"I never have, but"—Edric shrugged—"lads do grow up."

"Not that lad," said Caius. "I'm sorry to say it, but I see his character as fixed."

"I wouldn't want the little bugger hanging around me," said Edric. "But it isn't up to me. Nor any of us, really. Swift should get to decide if he'd come along. I'm sure Swift can handle him."

"I won't have to 'handle' Ash," said Swift.

"Whatever Ash might tell you of his intentions to help," said

Caius, "even if he thinks he's being honest—what support, really, could he actually give you?"

"He might not know medicine or academics," said Swift. "But he does know how to plan."

"You mean—plot," said Caius.

"I can focus really well with Ash nearby," said Swift. "I've made it through a whole book of Welsh legends, reading it to him."

"I talked to Ash plenty, while you were out," said Caius. "About you. About our accident. About the Tumble. About the box he found, which he couldn't stop blathering about, calling it his 'incredible treasure.' Through every conversation, he did nothing but compare himself to you. Believe what you'd like, but I'm telling you—Ash isn't going to change."

"He might not be perfect," said Swift. "But don't we all have flaws? I myself have imperfections, the worst of which is that I almost killed my brother. Isn't it better if we all just move on?"

Caius, watching Swift, leaned back. "Ash put those words in your mouth, didn't he?"

Those had been Ash's words. But it didn't matter. They were true words.

Swift concentrated on slowing his breathing. He placed his gaze back on his Sunstone.

Justus checked his phone. "Well, this is a relief. Elias says he can be here in a few minutes. He'll help us sort out the best course."

"There was no need to call in a negotiator," said Swift. "I'm telling you exactly what I need."

"A psychiatrist isn't a negotiator," said Justus.

Swift had known Elias all his life, and the thought of him lending his wisdom to a difficulty had always been soothing. But the idea of Elias dealing in this dilemma was terrifying. Elias was as objective as a cold wind, and he might not take Swift's side.

"Understand, lad, we must be very careful about seeing you through to healing." Justus glanced at Swift's chest, at the tip of the scab showing at his collar.

"I'm well on my way to healing." Swift spread his shirt to show the whole cut—red and presenting some irritation, but definitely healing. "This hurts far less than it did."

"You're not done with the fevers, though," said Caius. "You've had three since you've been home."

"That's not so many," said Swift. "Dr. Keats said recurring fevers were likely."

"It's three too many, in my book," said Caius.

"It isn't the risk of fevers that unsettles me." Justus rested his gaze on Swift's Sunstone. "It's—"

The doorbell rang.

"Well," said Justus. "I'd do better to let Elias deal in this."

Edric rose and went to the door.

9

"Would you rather speak to Elias privately?" Caius asked Swift. "It's up to you whether we're in the room."

Whether or not the others sat in, the outcome rested with Elias. If Elias even hinted at a hunch that Swift shouldn't go to Pembrokeshire, or spend time with Ash—if he remotely thought Swift shouldn't compete for the Practicum—Justus would put an utter end to everything.

"It doesn't matter," said Swift. "Stay if you want."

This feeling of being out of control had grown familiar. The isolation of drifting in the fisherman's longboat, Swift unable to even sit up—it'd felt like drowning in the night sky. And memories of half-waking out of the coma still visited him—memories of being handled, of having no way to communicate.

The feeling spurred a struggle for air, and now, at the mere thought of Justus and Elias deliberating on his fate, Swift had to mindfully keep his hand from rubbing at a phantom tightness gripping his throat.

He had to get a handle on this panic. He had to come up with a strategy to convince them to let him and Ash go to Wales.

It was the best way to both mend their troubled friendship and rebuild his constitution.

And through it, he just might coax Caius back to his university, back to reading medicine.

Caius watched Swift carefully.

Swift did his best to seem relaxed, but Caius certainly was seeing the anxiety. Swift could do little to conceal the bout of quick, shallow breathing the panic was forcing.

Edric led in Elias, beaming a smile as warming as the sun.

Elias took Swift's hand. "It's good to see you wakeful and home."

The way Elias was bending close, looking into Swift's eyes with such care, sheltering Swift's hand in both of his, anyone might've mistaken him for Swift's father. And he was almost a father. He'd been as close as any relative to Justus and Mum since before Swift and his brothers had been born.

Once they came along, Elias had undertaken a respectable share of the parenting. His wife and daughters had always felt like a family of sisters and aunties, and Swift's love of mythology, of sea stories and pirate fantasies, was shared with Elias and owed in large part to their nights spent together fireside, Elias entertaining the Kingsley lads with blue and watery tales.

"Have you had any fever relapses?" asked Elias.

Swift worked to hang on to enough air to speak evenly. "A couple. Near nighttime."

"Three, actually," said Caius.

"It's all part of recovering," said Swift.

"Take a look at his cut." Caius reached for Swift. "Can I show him?"

Swift widened his shirt.

"Why, it's looking loads better," said Elias.

"I'll take some credit for that," said Caius. "This has been under my tending since he's been home. Well—mine and Brooke's. As good as it looks, though, Mum won't be pleased until we erase every bit of that scar and bring the fisherman to her in handcuffs."

Swift startled a touch at the mention of the fisherman.

"It's Adara's right to be a bear at the moment." Elias rested his hand on Swift's cheek. "And I'll admit, I can still see the traces of a fever in those shadows around his eyes."

"I'm all right." Swift pulled back. "Or I will be."

He eyed Caius. Justus.

"I know what I need to do."

"Are we talking all together?" Elias glanced at the others.

"It's really fine if you'd rather talk to Elias alone." Caius scooted back his chair.

Swift hooked the leg of the chair with his foot.

The gesture was reflexive—an impulse he constantly felt to keep Caius close.

"I told you. You can stay."

Elias took a seat beside Justus, across from Swift. "What do you remember of the night of the accident?"

"Everything," said Swift. "Until we were picked up. Then I was sort of in and out."

"You did some panicking while unconscious," said Elias. "Were you aware of any thoughts in those moments? Any dreams? Any memories there?"

"I remember just flashes of what was going on. People talking. The brightness or darkness of the room. I couldn't respond to any of it. I thought about the *Strider*, her torn hull. And I asked for Caius. I hung on to the Star of Atlantis."

Elias glanced at Swift's hands, at his Sunstone nestled in its black cloth. "Well, I'll be. Is this it?"

Swift placed it in Elias' hands.

Elias studied the Sunstone with great care, though his attention never seemed to leave Swift.

Swift tried again to calm his breathing but still couldn't do much about it. The panic felt like an anchor bound to him—one too heavy to shake loose on his own.

Although Elias had to be seeing this, he didn't press the issue of why panic was striking. He was sharp enough to realize Swift would struggle to talk of it while in its grip.

Elias' quiet attentiveness, his patience and reserve, were qualities Swift had always admired. Because of how gentle he was, Swift felt more connected to Elias than to any adult, aside from Mum and Justus. Elias allowed one to speak, to act freely, without pretense.

Elias handed the Sunstone back to Swift.

At its coolness touching his palm, some of the constriction seemed to loosen from his throat.

"Did you hold the Star of Atlantis all the time you were in the coma?" asked Elias.

"Mostly," said Swift. "Others handled it, sometimes."

"No one handled it," said Caius. "We were all very frugal with touching it. Father did insist, though, on setting it beneath Swift's hand, at times."

Ash, though, had told Swift he'd held it. So—he must've taken it into hand when alone with Swift. Swift, unconscious.

"What's to become of that stone now?" asked Elias.

"We're consulting with a maritime museum in Pembrokeshire," said Justus. "It's small, but specializes on articles from maritime lore, which pleases me. From the pictures we sent of the Sunstone, of Swift's book and map, the curator believes this to be the actual Star of Atlantis."

All Octavian Krakau had to go on, though, to make that bold analysis, was one meager picture of the relics, along with details of where Swift had found them. Octavian had instructed them to take just one photo, and with no flash. In the picture, the small Cthulhu lurking at the map's edge was barely visible.

"Swift's Sunstone likely stood in that pitching sea cave for some centuries," said Justus. "That Swift's map led to the Sunstone—the curator calls it 'a miracle.' He apparently once sought the Star of Atlantis."

"So, what does one do upon discovering a legend?" asked Elias, watching Swift.

"The museum will appraise it," said Edric. "They'll present Swift with options. They told Father it's likely worth quite a bit."

"I, for one, think he should keep it." Caius watched Swift. "When I see you handling the Star of Atlantis, it's like watching you hold your own heart outside of your chest. I think that Sunstone's a part of you."

Elias asked Swift, "Do you want to keep it?"

Swift rested his gaze on the Star of Atlantis.

The fisherman, too, had told Swift to hang on to it.

And the myth spoke of the Star of Atlantis in terms of destiny, its finder chosen.

"Mum thinks I shouldn't keep it," said Swift. "She wants me to sell it or donate it—whatever I like. But she wants it out of my hands."

"Adara and I are in concord on this," said Justus. "I wonder, Swift, if separating yourself from the Star of Atlantis would help you move forward. What if it's that very stone, which you desired so greatly and won at such a price, that's blocking you?"

Everyone stilled.

Justus had spoken what it seemed they all thought but had been too sensitive to say outright.

The notion of actually parting with the Star of Atlantis brought wetness into Swift's eyes. Though, this troubling sense of heat might also be another fever starting.

"Do you want to divide yourself from the Sunstone?" Elias asked Swift.

"Ash thinks I should sell it," said Swift.

Caius screeched back his chair.

"Ash found a relic from the same era," said Swift, watching Caius cross his arms. "He wants mine displayed by his at the museum."

"About Ash," said Elias. "He's an old friend who hasn't been much of a friend. Yet I think he's visited you quite a bit since your accident."

Swift watched Caius, who was staring at his own hands, tightly knit, his knuckles white.

"Ash hasn't been much of a friend, it's true," said Swift. "But that's because he's been lost."

Elias, seeming to be keeping an eye on Caius, asked Swift, "Have you welcomed Ash's friendship?"

Swift still could hardly believe he and Caius had survived their ordeal. He could still feel the urgency, the resolute need to take Caius into the waters of Sterncastle Cove to save his life.

And he had saved Caius.

For Ash, too, he'd dare treacherous waters.

Edric captured Swift's glance. "You sure you don't want us to scram? Maybe you and Elias should speak alone from here on out."

"There's nothing to talk about that you don't already know," said Swift.

"Ash has visited Swift often," said Justus. "He's showing a warmth we haven't seen in a while."

"That he found a sea relic too," said Swift, "it sort of ties us together. I like having him near."

"Your father tells me reading has become challenging," said Elias. "Is that how you'd describe things?"

"I've had no trouble reading my sea legend books with Ash," said Swift. "You see, Ash returned all my books that he'd kept at his house, and—"

"You mean—the books he nicked from you," said Caius.

"One of them," said Swift, casting Caius a look, "talks of an ancient Welsh clan—these mage-like pirates called the Shepherds of the Stars. They were teachers and heroes. Wanderers who did interesting things like pillage kings and teach and take care of others and share books and keep wisdom and guard treasures."

"If you're having no trouble reading, why did your father mention it?" asked Elias.

"It's the medical texts—the books I'll have to master to compete for the Practicum," said Swift. "They're proving difficult."

Elias nodded at Justus.

Justus placed a book of anatomy on the table before Swift.

"Will you try and read a bit to me?" asked Elias. "Open it to any page you'd like, and read it aloud."

Swift flipped randomly to a section on muscles and ligaments. The print on the page, dense and small, drew him in. He wanted to know this science, these mysteries—all the clever biological mechanics and chemistry and quandaries and research kept here. But the harder he focused, the more the words seemed to twist. Trying to read them was like trying to comprehend the fisherman's strange speech.

"Take your time," said Elias.

"The words are elusive." Swift leaned closer to the page. "They're disorganized—sort of like disordered supplies jumbling inside a medical bag. I mean, the individual words, I can read—of course I can. *Ligaments...strength...connectivity...* but in trying to make out the meaning of a sentence, it's like I've forgotten how to put it all together."

"I've had him try copying down a passage," said Justus. "But even doing so, he can't manage much comprehension."

Swift squinted at the book. "Trying to read this is like trying to take in a story when the sun's set and it's too dark to see by. When the wind's too cold or too strong. I'm reading, but I'm doing it wrong. I have to figure out how to read this, though, because if I can't, I won't make the Practicum. If I can't, something bad will happen, and I won't know what to do."

Elias eased the book away from Swift and handed it to Caius, who slid it out of sight.

Swift, looking up at the others, read concern. Glancing down, he realized his hands were shaking.

"Seems another fever might be settling in." Caius felt Swift's forehead. "Damn."

"Can you think of anything that might make grasping those sentences easier?" asked Elias.

"I want to go to Wales, to our beach house," said Swift. "I want to walk the coast and wade in the Celtic Sea and breathe its mist. I want Caius to take me, and I want Ash to come."

"Swift drops into these fits of panicking often," said Caius. "And to get beyond the fevers, he has to keep his stress low. The idea of taking him to Wales terrifies me. Wales is where our accident happened."

"But so did our rescue," said Swift.

Justus glanced at Swift's Sunstone. "Does any part of you want to carry the Sunstone back there and leave it?"

Swift turned over his Sunstone.

The glow it seemed to maintain, even resting on its dark

cloth, charmed him. He ached to look through it and study the stars.

"The person to find the Star of Atlantis, legends say, is destined for it," said Swift. "Getting rid of it would feel like giving up on something important."

"Isn't it a bit of a contradiction?" asked Edric. "A boy of science, like you, believing so doggedly in something like destiny."

"There's nothing wrong with entertaining the idea of destiny," said Swift.

"It's a superstition," said Edric.

"No," said Swift, "it's a philosophy. It postulates that there could be more forces at work than what we understand; that some things can't be fully explained if we limit ourselves to the knowledge we have. And that's true, scientifically speaking."

"What destiny do you wish the Sunstone would lend you?" asked Elias.

"I don't know, exactly." Swift studied the crystal. "The seven-pointed Celtic star that those pirate mages drew—it stands for natural elements interconnecting. And the fisherman told me that I had a role to play. I certainly can't say he's right about that. But neither can I say that he's wrong."

"Consider, lad," said Justus. "Your ultimate goal is to earn your way into Dr. Keats' Practicum. Can that stone help you?"

"Well no, but—"

"Then let's leave the question of destiny for another day." Justus rested his hand on Swift's, covering the Sunstone. "Let's deal in the matter of how we might deliver you where you'd like to be. For my part, I think you'd do well to place the Sunstone behind you."

"What if I'd be sacrificing too much?" asked Swift. "Ash thinks—"

"Can we forget Ash for a bloody second?" asked Caius. "Elias wants to hear your thoughts, not his."

Elias held Caius' shoulder. "It's all right."

"What I was going to say," said Swift, "is that Ash thinks the rights to the Star of Atlantis likely belong to me. Just like the box he discovered, I found the Star of Atlantis on a stretch of coast that seems outside of all boundaries."

Swift stared at his Sunstone, its internal ligaments of fissures gleaming.

"It feels like this belongs to me." He glanced at Justus. "And I don't think it's blocking me."

"I'd like you to do an imaginative exercise, lad," said Elias. "Can you try?"

"Imagination is right up my alley," said Swift.

Justus glanced at Elias. "Which is mostly your fault."

Elias gently laughed. "I'd take the blame for that any day." He drew closer to Swift. "Close your eyes."

Swift leaned against the back of the chair. Let his warm eyelids fall closed.

"Imagine that you've traveled to Pembrokeshire," said Elias. "Imagine that you're in your beach house. That Caius has brought you. Your friend Ash is with you, and you've got all your sea legend books and your science and medical books, too. In your pocket, you carry the Star of Atlantis. Can you see this?"

Picturing it all was wonderful.

The path winding from the beach house down to the water would shine as though strewn with pearls. Blue flowers would peer from the sharp shore grasses. The sun setting over the dock would glow like a campfire ember. The sand would feel powdery beneath his bare feet as he waded the waterline.

He pictured trekking the fringe of the Wentletrap Forest— the Wentletrap, seeming to drink from the earth wisdom cast shoreward from an unceasing cadence of breakers—breakers full of starlight, full of the sun's garish set and its blessed rise.

He pictured the great moon—white and sailing, half-shrouded by a gentle blueness of shadow.

"I can see everything," said Swift.

"Picture yourself stilling in that lovely place," said Elias. "And decide—what would you most like to do?"

Swift, his eyes closed, his heart soothed, could almost feel a warm wind grazing his cheeks; could almost smell the raw spices of seaweed, of fish, of campfire smoke.

He saw their dock stretching out into petulant waters, and tied to it was the *Star Strider*.

The *Strider* off-kilter and coarsely patched, her sails cinched, her bow pitching dreadfully, rough waves overwhelming her bench.

He felt Caius' hand come to rest on his shoulder.

The grisly image of the *Star Strider*, drowned, sank away.

Swift pictured, in this imagined light of day, what the fisherman's stretch of beach would look like.

He visualized the turn of the coast where the longboat had been fastened.

But there was no longboat.

And no fisherman.

"More than anything," said Swift, "I'd like to return the longboat to the fisherman."

"And there it is," said Elias.

Swift opened his eyes to find Elias peacefully watching him. "There what is?"

"Your trouble with resolving the accident seems to have something to do with that fisherman and his boat. This likely isn't the whole of the difficulty, but—do you feel indebted, somehow?"

Indebted. That was it. That was exactly this feeling of drag, of incompletion.

He needed to tell the fisherman how grateful he was. He needed to show the man that he'd survived. He needed to ask him a thousand questions.

And if the fisherman couldn't be found, it would be some comfort to feel he'd at least set the beach back to rights, returning the strong boat that belonged to its treacherous waters.

Swift glanced at the anatomy book resting before Caius. "When I go at those medical texts, it's like I don't feel welcome to read them. My mind sort of traces what I'm responsible for." He watched Caius. "Sometimes I relive the torment of wronging you by chasing the Star of Atlantis. Other times I can't shake how I wronged the fisherman by dividing him from his longboat. I may have endangered his livelihood."

"You haven't wronged anyone," said Caius. "Not me, and certainly not that fisherman."

"And besides that," said Edric, "finding one lone, loony man in Wales with its hundred beaches—it rings impossible, right?"

"If I could just return the boat," said Swift, "even if it's only a gesture, it'd be a great way to show the fisherman my gratitude."

Edric quirked his brow. "You realize you're talking about the guy who cut you."

"You mean—who saved me."

Swift glanced at Caius.

"Who saved us."

"Have the police found any hints on the whereabouts of the fisherman?" asked Elias.

"Adara and I are quite frustrated," said Justus. "They'll keep Swift's case open, though at this point, with no leads having turned up, we're told it's unlikely any will."

If even the police couldn't find the fisherman, Swift certainly had little chance.

Yet he couldn't help harboring a glimmer of hope that they'd somehow meet.

"And the boat Swift was found in," said Edric, "they say with the number of fingerprints on it, it's likely a public commodity. They can't pair it with any one lunatic."

"The fisherman wasn't a lunatic," said Swift. "Once he fully woke up, he was ordered. He just seemed a little off-kilter, like a troubled soldier. Like Grandfather."

"Was he old?" asked Elias. "Perhaps dementia was at play."

"Not at all old," said Swift. "And yet—he was weathered. He struck me like an old older brother. Like Edric."

Edric sat back. "Ah, you're saying you think I'm an old man."

"To lads, every thirty-year-old seems sixty," said Elias. "My young man, Oliver, confessed to his mum that he estimates me at one hundred and three."

"The fisherman seemed just timeless," said Swift. "And vastly knowledgeable."

"What did he say to you?" asked Elias.

"That the dark feels like ambush. He called Sterncastle Cove 'his waters.' He talked in a muddled way about reconciliation and connection. He knew that the Star of Atlantis was a Sunstone—and he knew, somehow, that I'd taken it. He said ancient starfarers and seafarers used Sunstones; that Sunstones bring insights, not just to ships, but to people. He taught me how to navigate by it."

Swift, needing to catch his breath, paused.

Elias gave him a gentle moment, then asked, "Did he say anything else?"

"It got more bizarre at the end. He said there's a great question: what manner of strange really is out there? He said the truth is wondrous and treacherous—that it's star fields away. He said the truth is in my blood—that by taking the Star of Atlantis, I've got a role to play. He told me to keep my eyes open."

"All this superstitious prattle," said Edric, "and yet he wouldn't tell Swift his name."

"As he drew out his boat," said Swift, "he called himself 'one who knows many secrets of the sea.' Then we heard an odd sound coming from the Wentletrap—an animal's cry, maybe. Then he was just gone."

"The fact that he abandoned Swift like that makes me think he was dangerous," said Caius. "Who cuts a boy, then sends him out onto the North Atlantic at night?"

"I don't know why he vanished, but it seems not to matter," said Swift. "He really seemed to believe I'd be all right."

"Do you think of the fisherman as innocent, as Swift does?" Elias asked Justus.

"I'd answer any purposed assault on a lad of mine with Odin's wrath," said Justus. "But Swift's story doesn't suggest a purposed assault. I hope the police find something yet on the fisherman, so we might understand what transpired more clearly. But I'm resigned to believe that there's no real chance they will."

Elias leaned back. "Do you think the Coast Guard would release that longboat to us? I'd be glad to tow it to Pembrokeshire behind my yacht. It wouldn't take us half a day."

Something in Swift released. "Will you come?" he asked Caius. "And can we stay for a while?"

Caius caught Elias' glance. "Swift wants Ash to come along. Does that raise any red flags for you?"

"Swift needs support," said Elias. "Having a friend by his side—especially one who's been lost for a spell—that might make for some powerful medicine."

"It'll help Ash as much as it'll help me," said Swift. "He's been hurt, too. His mum left him a long time ago. I worry that the wound is still open. Our friendship—it feels like it's mending us both."

"Swift and I do need to get to the Pembrokeshire museum," said Justus. "It might be handy for Ash to come along, as he knows those ropes."

Swift felt like he was floating—Justus was actually getting on board. And with Elias agreeing that Wales might prove healing—so much so that he was willing to tow the longboat there—Justus wasn't likely to waver.

Swift focused on Caius. "Will you come with us?"

Once they were in Wales, Caius would soak in the beauty and calm of the place. He'd remember himself, and he'd want to study with Swift.

Maybe he'd decide to sign up for the fall term.

Caius lowered his gaze.

"Please—will you?" The words came more desperately than Swift intended.

"It's not that I don't want to," said Caius. "It's just—"

"Brooke," said Swift.

Caius didn't look up.

"Caius certainly wants to go with you," said Edric. "He's just got things to do here."

"Study with me," said Swift, to Caius. "Stay on that course 'til you aim to get off it. Don't just meander away."

"Is it troubling to you," asked Elias, "that you can't decide this for Caius?"

"Of course not," said Swift. "I know I can't control what Caius does. And I don't want to."

But he did.

Swift couldn't have imagined that Caius—whom he had relied on so completely—would ever need his help. But Caius had needed rescue off the islet, and Swift had carried him.

Caius flashed a glance at Swift. "You, of all people, should know I'm not meandering."

"As you know what's best for you," said Elias, "Caius knows what's best for Caius."

"That's fair," said Swift. "But hear me out." He studied his Sunstone. "Of course, Caius, you know what's best for you. But I just think..." What card could he possibly play to get Caius on board?

Caius was, again, staring at his fists—clenched.

Swift saw, now, that his fists weren't empty. He was grasping a bracelet Brooke had given him.

Its dark metal was catching the light of the moon streaming in—the romantic, bay scallop shell moon that shone far more beautifully in the Welsh sky than anyplace.

Swift rested back. "What if Brooke were to come with us?"

A pained tightness left Caius' forehead as he lifted his gaze to meet Swift's.

"You'd want Brooke with us?"

"Why not?" Swift shrugged to mask the revulsion and make believable his pitch. "You'd have Brooke to help you figure out your heading. I'd have Ash. If I'm to make any progress, I'll need a great teacher. I'll need you."

Edric, half-smiling, rose. He walked behind Caius and mouthed to Swift—*You've got him.*

"I must say," said Justus, "I like the idea of Brooke as a member of the party, considering that Swift's fever relapses seem not to be finished."

"And Brooke might like to see the beach house," said Swift.

"Mum's told her about it," said Caius. "It's beauty. It's solitude." He turned the bracelet in his fingers. "Brooke does want to see it."

Justus stood. "Elias and I will arrange to collect the longboat from the Coast Guard. That shouldn't take but a few weeks."

"Just think," said Edric, to Swift. "By early October, you could be sailing north and returning that bloody boat where you found it."

Elias stood, too, beside Justus. "Once there, you could take your lad to the museum and see about his relics. Then Swift, in the care of his brother and his friend, and under Brooke's eye, can heal."

"Marvelous!" Justus clapped Elias on the shoulder. "Except..." His face dimmed.

"What?" asked Elias.

"Adara." Justus met Swift's eyes. "Revisiting the grounds of the drifter who cut you—how will we ever get your mum on board?"

10

"Have you lost your mind?"

Mum's voice lifted above the clatter of a dish dropped into a watery sink.

"It's a fool's business, sailing the North Atlantic at the onset of autumn."

Swift and Caius rose off the couch and stood in the kitchen doorway.

Justus waved them back.

Swift had once heard Justus speaking to Elias about some disagreement Justus was having with Mum.

"I can put all my years of professional experience," Elias had said, "my ten years of medical schooling, and the sum of what wisdom my own life has yielded into one practical, irrefutable piece of advice."

"Well?" Justus had asked.

"Heed your wife."

And Justus did seem to be finding it difficult, crossing Mum like this. Of the two of them, Mum was the stronger willed.

"We won't be taking the *Regulus*," Justus told Mum. "Elias has agreed to sail us. His yacht is as comfortable and warm as can be. In it, we'd have a quick ride."

Though it was absolutely true that sailing to Pembrokeshire would be a breeze, Mum seemed little comforted.

Since she'd received Swift and Caius back home, she'd run herself ragged tending them, insisting that they receive large and nutritious meals made by no hands but hers, spending every moment at rest not at rest, but crocheting them blankets. It was like, now that their wellbeing could be influenced by her care, she couldn't hold still.

"The sea affords no comfort, in the best of times," said Mum. "The wind will be up, the waves strong. Even in a yacht, it'd be a sea-sickening and wearying trip."

Justus gently touched the back of her neck, where auburn tendrils had slipped from her high bun—her hair tied up and out of her way in a manner she never had worn, but told how little time she was willing to spend on herself.

"My love, we've had many pleasant trips on that yacht," said Justus. "And we've sailed a good deal further north than Pembrokeshire."

"Not with two injured sons on board," said Mum. "And in the first place, Swift and Caius have no business going anywhere near Sterncastle Cove."

Bubbles, flung from a spatula, left froth on Justus' sweater.

"We won't be sailing into Sterncastle Cove." Justus brushed off the bubbles. "We'll be well south. Swift will tie the longboat where he remembers the fisherman giving it to him. And that will be that."

Mum turned off the water. "And what if the fisherman is there?" She settled her hand on her hip. "With his knife?"

"Dr. Keats was right." Caius stepped in. "Chances are, that fisherman's long gone."

She glanced at Caius in the doorway, then at Swift, peeking in. "None of you sees this as less than wise?"

Swift, Justus, and Caius only glanced at each other.

"You must agree that the fisherman needs help," said Swift. "He ought to at least have his boat."

"His right to have his boat vanished when he drew your blood," said Mum. "And what if you were to find him?" She pointed the spatula at each of them. "He might make quick work of the lot of you."

"Seeing his boat back to him is our responsibility," said Swift. "The Coast Guard won't get around to towing it back there for ages—they're willing to let Father and Elias do it."

Mum plunged her hands into the dishwater.

"Mum," said Caius.

She glanced over her shoulder.

"Lad's not at peace with the way things lie. He needs this."

"What he needs is safety, and—"

"Swift needs closure on the score of the fisherman," said Justus. "And that diagnosis is coming from Elias. Caius and I would like to help him to it."

"So would Ash." Swift glanced at Caius. "And Brooke."

Mum turned. "Brooke would be traveling with you?"

"Our lad will be in quite good hands," said Justus. "Swift and I will first meet with the curator, Octavian Krakau. I'll then come home, while Brooke and Caius, along with Ash, remain at the beach house with Swift for a week. Maybe two if he finds he's making good progress in such a restful environment."

"Swift has asked for my help," said Caius, "and Brooke's. We'll structure his time carefully. He'll be doing little besides reading from his medical texts."

"I know my lad," said Mum, her eyes arrow-focused on Swift. "You place him in Wales where his treasure came from— it'll only spark his drive to explore."

"Perhaps he does need careful watching," said Justus.

"I don't—" Swift stepped in.

Justus gestured for him to be still. "Caius and Brooke can provide all the oversight Swift may need."

As difficult as it was to bear the insult that he needed oversight, Swift kept quiet. When it came to communicating with Mum, Justus knew what he was doing.

And he was moving their argument along.

"I'm afraid it'll be a burden for Brooke," said Mum, glancing at Caius, still on crutches. "Caius couldn't be expected to do much."

In truth, though, Caius had adapted quite well to his limits.

Even on crutches, he could manage just about everything on his own.

It was just that when Mum was around, she wouldn't let him. In a couple of days, Caius would switch to a walking boot, which would give him back nearly all his freedom.

Swift sometimes went a little tired when a fever would strike, but that was all. There'd been times when he'd been cooking with a fever without even knowing it.

It was often only during his nightly checkup with Caius that he'd realize he had one, or when Brooke or Mum detected it. Even with fevers so often simmering, he, too, had grown perfectly capable of taking care of himself.

"Swift and I are doing a pretty good job looking after each other," said Caius. "And just think—we'd be in our beach house —such a beautiful place. Brooke and I can help Swift focus on his studies."

"What sort of oversight do you have in mind?" asked Mum, her eyes still somewhat narrowed.

Caius stared at Swift, the look on him severe. "If he so much as opens a legend book, I'll keep it 'til we've come home."

"Hang on, I didn't agree to surrender my books—"

"Your aim is to relearn to read medicine," said Caius. "That's the whole of it."

Mum folded her arms. "Not one of you is to set so much as an oar into Sterncastle Cove. Can I count on you to abide by that?"

"I daresay we can." Justus squeezed her shoulders. "You can count on us to abide by the first rule of sailing. We'll certainly all come back alive."

He kissed her ruddy cheek, then backed out, herding Caius and Swift from the kitchen.

11

Swift stood on the bow of the yacht at its rail, beside Ash, as Elias pulled away from Clovelly's dock.

The North Atlantic was losing the cool blue atmosphere of high summer. Now, tending toward autumn, it was all gray water and sinking clouds.

Seagulls swooping near the wave crests looked like shreds of storms—pieces of the pearl-gray sky clipped by shearing winds. And the sea itself, agitated by near storms, shivered like a troubled sleeper.

The Devonshire shore appeared dull, the sunlight having vanished from its sand. Receding in the bleak morning fog, it struck Swift as foreign.

Barely a month had passed since the accident, and Swift was left feeling equally unfamiliar to himself. It was as though the unrest in his body, in his mind, was spurred by a changing of internal seasons, of winds.

Justus, Caius, and Brooke sat talking together in the yacht's warm cabin, with Elias at the helm. Swift and Ash had chosen to ride on the open deck—Swift wanting to taste the salt in the air and face the fisherman's beach head on; Ash saying he wanted just to be with him.

Elias caught Swift's attention with a wave. They'd traveled far enough that he could punch the motor.

Swift and Ash took seats on a stow box against the rail and waved back.

Brooke, eyeing them, arms crossed, said something to Justus.

She clearly didn't like Swift riding outside in the strong wind. Probably, she feared it would trigger a fever.

But the relapsing fevers had been occurring so frequently, it seemed Swift was doomed for one, whatever he might do.

Justus, rubbing his beard, seemed to be considering calling Swift in.

Caius glanced at Swift, then said something to Justus, to Brooke.

They all sat back down.

Caius knew Swift didn't belong in there. He needed to stay on the brink of the boat, where he could connect with the trails of water leading to Pembrokeshire.

The only other member of the party preferring the cold wind to the cabin was Elias' six-year-old grandson, Oliver—a wriggling bundle of life-jacketed joy buckled onto a bench wrapping the cabin's windows.

Though Swift would've rather been alone with Ash, he couldn't help but feel fondness for Oliver.

The boy's face was pale, his eyes stark, as though he were trying to see everything at once.

The only sound breaking the whoosh of the wake was Oliver's little fist tapping the cabin window, trying to get his grandfather to look, look at that wave! Look at the beach we're coming on! Look at those reef rocks! Oh, look at those birds! Look at all this!

Swift gave the wonderstruck boy a small smile, then leaned against the rail.

He let the fisherman's longboat, at the tail of the yacht, capture his gaze.

The longboat, tethered to the yacht's stern, skipped along in stride like it was chasing them.

"What are we going to do with that boat?" yelled Oliver, over the cacophony of the wind and the engine.

"Sail her to a beach," called Swift. "Leave her for her owner."

"Who's going to sail her? Can I?"

"I don't think so, lad."

Swift's voice caught. He'd never before felt old enough to call another boy 'lad.'

"I could do it," said Oliver. "I've sat on Grandfather's lap before and put my hands on the wheel of the sailboat and guided her true."

Swift offered an affirming, brow-lifted nod.

The yacht dashed in skips over the open sea, all its summer lacquer gone, brewing storm winds keeping it in a state of petulance.

Or perhaps the water was pressed to turbulence by the dipping near of a hundred million tugging stars winging in their courses, invisible now.

Swift's hand reflexively went to his pocket to draw out his Sunstone.

Anytime the sky captured him, he'd fallen into the habit of lifting the Sunstone to study the canopy, to peer at the brighter stars beyond the clouds, ensconced by the day.

But his pocket was now empty.

Caius had carefully packed Swift's relics and forbidden him to unbox them—not until they were at the museum, for fear Ash might be tempted to meddle with them.

Or steal them.

Those seemed like most irrational fears.

How in the world could Ash mess with or steal anything from Swift when they were all together, Caius watching like a hawk?

But Caius wouldn't be moved.

Ash, glancing at Swift's hand, seemed to pick up on the craving.

"Whether or not you'll get to keep it, the Star of Atlantis will certainly be in good hands."

Swift drew his fingers away from his pocket. "I'd rather it stayed in my hands."

"Why, though?" asked Ash. "Wouldn't something so valuable be better off in a museum, under the care of someone who understands its worth?"

It was precisely because Swift understood its worth that he'd sought to claim it.

And he had claimed it.

Now, as anxious as he was to find his way out of these dark woods and back to his medical texts, the Sunstone with its mystical nature of capturing light, with the sense of destiny it carried—it seemed at least to offer hope that he could.

"If they make me give it up," said Swift, "I'll feel lost."

"I could see why," said Ash. "That stone kept you on course after you left Caius on the beach for dead."

Swift leaned away from him and watched the hypnotic flashing of water coursing past.

"Maybe you should try acknowledging," said Ash, "that it wasn't the Sunstone that saved you. It was that Scottish crew who plucked you from the sea."

Swift couldn't answer Ash.

He couldn't even look at him, nor take his eyes off the water —because the low sun was slicing in through parting clouds, coaxing an illusion on top of the waves.

Little ships seemed to have grown out of the sea. Little ships, stacked with little sails, seemed to be teeming over the water, like some country of North Atlantic faerie folk had emptied their boroughs and crowded the Celtic for boating races, or for setting off to battle by the billions.

Swift clung to the rail.

He couldn't look away from the fantasy. He couldn't even blink.

Every place on the sea his gaze met, the little ships manifested—their sails made of light, their hulls of water shadows.

He shook himself to try to clear the mirage, but once he'd learned to tease the illusion of little ships skittering over the waves, he couldn't unsee them.

The fisherman had spoken of extraordinary things being real—of destiny, of hidden worlds; of ancient seafarers and starfarers; of so much allure, star fields away.

Swift was deeply aware of how brightly the stars hung, though he was blind to them in daylight without his stone.

If there was anything that captured him as much as sea legends or medicine, it would be astronomy—the study of those distant suns and planets, their mathematics and chemistry, their mind-blowing physics, their winging through the unending ocean of the windless Universe—astounding.

Watching the Celtic Sea with its fleet of watery faerie ships, seeing the sky, its star fields veiled by light and low clouds—it lent a stark sense of how minimal was his knowledge of the natural Earth, much less of the distant reaches of space.

The illusion of the tiny ships was interrupted by Oliver, suddenly at Swift's side, buckling himself to the bench Swift was sitting on.

The boy was little for his age, and an only child. Swift pitied him for having no Caius.

Swift knelt before the little boy and saw his seat-belt secure. He zipped up Oliver's small jacket to his chin and pulled the flaps of his headband tight over his ears. "You okay?"

"I'm okay. I'm on the lookout. Want to help?"

Swift let out a gentle laugh. "What are we on the lookout for?"

Oliver twisted around and gripped the rail with his small, gloved hands. "The sea is swarming with monsters, Grandfather says. We'd better watch out for them."

Swift glanced into the cabin at Elias' jovial face, smiling easy as he talked with Justus.

"Belonging to Elias as you do," said Swift, "you're probably stuffed full of stories all day."

"Oh, yes. All day." Oliver rested his chin on the rail, his gaze sinking into the distance.

"Which are your favorite stories?" asked Swift.

Brightness seized Oliver like fever. "Ocean voyages. And stories of being a pirate king."

Ash glanced at Swift, then—half-smiling—looked away. They together, at Oliver's age, had reigned as pirates over many dreamed seas.

The yacht set into a canter as it angled landward.

Swift stood again and took the rail.

Beside him, Oliver's copper head shone in the pale sun, and his cheeks were chapped red from the wind. But he seemed to feel no ache, no cold, no stinging of sunlight nor of mist, for the heights his imagination was flying.

Swift watched the coast with Oliver, trying to see what he might be imagining.

Fleets of battered pirate ships, perhaps, flying black flags to warn off death, lashed to every dock they passed.

A brute giant squid slithering tentacles out of the water and bashing one of those ships.

A clattery break in the waves—the surfacing of a shoal of mermaids—devastatingly beautiful—waiting for a prisoner to trip off a plank.

Somehow the fantasies failed to incite the thrill they would have just weeks ago.

Swift's heart sank at the realization.

Yet taking in these coastal waters and rocky white shores, their boundaries drawn by beaches of brown-sugar sand—the natural world seemed as entrancing as any fantasy. Perhaps even more so.

Just as the waves had seemed to shift into armadas of faerie ships, the plain coast seemed to display a new magic—not a magic spun by Elias or any great story weaver, but a magic conjured by the Earth, delicious in its ordinariness, dense with science, with botany and biology and physics, with history.

The jetting rocks represented an account of the comings and goings of tides, of eons.

Those crags bore fossils that bespoke the passing of geological eras.

And every grain of sand seemed a tiny miracle, grand at the cellular level, each—one of billions—a microcosm, a moon, swarming with elfin gastropods.

The coast seemed a microcosm, too; a slice of a wide world that Swift could examine. The coast was a slip of land peopled by birds, by woodland animals, by constant stars.

Its shallows rimmed a water world occupied by schooling fish, by coasting sharks, by blue-starred black octopi; by hardened Welsh fisherman harboring ancient secrets, carrying knives fashioned of metal spirited to Earth on the tails of fallen stars.

Inland, people like Dr. Keats labored, making miracles happen. Caius might soon be among such angels. And maybe Swift would as well, someday.

Oliver, his face joy-filled, glanced up at Swift.

"It's all beautiful, isn't it?" Swift asked him.

"Beautiful because the beaches are made of silver and gold coins," said Oliver. "And the water." He pointed. "See it shimmering? That's because, there—right there—mermaids are swimming."

The sea was indeed glittering intensely in a single patch, about a quarter mile from the yacht. But that shine was no shoal of mermaids, nor any magical beast.

It was the reflection of a star—a sun, ninety-three million miles away, and yet right there it was piercing the clouds, acting on them, the heat of its roiling core transforming the Celtic Sea into mist and shedding the light of its heart on the water.

"Mermaids!" cried Oliver. "Do you see them?" He turned his eyes up to meet Swift's, his expression demanding that Swift participate in the fiction.

"Yes, Mermaids." Swift offered Oliver the most captivated look he could conjure.

In that moment of seeing Oliver's rapture, of feeling a keen wonderment of his own, sparked by a very different source, Swift realized he no longer needed pirates or mermaids or monsters to muster a sense of enthrallment. There was so much in the natural world to investigate—plentiful actual wonders to fathom.

He glanced down at Oliver.

The lad was still fixating on the waves, maybe imagining

mermaid tails, maybe caught up in the vision of illusive faerie ships, which Swift still couldn't shake.

"Do you have many seafaring storybooks?" Swift asked him.

Oliver came out of his fit of astonishment and met Swift's eyes. "Not many books. My grandfather tells me stories from his own mind."

"I have a pretty expansive collection of seafaring histories and legends," said Swift. "They're full of pirates and monsters. And plenty of them are true. Would you like to have those?"

Oliver's mouth made the roundest "O" Swift had ever seen. "O—Oh, yes. Could I really?"

"Consider them yours. After you drop us off, you and Elias can go on to my house and pack them."

Oliver threw off his buckle and hurried to the window containing his grandfather and banged on it, shouting the good news through the glass.

Elias smiled and shook his head, pointing at his ear.

Oliver shouted more loudly and more articulately—"He's giving me his pirate and his water monster books. It's going to be great. You're going to read them all to me. Tonight!"

Elias nodded at what he probably still couldn't hear.

"You sure you're ready to part with all that?" asked Ash.

Swift shrugged as he guided the lad back to his bench and buckled him in.

"The only legend book I need to hang on to is *The Star of Atlantis*."

"But you might not be able to," said Ash. "If the museum takes your relics, you'd have nothing."

The truth was, though, if the relics proved fake, he might already have nothing.

Oliver snatched up Swift's hand and gripped it as he laid his gaze again on the sea.

"It's all right." Swift snugged Oliver's ear warmers closer against his small head. "I think."

Swift lost himself in the coursing of waves, in the unscrolling coast, until finally in the distant north, a dancing wisp of a dark cloud caught his eye.

It was the cyclone of circling birds—a sign that they were advancing on Sterncastle Cove.

Swift glanced back at Elias and nodded.

Elias angled the yacht toward a beach stretching far to the bleak north.

12

Caius came out from the yacht's cabin and stood by Swift. "You ready for this?"

Swift stared at a grim stretch of land, rolling away north, stopping short of Sterncastle Cove.

He needed to be here, certainly, to reach the closure Elias hoped this place could bring.

But the sight of those rough waves, that foreboding landscape, was fearsome.

"I have to be ready," said Swift, pressing back agonizing flashes of their accident. "This is the best way to deal with what happened."

Caius peered through binoculars at the beach where Swift had left him. "I'm not giving up, you know."

Swift glanced at him.

Caius handed him the binoculars. "That remark you made —admonishing me not to meander."

"I know you're not meandering," said Swift. "I only meant—"

"The thing is," said Caius, "sometimes, I feel I never could keep on with medicine. As much as I want to, it strikes me, at times—I might not have the choice."

Swift adjusted the binoculars and through them studied the prismatic rocks marking Sterncastle Cove.

"I'll have loads of support, no matter what I do," said Caius. "That feels good because"—he lowered the binoculars away from Swift's eyes—"I don't believe a person is bound to only one path. I don't believe I'm a trauma doctor and nothing else."

"You're trying to tell me something, aren't you?" asked Swift.

"It's just—I don't quite believe in destiny, though you seem to." Caius lowered his gaze. "There are many paths, many things I could do, all fulfilling."

Those final words sounded like Brooke's. And the way Caius had spoken them, he sounded resigned. It felt like he was nudging Swift to consider resigning with him.

"There might be lots of paths," said Swift. "But I'm a medical Practicum student. That, I can feel."

"That's where you're at, I know. But—were you to change your mind—I'd still be here for you."

"I'm not going to change my mind."

Caius, squinting in the sun, focused on Swift. "This world is full of people who'll tell you there's a right way and a wrong way to be. And of course they believe that the right way is their way."

"I know there are people like that," said Swift. "But you can't think I'd be so easily pressured."

Caius sent a fleeting glance toward Ash—leaning over the rail with Oliver and pointing at a school of fish darting at the skim. "Some people are highly controlling."

"I know," said Swift, watching Ash, too.

But being controlling—that wasn't such a terrible quality. Ash would try to press. It was his way. And it was true that, at this point, he couldn't be wholly trusted. But for all that, Ash's camaraderie, Swift needed. And Swift understood why Ash was controlling. He ached for Ash because of it.

"Controlling people can be very smart and cunning," said Caius. "You must learn not to heed them."

"And how about you?" Swift glanced back through the

cabin window, at Justus. "Do you think you've ever been manipulated?"

Caius, glancing at Justus, too, smiled a bit. "No. I've always felt medical school was my fit. And Justus—he doesn't control or manipulate. He aims us, then lets us find our own way."

Ash was holding Oliver now, and they together were pointing at the beach.

"Is that a person?" Ash glanced at Swift. "Oliver's spotted something on the beach."

Swift struggled down a flashing thrill at the thought of encountering the fisherman—of speaking to him, of asking him questions.

But whatever was on that beach, surely it wasn't the fisherman. There was no way he'd be so lucky as to find the man immediately.

Swift peered through the binoculars.

The beach was mostly clear, except along its northern edge. There, a darkish hump rested.

Even with the aid of the binoculars, Swift couldn't decipher what it was.

It might be a person. Or a blanket. Or a heap of rubbish. But beside it stood a clear fire pile.

He handed Caius the binoculars. "Can you make that out?"

Caius looked. "I see kindling. There's no smoke, but toward the center of the stack, the branches are blackened. Seems like a fire might've been lit, then doused quick."

The kindling pile, though mostly unburnt, was a bit strewn.

Perhaps the pile was old. Even so, it was possible it'd belonged to the fisherman.

Maybe he'd camped here recently, somehow evading the police.

"If that fisherman's here..." said Ash, almost to himself.

The look on him was greed. Hunger.

Seeing something on that beach—seeing Ash's gaze fixed on it, Swift realized the last thing he could bear would be Ash meeting the fisherman. Ash hearing his remarkable words. Ash pressing him.

Then and there, Swift made a pact with himself that any pursuit of the fisherman, he'd do without Ash.

Probably, though, the fisherman was long gone. In all likelihood, they'd find zero evidence tying the remnants of this campsite to him.

Swift jolted at the yacht's engine dropping into a low gear.

The closer to shore they pulled, the more disheveled the kindling pile looked.

"I think they're wanting us," said Oliver, pointing at the cabin.

Swift guided Oliver to the door, steadying him against the pitch. He opened it, letting out a flash of heat.

Oliver rushed to his grandfather and climbed onto his lap.

Brooke drew Swift in. "Why don't you sit down a moment? Warm up."

Swift moved away from her, toward Elias.

"Is this the place?" asked Elias.

"Without a doubt," said Swift. "Those square rocks straight ahead—they stand at the entrance to Sterncastle Cove. And this is the coast I set out from in the longboat. On its beach, we just spotted a wood pile that looks burned."

Justus stood and zipped his coat.

Swift led them out and to the stern. He got to work reeling close the fisherman's longboat.

He turned toward Caius. "You'll help me draw her to shore, right?"

Brooke grasped Caius' arm.

He held her hand tightly against him a moment, then said to her, "I'll be all right."

Not letting go, she drew him back toward the cabin and whispered something.

Swift caught—"I didn't expect you'd want to," and "your leg might not handle it well."

Caius seemed to say something back to Brooke, something about "needing to be with Swift." Something she apparently didn't like, judging from the chilly look taking her.

Caius, tending remorseful, whispered something else. He offered her a small kiss.

At that, she softened. She held Caius close for a longer kiss.

Swift grew uncomfortably hot—not at just the sickening sight of their intimacy, but at the sting of Brooke deliberately keeping Caius entwined when he'd told her he wanted—he needed—to be with Swift.

Swift made himself exceptionally busy tending to the longboat's ropes.

Justus, likewise, seemed purposefully tuning out their discussion. Ash, clearly entertained by the argument, discreetly watched.

Caius came away from Brooke. "Look, Swift. I actually don't trust myself to go easy." He offered Swift a mere glance. "I'm not sure my leg could manage that beach."

"It's fine," said Swift, avoiding looking at him as well. "I wouldn't want you to risk anything."

While Caius rejoined Brooke, Swift watched the waves swamping the rocky shore. He gazed at a sheet of mist blowing over the rough terrain marking the brink of the Wentletrap Forest.

At seeing it all so crisply, so immediately, his memories of the fisherman struck hard.

"I'll help you draw the longboat." Ash took the boat's rope from Swift.

"You?" Swift swallowed. "No, don't feel like you have to. I mean—this is intense." He glanced at Brooke. "I imagined Caius might want to go with me, but my father and I can manage."

"Are you kidding?" Ash towed the longboat nearer. "I'm dying to see where you wrecked, where you climbed to reach the Sunstone, where you left Caius behind."

"The three of us will go," said Justus. "And I'll have you lads following my lead. Understood?"

Swift relaxed a bit at seeing the sternness on his father. In the unlikely case that the fisherman were here, Justus would surely keep Swift—and Ash—well-distanced from him.

Swift scanned the edge of the Wentletrap Forest, looming

behind the strewn kindling. "I'd like to walk along the forest's edge—to see, by day, the course I took."

Justus nodded.

"I'll idle the yacht at the end of that prominence, just south," said Elias. "Let your hiking lead you there." He tossed Justus a two-way radio. "Call if you get into a scrape."

Justus followed Ash over the yacht's rail and dropped beside him into the longboat.

"It would've been nice if the Coast Guard had bothered to clean this," said Ash, spotting Swift in. "Be careful, there's caked sand everywhere. It's slick."

At placing his feet in the longboat—Swift froze. It was as though his body were remembering the feel of its density, its strength, the sense of water coursing under its heavy wood.

And the Celtic Sea stretching forever, the slosh and gurgle of waves twisting around the longboat's hull, struck him with exhaustion and burned in his cut.

"There's room here on the bench," said Ash, reaching for him.

Swift remained standing, holding tightly to the yacht.

A sense of brutality was resonating off the coast's jagged rocks, the rough water breaking on them. And the fierceness he'd felt in the slash of the fisherman's dagger—he was sensing it viscerally.

At this moment, the idea of drawing the longboat, of revisiting the fisherman's beach, seemed gravely dangerous.

"You all right?" Ash rested his hand on Swift's leg.

The waves coursing to the shore were calamitous. And the tide would've been a bit higher, a bit stronger on the night of the accident. How he'd piloted this craft into them seemed inexplicable.

Until he noticed a broad coursing riptide jetting out straight from the beach. He turned enough to focus on it.

That same current must've been at play when he pushed off. It must've lent the power that let him clear the breakers.

"Swift?" Justus sat forward. "Would you like to remain in the yacht?"

Swift let go of its hull and sank onto the longboat's bench.

The fisherman must've known that current.

That would explain why he'd been so confident Swift would make it out to open water.

Swift's conceptualization of the fisherman took a warmer tone.

He hadn't set Swift adrift on barbarous waters. He'd placed him in a craft that would carry him far west, toward help.

Swift reached to lift one of the oars from its hooks.

Ash stopped him. "Let me."

Swift took the oar. "I can manage." And truly, the oar felt lighter than the last time he'd held it.

Justus removed the oar from Swift's hands and gave it to Ash. "Helping Swift go easy will be your main occupation in Pembrokeshire, I think."

Justus lifted the other oar and, together with Ash, turned the boat.

"That sharp boulder with ridges, at the beach's north edge" —Swift pointed at the group of rocks, the blind out from which the fisherman had drawn the longboat—"the longboat was tied there."

Justus and Ash aimed their heading for the point, a stone's throw south of the towering entrance to Sterncastle Cove.

Swift glanced back at the horizon, which he'd frantically chased, searching for a ship.

That open water looked more desolate, more hopeless than the coast had. It spoke of lostness. Dismemberment.

And seeing the bow of the longboat cutting through the water, the hallucination he'd suffered—Caius as a spirit, seated at the longboat's bow—it struck as clearly as starlight.

"You all right, lad?" asked Justus. "Feeling seasick?"

"Not seasick," Swift whispered.

Old Norse myths had it that the day of a person's death was written by seers on the day of his birth. As harrowing as their ordeal had been, Swift couldn't help feeling he'd evaded death.

Sitting again in the longboat, it felt as though today, he

himself was like a spirit, come back to haunt the waters on which he ought to have died.

What if, for his escape, death now would be hunting him?

The bow of the longboat struck sand.

Swift steadied himself. Of course it was foolish to entertain such troubling and far-fetched ideas. Edric viewed destiny as a mere superstition, and Caius saw it as a means of manipulation.

Though Swift could see both points, they seemed slightly off the mark. Destiny, to him, was like that ocean riptide, still coursing visibly—something present to carry him onward when he himself was too blinded or damaged to advance on his own.

Swift climbed over the gunwale and dropped into the shallows.

The sucking pull of seawater constricted his thighs, and the air hung thickly with the scent of kelp, tinged rustic by the smell of an old fire.

The whole of the landscape with its metallic streaks and cold colors, with its swollen moon—pale as death on the watery horizon, was a relic of his nightmare. A flurry of panic rose—a panic of feeling that Caius was alone and in danger.

"Hang tight, lad," Justus trained Swift's hands to the boat's gunwale. "Hold steady while we fix her to the rocks."

Under the boat's rim, Swift's fingers fell upon something cool. Metallic. Something sharp-edged—a metal plate, framing a long cylinder. It felt like a hinge.

Ash helped Justus loop a length of the longboat's tow rope over a pronged rock. They busied themselves tying it firm.

Swift discreetly ran his hand along the boat's interior curve.

Underneath the piled sand, there seemed to be a fissure in the wood—almost flush but betraying what seemed to be the outline of a small stow.

But it couldn't be. Surely, the Coast Guard would've discovered any stow and emptied it.

Justus climbed onto the beach and trekked up to the dry sand, measuring, as he went, the rope's hold.

Ash tugged at Swift's elbow. "She's fixed steady. We'd best get you out of the water."

Swift couldn't bring himself to step away. A stow in this longboat might mean a lead to the fisherman.

Ash couldn't find out about this.

"What's the matter?" Ash was watching Swift carefully, like he knew Swift was hiding something.

Swift stood frozen in the chilling waves, the idea of something hidden here gripping him, the desperation to keep it from Ash paralyzing him.

"Why are you just standing there?" asked Ash. "You'd better come dry off."

Ash, glaring at him, petrified him further. Ash wasn't just coaxing him.

This was pressure. Control.

"What's wrong with you?" Ash climbed a yard up the beach. "I said, come away from the boat."

It was a familiar feeling, of course—Ash controlling him. And it was a terrible feeling.

Caius had been right—Swift needed to find a way to deal with this pressure.

But he couldn't think how. He couldn't think at all, with Ash watching him. All he could do was gently pull his hands out of the boat lest Ash realize he was, in fact, hiding something.

Justus, from up the beach, turned. "Lads? Is all well?"

Ash's expression changed to a cool shade of caring. "Do you need help?" He came a few steps down.

The concern in the question sounded genuine.

Was it?

Ash climbed further down, into the cold water with Swift. "Why don't we go together?"

The sickening sense of being controlled shifted into the soothing sense of being guided.

Ash reached out his hand.

Swift stepped away from the longboat. He'd figure out a way to come back—alone—to investigate that hidden stow.

He took Ash's hand.

Ash led him out of the water and onto dry sand.

"What's going on?" asked Ash. "Why do you look so lost?"

"That night, setting out from right here," said Swift, "a part of me felt I was leaving Caius to die."

Ash rested his eyes on the deep coast. "Then, let's move on."

Swift followed him further up the beach.

Just beyond the waterline, Swift's shoe caught on the tail of a rope. He unburied it and traced it to where it was tied off. He studied the rope's fringes—severed cleanly.

The knife the fisherman had used to cut this rope had been the same knife that'd cut Swift.

Swift lent his attention to the wind, moving through the Wentletrap like a current—for standing here, he could clearly recall the sound of bestial crying he'd heard just before the fisherman vanished.

Nothing moved, though. Nothing wailed, save the wind.

Justus, having checked the kindling pile, was walking back, his gaze fixed on the rope in Swift's hands. He seemed likewise to be reading it, a sense of solemn certainty dawning on his face.

Swift handed the rope to his father.

"Perhaps we should leash her with this rope as well," said Justus. "The fisherman might conceive in its binding the assurance that the lad he sent out to sea has survived."

Justus carried the rope back to the water and threaded it through a hook on the longboat's bow.

Ash climbed onto a high rock and scanned the beach.

Swift followed and crouched beside him at the rock's pinnacle.

Ash, seeming frantic to find something, Swift, fearful that they actually might, together searched the beach for footprints, for any sign of a presence.

The whole landscape looked salt-washed and dead, its pale sky carrying gulls bawling with hunger, its misted wind whipping the tall grasses, its shore waves tumbling in petulance, grumbling over sharp rocks.

Swift gazed to the south, toward Elias' yacht, inside of which Caius was surely warm and very glad about the solitude Brooke had won them.

Swift touched his chest where the dagger cut crossed him.

Though healing clean under Caius' care, it was blossoming into a pink scar that was tender.

Touching that line of scarred skin through his jacket was like running his fingers over a threshold.

The night of the accident, though keenly felt, was frozen in form, in the past.

Perhaps he could leave its terrors here on this horrific beach, leashed like a beast, with the longboat.

The yacht moved into deeper water and set a course for the prominence.

Justus waved for Swift and Ash to climb down. "I'd like you to see the kindling pile."

They scaled down and trudged after him to it.

"This is clearly a campsite," said Justus, "though, quite old and wasted. A blanket lies there, but it's swamped with blown sand."

"The tinder looks barely used," said Ash. "And freshly cut."

Justus knelt. "It's quite scattered. Whoever built this likely moved on days ago, if not weeks."

Swift pointed through the brush. "That's the stretch I hiked. It isn't easy going, but I did manage it."

"Lead the way," said Justus.

The way, now a month into autumn, was trickier than it'd been on the night of the accident. The ground was dense with leaf litter, the weeds and vines stiff.

Soon enough, though, Swift was through it and looking over the beach arcing around Sterncastle Cove.

In one sweep of a glance across the water, he saw everything—the cove's islet, its peaks sharp, the slick of them shining; the reef that'd tipped the *Strider*; the knob on the islet where he'd leashed her; the patch where, on that narrow shelf, Swift had lain, frozen, near-drowned; the holds he'd used to make that chancy climb; the sharp rock at its base that broke Caius' leg.

Justus stood beside Swift, so closely their arms were touching, sharing warmth. They together stared at the water in Sterncastle Cove, at its anguished state.

Its temper looked even deadlier than Swift recalled; more furious, cursed to churn, it seemed; to never find peace.

"I don't know how we swam that," Swift whispered.

Justus' gaze seemed locked on the fraught water. "Nor do I."

"Is that the islet where you found the Star of Atlantis?" asked Ash.

The islet's pinnacle seemed to twist, like two hands wrung. The crevasse at the top of the tower, leading into the cavern, gaped like a mouth.

"Inside that cave," said Swift. "The whole place is treacherous."

Justus squeezed his shoulder. "Let's carry on."

Swift crossed the beach, to the rocks where he'd sheltered Caius, bleeding and unconscious; the rocks where he'd left Caius.

He approached them gingerly, fearful of finding a stain of blood.

But there was no sign of their presence, the sand having been turned over and over by wind and scavengers.

Swift stopped at a place where the sand rose into a mound. Sweeping at it, he uncovered the torch he'd left, trained toward the sea beside Caius.

"This was the beacon I placed by him," said Swift. "I had to leave him in the cold night with only this."

Justus knelt beside Swift. "And it was a beacon that guided your rescue ship to him." He unburied the torch and tried to turn it on, but the batteries were wasted. He tucked it inside Swift's rucksack.

The weight of it felt like a drag on the back of a skiff. It was as though, carrying the torch away, Swift was silencing a light-house that needed to remain.

But part of him wanted to keep the torch. If he'd done anything well that night, it was placing this light beside Caius.

Justus—seeming in a bit of a rush to leave—turned back the way they'd come. Swift and Ash together followed him through the brush and over the fisherman's beach, toward a narrow trail leading to the prominence, where Elias would be idling.

Swift stepped onto the trail, but there paused.

Ash watched him. "Is something wrong?"

Swift glanced toward the fisherman's longboat, straining at the ropes binding her to the rocks. "I need to go back for a minute."

"Whatever for?" Justus held out his arm. "We've lingered here plenty."

Swift stepped back. "I'd like to see the longboat. One last time."

Ash approached. "I'll go with you."

"No." Swift tried to conceal his desperation to get to the boat alone, to explore the hinge in secrecy.

But a casual expression wasn't too difficult to manage. In truth, even if the hinge signaled a stow, it was probably empty.

Swift glanced at Justus. "I'd like to go alone."

Ash narrowed his eyes the tiniest bit.

"I'll just be a moment," said Swift. "You can both go and meet up with Elias. I'll follow."

Ash faced Justus. "Is it wise for Swift to go back there alone?"

Justus spent a moment in thought. "I'm confident that Swift knows what he needs." He walked back to Swift and handed him the two-way radio. "Make it quick."

Swift held steady at the trail's mouth until Ash had turned and was following Justus away, toward the prominence.

Finally, they together disappeared around a bend.

Swift turned and raced over the sand to the longboat.

13

Swift slid his hand along the gunwale of the longboat. He glanced back toward the trail Ash and Justus had disappeared into.

It lay empty, its shore grasses gently bending in the wind.

They were probably reaching the prominence and would board Elias' yacht.

Still, Swift took a moment just to lean on the longboat's gunwale, thoughtfully, in case they somehow could see him and were watching.

He slipped his hand inside the boat; discretely felt for the inch of cold metal—the plate and its cylinder. He laid his fingers on what certainly was a hinge.

Tracing it to the barely detectable line told how well-concealed was the rim of what was definitely a stow.

He fully faced the boat and studied its inner curve.

Bow to stern, the longboat's base was piled with cracking sand. It seemed the Coast Guard hadn't cleaned any part of it.

He brushed off the hinge.

It was scratched up but not rusted. Probably, it would open. He followed the line, crumbling off sand.

About a foot from the hinge, he uncovered another slip of

cold metal. He smoothed away sand from the boat's base until he had the keep fully unmasked.

Its door was cobbled with skill to curve perfectly along the turn of the boat.

At its base rested a tiny divot. Swift could barely fit the tip of his finger inside, but he managed it and tugged.

The stow creaked open.

He found the space within rather small. It held a coiled rope. A few rags. And beneath them—a book.

Swift checked behind him.

Ash and Justus still were nowhere in sight—although, Swift could now hear voices on the wind. Justus was probably reporting to Elias that Swift had gone back to the longboat and would soon be on his way.

And certainly, if he didn't join them in a few minutes, they'd come looking for him.

Swift drew the book from the stow.

It was thick, about the size of a textbook, and seemed old. One edge of the cover was vaguely water-stained, but the pages were undamaged. Its binding was crafted from a firm braiding of rope.

This book was steady—as steady as if it'd persisted through centuries and would last centuries yet. It was steady like an ancient oak, imperiled by storms, but not broken.

The book's cover was dusky with fine sand.

Swift smoothed the filth away, bringing it out clean.

It was deeply blue. Its worn silver title read—

The Shepherd of the Stars.

Star Shepherds. Cynfael Maddox's people. The Welsh clan of mage-like seafarers. The clan of pirates with Icelandic origins. The clan known to plunder and guard treasures. To enlighten.

The museum curator believed Ash's box held records kept by this clan, thriving in their renaissance on what treasures they'd managed to protect.

Swift opened the book.

Inside, he found nautical notes about winds and currents

from the coast of Wales up to Scotland, then to the Faroe Islands and beyond, trailing to Iceland.

Flipping through, he found locations scribed—coordinates of longitudes and latitudes noted alongside sketches of coastal ports.

Forging on, Swift discovered many pages holding notes on astronomy. Maths formulas.

He knelt on the beach and studied them closely. Here were physics calculations. Chemistry equations.

And he could read them. He could read everything.

Hardly able to breathe, he searched on.

The handwriting throughout struck as familiar—it seemed similar to the handwriting in *The Star of Atlantis*. And odd markings traced the top of each page—the same cryptic symbols found in the *Star of Atlantis* book, and on its map.

He closed the book and stared at it.

Was it possible this was written in the same period as *The Star of Atlantis*?

The sense of a destiny guiding him swelled.

The voices of Caius and Edric, in the back of his mind, also strengthened, whispering how foolish was the notion of destiny. But holding this book—*The Shepherd of the Stars*—Swift found their criticisms easy to ignore.

If this book was somehow tied to the Star of Atlantis—if Swift had been destined to find the Sunstone, could he not be destined, too, to find this?

Whether he were meant to come across it or not, discovering this book was fortunate. It might shed more insights on the Star of Atlantis myth. And—what if it referenced the Cthulhu? This book might lend insight on whether the Sunstone was authentic.

And it might hint of where the fisherman could be found.

Swift started to slide the book into his rucksack, but paused.

What would the fisherman think if he discovered his longboat returned but plundered?

Swift again studied the stow.

Everything in it was grimy. It was unthinkable to leave the

book in that muck, in a boat tethered to a treacherous coast with no guarantee of its owner ever returning.

Swift felt an honest responsibility rising, alongside his desire, to take the book. To keep it safe.

But how could that not be stealing? This belonged to the fisherman, as much as the longboat did.

And if Swift did take it, he might be obligated to report it.

Swift swept a last streak of sand from the book's cover.

He'd given his childhood collection of legend books to Oliver. He might have to surrender *The Star of Atlantis*, the Sunstone, and the map to Octavian Krakau.

But right now, nobody knew about *The Shepherd of the Stars*.

Keeping it seemed like doing right by the fisherman. And doing right by himself.

And in following the trail of sciences recorded here—maybe he'd re-learn to read academic texts. And so he might find himself on a journey beyond the Star of Atlantis, chasing the Practicum with Dr. Keats—a yet more magnificent star.

Swift slid the book into his rucksack and shouldered it.

The book, beside the torch, compounded the weight.

Both were relics of a nightmare that perhaps ought to be left in these wilds.

But how promising was the book, so dense with insights.

The Shepherd of the Stars seemed suddenly the center of Swift's world—a world of childhood dreams, of chasing legends and waking sea monsters; of destiny and legends arriving to him in the unlikely form of a Sunstone; a world of science and secrets, of chemistry and maths, of physics and stars.

He found he could conceive of the weight of the book and torch together less like a deadweight and more an anchor.

He closed the stow.

"Swift?"

Swift startled and turned, guarding the stow with his body.

Justus had climbed onto a rock at the prominence and was waving. "Time to go!"

Swift held on to the longboat for a final moment, then discreetly concealed the stow.

He turned to fully facing his father and waved back.

Justus climbed down from the high rock and vanished from sight.

Swift trekked through the sand toward the trail.

Halfway to the prominence, Ash met him, emerging from a blind in the trail's bend.

14

Justus pulled up to the Welsh maritime museum.

Swift, from the passenger seat, noticed a shadow inside the museum's door.

"That's the curator," said Ash, from the back seat. "Octavian Krakau. You're going to love him. I do."

Octavian Krakau. The curator who'd bought Ash's treasures. The curator who wanted to keep Swift's. A man who'd once searched for the Star of Atlantis.

"He's vastly knowledgeable," said Ash. "So interesting."

Octavian Krakau, a renowned historian who shortly might declare Swift's Sunstone, his *Star of Atlantis* book, and its map all counterfeits.

"Wait until you see his rustic weapons collection!" said Ash.

Octavian swung wide the door.

Swift pulled from the floorboard his box of Star of Atlantis relics.

He started to climb out, but paused at seeing Octavian's eyes narrowing.

He was a big guy. Strong-seeming. He looked a decade older than Justus, and those slitted eyes painted him a little mean, like a winning prize fighter.

Octavian shifted his gaze to the box Swift was clutching.

Swift gripped the box tighter.

Whether or not his relics were authentic, if it was decided Swift had no rights to them, Octavian was the person he'd surrender them to.

Ash, his eye keen on what must look like terror on Swift, widened his car door. "Octavian looks tough as a bull, I know. But he's actually nice as can be."

He turned and waved.

Octavian, smiling, waved back.

And of course it wasn't fair to judge Octavian by just a glance.

Still. Swift couldn't help noting a sort of duplicity in his expression.

Octavian clearly wished to appear "nice as can be." But there was definitely something dark behind that smile.

Justus, too, seemed to perceive something off. He was walking toward the museum slowly, and not once did he take his eyes off Octavian. He seemed to be sizing him up.

The only drive that Swift found to coax him on came from thinking about his secret of *The Shepherd of the Stars*.

Octavian might very well strip Swift of the treasures he was holding—this last bit of his boyhood. But with *The Shepherd of the Stars* carefully concealed inside his rucksack at the beach house, though Octavian might do some significant damage to Swift today, he couldn't destroy him.

"Welcome!" Octavian hurried them on with a wave.

Justus—always jovial and warm, though never without the gravity that made him an excellent anesthesiologist—did not return the man's smile.

Even in how Octavian moved, there was an odd fluidity and quickness.

It seemed he'd have the dexterity to strike out one of those strong arms and land a hard punch. Or snatch up what he wanted and flash off like a greedy squid.

Ash ran right to him.

"What an honor," said Octavian, "to host these two young treasure finders of Devonshire."

Ash shook Octavian's large hand. "Are you taking good care of my incredible treasure?"

"Oh, yes, Mr. Emberly!" Octavian's voice, singsongy with his Welsh accent, still managed to sound a bit sinister. "The most exquisite care."

He guided them along a corridor lined with display cases containing what Ash had mentioned—the rustic weapons.

Case after case held blow pipes and dart guns classified according to their origins and gruesome capabilities. *For close range conflict*, read a heading placed over a decrepit vial whose label read—*Viper poison. Affects the nervous system. Lethal.*

On the wall above the cases hung various styles of bows and arrows, of clubs holding sharp stones embedded.

And further on stretched a row of rudimentary swords attributed to early Gaelic peoples, to Roman and Chinese armies, to Scythian nomads.

And finishing the display was a bone chilling line of serrated, long spears, laid with the names of South American tribes.

Octavian led them on, into a lofty main corridor, where fine wires tied the skeleton of a whale to a crook of high rafters. A rusty harpoon dangled alongside, frozen in aim at the creature's vast flank.

"Don't let old pinstripe frighten you." Octavian wiggled a finger up at the expired whale. "We've a robust whaling history in Pembrokeshire. She's just doing her part for posterity."

Though it was only bones hanging there, the gist of the creature was caught well enough to lend a hint of her character.

She looked joyful. She seemed not to understand that she was divided from the water; that Octavian had a harpoon pointed at the vault where her heart should belong.

"She looks somehow alive," Swift whispered to Justus, who'd stopped, too, and was staring up at the monstrous bones.

"They've captured her," said Justus.

"Inside here, please." Octavian drew open a gilded, heavy-looking door.

He watched with an expression of enthusiasm not unlike hunger as Swift moved through, into an office.

But such excitement was probably natural.

The discovery of the Star of Atlantis likely meant the onset of a new era for the little museum. As great as Ash's treasure box was, being also from the age of Icelandic piracy, it held scant notoriety. But anyone interested in Celtic maritime history would've heard of the Star of Atlantis.

"Kindly place the box on my desk," said Octavian.

Swift did so but found himself unable to step away. It was as though the Cthulhu, at play on the map, in *The Star of Atlantis*, had him gripped.

"I see you're uneasy, Mr. Kingsley," said Octavian. "But you need not be. I've followed the story of your accident on the water, of your recovery, and your brother's. Your lingering peril. You must be quite exhausted by all you've been through. Our museum is highly capable of taking excellent care of your finds."

"Just a moment," said Justus. "It's yet to be determined what's to become of Swift's relics. No?"

Octavian bowed away as though genuflecting to Justus. "I only assume the authorities will ascribe them to me. Considering their delicacy. Considering the specialty of care they'll require."

"This has nothing to do with specialized care," said Swift. "The Welsh authorities will either declare these mine or not. If they're mine, then it's up to me to judge what's best for them."

Octavian smiled with a humility that seemed forced. "True." He glanced at Justus. "You have a shrewd lad, I see."

"He is shrewd," said Ash. "Shrewd enough to realize how important it is that historical things be preserved. Swift and I, you see—we're the same. We've both always loved treasure hunting. We both value sharing our finds. Isn't that right, Swift?"

Swift drew breath to argue that he did have his own thoughts on the matter, but Octavian moved in.

"Shall we see your finds, then?" he asked.

Caius had said that Swift, holding the Star of Atlantis, seemed to be holding his own heart outside of his chest.

And so it felt, as he removed the tape from the box.

For doing so placed him on the cusp of revealing a most painful doubt to Octavian.

He'd find out—within minutes, now—whether his treasures were fake.

He focused on the fact that Octavian was a renowned historian. Despite the power he wielded to declare these discoveries worthless, or even to legally rob Swift, he also had insights.

"What do you know about the Star of Atlantis myth?" Swift asked him.

Octavian peered inside the box. "Having the relics themselves at hand—this quite broadens our grasp on the Star of Atlantis."

Swift reached into the box.

In a quick burst, Octavian knocked Swift's hands away.

Swift strayed back, his hands stinging.

"Apologies, Mr. Kingsley," said Octavian. "We mustn't touch the relics with bare fingers."

Swift stood frozen by the shock of how aggressive that'd felt.

Octavian had asked him to take out the relics. It was like he'd purposely set Swift up for that reprimand.

Octavian nodded to Ash, who was pulling down from a shelf a box of gloves. "Slip those on, and I shall do the same." He glanced at Justus and Ash as he drew out a black cloth and laid it beside the box. "Only Swift and I—gloved—may handle the artifacts."

Octavian seemed aware he'd offset Swift. And he seemed to be relishing it. Neither Justus nor Ash appeared cognizant, though, of the satisfaction brightening Octavian.

Swift pulled the gloves onto his smarting hands.

"Now." Octavian wriggled his own gloved fingers. "Let's have a look."

Swift, drawing out the map, felt a stroke of shame at how tattered its edges were, from the many times he'd handled it. He gently straightened it atop the cloth.

He pulled out the book—seeming also more worn than he recalled, its nicks and minor dents blaring beneath the strong overhead lights.

He placed it alongside the map.

Octavian bent over the map. With a magnifying glass, he examined it, corner to corner.

His eyes, his magnifier, traced the drawing of the Cthulhu.

Swift held his breath.

Octavian cast Swift a slight look of judgment. "These have tasted a bit of Celtic wind, haven't they?"

Swift relaxed some.

Octavian's disapproval was unpleasant, but his glass had precisely surveyed the drawing of the Cthulhu, and he hadn't seemed to note it.

Octavian opened *The Star of Atlantis*. He flipped the book's pages so carefully, as though they might crumble.

"Do you have any sense of how old that book is?" asked Swift, trying his best to keep his voice from betraying his terror at what the answer might be.

"Quite old. Centuries, I'd say." Octavian angled a lamp to shine straight on the pages. "This book presents a masterful example of retting—a paper making technique involving fermentation. The practice died out in the 1700's."

"The book, then, was written in the 1700's?" asked Swift.

"Earlier, I deduce."

Octavian held his magnifier closely against a page.

"The ink, when held at an angle in the light—do you see that?"

Swift peered through the magnifier.

"It looks iridescent."

"The ink is oil-based," said Octavian. "Inks used beyond the 1600's no longer contained oil, which, though challenging to work with, lent them a quality of permanence, of near immortality. This book was made, as they say, when things were built to last. Its creator clearly intended it to have a long life."

Swift felt like he might lift off the Earth.

The presence of the Cthulhu was a conundrum, still. But

the question of the authenticity of the book and map seemed resolved.

Swift brought out the Star of Atlantis itself—his Sunstone—nestled in bubble wrap.

Octavian hovered his hands beneath Swift's, like Swift were a small child and liable to drop it.

Swift peeled off the wrappings, revealing the shining clear stone.

He rested it on the cloth.

Lying against its shed plastic, the crystal looked like a sun blooming out of clouds.

Octavian licked his lips. "Marvelous."

Swift tried to envision stars levitating in the core of the Sunstone—Mintaka and Orion's starry form ascending in the west, drawing him to rescue.

But lying in Octavian's office, beneath his great shadow, groped by his rubbered hands, the Star of Atlantis seemed not at all a wondrous Icelandic seafaring device.

More, it seemed a corpse awaiting autopsy. Or a living soul awaiting vivisection.

"Have you ever before seen a piece like this?" asked Justus.

"I do have a Sunstone, loaned from a museum in South America," said Octavian. "Though, it isn't a navigational stone, as this is." He screwed a gem lens over his eye and bent low over the Sunstone. "My South American specimen is in quite poor condition, with one edge shattered. A piece like this—intact and purposed for navigation"—he glanced up at Swift—"it's a rarity."

Swift relaxed even more. Though creepy, Octavian clearly knew about Sunstones. If Swift's Star of Atlantis were any manner of counterfeit, Octavian would certainly be spotting the signs.

"Do you believe any part of the myth surrounding Sunstones might be true?" asked Swift.

Octavian straightened. "According to both South American and Norse legends, Sunstones are discovered by those destined."

The notion summoned a rising excitement. Swift worked to conceal it, for Justus certainly wouldn't be pleased at Swift giving too much credence to the idea.

"Destined for what, though?" Ash lifted a bamboo dart blow pipe from a display on the wall.

"Some believed the finding of a Sunstone was auspicious—a sign of good fortune," said Octavian, seeming not at all to mind Ash toying with the blow pipe. "Others saw it more as a storm crow—a portent of disaster. Some even claimed the finding of a Sunstone would signal the first seismic wave in a calamity that will bring our world, as we know it, to an end. Many have sought Sunstones. And more never dared. For on top of being a mythical omen of doom, the hard fact is—many seeking Sunstones have died violent deaths."

Ash, fisting the blow pipe, crossed his arms. "Then Swift is no exception. He almost died trying to reach this. He almost killed his brother, too."

Justus glanced at Ash, at Swift. He seemed to be trying to read them, to discern the extent of what injury those words had dealt.

But Swift didn't feel any new injury at the cold truth Ash had voiced.

The accident had come about by Swift's actions. His competitiveness. His bullheadedness. His greed.

"One narrative on Sunstones," said Octavian, "describes watchers posted near to where they're hidden."

"Watchers?" Swift looked up at him.

"With such tales of destiny, of doom," said Octavian, "there'd be those keen to see who might be purposed for mighty deeds. Or who might reap calamity." He took a step nearer to Swift. "If you could glimpse the onset of the end of the world, wouldn't you?"

Could it be that the fisherman was an actual watcher, as spoken of in myths? A watcher anxious to see what would befall the champion taking the Star of Atlantis.

Justus scoffed. "How wildly out of hand legends can grow."

It was outlandish. Ridiculous.

And yet—Swift's world had ended, in a sense, on the night of the accident.

Both his life and Caius' had irrevocably changed.

"I also can tell you a bit about the crystal itself," said Octavian. "It's termed a 'Sunstone' for its use in navigation, but it's actually a prism of Icelandic Spar."

He went to a shelf and tapped his fingers across a row of books. He pulled out a geology text and handed it to Swift.

"On page 73 begins the piece on Icelandic Spar. You're welcome to take that book with you if you'd like."

Swift opened the book. "Is Icelandic Spar common?"

"Not the navigational variety," said Octavian. "Except, oddly, they're sprinkled all over old maritime myths."

Ash stood away from the wall. "Does that mean more Sunstones might be out there?"

"I wish I could tell the difference between history and myth," said Octavian. "What we know for sure is—there are other myths."

"And what do the other myths say?" asked Ash.

"They propose that the mineral didn't originate in Iceland," said Octavian. "Rather, they claim it fell to the Earth encased in metal, as meteorites."

Justus and Swift glanced at each other.

"Some myths say Sunstones were used symbolically by ancient Welsh clans," said Octavian. "Clans who viewed these prisms as symbols not just of destruction, but of connection; as the turning of fate, for the better or worse. Yet, few Sunstones have been found."

"All that symbolic rubbish seems far-fetched," said Ash, tapping his thumb on the blow pipe.

Octavian glanced at Ash. "Take heart, lad, that more Sunstones, more destinies, might wait."

And perhaps it was far-fetched to imbue a mere rock with such meaning.

But these insights sounded eerily similar to what the fisherman had told Swift of the Star of Atlantis.

"There might be kernels of truth to be found at the center of legends." Swift adjusted the Sunstone on the desk, aiming it to catch more of the light. "Like an acorn buried beneath seasons of leaf fall in a forest."

Octavian shooed Swift's hands away. "I expect that legends do grow in their eccentricities, not unlike a timeworn forest draped with lichen and mosses. It takes careful inquiry to separate facts from fables."

An inquiry into *The Shepherd of the Stars* might serve precisely to separate these facts from their fables.

Thinking of all it might tell, of how it might enlighten, his hands grew jittery to thumb through it.

If Octavian were right that more Sunstones were out there, *The Shepherd of the Stars* might hint where they'd been hidden.

The Shepherd of the Stars was, after all, a book kept by a mystical wanderer who perhaps knew more about the Star of Atlantis myth than even Octavian.

At considering the notion, a spike of hot anxiety struck Swift like a wash of livening medicine—a madness to get back to the beach house, to slip out alone and explore *The Shepherd of the Stars*.

Since he'd found the book yesterday, he hadn't had more than second to himself—he'd barely even managed to hide it.

"From the research you've done," said Ash, his gaze piercing Swift, "do you think any hard evidence exists that might lead to more discoveries of Sunstones?"

This was the look Ash wore when trying to read Swift, to manipulate him into giving something up.

Was there any chance Ash had seen him swipe the book from the longboat?

When Swift had returned to it alone, he'd kept vigilant. There'd been no sign of anyone's eyes on him until Justus had called from the high rock.

And that had been way too great a distance for him to have seen what Swift was up to. And when Swift trekked back to the trail, the book carefully concealed in his rucksack, Ash had rounded the bend, as though coming all the way from the prominence, to meet him.

No. Ash couldn't have seen.

"I have no idea whether more evidence exists," said Swift. "Though, I'd like to believe so."

He carefully lifted the Star of Atlantis, despite Octavian widening his critical eyes. "It's difficult to imagine that this could've dropped to Earth as a meteorite. Meteorites mostly burn up in the atmosphere. Whatever does find its way to the ground is usually granular."

Octavian took the Sunstone from Swift and rested it again on the desk. "That the Star of Atlantis myth panned out to be quite true—I feel this suggests that other myths could be substantiated."

Ash's gaze on Swift remained sharp. "Swift is skilled at locating leads. He might find more."

Even if Ash hadn't seen Swift take the book, he could be sensing that Swift was hiding something.

Justus, seeming to detect some tension between them, rested his hand on Swift's shoulder.

Ash removed his gaze from Swift.

Like a fish let off a hook and into a current, Swift could breathe evenly again.

"Let's move our discussion to practical matters," said Justus. "When will you know Swift's options?"

Octavian, removing his gloves, rounded his desk. "I expect a decision from the Welsh authorities any day."

He sat.

"Although, I do have one directive. The book and the map must remain in my care until a decision is made."

"What?" Swift moved closer to the desk, to his map, his book.

"I apologize, lad," said Octavian, smiling. "To ensure proper handling, the book and the map are to remain here." He handed Justus a document.

"I bought the book and map with my own money," said Swift. "The Welsh government can't claim any rights over them."

"But I'm afraid they can," said Justus, perusing the document. "To ensure the safekeeping of the book and map, Octavian has been instructed to confiscate them."

A trembling came into Swift's hands. "What about the Sunstone?"

"There's no mention of the Sunstone." Justus turned over the document. "Must Swift surrender it?"

Octavian was quiet for a moment, then murmured, "No."

He drew out a pad of paper.

"Because of where it was found, as much as the authorities ought to be able to confine it here, they can't."

"What's this that I read of a consignment stipend?" asked Justus, angling the papers toward Octavian.

"For resigning the book and the map to me—temporarily," said Octavian, "I'm prepared to offer compensation." He tore off a slip of paper and scribbled on it. "What would you say to this?"

Swift glanced at the note. It was more money than he'd ever imagined receiving at one time.

Looking at it, nausea welled. He could never seek to profit off a venture that'd almost killed Caius; a venture that still might cost Caius his future.

"And were you to leave the Sunstone, too, in my care, just for the night"—Octavian captured Swift's glance—"I could double that."

Ash, his mouth gaping, moved nearer.

Swift felt none of that astonishment. The idea of surrendering all his relics to Octavian incited a deep pain, like what he'd suffered when he'd left Caius on the beach—a part of himself forsaken.

Swift rested his gaze on his Star of Atlantis—the crystal that'd unveiled for him the summer stars, guiding him.

"The Sunstone, I'm keeping."

Octavian drew from a drawer a packet of papers. He crossed out a line or two, made a note in a margin, then handed it to Justus.

Justus slid on his glasses and read through the packet.

"Do realize," said Octavian, writing a check, "if the authorities judge that you can't keep the Sunstone, to hold on to it would be theft."

Justus set a page before Swift, pointing to where he should sign.

Swift looked at the pen Octavian was holding out, still uncapped from writing the check. "I don't want any money."

"Come, lad," said Justus. "It's a fair exchange. You're consenting to temporarily surrender your book and map—artifacts that belong to you at present."

Swift could only stare at the check.

The blood money.

"As Swift is a minor, am I right in assuming I'd be steward of the check?" asked Justus.

"Yes, Sir," said Octavian.

"Sign that line, lad," said Justus, his voice gentled by a close understanding. "I'll be the one taking the money. We'll add it to your college fund if you like."

"I'm going for the Practicum—I might not need a college fund."

"Maybe you don't care about it today," said Ash, his gaze fixed on the check. "But one day you'll regret forfeiting that."

Swift eased away.

"That you should receive this, there's no question," said Justus. "What you'd like to do with it—well, that's a quandary we'll explore another day."

Octavian held the pen closer to Swift.

Justus was speaking reason. Yet, to sign felt like a betrayal toward Caius. It was Caius who'd ferried him to the mouth of Sterncastle Cove. Caius, who'd dared its waters with Swift. Caius who'd drawn him from their depths when the *Star Strider* flipped. It was Caius who'd bled into its waters.

Justus carefully watched Swift, as though perceiving what his mind was tracing. "Caius would want you to sign, I assure you."

"Would Caius let me share that with him?" Swift eyed the check. "Could it pay for part of his medical school?"

"I daresay he'd consider it," said Justus, "if those were your wishes."

Swift, gripping the Sunstone, took the pen. Signed.

"If you're called to permanently surrender these items," said Octavian, "please be assured that I'll steward them with the greatest care."

Octavian's words sounded so confident. So final.

Swift met his eyes. "But I might not have to surrender anything."

"True." The smile on Octavian twitched. "In that case, you could sell them. For permanent possession, I could offer you a handsome fee."

"What sort of fee?" asked Ash.

Octavian grinned. "It's a spot more than what I paid you."

Ash's eyes expanded. "Swift—sell everything. Take the fee!"

"It is a handsome offer, to be sure," said Octavian. "But a lad like you, Swift, altruistic—you certainly can grasp what value the Star of Atlantis would offer to other good folk like yourself, hooked by the lure of the sea. One-of-a-kind pieces, such as these, would be a delight to a maritime museum's patrons."

"Yes, and these relics could be placed beside mine, couldn't they?" asked Ash.

"That, they could!" said Octavian. "And in fact, your box and its contents are on track for exhibition tomorrow. If you'd like, before you go, I'll show you where they'll rest."

"So—this very day, my incredible treasure will be displayed?" asked Ash.

"It will require working into the late hours," said Octavian. "But yes."

"Could I stay and watch the work?" asked Ash.

Swift flinched at Ash's eagerness to remain with Octavian. It felt like a small betrayal—Ash choosing Octavian over him.

"That is"—Ash lifted the blow pipe and peered through it at Swift—"if you don't mind."

But Ash couldn't be blamed for that enthusiasm. To see his treasure box placed on display would be meaningful. And,

Swift, relieved of Ash tonight, would have a better chance to get alone with *The Shepherd of the Stars*.

"It seems like a great opportunity." Swift tried to steady his voice beneath the urgency mounding to get back to the beach house.

"Excellent." Octavian moved to the great, gilded door and pulled it open.

Ash joined him. Stood behind him.

Swift packed the Sunstone and lifted the box. He followed Justus into the museum's dark corridor, lined with brutal instruments of warfare.

15

Swift stared at the quiz questions looming at the end of his biochemistry chapter.

The semblance of an approach to answering the third question—the hardest one—was beginning to form.

"Well?" asked Caius. "What've you come up with?"

The impatience that'd been growing on Caius made it clear he wanted to be someplace else. Namely, upstairs with Brooke, who'd just turned off the shower.

"I can't think with you rushing me," said Swift.

And indeed, at the interruption, all the progress he'd made dissipated—a slip of twilight suddenly gone.

But Swift, too, was wanting to be someplace else.

Ash was still at the museum, and Swift hadn't found any chance to slip away with *The Shepherd of the Stars*. Caius hadn't let him off the hook for even a moment, but had insisted that he keep trying to read text he couldn't read; to conjure answers to questions he couldn't wrap his head around.

Swift glanced up from the text. "Can you set your hand on my shoulder, the way you did yesterday?"

It seemed such a small thing. But with the weight of Caius' hand resting on him, with his eyes intently watching Swift, the task of comprehending and strategizing seemed easier to manage.

Caius warmly settled his hand on Swift's shoulder.

The feel of it was just right. It made Caius seem present. Patient. As though he were really wanting Swift to succeed.

"All right," said Caius. "Question three. Give it a go."

Swift narrowed his eyes at the text. Question three was complex. Interpretive, not straightforward. He struggled to reread the question; strove to assemble an approach. But he couldn't come up with anything.

Caius tightened his hand on Swift's shoulder.

Swift stared up at him, as though he might siphon an answer from his brother's expression.

But all he read on Caius was distraction. He kept sneaking glances at the stairs, as though hoping Brooke would come down. As though he were weary of trying to teach Swift.

Swift had to come up with an answer to question three. He had to show Caius he could do this. If he couldn't prove he had some skill yet, Caius might wholly give up on him.

Swift tried again to read the question. It had something to do with the chemistry of blood cells.

But even focusing so intensely, he won no comprehension. All his mind would latch on to was the opalesque moon ascending behind Caius, beckoning through the tall kitchen window.

The moon was almost full this night, bright as gallium, broad as a taut sail and climbing a pink twilit sky. With its pockmarks and fissures, it seemed like a Sunstone in its own right, capturing the light of a star and presenting a pathway for Swift. A path leading away from the beach house and into the wilds.

The prompting to bathe in that moonlight, to meld with the onset of dusk, to slip to a place where he could secretly explore *The Shepherd of the Stars*, was more a craving than a simple wish.

The sound of Brooke's feet, light on the stairs, drew Caius' gaze.

Brooke—wearing Caius' bathrobe, blotting her dark hair

with a towel—stopped in the doorway. "How's the studying going?"

"Slowly," said Caius, his voice weary, his eyes trained on Brooke.

"But I have gained some distance," said Swift. "I managed to answer two comprehension questions."

"Well, that's good!" Brooke came over and stared at the page. "That's some difficult material. You should be proud of your progress, and proud of even your struggle." She glanced at Caius. "For I know how demanding Caius can be when he wants an answer."

Caius let go of Swift's shoulder. He settled back in his chair, arms crossed, and watched Brooke.

Swift set his own hand on his shoulder, grown instantly cold.

Brooke went to a utility drawer. "Please don't let me stop your work. I just need an extension cord for my hair dryer." She rifled through the cluttered drawer.

She was clearly having difficulty navigating it, but Caius didn't offer to help her. He only watched her, his gaze seeming to settle on her bare feet; on the flashes of thigh the bathrobe—rather skimpy on a woman—was baring.

Those glimpses of skin were irritating, like sunlight disturbing a headache. Did Brooke not realize how much of herself she was showing? You'd think in a house having three boys, she'd try to be more modest. And with her long hair wet like that, with Caius' bathrobe frumpy on her, Swift was surprised she was willing to come down at all.

She didn't seem embarrassed, though. And the way Caius was watching her, one would think she was dressed to go out and hit some pubs.

"Ah, here we are." Brooke wrangled a knotted cord from the back of the drawer.

Caius, his cheek resting on his hand, his gaze tracing Brooke, said, "You think you could find another in there?"

She cast him a look as she sidled up beside Swift. "Still feeling okay?" She placed her hand on his cheek.

Swift was polite enough not to duck away from her, though he wanted to.

"You feel nice and cool." She smoothed Swift's hair, as Mum might. "I'll leave you two to finish." She smiled at Caius as she slipped up the stairs.

Caius kept his eyes on her until she disappeared.

When the bedroom door creaked shut, Swift pulled the book nearer and focused again on the question.

Caius shifted his attention back to Swift. "Why don't we just forget the question itself and work on your thought process?" He leaned in, his elbows on the table. "Can you talk me through the strategy you might use to approach it?" But something like doubt or distraction was lingering in Caius' eyes.

Swift believed, 100%, that Caius could get past his challenges and pick up his studies where he left off. And Caius often said, in his ever-hopeful way, that he believed Swift could do the same. But he hadn't demonstrated that confidence.

"I'm sure I can answer this," said Swift, looking not so much at Caius, but at the moon and how it was decanting a silver glaze on the treetops sloping up in the distance. "Though, I don't quite know how."

Caius glanced out the window. "I can see that the moon's capturing you." He studied Swift. "And I don't think I'm getting you back."

"Some fresh air might clear my head," said Swift. "I could walk the coast for a bit, then try again."

Caius leaned back, his gaze on Swift more a doctor's than a brother's. "If you'd like a short walk, that's fine. But promise me you'll not push yourself. I expect you to give this another go in the morning."

Swift hustled to the door and crammed his feet into his shoes.

"So let's have you home at a reasonable hour—say, nine?" asked Caius. "In the meantime, I'll aim to study with Brooke."

Enthusiasm brightened his eyes as he spoke her name— hunger pangs clearly visiting him, too.

Swift snatched his rucksack from the kitchen cabinet he'd hidden it in.

Caius gave him an odd look. "What on Earth was your rucksack doing in the sugar pantry?"

Swift hurried past him. "Ash hasn't texted you, has he?"

Caius, standing, checked his phone. "Not a word from him. He must be relishing watching that curator situate his 'incredible treasure.'"

Swift hustled out the back door and picked up his bike. "When he does text, you'll go get him, right?"

Caius took a mug down from a cabinet. "Yeah."

"And do you promise to be nice to him? Even if I'm not with you?"

Caius placed his mug under the spout of an espresso machine.

"Not to worry, I'll be civil."

~

SWIFT BIKED AWAY from the beach house, north—toward a prominence that climbed to a cliff overlooking the coast.

Beneath the cliff, to the north and east, stretched the great Wentletrap Forest rolling in gentle waves of elevation. To the west spread the sylvan circlet of Coracle Bay, its sharp waters crashing on striated rocks. And beyond swelled the sapphire expanse of the Celtic Sea, lilting as though rocking the whole kingdom to sleep.

Swift biked up a small rise to reach the pinnacle of the overlook, and there rested his bike against a broad tree. He sat at the precipice, soaking in the view of the Wentletrap and the white breakers lashing its pale, slender beaches.

He opened his rucksack and pulled out *The Shepherd of the Stars*.

The twilit panorama reflected itself in the title so brightly, the script seemed to cast light around him.

Bathing in that light, in the beauty of the coastal dusk, Swift stilled.

As breathtaking as the bay was by nightfall, shining beneath the corals and reds of a slow sunset, it was the darkening forest, its shadow vast before him, that held him transfixed.

How awe-striking it was to think that the Wentletrap, this wise and expansive clan of trees—mages in their own rights, had watched over the Pembrokeshire shorelands for so many centuries. The forest was haunting when misted at dusk, its ancient trees crooked and colossal.

Swift's own house in Clovelly opened on a forest. But that glade—old as it was, its oaks planted by his great-grandfather—wasn't near the age of this place.

And unlike those small woods behind his home, the Wentletrap was known to be deadly.

Every year or two, as long as Swift's family had owned the beach house, reports would flitter about the coast of some rare hiker the Wentletrap had claimed.

The entire forest was a preserve—someone's property, but it was sprawling and wild. And the stories of hauntings, of ramblers vanishing in the trappings of its trails, seemed to hang in its mist, settling now.

The Wentletrap was such a thick wood that even at high noon its interior looked inked with shadows. And at this point in twilight, even its fringes were growing dark enough that Swift had to strain to make out the shapes of the trees.

Those shadows themselves, cast by trees old enough to witness the shaping of this rocky coast—old enough, even, to sense the shifting of Polaris' stronghold in the northern sky—Swift found himself hungering for the Wentletrap as strongly as he'd been hungering to bathe in the moonlight. For as dark as the ancient forest was—how enduring. How steadying.

Sitting on the overhang's edge, so close to the Wentletrap that he could smell its rich earth, it seemed that the cells within his own blood might harbor an inkling of xylem; that he might find himself nourished by the Wentletrap's mists—mists struck blue by that coasting moon, by these shimmering stars, dressed in their finery of twilight-gilded clouds.

The air kept in the Wentletrap's darkly green shadows

looked delicious to breathe, streaked silver as it was with a glazing of sea vapor—drifting, it seemed, from the paths of the stars gently waking.

Mum and Justus had never let any of their lads wander into the Wentletrap, for how easy it was to get lost. As a small boy, though, Swift had sometimes managed to let his play lead him to its brink.

Peering inside its deep corridors, he would imagine seeing skeletons—skeletons of long dead hikers rotting on the leaf litter; skeletons of marooned sailors wandering in to hunt birds, to gather nuts, but confounded and killed by the Wentletrap's poisons and spells.

Swift, now, could smile at the fantasies. Ash had played with him along the skirts of the Wentletrap in their boyhood, and its savagery and mystery had certainly juiced up their games. This was a wild slip of land with no habitation, few roads, and hardly any foot traffic of any kind.

Even now, at fourteen, Swift couldn't help watching the edge of the Wentletrap, wondering whether he might spy something terrible moving inside. Not skeletons, perhaps. But— something.

Swift drew the Sunstone from his pocket. He trained the crystal on the starfield—barely visible with the deepening of twilight.

From these clear-skied tracks, the stars lighting the stone blared.

The Sunstone, here, seemed less a solid mineral and more a jar into which he'd snapped a bundle of cosmic fireflies, levitating in a mist of refraction cast from the fissures in the crystal.

Through the Sunstone, even the starlit tops of the trees appeared bright. Through the Sunstone, it seemed the forest held a great consciousness—something present with Swift.

It felt as though these stars, these woods, this curve of ocean held something to teach him, something to help him, if he could just hear it.

Perhaps inside those knots of trees waited something companionable, the way the sea offers company, for all its peril.

Swift lowered his gaze to *The Shepherd of the Stars*, promising, by its own right, to keep wonders.

Brushed by an easy wind, dusted with the strengthening starlight, Swift opened the book.

On the first page lay an oath which he knew—the oath written in *The Star of Atlantis*—

Come hell. Come storm waters. Come the Kraken. I'll forsake all sound shores for the night-lighted passageways—untrodden reaches—for sun-brightened visions, for insights of stars.

And the handwriting.

Swift held the book closer.

It certainly did seem similar—perhaps even identical—to the handwriting in *The Star of Atlantis*.

But he'd lost all access to *The Star of Atlantis*. All he could do now was speculate, to try and envision how its handwriting had looked.

Swift pulled a penlight from his rucksack. He turned the page to find a description of the properties of Icelandic Spar—a description ten pages rich.

These words, this matter, presented no challenge, his eyes drinking in every letter as though he were parching for them.

As he sped through the text, peals of relief struck. This was just how he used to tear through his medical texts. Had Caius been here to quiz him on the properties of Icelandic spar, colors would've been flying.

Swift pulled from his rucksack the geology text Octavian had given him.

He scanned through the section on Icelandic spar and found he could read it just as well.

Dr. Keats' speculation that the coma might've damaged Swift's brain seemed an overwrought concern. For here, he was proving it not to be the case. These weren't medical texts, but neither were they legend books.

The material here was scientific.

Why the medical texts were so problematic remained a

mystery. But perhaps that issue wouldn't persist for much longer.

In his hands, the book's cover warmed, lending the impression that it was aglow.

He could easily imagine that the book itself, its leaves cobbled from reeds as old as the Wentletrap, had soaked up some guiding starlight.

It was as though *The Shepherd of the Stars* were a rescue boat sent out to reach him.

And because the book taught about Icelandic spar, whoever wrote this didn't just know about the legends for which he thirsted.

They knew about Sunstones.

Octavian and Ash had both speculated that the people guarding the Star of Atlantis—the Shepherds of the Stars—had hidden other treasures. Other Sunstones.

The last bit of western sky flashed gold like the strike of a match blazing—the sun setting a low cloud on fire as it finally crashed into the waves.

The Wentletrap Forest and its twisting mists shone a moment in gossamer silver—and then in blew a heavier mist, bringing all to darkness as though the world were a wick and its flame had been snuffed.

Cradling *The Shepherd of the Stars*, Swift turned pages. By his penlight, he scanned the section describing Sunstones, comparing it with the geology text.

Both books held that Icelandic spar was indeed meteor-based, though there was some admitted uncertainty. The geology text mentioned multiple minerals carelessly called "Icelandic spar," some of which were common—not worth much and mined in many places throughout the Earth.

True Icelandic spar, according to *The Shepherd of the Stars*, was extremely rare.

It derived its name by its frequent appearance in Norse seafaring accounts, and by its clarity and similarity to ice. And the book told that true Icelandic spar acted as a polarizing agent on light.

"Of course."

Swift bent closer to the text.

"Light polarization."

This would explain how his Sunstone could tease starlight from the day-blue sky, from mists and from clouds, from the most light-starved nights.

And from *The Shepherd of the Stars*, Swift learned that true Icelandic spar could create odd effects when laid atop written words.

Sometimes it distorted or doubled them. Sometimes it brought out secret features, written in the lettering by a knowing hand but not visible without the effect of the stone.

"No freaking way." Swift snatched up the Sunstone and rested it on the page.

He shone his penlight through.

There was a slight doubling effect to the letters, but nothing truly odd.

No secret text revealed.

But. He was just at the beginning of the book.

He flipped through to pages where lay scribblings of chemistry, of maths, of physics; he thumbed through a section of nautical coordinates; through a few chapters seeming tied to astronomy; through tales and anecdotes—what looked like bits of insight about the Shepherd of the Stars clan.

Upon encountering each scientific notation, each sliver of history, a millimeter of his anguish seemed to stitch itself closed. Not only was this book created by a soul kindred to his own, but most of this science, Swift could comprehend.

Some of the chemistry formulas, he found incomplete. Markings looking like gibberish lay interspersed among the equations.

Swift carefully rested the Sunstone atop a sequence of formulas.

Through the stone, the formulas shone whole. Through the stone, they presented the molecular and empirical representations of potassium dichromate and magnesium phosphate.

He flipped through a half-dozen pages and found the effect

repeated again and again—chemistry formulas and mathematics equations shifting from nonsensical to complete.

The wind picked up, bringing the hickory smell of campfire smoke from the south.

Caius and Brooke, "studying," must have lit a campfire on the beach.

A glance at the bare stars told Swift it was well after eight. Caius would want him to start the ride home soon.

Swift slipped the Sunstone back into his pocket.

But he couldn't bring himself to leave.

The thought of the beach house—even the thought of a lovely fire blazing near the ocean—was suffocating.

For at the beach house, Swift would be fated to see Caius and Brooke by the campfire, assuredly not studying. At the beach house, he'd face the pressure of their glances, as though both of them were keeping a polite, cruel secret that Swift was bound to utterly fail in his study of medicine; that they were just patiently waiting for him to realize it.

Even though the dark notion struck as actual, Swift recognized it more as paranoia than legitimate.

There was some truth, though, to the sense he received from them at times—that they somewhat believed giving up on the medical Practicum might be his best course.

But sitting in solitude on the border of the Wentletrap Forest, discovering insights in *The Shepherd of the Stars*, reading them fluidly, Swift felt he was receiving strong medicine—a strengthening current delivering words, delivering chilled wind, deliciously bitter with ozone kept among densely grown trees.

Swift again focused on *The Shepherd of the Stars*—a book whose heaviness, whose bright pages seemed to whisper that he should never give up.

As the Sunstone applied to a page in this book made it whole, it seemed the Star of Atlantis, by all its myths and its truths, was rendering him complete, too.

Turning the page, Swift found a listing of elements—a periodic table following the method of Antoine Lavoisier.

Swift straightened with a thought striking.

By the science recorded here, could he not gain clues—textual evidence—as to when this book had been written? And not only this book, then, but *The Star of Atlantis*—if they in fact shared an author.

Swift rested his eyes on the dark Wentletrap as his mind traced what he knew of the evolution of chemistry. Lavoisier had created his tables in the 1700's.

It made sense that this book, too, might've been written in the 1700's. That agreed with Octavian's deduction of when *The Star of Atlantis* was penned. And it was around that period when Cynfael Maddox was said to have sailed, when the Sunstone was allegedly hidden.

Turning a few pages more, Swift found Mendeleev's periodic table—one of the most beautiful inventions in chemistry—well, in all sciences.

"Hang on," Swift whispered.

Mendeleev created his tables in the late 1800's—tables that included gaps which anticipated new elements, then still undiscovered. And yet in *The Shepherd of the Stars*, those elements were included, the noble gasses—argon, helium, and others.

"How could this be?"

The ink and paper of *The Star of Atlantis* had dated much earlier than the late 1800's.

Swift flipped on to find hieroglyphs and illustrations of well-known archaeology relics, including the Stonefire pictograph—an ancient artifact that, like rare Icelandic spar, had been unearthed worldwide.

He found drawings of stars and constellations, true enough to the real night sky that he could recognize the patterns of stars that would light up midsummer.

These drawings captured him the way real stars did, their features striking with a semblance of home.

Someone very engaged with watching the stars must've drawn these.

Exploring on, Swift found galaxies—four sharply drawn, sweeping galaxies. Their renderings were so perfect, Swift knew them on sight.

Here lay the Andromeda Galaxy, the small and large Magellanic Clouds, and the Triangulum. They were even placed in context—the constellations in near proximity included.

Swift gathered his knees underneath him and leaned closer over the book.

Galaxies weren't formally discovered until the 1900's. For this author to have drawn four galaxies visible to the naked eye, he or she had to be familiar with relatively recent astronomy.

If this book were very old, could its content have been created over a long span—the science in it unfolding like a timeline?

Swift closed the book and again studied its cover.

If part of this book, even a small part, were recent—could that mean someone contributing to it was still alive? And who was this "Shepherd of the Stars," singled out by the title? Was the Shepherd of the Stars the author? Or perhaps this was a biography.

Or—could the fisherman be the Shepherd of the Stars?

The exhilaration of the idea brought Swift to his feet.

A wash of wind carried the sharp cologne of pines up the rise and called his gaze to the deeps of the Wentletrap Forest.

The *Star of Atlantis* map—though it was a map of Sterncastle Cove, and though it laid out the coastal features leading there—it was also a map of the Wentletrap Forest.

The larger part of it, actually, was of the Wentletrap.

What if something, then, some insight or secret—some treasure—rested in the Wentletrap Forest?

The notion he'd felt earlier—a presence in the Wentletrap—washed back.

The only sign of life he could sense in the expanse of trees now, though, was the occasional gull taking flight, stirring the silver mist and coasting to reach a roost by the sea.

And yet the thought of exploring the Wentletrap, of feeling enclosed by its cherishing limbs and bathing in its scent—musky and dark, spiced with brine and earthy with crumbling wood, of green leaves unfurling, of roots spreading—it conquered him.

For what might this forest reveal of the Shepherd of the Stars? In the deeps of those trees—what might he be destined to learn?

Cradling *The Shepherd of the Stars*, he couldn't help but wonder whether it'd been he who found it, not to mention *The Star of Atlantis*, its map, and its Sunstone—or if they, perhaps, had found him.

Inside the woodland—not far from its edge—something flickered.

Swift knelt at the overhang's rim and peered among the dark limbs of trees.

Something inside the forest was moving, was glowing.

The light wasn't quite like a torch—it cast no beam. It sputtered and swelled like one of the beach house's old-fashioned lanterns.

The light was meandering, too, like a lantern being carried.

Keeping his eyes on the light, Swift slipped his books into his rucksack and shouldered it.

Charmed by the scent on the wind, entranced by how the mist was catching the stars, unseated by the sight of the tallest trees netting the rising moon—Swift couldn't help but join with the forest.

He had to move in it, like that light was moving; to travel its starry trails toward its twisting heart.

Perhaps this feeling issuing from the Wentletrap Forest told more of its nature than did the rumors of its hikers meeting their deaths.

Maybe the Wentletrap wasn't perilous, but just secretive. Maybe that somebody carrying a lantern felt adrift, as Swift did, and had sought the Wentletrap, had crossed its alluring threshold, to receive nourishment by these grounding trees.

The light in the forest shifted from sharp to glowing, like a bright star submerging into a thickening mist.

And then it was gone.

Swift, his every quick heartbeat seeming to sparkle with destiny, trained his penlight on the ground.

Following the cliff's edge, he discovered a trail winding down—a trail seeming to lead into the forest.

The trail was shallow and wide enough to dare at this newly dark hour.

And the moon, so strong, painted clear shadows where rocks lay that might trip him. Even tonight's stars seemed bright enough to cast shadows.

It took not five minutes for Swift to reach the base of the trail and find his way to the Wentletrap's brink.

He stood before its magnificent boundary of pines and oaks, looming like giants posted at the gateway to Loki's dark forest, Myrkviðr.

Inside the forest, the lantern's shine again woke.

And not only was there a light. There was a sound, now.

Someone was humming.

An urge rose in Swift to call out, but with it came a wave of fear and a strike of remembered pain in his chest. The last time he'd happened upon a person in the desolation of this coast, he'd caught the blade of a dagger.

As silently as he could, Swift slipped inside the forest. He crept tree to tree, following the swaying light as closely as he dared.

16

*B*y the sound of the humming, it seemed the person weaving through the Wentletrap was a man.

Swift followed behind him, keeping well inside shadows.

The man was running his hand along the gnarled trees he passed, their great roots heaving from the earth like tentacles.

Swift, as far back as he was, couldn't make out the man's face. Who knew but that this might be the fisherman?

If the fisherman understood the science in *The Shepherd of the Stars*—if he'd written that science—maybe he could teach it. As advanced as Swift was in maths, much in the book baffled him.

The fisherman—what if he could be the teacher Swift needed? The teacher Caius, perhaps, no longer was.

As soon as the thought struck—the fisherman as a teacher, it felt true. The fisherman, with his cryptic talk, had lit a fire in Swift's heart in a way that only a teacher can; a fire that'd been kindling all through the coma, a fire that seemed now to be quickening, stirred by *The Shepherd of the Stars*.

In a sudden burst, lights woke above Swift, high in the canopy. Lights flickering. Lights like white stars. Lights glazing the forest, giving form to the shape of the man—holding a lantern and cloaked.

He looked ethereal. Phantasmic.

The cloak draping him was a very deep blue and fastened at his shoulder, asymmetrically. It looked fine—fine as though tailored, like something formal and from an era long-passed. He looked about Justus' age, or perhaps younger. But he carried great austerity.

Kingly was the only word Swift could conjure to describe this cloaked man holding an oil lantern.

Mesmerizing though he was, Swift felt a twinge of disappointment.

He definitely wasn't the fisherman.

Swift studied the great heights of the trees, searching for the origin of the lights.

Though bright, they were beaming from places he couldn't see well.

But they lit the man in perfect clarity.

The man seemed completely at peace in this bizarre place—the deadly Wentletrap Forest, at this very odd hour.

He didn't seem lost, nor in need—though perhaps he wanted to be left alone. As strange as his clothes were, they cast him as a perfect fit for this forest—like he were wearing the finery the Wentletrap merited.

The man faced Swift.

Swift froze in a shock of embarrassment at being caught following.

The man didn't speak or advance. He only raised the cloak's hood, darkening his face.

The man's eyes, barely visible, still seemed to be watching Swift. Despite the hood shading them, they seemed gentle.

Still, nothing hinted at whether the man might be friendly. Swift felt no direct threat, but neither could he gather any sense of peace.

And nothing about the man prompted Swift to approach.

He seemed to be considering Swift—but for what reason?

The man lifted his lantern and blew out the flame.

All at once, all the lights in the canopy went dark.

The blazing stars and soft moon, seeming to follow the command of the lights in the forest, grew obscured by clouds.

Inside this deepness of trees, little starshine could reach the Earth, and Swift's eyes were blinded from gazing beneath lights so bright. He couldn't see but a few inches in front of him.

Up welled terror, a heart-stopping sense of vulnerability.

Was the man coming closer? Was he unsheathing a knife?

The earthy air of the forest seemed to transform into water. Unbreathable.

Swift sank into a low crouch, beside a broad tree.

He couldn't name anything he'd seen of that wanderer as explainable. Rather, those ghostly, bewildering lights, this cold mist, coaxed up paranormal explanations.

His legend books spoke of sightings—documented sightings —of figures wandering the coast of Wales.

Some believed them to be the spirits of the original Star Shepherds—of Cynfael Maddox and Griselda Jib and Chance Merriweather and Bones Cooper, and of all those other mages— crew members of the *Checkered Whelk,* killed for ransom or dispersed to live or to die off the land.

Swift leaned into the crook of the tree, buttressed by roots before and behind. He lay against its cradle of lichen-laced bark until he could breathe steadily, until he could shake the belief that he'd just seen a spirit.

Swift checked the positions of the few stars he could recognize in the gaps between branches and clouds.

A quick calculation of their angles told it was well past nine 'o clock.

Caius would give him a few minutes, but it wouldn't be long before his own imagination would get the better of him—he'd be picturing Swift stricken with fever or lying at the base of a ravine from a fall.

But Caius would never come looking for him here, inside the Wentletrap Forest. Swift had to start the hike home.

And he could. He could slip away from this blind. In all likelihood, there wasn't a cloaked man holding a knife—a knife keen enough to cut through his clothes; a knife hewn as a mermaid, her eyes of cold diamonds; a knife held by a ghoulish man advancing, now just on the other side of this tree.

Swift tightened his grip on the tree's coarse roots. He told himself to stand, to just stand, to walk straight back south. No one would follow him. No one would jump out of the dark and flash the chill of a blade across his chest.

There were no ghostly hands reaching their iced fingers to touch him.

The thought of reaching, dead fingers constricted him into a crouch.

And there he froze. For from the forest's deeps rose a sound.

The ground litter rustled.

A twig cracked.

Swift peered over the tree's buttress.

A new sort of light was aglow in the forest.

Two lights were moving in the darkness. Eerie green-blue lights, like the scarce moonlight was reflecting off the retinas of an animal. A massive animal.

Or could that hulking thing be the man, his eyes assuming qualities of a beast?

The eyes were pale, ghosted—like the luminous eyes of a Viking, undead and desiring his treasure.

Swift held still as more lights emerged. Small lights. Lights slipping near to the ground as though shining from the faces of great snakes.

Swift held on to his chest, pressing it like Justus did, like Caius did, when he slipped into panic.

Whatever creatures these were, they seemed as unearthly as the wanderer had. There weren't any wild animals as big as that in Wales.

A sharp energy pricked Swift to want to run, but—running would be foolish. Outrunning whatever that was seemed unlikely.

But neither could he stay here, waiting for whatever that was to stalk nearer.

Adrenaline stinging his legs brought him to his feet. If that thing pinned him against this tree, he'd certainly freeze with horror while it tore into him. If it was, in fact, a hunting animal, he'd have nowhere near the strength to fight it off.

And if it wasn't an animal—if it was something unearthly—fighting wouldn't make any difference.

Swift spent a moment breathing deeply, mustering the courage to sprint home.

But—he gripped the tree's trunk—which way was home?

He'd followed the wanderer around several twisting forest corridors. It was impossible, now, even to grasp from which direction he'd come.

Keeping his eyes on the glowing disturbances, Swift worked the Sunstone out of his pocket.

The creatures didn't seem to be nearing, though there were even more of them now. Six pairs of eyes, at least.

Swift slowly lifted his Sunstone to the sky.

With the Sunstone brightening the stars behind moving sheets of mist, it didn't take him long to figure out which track through the trees would lead south, toward the beach house.

How lucky that he'd been bold enough to refuse to part from his Sunstone today. If it helped him reach the edge of the forest before those creatures reached him, this would make twice that the Star of Atlantis had saved his life.

A snarl.

Swift's heart jumping jolted him to run.

Shining his weak penlight before him, he raced along the curve of a trail.

At its fork, he skidded to a stop and stood petrified, his heart thundering.

There were no lights behind him. There was no spirit. No cloaked figure bearing a lantern. Nothing moving toward him. No sound of any animal.

There was just a faint veil of mist. Leaves dandled by a soft wind. A gentle moving of branches.

The wind coursing through the trees was a hum, but otherwise there was no voice. The only clear sound was the distant crashing of waves in the bay.

Swift checked the stars through the Sunstone and darted along a counter-intuitive right-hand path, which led more southward—though it twisted to the point that he didn't feel he was going south.

He raced on until he reached a small clearing nestled between two bowed lines of trees.

He sprinted along their arc and onto another trail, stopping when the path widened and studying the sky through the Sunstone. At each glimpse, he adjusted his course to keep to trails leading south.

After winding through the corridor several turns, he found himself doubting his own skill of perception, of reading the stars.

It seemed these forest trails had been cut in dizzying spirals that would spin him into the tangle of trees more readily than it would spin him out.

No wonder people got lost in the Wentletrap. Died in the Wentletrap.

A light in the canopy, just above, flickered. It flashed brightly, like lightning striking a tree.

The flash didn't dissipate but materialized into a square—high in the crown of an oak.

Swift stared up in wonderment, but before he had time to process it, the light snapped off.

Another light, a bit farther ahead, lit.

This one dazzled long enough for Swift to deduce it was some kind of sign.

It held writing—one word, rendered in the cuneiform wedges of Celtic Akkadian.

It read, "shepherd."

Swift ran to it, but just as he drew near to it, it flashed off.

Another ignited—another Celtic Akkadian symbol. It lingered behind a veil of mist that obscured its details, making it illegible.

Running toward it led Swift along what felt like a series of doubtful turns.

Maybe this was the trick of the Wentletrap. Maybe this was how it spun its victims to lostness and death.

But driven by a sense of flight from the man perhaps holding a dagger, from terrible incandescent eyes, Swift ran on, following sign after sign.

Finally, he broke through a line of trees and found himself stumbling out of the thicket.

Looking up, he discovered himself at the base of the very same rise he'd climbed down.

Leaving the cover of the Wentletrap brought a wind stronger, colder, and tainted with sea spray.

Swift stared behind him, into the dense forest.

No lights shone now—no lantern, no creaturely eyes, no signs, no flash of any blade in the moonlight.

Using his penlight, Swift searched out the trail cut into the cliff's face that he'd followed down. He trekked up its folding course to the top of the overhang.

At its edge, he crouched.

His mind's eye, firing with surges of adrenaline from his manic heart, kept him certain he'd seen something extraordinary. Spiritual.

He studied the forest, scanned its deeps for anything glinting. But all remained dark.

Whatever animal that'd been, it seemed not to have followed. And there was no trace of the man.

Swift felt, through his backpack, the sharp corner of *The Shepherd of the Stars*.

He clawed off his rucksack and pulled out the book. He raced through it to the section on Welsh clans.

He found a few cryptic lines on the power of Sunstones— *"lighting the way over strong seas, through vast time, to distant worlds."*

But he could find nothing—no fable nor history—about forests holding creatures or spirits.

As he flipped through, his eyes were continually drawn to the top of each page.

Every one of them held strange markings—hashes like what crossed each page in *The Star of Atlantis*.

It seemed beyond any doubt that these were cyphers belonging to some symbolic or cuneiform language.

But if so, they seemed quite incomplete. Of all the languages Swift had studied, no script looked like this.

Like sunlight shafting from a cloudbank, the words he'd read in the section on Sunstones drifted back—*"True Icelandic spar can create odd effects when placed over letters."*

Earlier, Swift had checked the words in the book, the science formulas, by the Sunstone.

But he hadn't tested these markings.

Swift placed the Sunstone on a row of marks crossing the top of a page. He shone his penlight through.

Bold letters appeared inside the clarity of the stone.

They were indeed cuneiform symbols. Ancient symbols. Symbols Swift could read.

Symbols of Celtic Akkadian.

The symbols spelled out: *"The House of the Shepherd of the Stars."*

Swift flipped to another page and rested the Sunstone against the hashes at its top.

Some of the characters were illegible—he didn't know Celtic Akkadian completely. But he knew enough to make out the gist: *"At last, peacefully rests the Shepherd of the Stars, at the pinnacle of the shell's crown."*

The House of the Shepherd of the Stars...did that refer to an actual house, belonging to the Welsh clan? Or—*"peacefully rests"* sounded funereal. Was this speaking of a tomb?

He turned the page and read another line through the crystal: *"In the heart of the coiling trees may he always be found."*

And on another page: *"Look to where treetop meets sky."*

Coiling trees. A forest's heart.

Swift had discovered this book on the brink of the Wentletrap Forest. And a wentletrap, by definition, was part of a seashell—the inner column twisting up to the pinnacle, like a circular staircase.

Swift turned the page and read the cuneiform through his stone.

It spelled—"*Cynfael Maddox.*"

Cynfael Maddox—the great seafarer and Captain of the *Checkered Whelk*. Cynfael Maddox—the Icelandic pirate who stole and stowed the Star of Atlantis.

Beneath the name, Swift read:

"Cynfael Maddox came to be known as "The Shepherd of the Stars" by his peculiar fondness for wandering through ancient oak forests by night, speaking wisdom to the trees, and casting what might be called spells on the people he happened upon."

Swift had to stop for the shock of the words. That was almost exactly what he'd seen.

He angled the book more into his penlight's glow and read on.

"Over time, legends grew around Cynfael Maddox, twisting about his persona as the roots of ancient trees enclose stones. Rumors spread through the coastal villages of Cynfael's time-lessness, of his immortal wisdom, of the visions seen by his clan. And reports of his spirit, sighted along the shore on starlit nights, span centuries. A house stands in the center of Cynfael's forest, where ancient trees reach for the sky."

"The Shepherd of the Stars," Swift whispered. "That was Cynfael Maddox."

And Cynfael Maddox might once have been found at the heart of the Wentletrap Forest.

Swift again scanned the forest for a lantern, for signs, for bright eyes. He listened for humming.

But the Wentletrap remained silent and calm, like a primordial sea set back to rest with a Kraken's retreat.

Swift turned the page and read on:

"Though few have seen the house, allegedly the hideout of the Checkered Whelk's crew, many have looked for it. Some claim it to be enchanted—coming and going with the whims of the

mist. Some say there rest Cynfael Maddox's most illustrious treasures. Treasures protected by foresight. By time. And by spells."

Could the Shepherd of the Stars still somehow be at the heart of the Wentletrap Forest? Was it possible the ghostly wanderer Swift had seen was—somehow—him?

The map to the Star of Atlantis—the map of the Wentletrap Forest—flashed into Swift's mind.

It, too, held these mystical hash marks. And in this same way, with his Sunstone, he could likely decipher them.

If only he had the map now.

He could visualize the details of its markings, some tracing the map, others set in a list—like ordered notes or numbers.

Might those be directions?

And on the map, hash marks were drawn inside the boundary of the Wentletrap Forest.

Maybe the map led—not just to the Star of Atlantis—but to the Shepherd of the Stars.

To his house. His tomb.

"I knew it—" rang a bitter voice, from behind.

Swift jumped to his feet and spun.

Leaning against the tree beside Swift's bike, his eyes fixed on Swift—was Ash.

17

The expression Ash wore, traced by moonlight, was terrifying.

He seemed ready to scream at Swift.

To throw punches.

Swift shifted *The Shepherd of the Stars* behind his back.

"I saw you take something out of the longboat." Ash advanced. "I know you're hiding something."

The way Ash was staring, heat in his face, tears in his eyes, crowded Swift to back up, almost to the cliff's edge.

He peered over his shoulder, checking for any lights in the trees, for glimmers of shining eyes.

"You knew the longboat held something," said Ash. "That's what this whole trip has been about."

Swift watched over the cliff's edge to see the forest remain dark.

Then he turned and met the hurt in Ash's eyes.

"This trip is about getting back on track," said Swift.

"Then what is it that you've found? What's so important that you'd go off sneaking around?"

Sneaking around. That's how Ash described his mum's deception before she abandoned him.

Swift relaxed some.

Maybe this anger was partly Ash's old fury at his mum.

Still, for how hard Ash was coming down on him, for the panic from the terrors of the forest, Swift couldn't meter his breathing.

"I wasn't meaning to dodge you," said Swift. "I was going to tell you about this."

The feeling of straining to find enough air was coming now with dampness collecting on his forehead, and his heart wasn't slowing. A fever was probably sparking.

"You're lying," said Ash, through set teeth.

And Swift had lied. Sort of. Though he'd never meant to be hurtful, he had been sneaking around.

"You obviously wanted to add to your tally," said Ash. "You wanted to cast me behind you. Again."

Ash's words took the wind out of Swift. The last time he'd seen Ash this angry was right after they'd nearly drowned.

But he couldn't defend himself. He couldn't be honest about why he'd hidden what he'd found in the longboat. He couldn't admit that he knew Ash himself had an agenda on this trip; that Ash was aiming to add to his own tally.

"I just needed some solitude to wrap my mind around something," said Swift.

Ash folded his arms.

"But what do you care what I'm up to?" Swift tightened his hold on the book behind his back. "You spent the whole day at the museum with your box, with Octavian, instead of helping me study."

"You can't be mad at me for that. You yourself said I should stay with him."

Swift glanced back toward the forest.

He found no lights. There was no sign anything had followed him out.

But that didn't mean nothing had.

"Why do you keep looking behind you like that?" asked Ash.

"We should get back to the beach house," said Swift.

"I can see you're keeping something from me," said Ash. "I'm not going anywhere until you say what it is."

"It's just...in the forest..."

But Swift couldn't dare say what he'd seen.

If Ash knew Swift had sighted a mystical man wandering the Wentletrap, that in its deeps shone signs written in a language also found in *The Shepherd of the Stars*—a book that referenced Sunstones and included a code, Ash would be wild to investigate it.

Any seeds of genuine interest Ash might have in Swift, any support he was willing to give, would disintegrate.

But the truth was, by sneaking around, by hiding the book, Swift might've already lost Ash's support.

"It's late," said Swift. "We absolutely need to get home."

"You were pleased enough to come out here on your own and stay way past dark," said Ash. "But now that I've caught you keeping secrets, you're anxious to get home?"

"You're misunderstanding—"

"You look bloody bad, by the way, with how you're trembling, how you're sweating," said Ash. "You're probably getting a fever again, and all because you're going to lengths to outdo me, coming out onto this cold ridge and hiding something, breaking curfew for the sake of it."

Swift lowered his gaze. "Caius is probably too lost in Brooke to have noticed I broke curfew."

"Caius is worried sick, bloody controlling as he is," said Ash. "He made me come out looking for you."

"Caius was worried about me," said Swift, "and so—he sent you?"

If Caius were truly worried, he wouldn't have trusted Ash to come looking.

"But of course Caius sent you," said Swift. "All he wants is to be alone with Brooke."

"No, Caius thought you might've biked too far and gone weak with a fever," said Ash, his voice breaking.

"Please listen," said Swift.

But Ash was withdrawing his focus.

This was how Ash isolated himself from others, creating a psychological chasm and breaking all connection.

It was a tactic he'd used since childhood, when he needed to reach a place where his mum's yelling couldn't touch him. And it was how he sent a message to people he'd grown to despise that he wanted nothing to do with them.

Rarely had he used this on Swift.

But he had used it.

And now, like in the past, the gesture incited a literal, deep pain in Swift's chest, a sharp panic—the terror of Ash exiling him. Again.

"I worked so hard all day with Caius," said Swift. "The truth is—I did want a moment to myself."

"If we were really friends, you wouldn't need to keep anything to yourself. And Swift, just think for a second about how shabby this is. Instead of trusting me, you manipulated your way into getting at that longboat so you could plunder it."

Swift couldn't deal with such an unjust twisting of his motives.

"You're slanting this." Swift tried to catch his glance. "I didn't know anything was in the longboat. I purely intended to bring it back to the fisherman's beach."

Ash met his eye. "Then why are you still hiding something?"

Swift—his hands shaking—brought out the book. "I really was going to tell you."

Holding it before Ash seemed entirely foolhardy—a self-betrayal. But bearing that seemed less painful than owning Ash's accusations, his assumptions that Swift's motives were malicious.

Ash stared at its title.

"While we were tying off the longboat," said Swift, "I noticed a stow. Before then, I had no idea the boat held anything—I swear. Was I crazy to want to look in it? You would've done the same."

"No, if I'd discovered a stow in that longboat, I'd have told you. But you hid this entirely, and not just from me. You hid it from Caius and Brooke, too, and from your father." His eyes narrowed. "And from Octavian Krakau."

Ash, standing in this mist-heavy darkness, keeping back all understanding, all warmth, seemed a wholly different person from the Ash who'd comforted Swift on the rescue boat; the Ash who'd promised at Swift's hospital bedside to do anything to help him.

Ash shook his head. "Jesus, Swift—when will you stop trying to outperform everyone?"

Perhaps it had been shabby of Swift to hide the book. But he'd done it for good reasons.

And the extent to which Ash was taking the offense—it was striking, now, like a massive overreaction.

Swift rested his hand on his cut, throbbing. "I just wanted some solitude, because...I don't know. For my own reasons."

"You do have your reasons." Ash turned away. "You've always had your reasons to be selfish."

Selfish.

The word struck like a slap in the face.

How could Ash call Swift selfish? Swift—who'd once nearly died trying to save Ash's life. Swift—who hadn't forced Ash to give back the books he'd stolen all those years ago, but just walked away.

"I'm not the one being selfish." Swift regretted the words the instant they were out.

He was dangerously close to letting Ash see the truth—that he knew Ash cared little about him.

Ash rested his gaze on Swift. "I know exactly what's going on here."

Swift met his eyes.

Did he? Did he realize Swift believed Ash's friendship was a pretense?

"Those Star Shepherds are named so for a reason," said Ash. "They guarded Sunstones. We've both read about that, and Octavian thinks it's true. You must believe your fisherman's one of them. So here you are, having found a lead to more treasures, and yet you're refusing to share it with me, even when I've done nothing but be on your side."

Except—Ash hadn't been on his side.

Since they'd been in Wales, he'd been nowhere near Swift's side.

On the fisherman's beach, he'd done little to actually help Swift confront those painful memories. He'd mainly been interested in seeing the islet and the evidence of the wreck.

And since then, he'd spent most of his time with Octavian.

Swift unzipped his jacket to ease an uncomfortable heat churning in his chest.

"Do you think this is being on my side? Yelling at me like this when you're supposed to be bringing me back to my brother?"

"Some people never change." Ash shook his head. "You hoard things and hide things and try for wins that I have no chance at. You've always hated sharing with me."

Ash's words were so poisoned, so stunning, that Swift scarcely could see.

"I've hoarded?" He moved in so close he could feel the heat coming off Ash's body. "You promised Edric you'd return all my books, and yet you keep one. It's been you who's stolen and lied. You're the one who's struck up savage competitions, leaving no room for comradery. I've wanted to trust you—but don't you see that you're teaching me not to?"

"Don't turn this around," said Ash. "This isn't about me, or about that last book—which I did return. This is about you, and the lie that you told today, and the book that you're holding."

Swift glanced at it.

"But it's not even about that book." Ash walked away, toward the tree where his bike was leaning.

The fury and disapproval radiating from him seemed to warn he was fully capable of leaving Swift, of finally abandoning him.

"It's about what that book means," said Ash. "You're keeping me at a distance. You're just like my mum—only interested in yourself."

Swift shrugged off his jacket and let it fall.

He tried to muster words to defend himself, but he was now seeing an awful angle to himself which Ash was spotlighting.

Although he genuinely had wanted to rebuild a connection with Ash, he hadn't been willing to risk trusting him.

He'd kept this book from Ash. And before that, he'd kept from Ash the anachronism of the Cthulhu. And now he was wanting to hide how he'd come to suspect *The Star of Atlantis* shared an author with *The Shepherd of the Stars*. And he certainly couldn't imagine revealing that the author might be—whether entombed or alive—in the heart of the Wentletrap Forest.

This impulse Swift felt to keep secrets—did it mean Ash was right? Was Swift selfish?

But Ash was clearly still stinging from the agony of his mum leaving him. Maybe that was a sign that this argument was, more than anything, another cry for help.

To heal, it seemed he'd need Swift to be forthright with him. To take risks. He'd need to feel Swift was willing to extend trust.

"Look." Swift backed off a little. "I'm sorry."

Even Caius had often told Swift that friendship must run both ways. Maybe it was Swift, this time, who wasn't holding up his side of the bargain.

"I can see that I was being selfish," said Swift.

The words felt good to say. And they seemed to ease Ash some.

"You admit, then, that you did intentionally hide that book from me?" asked Ash.

Part of Swift still wanted to put some distance between Ash and *The Shepherd of the Stars*. But at the same time, an impulse was striking to just hand Ash the book.

In doing so, he'd be demonstrating his refusal to let another book ruin their friendship—a friendship for which they both were desperate.

But he couldn't do either. He couldn't stow the book, and he couldn't hold it out to Ash.

The heat in him was intensifying, and the misted wind was

making him shiver. All he could do was hang tightly to *The Shepherd of the Stars* as though it were a shaft of driftwood floating atop a wild sea.

"Can you at least admit that you were wrong to hide that book from Octavian?" asked Ash.

On this point, Swift felt blameless.

"Octavian has no rights to it." Swift rubbed his forehead, at an ache setting in.

"What makes you think you have any rights to it? You swiped that from a longboat belonging to somebody else."

"No one could accuse me of not reporting this book just a few hours after finding it."

"You know what?" Ash shrugged a laugh. "It probably won't even matter. Octavian says it's unlikely you'll get to keep any of your relics."

Swift could hardly take air for the visceral feeling of losing everything—all that had guided him to find the Star of Atlantis; the Sunstone itself and the sense of destiny it imparted, which Swift had come to own as an inner strength.

"I thought you were hoping I'd get to keep them," said Swift. "Because it would mean you'd get to explore them, too. For tonight, the Sunstone is ours. And so is this book."

"Our Sunstone," Ash whispered, as to himself. "Our book."

The anger on him seemed to dissipate like a sea vapor vanishing at the striking of dawn.

After a moment, he let a smile come. "What are we doing?"

At seeing Ash lighten, tension evaporated from Swift. "I don't know. I don't want to fight with you."

"Well, for my part," said Ash, "I'm sorry I laid into you."

Despite how rapid as the alteration was, Ash seemed genuinely apologetic. He seemed to have suddenly and completely let go of his determination to act as Swift's accuser, his competitor.

Maybe if Swift was naturally selfish—as Ash claimed, Ash was a little bit naturally mean.

But that was forgivable. Friendship meant accepting the best and the worst in someone.

Ash glanced back toward the trail leading to the beach house. "You won't tell your brother we got into this scuff, will you?"

From distantly in the forest, came a cry—a low cry, difficult to distinguish from the churning of waves in the bay.

But the cry was distinct.

It sounded like an animal howling. A wolf.

Ash moved a step closer. "You won't tell Caius, right?"

Had Swift imagined that—a ghostly wolf's cry? It sounded just like the wail he'd heard rising from the Wentletrap after he and Caius wrecked.

Ash, awaiting a response, appeared not to have heard anything.

And there were certainly no wolves in Wales. There hadn't been for hundreds of years.

Swift let the sight of his oldest friend draw him out of the mortification that he might be hallucinating with this fever.

"Don't tell Caius," said Ash. "All right?"

If Caius were to find out about this fight, he wouldn't care that Ash needed compassion; that Swift felt lost without him. He'd send Ash straight home.

Swift shrugged. "There's nothing to tell him."

Ash smiled. "That's just what I think."

Swift met his eyes. "Can you forgive me?"

"Be honest." Ash lifted his head, so he was looking down on Swift. "Were you really planning to tell me about that book?"

"Of course. I just needed some time with it. I didn't know if I could even read it."

"Have you tried reading it?"

Swift cradled the book. "Reading this—the words are like water. They flow right into me. It feels like this book might be my way back to grasping academic texts."

"Then—that's wonderful."

Swift returned Ash's genuine smile. "I'm truly sorry I hurt your feelings by keeping this a secret. But it wasn't because I wanted to keep score. I'm not like that."

The mean Ash seemed to have disappeared, leaving in his

place the caring Ash. Maybe that outburst had just been a bit of emotion he needed to vent.

Maybe Ash was actually on the verge of truly extending the friendship Swift so desperately wanted.

"You know what?" Ash guided Swift's bike to him. "I believe you."

Swift felt so much relief, he could've embraced him. The churning heat in his chest persisted, but that wasn't so surprising, coming out of such a painful conflict, and such a harrowing trek through the forest.

Ash lifted his own bike. "Let's hear what's in that book."

With Ash standing so near to him, looking so kind, so inquisitive, things felt normal again.

Ash was a beautiful-looking person at the worst of times, and seeming so cheered like this, so aligned to Swift once again, Ash simply shone. Maybe Ash, likewise, was feeling Swift's caring.

"It speaks of Sunstones." Swift held out the book to him. "It speaks of Cynfael Maddox, in Celtic Akkadian. And there's some Old Norse as well. It has chemistry and physics formulas —and some very complicated maths. And it includes some astronomy, too. Isn't that so odd and wonderful? And..."

Swift almost let slip that the handwriting seemed a match to the penmanship in *The Star of Atlantis*.

"And what?" Ash stared at him.

Swift swallowed the reflex to withhold. After all, Ash would probably notice the similarity himself, tomorrow, when he looked closely at Swift's *Star of Atlantis* book and map.

The real secret, anyway, was that the author might be entombed in the Wentletrap Forest. Or that the author—one of a series—might yet be living.

Ash wouldn't deduce that just from knowing about the shared penmanship.

"And it seems," said Swift, "that the handwriting here matches what's in *The Star of Atlantis*."

"Whoa." Ash took the book and opened it. He eyed its

Celtic Akkadian, its Old Norse. "Did you say you could read this?"

"There are a few cyphers I don't know, but"—Swift gazed at the hashes, the code—"I can read most of it."

Ash turned Swift around and settled the book safely in his rucksack. "We should get you home. Your brother will be at his wit's end with worry."

But Caius probably wasn't thinking at all about Swift. He was certainly glad that Ash and Swift were both elsewhere, giving him some privacy with Brooke.

Ash walked his bike to the trail's mouth. "Caius and Brooke built a sickeningly amorous campfire by the sea." He glanced at Swift as though reading him. "Want to crash it?"

Swift smiled, though a sharp shiver quelched that. The thought of sitting by a piping campfire sounded good. And the thought of interrupting Caius and Brooke's intimacy sounded great.

A wind lifting brought a sensation like ice on Swift's skin.

Ash seemed to notice the flash of agony crossing him. "Do you think you should ride?" He picked up Swift's jacket from the ground and settled it warmly around Swift's shoulders. "I can hurry to the campsite and tell Caius you're getting feverish. He and I could together help get you home."

Swift zipped his jacket. "I'll be damned if I tell Caius anything. He's getting tired of caring for me."

"Who knows if you'll manage to keep that book," said Ash, "but you're right that we do have tonight. By the campfire, we can map out its contents. You can practice reading it to me."

"Only," said Swift, "I can't show the book to Caius. He'd be even more furious about it than you were. He'll say this is why I couldn't make any headway in the med texts today, which is absolutely not true. I don't know if I can handle two fights in one night."

"Then we'll keep your secret together." Ash cast him a grin. "You should see what Brooke's wearing—this way-too-tight sweater and a minuscule skirt. Leggings that show every curve."

Swift shook off a little revulsion. Brooke was pretty, yes, but exclusively in a big-sister way.

"Caius will be well-distracted," said Ash. "And by the end of tonight, you and I will have learned all about what's in that book—about any secrets it keeps."

Swift shivered at the thrill of Ash hatching a plan. A great plan. Their plan.

"I truly am sorry." Swift held Ash's glance. "Can we forget that I hid the book from you?"

Ash steadied Swift's bike while Swift climbed on. "Sure."

Swift followed Ash, riding easy down the path toward the rocky coast.

18

Swift stilled his bike at the end of the trail, opening onto the beach.

Ash braked behind him.

They together looked over a ten-meter stretch of sand toward a ring of logs surrounding a campfire.

A hearty flame was dancing upon the woodpile, casting broken light over Caius and Brooke.

A few dozen meters beyond the fire stood a dock, stretching far out into the water.

It was from that gray pathway, leading into dark waves, that Ash had fallen when they were eight. It was here, on this rocky slip of shore, that their friendship had splintered.

And tied to the dock was the *Star Strider*.

Or what was left of her.

The *Strider's* sails were tied down and constricted against their poles so tightly that, watching them pitch in the moonlight, Swift found it difficult to breathe.

Her starboard hull, gouged by the reef they'd struck, was patched—but only well enough to keep her bones dry.

The covering was bulky and coarse, so she suffered a constant tendency to tip.

The way she still dragged on that side—it seemed she could yet remember her near-drowning.

It seemed she might be despairing that by it, she might still suffer death.

As much as Swift wanted to believe he could sail her again, the hope seemed foolish. She was, for all practical purposes, gone.

Justus didn't want to scrap her, but in the end he would probably have to.

Caius and Brooke were sitting together on a log, Caius behind her, holding a blanket tightly around them both. The sand at their feet cradled two glasses of wine.

Swift and Ash together rolled their bikes to the edge of the campfire ring.

"There you are." Caius stood, bundling Brooke alone in their blanket. "Thank God."

"You mean—thanks to Ash," said Swift. "It was Ash who came looking for me."

Caius rounded the fire. "I checked all up and down the beach and called for you. Where were you?"

"You didn't ask me to stay within earshot." Swift dropped his bike against Ash's, on the sand.

Ash settled down on a log, close to the fire—his back to the dock.

"Even if I give you that," said Caius, "did I not ask you to be back by nine?"

Brooke reached for Caius and traced his arm. "He was just enjoying the coast. Weren't you Swift?"

Swift glanced at her. "If you have to know, I wanted to see a bit inside the forest."

Ash's eyes expanded. He, as well as Swift, had been forbidden since infancy to step a toe into the Wentletrap Forest.

Caius lifted his brow. "You went into the Wentletrap?"

"That's right," said Swift.

Rarely was he brash like this with Caius.

When Swift gave this kind of attitude to their parents, it was usually Caius who brought him back to civility. But it was feeling good to cast a little defiance Caius' way.

"You wandered into that forest at night?" Caius closed in. "Alone?"

Swift had never been able to stand the feeling of Caius upset with him.

But at this moment, he suffered not at all, clouded as the discomfort was by the anguish of Caius pulling away from him, toward Brooke.

"It isn't a big deal." Swift sat down on a log, close to the fire. Close to Ash.

"People have gotten lost in that forest. Died in that forest." Caius stared down at him. "You know this."

"I couldn't have gotten lost. I had my Sunstone."

Caius watched him as though evaluating him.

He might be reading a lingering panic in Swift—panic because Swift actually had gotten lost in that forest.

He'd been scared out of his mind that the person—or whatever it was—had been coming for him; that those ghostly eyes had been staring from the face of a creature that was sizing him up for a fight.

And anxiety from his scuffle with Ash was still ringing.

"Are you feeling feverish?" Caius crouched before him.

Caius offering some care felt good. But Swift was too far gone in frustration to cut him any slack.

"No."

Caius took hold of Swift's wrist. "Your heart's a bit quick." He felt Swift's cheek. "And you're warm."

"Of course I'm warm." Swift stood and stumbled back over the log. "I just biked half a mile."

"All right." Caius stood, too. "I was just very worried. I guess I still am."

But, of course, he wasn't worried. He was glancing back at Brooke.

"Are you going to send us to bed, Mr. Caius?" asked Ash.

"Don't get funny with me—it's just Caius." He pressed Swift with a weighty stare. "I need you off to bed if you're tired.

I was serious when I said I want you fresh for studying in the morning."

"I'm not tired." Swift settled back down on the log.

"I thought you'd say that." Caius lifted a textbook from beside Brooke's leg. "Why don't you use this bright fire, this sailing moon, to try and read a bit of biochemistry." He handed Swift the text. "Read again the chapter we worked on today, all right?" He glanced at Ash. "I'm sure Swift would appreciate your help."

"Of course I'll help him." Ash drew Swift's backpack off him. "Swift, do you have a"—he raised his brows—"torch in here?"

"I sure do," said Swift. "Would you be so kind as to get it out for me?"

Caius cast an odd look at them both as he traipsed back to Brooke.

"Now." Caius slipped into the blanket behind her. "Where were we?"

"*Now...where were we?*" Swift mimicked in a whisper, making Ash smile.

Ash opened Swift's rucksack, and in a tandem maneuver, they pulled out *The Shepherd of the Stars*, nesting it perfectly inside the biochemistry book.

This comradery with Ash lent a sense of elation, of strong friendship. This was exactly what both of them needed.

"I saw something strange," whispered Swift, "in the forest."

"You really went inside the Wentletrap?" whispered Ash. "I thought you said that just to set Caius off."

"I got good and lost in there, too," said Swift. "But I'll never admit that to him."

"What did you see?" asked Ash.

Caius, nuzzling Brooke's cheek, glanced at Swift. It was like he was secretly watching. Listening.

"Can I try reading this to you—aloud?" Swift asked Ash, strongly.

"Sure!" Ash replied. "Whatever helps."

Swift started in on the first paragraph of the biochemistry text, while Ash shone the light.

Brooke gently whispering to Caius brought an end to his surveillance.

"I saw a person," Swift whispered. "Or—something. Someone carrying an oil lantern. He was humming and talking to the trees."

Ash's eyes expanded.

"Could that have been your fisherman? He sounds mad enough to be."

"It wasn't the fisherman," whispered Swift. "I caught a glimpse of his face—just before he disappeared, like a ghost! And then, something even more bizarre happened. I saw something glowing. Eyes, I think. Dozens of them."

"What in the Wentletrap Forest could have glowing eyes?"

"They looked like animal eyes reflecting the moon," said Swift. "I couldn't make out exactly what they were. Something big. When you found me, I was searching this, trying to make sense of what I saw. I mean, if this book is about that ancient Welsh clan—ghostly wanderers—don't you think it might hold some explanation?"

"It sure could." Ash bent more closely over their secreted book. "And if it tells about those wanderers, it might tell of the treasures they protected."

"This book might be a biography," whispered Swift, "about someone called 'The Shepherd of the Stars.' Or maybe it's a journal, written by someone from that clan. And look"—he flipped to the opening section—"here, it tells about Icelandic spar."

Ash ran his finger down the page. "This is amazing."

"Ash—I could read all of this."

Ash flipped on. "Whoa—are these the science formulas you told me about? Can you understand them?"

"Some," whispered Swift. "I've studied higher maths, but I've never seen anything like this. And then—there are all these physics calculations."

He turned more pages.

"And these—I think they're astronomy notations. And here are chemistry equations. Looking at all this—does it not seem that the Shepherd of the Stars was a scientist?"

"You might be right." Ash leaned nearer to Swift.

The feel of him close, in a covert discussion, both of them aiming to thwart Caius, both of them craving to read *The Shepherd of the Stars*—Swift's guard fell completely away.

"Ash..." Swift lowered his voice more. "There's special writing in this book. Writing that's hidden."

"What do you mean, 'hidden?'"

"It's really clever, actually." Swift pointed to a page thick with physics equations. "Look at these cryptic marks, at the tops of the pages and scattered inside the equations. Icelandic spar can produce a distorting effect. This means letters can be drawn —letters illegible on their own, but clear when seen through a Sunstone."

Ash's eyes expanded. "Like runes from Norse mythology." His face lit more brightly than Swift ever had seen it.

"I can't say they're as meaningful as runes," said Swift. "The characters are English and Celtic Akkadian—not Old Norse."

"Still, if they were secretly written, they might be runes, said Ash. "Runes that invoke power. Runes that only reveal themselves to someone who's open to fearful insights and terrible abilities. You—or you and me both!"

Swift, studying Ash, worked to deduce whether he was really letting himself believe such an extraordinary thing.

"It's a wonderful idea as mythology goes," said Swift. "But you can't think what's written here was placed specifically for us."

"How can you dismiss it?" asked Ash. "You're the finder of the Sunstone. I'm the finder of a box marked with a Celtic Star."

"What we know is that these letters can only be read using the Star of Atlantis," said Swift. "When I placed the Sunstone on the page and shone the light through, letters formed. Numbers. Some of the formulas are incomplete and just meaningless—until deciphered by the Sunstone."

"Whoa." Ash dropped the penlight.

"You guys all right?" Caius pulled away from Brooke.

She grasped a handful of his shirt, keeping him close.

Swift snatched up the penlight. "We're fine."

"He's making real progress," said Ash.

Caius gave them a warning glance but turned again toward Brooke, who was saying something softly to him.

"Keep the books steady," whispered Swift, sneaking out his Sunstone. "I'll show you."

Ash did his best to hold both books while Swift held the Sunstone over the markings crossing a page.

The stone, beneath the penlight, glowed.

Like magic, the markings shifted to Celtic Akkadian letters.

"These are Celtic Akkadian symbols," Swift whispered. "They read—*The House of the Shepherd of the Stars.*'"

"This is incredible," Ash murmured. "What could it mean?"

Swift held silent. Despite how open he was feeling, he found he couldn't disclose more.

His theory that this "house," likely a tomb, waited in the Wentletrap Forest—that in it, more treasures might rest—would be simply too enticing to Ash.

Ash turned the page. "Do another one."

Swift peered through the Sunstone. "This reads—*'The People of the Stones.*'"

"That sure sounds like our Welsh clan," said Ash. "Protectors of the Star of Atlantis—of Sunstones. What if this book leads to more treasure?"

Ash had said "treasure" loudly, and at it, Caius stood.

"I told you these two would just mess around if I let them stay up," said Caius.

Swift and Ash carefully, together, lowered the two books.

Caius limped to standing before them.

"If you're not going to use this time productively, you might as well be off to bed."

"We're not messing around," said Swift.

Swift and Ash, in unison, lifted the medical text, keeping *The Shepherd of the Stars* carefully concealed.

"You see," said Swift, "I accidentally read this phrase—'tertiary structure' as 'treasure.'"

Caius eyed them both, then in a quick swipe lifted the biochemistry book, sending *The Shepherd of the Stars* tumbling out of their hands.

Caius picked it up. Studied its cover. "Where did you get this?"

At the dark tone in his voice, Swift stood.

So did Brooke.

Swift considered conjuring some lie. But Caius could always tell when he was lying.

And it felt awful, anyway, lying to Caius.

Even Swift's current posture of defiance was starting to feel a little sour.

"Is this yours?" Caius looked down at Ash. "Or is this another book from my brother's collection that you stole?"

"Ash returned everything, and you know it." Heat flashed into Swift's face, burning all contrition. "I found that book in a stow in the longboat."

"In the longboat?"

Caius opened it to the first page and seemed to be reading the oath.

"How could the Coast Guard have failed to spot this?"

"The longboat's base was concreted with piled sand," said Swift. "The stow would've been easy to overlook."

Caius turned the book over. "Seems they would've searched for—and found—any stow in that longboat."

He glanced at Ash.

"I'm not lying," said Swift. "The Coast Guard did a shabby job cleaning the boat. You saw it, how dirty it was. They probably wanted to leave it as it was found, right? In case they needed to check it for more fingerprints or something."

"You shouldn't be upset with Swift," said Ash. "He's figured out a way to decipher some of the words in that book which are cryptic."

Caius tapped the book's spine against his palm. "What I'm

deciphering is that your mind has been on this rather than dealing in your med texts."

"You're misunderstanding," said Swift, "I've been trying—"

"No wonder you've been so distracted." Caius reached the book behind him to Brooke, who took it.

"But I've managed to read that," said Swift. "Don't take it from me."

Caius seemed no longer willing to meet Swift's eyes.

"It's wonderful how easily I can read it," said Swift. "It even has some Celtic Akkadian and Old Norse. Some words are hidden except when seen through the Sunstone." He eased forward. "And Caius—it includes science notes. I've had no trouble, not even with the other languages. Not even with the academic material. I think that book is my way back to focusing."

Caius glanced at him. "I have to say—I'm surprised at you, Little Brother."

Little Brother. That's the moniker Edric used when he wanted to diminish Swift. Swift couldn't remember Caius ever using it.

"You've lied to the authorities, to that museum curator," said Caius.

"I didn't lie to Octavian," said Swift. "I just didn't tell him about this." He glanced toward Ash, hoping he might act as some defense.

But Ash was just watching, wide-eyed like he was enjoying the argument.

"It was deceitful of you," said Caius. "And don't tell me you can't see it—I know you can."

Ash perked up. "It wasn't just deceitful, but witless. Octavian would pay a fortune for *The Shepherd of the Stars*, I'm sure. It's clearly connected to *The Star of Atlantis*."

Swift stared at Ash.

Ash patted Swift's leg. "I'm just trying to lighten things."

"There's nothing light about this," said Caius, to Swift. "I've never known you to flat out lie to me."

Swift moved toward Brooke. "Please give me my book back."

She only cast a helpless, "I'm sorry" sort of look from behind Caius as she slipped the book into her satchel.

"Tomorrow, that book's going to the museum." Caius crossed his arms. "I hope you can accept losing it, because the museum will likely confiscate it."

Swift advanced. "Do you want me to keep bumbling around, out of focus and in the dark?" He stopped right before Caius. "Or do you want me to heal?"

Caius glanced toward Brooke. "I'm sorry you're having to see this. He's not usually like this. He's probably just really tired."

"I'm not 'really tired,'" said Swift. "And I'm never 'like' this. I'm not 'like' anything."

"Then can you explain what's going on with you?" asked Caius. "What was the point in hiding that from me?"

How could Caius not see what was going on?

"The point is"—Swift unzipped the front of his jacket, letting in the night's cold—"you're really making me bloody mad."

"Oh, so this is my fault?" asked Caius.

Brooke touched Caius' shoulder. "Maybe now isn't the best time to talk this through. I'm sure you're right, that Swift and Ash are tired. You're probably pretty tired."

Caius seemed to ease up a little.

Brooke drew her hand down Caius' arm. She wrapped her fingers around Caius' thumb and pulled. "I myself am pretty tired."

The gesture was so obvious, so raunchy, so sickening, that Swift had to turn away.

Ash, seeming beside himself with pleasure at all this drama, was full-on grinning.

Caius gently pulled his hand away from Brooke's, but he didn't take his eyes off her. "You—I'll put to bed soon enough."

Caius, being so hard on Swift and so nauseatingly sweet

with Brooke—it invoked a thickening in Swift's chest. He was afraid to draw breath for fear that tears might rise.

He backed away from the fire. From Caius. "You can quit pretending that you care anything about me anymore, because I know you don't."

Ash rested back against the log, his hands knit behind his head.

Caius took a limping step toward Swift. "That's nothing close to true."

Swift stood still, his eyes dampening, his heart galloping. "But it is."

Caius' expression was going stony, making him look exactly like Justus, when one of the brothers had gotten into big trouble.

"Can we speak in private?" Caius glanced at the waterline.

"You willing to leave Brooke's side for ten seconds?" asked Swift.

"You willing to drop this ugly attitude?" asked Caius.

Swift started toward the waterline. The waterline that'd once nearly divided him from life. The waterline that once had divided him from Ash. The waterline over which Caius had pulled him, drawing him clear of the strangling breakers.

"Are you coming or not?" Swift called back.

Caius limped through the sand after him.

19

Swift stopped when he reached the breaking waves.

Caius stopped behind him.

"What's gotten into you?"

"I just—" Swift faced him.

How to put this into words?

How to describe for Caius the person Swift was watching him morph into—a person willing to displace their brotherhood for a girl; a person no longer interested in caring for Swift but just in ordering him around? Ash was right. Caius was bloody controlling.

"You're not being the teacher I need," said Swift. "I don't like how controlling you've become."

"Controlling." Caius, seeming stung, glanced off toward Ash, like he knew Ash had called him that.

"And you're not listening to me," said Swift. "You're ignoring what I'm trying to tell you." He gestured toward the campsite. "That book was an incredible find, and yet all you've done is criticize me about it."

"I'm not being dismissive or controlling," said Caius. "I'm acting in your own best interest. Do you not recall that I agreed to come here because you asked me to?"

"Maybe you shouldn't have." Swift kicked a pile of sand. "If you'd stayed home with Brooke, I'd be no nuisance to you at all."

Caius moved in. "If I hadn't wanted to come, I wouldn't have. I'm aiming to help you by removing your distractions. That book's a distraction. I see it. And you know it."

"It's no distraction—it's a relief. I was bewildered at how easily I could read it. And then I discovered it held cryptic words—words I could understand, using my Sunstone." Swift faced the water. "I thought you'd be proud about that, not furious."

Caius limped to standing beside him.

"You expect me to be proud of you for stealing a book, and then lying about it?"

"That isn't what happened."

"Then why didn't you tell me about it? Why didn't you tell anyone? If you'd taken that book to the curator, who knows but that he might've even paid you to consign it to him for analysis."

"Right, like I want more blood money."

"You're looking at this all wrong," said Caius. "You're viewing that curator in a negative light, and you're perceiving things as yours that aren't."

"How I'm perceiving things isn't the problem," said Swift. "Something about Octavian is off. After dealing with him for five minutes, I was sure I was right not to bring that book to him."

"Is your judgment of him fair?" asked Caius. "After all, he wants the same thing you do. You probably can't see him as anything but a rival, when really he's an expert you should trust."

"No. He's manipulative and prying. And...I don't know."

"Exactly," said Caius. "You don't know."

"There's something mean-seeming about him," said Swift. "Like he wouldn't play fair."

"Swift—that's not based on anything."

"You would've noticed it yourself if you'd come to the museum." Swift flicked a mortifying wetness from the corner of his eye. "If you'd forced yourself to be with me instead of Brooke."

Caius limped a step nearer. "More than anything, this is about Brooke, isn't it?"

Something in Swift's chest twisted at watching Caius standing there in the cold sand, putting his weight on just his good leg.

"Everything in your expression tells me how much you dislike her," said Caius. "She knows it, too. With how you go on about gratitude—gratitude for our rescue, gratitude for that fisherman—can't you spare any gratitude for her?" He had to take another limping step to keep his balance in the shifting sand. "She's been a great help to us both."

Swift's eyes were growing wetter for the heat flashing through him. And standing at the sea's brink was reviving the raw sense of desperation he'd felt, standing on the beach beyond Sterncastle Cove, Caius lying unconscious behind him.

That horrible sense of Caius fading out, of tasting the bitter realization that Caius might die—it surfaced viscerally, bringing a tang of bile to Swift's throat.

Now, here was Caius, alive and on his way to a near-full recovery—and yet Swift was still losing him.

Only it wasn't death snatching him away.

Caius was choosing to set Swift aside. Caius was choosing to leave him.

"Brooke had to help us because of me," said Swift. "Because of me, you risked losing your chance at medicine when you'd hardly begun." He felt a tear speed down his cheek. "If I hadn't been set on going after the Star of Atlantis, you wouldn't have gone to the hospital at all. If I hadn't asked you to take me to that bloody cove, you wouldn't have met Brooke, and we'd still be proper brothers."

Caius stood stunned, it seemed, while Swift's raw confession hung between them.

Swift dropped to sitting in the sand.

Caius eased down to crouching before him. "We still are proper brothers. No girl can ever change that. No matter how beautiful she is. How special."

Swift turned away.

"Hey, keep talking." Caius brought Swift's hands down from his face. "I want to understand."

"I can't deal with the distance she's drawing between us." Swift couldn't look at Caius. "I almost lost you in the cove, and that was bad enough. But now I have lost you."

Caius scooted closer, moving his bad leg gently. "I'll concede it. I've been a bit preoccupied with her."

"A bit preoccupied? You're never apart." Swift wiped his cheek on his shoulder. "It seems the Star of Atlantis does bring about curses and the endings of worlds."

"Hm." Caius glanced off. "Curses that bring around girls like her are my kind of curses. You'll see that yourself, one of these days."

Swift angled away. "She's been around constantly. And it's my bloody fault."

Now that Swift was speaking his honest feelings about Brooke, black energy seemed to be bubbling up, making him contract his arms tighter around his knees to distance himself more from Caius.

"You've got it quite wrong," said Caius. "Brooke and I met months before the accident. Before you even found your map to the Star of Atlantis, in fact, Brooke and I were friends."

Swift glanced at him.

"We met last term, when my professor invited her in as a guest lecturer on doctor-nurse dynamics. We went out afterwards and sort of hit it off. My being in her care for a week—it only served to speed things along."

"She's probably wishing that I wasn't here," said Swift. "That she had you to herself."

"Not at all," said Caius. "She knows how tight you and I are. And she wishes you'd give her a chance. Her eye is on you, and that comes from a place of genuine caring."

"That's hard to buy. She's acting every bit as obsessed with you as you are with her."

Caius studied him. "I can't help but suspect that some of these dark thoughts might be stemming from a fever starting up again." He reached for Swift's forehead.

Swift ducked away.

"I don't think I've ever seen you as agitated as you've been tonight, actually," said Caius. "Perhaps it isn't all about Brooke."

A shadow, inland, caught Swift's eye. Someone moving in front of the campfire.

Swift blotted wetness off his face. "She's coming."

Caius glanced toward her. "Just try to think on how kind she's been to us."

Brooke stopped beside Caius. He took her hands, allowing her to help him stand.

Swift pushed to his feet and walked away from them.

"I'm afraid Swift's fever might be back," said Caius. "But he won't let me see to him." There was sorrow in his voice, as though he were aching, too, at the distance stretching between them.

A part of Swift wanted to close that distance, of course. To go back to Caius and apologize. To tell Caius how intense this heat was becoming. How his head was aching and how tight his neck was. But, within the distance dividing them, stood Brooke.

Swift walked faster away from them, back toward the campfire.

"I shouldn't have let him go wandering," Caius said to Brooke.

"The best thing for Swift right now, if he is unwell, is rest," said Brooke.

Swift climbed over the log in front of the campfire and sat beside Ash.

"Is he going to give you your book back?" asked Ash.

Swift speared a stick at the fire. "I doubt it."

Brooke and Caius, holding hands, passed before them into the ring of logs.

"If you ask me," said Brooke, standing before Swift and Ash, "everyone just needs to try and relax." She smiled sweetly down at them. "Why don't you two be off to bed? You have to be at least a little tired. And listening to the ocean through the beach house's windows as you fall asleep—doesn't that sound lovely?"

Caius discreetly took her by the waist and pulled her close.

He seemed to think he was speaking too low for Swift to hear as he whispered, "I think I know how to help you relax."

Brooke flashed her gaze onto Caius.

Ash, grinning at Swift, whispered, "They're making this into a porno!"

"I can't handle another second of this." Swift took Ash's arm and pulled him to standing.

"Whoa, Swift," said Ash. "You're hand's piping."

"I'm just set off is all." Swift glanced at Brooke's satchel, where she'd tucked *The Shepherd of the Stars*. "Can I at least take my book to bed with me?"

"That isn't a good idea," said Caius. "It'd keep you up late and wear you down to nothing. You need to be rested if you want to go at your med texts tomorrow."

Brooke slipped her hand into Caius' front trouser pocket. She drew it out and presented two capsules.

"What you can do is take these." She held them out to Swift.

It was a medicine Dr. Keats had prescribed, for staving off a fever that might be escalating.

"They'll help you relax and will keep you asleep through the night," said Brooke. "Take care that you make your bed warmly and remain quiet. Doing so should keep any fever at bay."

Swift didn't look at her. Couldn't look at her.

Ash held out his hand. "I'll see that he takes them."

Brooke gave him the capsules. "I'd like him to have a full glass of water with those, then straight to sleep."

"You got it." Ash tossed his arm around Swift's shoulders and guided him toward the beach house.

20

Swift struck a match, brightening Ash's face.

He hushed the flame inside an old oil lantern, keeping its wick barely simmering.

He glanced at Ash.

It seemed, at this moment, Ash could be trusted. That finally they were salvaging what they'd lost. What they'd broken.

"Where could Caius have hidden your book?" Ash whispered.

The beach house wasn't large, but it kept plenty of great places to conceal *The Shepherd of the Stars*. Swift's only hope lay in the possibility that Caius hadn't tried very hard to hide it.

Perhaps, though, he hadn't.

When Caius had stumbled through the front door in the wee hours, his face bright and cheered by his wine, his hand clasping Brooke's, they'd spent just a minute downstairs before stumbling up to the master bedroom.

"I bet he stuffed it someplace by the front door." Swift picked up the lantern and led Ash toward the entryway.

At the base of the stairs, he paused.

Caius and Brooke, up there, behind the closed door, were speaking softly. Laughing quietly.

"What if they took it up with them?" asked Ash.

Caius and Brooke's laughter changed. Into something...else.

Swift snatched Ash's arm and pulled him away from the stairs.

As gently as he could, Swift opened the coat closet in the entryway, while Ash rifled through a cabinet, drawer by drawer. Both came up empty-handed.

A storage trunk, its old blue wood silvered by light shafting in from the cold autumn moon, caught Swift's eye.

Swift whispered, "He wouldn't have."

He opened the trunk.

The blue moon streaming in through the beach house's windows tumbled across the silver print on the aged cover of *The Shepherd of the Stars*.

"Nice work!" Ash lifted the book from among the woolen folds.

Swift and Ash together startled at the floorboards above them creaking. Rhythmically.

"We have to get out of here." Swift hurried to the front door.

Ash, staring up the flight of steps, stalled. "Don't you sort of wonder what they're doing?"

"God, no." Swift quietly lifted the lantern.

Ash crept back to the trunk.

"What are you doing?" Swift whispered. "We don't have much time."

"Getting blankets," said Ash. "If your fever spikes again, we won't be able to get to the museum tomorrow."

Ash was right. They had to be cautious. Swift had to stay well enough to make it to the museum. The pills Brooke had given him, he'd flushed.

"Warmth and quiet."

Ash handed Swift a blanket.

"That's what Brooke said you need to stay well."

Swift softly opened the front door and slipped out, Ash following.

They together broke into a run, racing each other beneath

Pembrokeshire's blazing constellations, Draco the starry black dragon and Cygnus the blue swan bright in flight straight above.

They tore to the campsite on the beach, its kindling cold now, where they'd been reading *The Shepherd of the Stars* before Caius confiscated it. Before Brooke slipped it into her satchel, keeping it. Damn Brooke.

Ash won their race, reaching the charred firewood an instant before Swift.

He hollered.

"Hey, quiet." Swift, needing to catch his breath, knelt in the cold sand.

"We don't have to be quiet anymore," said Ash. "I mean, Brooke and Caius couldn't hear us from all the way out here."

"Caius seems to have a sixth sense when it comes to what I'm up to." Swift swelled the flame inside the lantern. "I'd rather not tempt fate."

Ash checked the dark house behind them. "Any chance they'll see our light?"

"Their bedroom doesn't look out this way. They won't see us unless they come downstairs."

Swift dropped back to sitting in the sand.

Ash knelt before him. "Well, open the book to where we left off." He inched closer. "Let's find out if it talks about those old Welsh clans—whether they're still around. What secrets they might've kept."

A noise sounded—far off, from the north. From the Wentletrap Forest.

It was like a dog's howl, but more savage. Like something hungry or in pain.

It was the same sound that he'd heard earlier tonight.

And he'd heard something very like it, too, on the night of the accident. It was the sound the fisherman had said was "a summons."

Swift stared at the forest's deep shadow, looming up the coast, delivering to the wind a smell of wildness, of leaf litter, of pine.

The noise struck louder—its shrillness, its ferocity sending a chill through him.

"Have you ever heard a noise like that?" asked Swift.

"Probably." Ash shrugged. "It's just a night noise. Only someone's dog."

The howl—the creaturely scream—rang again.

That was no dog. And there were no people around here to have dogs.

But Ash seemed unafraid. He seemed hardly to have noticed.

"Go on," said Ash. "Try to read more of your book. Like you said, we don't have much time."

Swift flipped through the stiff pages of *The Shepherd of the Stars* to where he and Ash had left off—to a section entitled, *The People of the Stones.*

There lay a woodblock illustration of an ancient oak tree, sharp points of starlight descending in the background.

A man was drawn at the base of the tree, holding a streaming lantern.

Looking at this picture brought a strong sense of what he'd seen not two hours ago, when, in the Wentletrap, he'd spied a ghostly person moving by low lamplight.

But he couldn't really say it was the same. The fevers made him second-guess his perception, and even now he was struggling through a fit of chills that signaled the onset of an intense one.

But who knew? The eerie person in the forest with his lantern could've been a hallucination. And the glowing eyes Swift had sighted—that'd sighted him—what if they'd been nothing more than a waking dream?

Swift laid the book in the sand. Closed it.

"What's the matter?" asked Ash, a tint of frustration in his voice. "We have to keep reading."

But Ash looked more than frustrated. Was he angry?

Swift watched him, waiting to see which side might get the better of him.

Ash asked more softly, "Don't you want to keep reading?"

He was trying to recover his patience. And of course Swift should give him the space to check himself.

"I know you can do this," said Ash, more gently still.

"What if Caius is right, though?" asked Swift. "What if I'm only creating distractions by exploring this? Caius wants me to set aside all these fantasies."

Ash crouched closer. "Think about what you saw in the Wentletrap."

"What if what I saw wasn't real?"

"Look." Ash shifted to sitting by him. "You have to keep your brother out of your head. He means well, I'm sure, but he's bloody controlling."

He pulled the book back onto Swift's lap.

"And besides, he doesn't understand these books like we do." He caught Swift's glance. "They aren't fantasies. They're histories."

Ash cast a puckish expression, and by it Swift felt he was slipping straight back to his childhood.

He glanced back at the beach house, where Caius and Brooke were certainly knotted up together in the sheets.

It suddenly seemed not to matter whether *The Shepherd of the Stars* was history or fantasy, whether it was a distraction or a support. There seemed to be enough truth in the fact of himself and his best friend venturing through it together, entranced.

Swift shifted to kneeling in the cold sand.

By the light of his lantern, he opened *The Shepherd of the Stars*.

Ash settled in front of him, beside the cold embers. "Read it to me like you were doing before they caught us. It's okay if you have to go slowly."

Swift smoothed the page. "This bit mentions Cynfael Maddox."

"That's incredible," said Ash. "What does it say?"

Swift read—

"Cynfael Maddox came to be known as 'The Shepherd of the Stars' by his peculiar fondness for wandering along starry

beaches, through ancient oak forests by night, speaking wisdom to the ocean, to the trees. Some say he cast spells on the people he happened upon."

"Whoa," said Ash. "That's precisely what you described seeing tonight. Do you think that man you saw cast a spell on you?"

"I don't know—he didn't come near me," said Swift. "Or—I don't think he did." He wiped at his eyes, tearing from the wind, and from a heat welling in his chest.

The lighthearted expression faded from Ash. "That fisherman you saw the night you and Caius wrecked—if he's some sort of descendant from Maddox's clan, maybe he didn't just land that knife cut on your chest, but actually did cast a spell on you. The Shepherd of the Stars clan—if they do have mystical powers and foresight, maybe your struggle to read, to focus, is because of a spell. What if your whole fever disease is some sort of curse?"

Swift laid aside the book.

"We have to keep going." Ash glanced at the beach house.

"I want to." Swift shivered. "It's just—I'm getting so cold."

Ash threw one of the blankets around Swift's shoulders. "Should we light the campfire?"

"No way. We can re-hide the book well enough, but when Caius wakes up, the first thing he'll do is come out here and make sure the embers are dowsed." Swift pulled the blanket tightly around him. "He'd definitely notice if more wood were burned."

"Can't you read any more?" Ash tucked the second blanket around Swift. "Try. Or let me."

Swift handed him the book.

Ash rifled through. "I'll see if I can find anything more about Maddox's spells."

Swift snugged the blankets up around his neck and ears. They were woolen blankets and very thick—where they enclosed him, heat blazed. But the cold wind drifting from the ocean, trickling through the gaps, felt like a drenching of icy seawater.

Ash bent low to the lantern and studied a page. "You said this handwriting here is like the penmanship in *The Star of Atlantis*?"

"I think it's the very same. But I'll need to get that book back from Octavian to be sure."

"What if that book is cursed, too?" asked Ash. "What if the bloody Sunstone is cursed? What if all this is the reason you and Caius almost drowned, when you led him into that deathtrap of Sterncastle Cove?"

Swift lowered his gaze.

"Oh! Here's something." Ash laid the book on the sand before them.

"Those encountering Cynfael Maddox often reported leaving his presence dazed."

Ash pulled closer the lantern. "You had to be dazed as you sailed off from that fisherman into those deadly night waters." He glanced at Swift. "Weren't you dazed?"

"I guess, but that was the fever disease starting," said Swift. "Not a curse."

"And I'd say you're looking a bit dazed now," said Ash. "You might be lucky the man you saw tonight didn't cut you."

"If Cynfael Maddox and his clan cut everyone stumbling onto their path, wouldn't the book talk of them as villains more than heroes? And wouldn't it speak plainly of his violence if people left his presence cut and blood-poisoned rather than 'dazed?'"

"Cut and blood-poisoned." Ash held up the lantern. "Are you all right? I mean, even in this poor light, I can tell the color's gone out of your face. That's one of the signs Brooke told me to look out for—it might mean a fever's starting."

Swift was unable to control the shivering now. "We should go in."

"One more second." Ash flipped through more pages. "Whoa—listen to this—

"The so-called 'spells' Cynfael Maddox used—some believe these to be bits of great thoughts and wisdom. Insights about the Celtic seven-pointed star, about seafaring, astronomy, and mathematics."

Ash thumbed back a few pages. "That would explain why there are so many maths formulas and chemistry looking things and such rubbish scrawled all over the place in this book. These might somehow be Cynfael's pieces of wisdom. Or somehow his curses."

"Ash," Swift whispered.

The fever was definitely spiking. Swift's skin and muscles were quaking with the sensation of ice touching him, but inside his chest and belly, it seemed lava was boiling.

"Listen," said Ash.

"People encountering the spirit of Cynfael Maddox, over centuries, often reported that they felt a sense of destiny, a great wisdom imparted. Many think of him as a true renaissance man—a magnificent teacher with endless ideas and knowledge. And some in his company were known to be gifted with foresight."

Swift tried to catch Ash's glance. "I need..."

Ash read on—

"And their lives, after meeting Maddox, often were changed."

Ash finally looked at Swift. "Your life certainly did change. But do you think that the fisherman imparted any wisdom?"

Swift lost all strength and fell to his side.

"Swift?" Ash knelt over him.

Swift couldn't speak. Couldn't breathe.

The trembling from the fever seemed more than just chills.

His body was spasming.

Seizing.

Dr. Keats had said seizures were possible. And Swift was losing all control of his body.

"Get Caius," Swift said, or tried to.

In what seemed like seconds later, Caius was kneeling over him, pushing back the blankets, clearing away the kindling pile Swift's wild hands were hitting.

"You're okay." Caius held on to Swift's shoulder. "I have you."

Brooke knelt at Swift's head and gently guarded his face from the sand he was kicking up.

"From the porch, I saw him tip," Caius said to Ash. "Was he seizing before then, or did this just begin?"

Ash's face was tear-streaked. "I don't know."

Brooke filled a syringe. Caius held down Swift's arm as she injected it.

The shot incited a pleasurable buzz that took Swift's mind off the fact that he hardly could move. After a moment, his body calmed, and he dropped into a state of complete exhaustion.

"Is he not breathing?" asked Ash. "What's happening?"

"This is a febrile seizure," said Brooke, calmly. "It looks scary, I know. But he'll be all right."

Caius, seeming to catch Brooke's half-lie, glanced at her.

Swift knew exactly what Caius was thinking. It was a bad sign that a fever had stricken so hard as to spur this.

Caius carefully dusted sand from Swift's face. "If we hadn't happened to come down just then…"

Ash bent closely over Swift. "Is he through it?"

Caius moved Ash back. "What were you two even doing out here?"

"My fault," Swift whispered.

Ash, clever as always in a tight place, slid their contraband book beneath a discarded blanket.

"No, the fault was mine," said Ash. "Swift said he was hot. I thought coming outside would help."

Caius pinned Ash with a glare. "Next time, check with us."

"We were going to"—Ash glanced from Caius to Brooke—"but…"

Caius' look sharpened. "Understand, lad. If you can't help

us care for Swift—if you interfere with the rest that he needs—then you're gone."

Ash, gone. Ash—the only help Swift really had, with Caius well-claimed by Brooke. Ash—Swift's only link to feeling that he was in any sort of control.

"I'm sorry," said Ash. "I can't tell you how sorry. Of course I want to care for Swift. Please, let me stay. I've tried to help him. I'll keep trying."

"You can save your begging," said Caius. "I really don't buy it. You're proving more distracting to him than any legend book."

The words seemed to sink Swift.

Brooke offered Caius a gentling look. "This may have happened to Swift whether they came out here or not. You know that, right?"

"This shouldn't have happened." Caius glanced at Ash. "Trusting him seems to have been a mistake."

Darkness encased Swift. Whether he was losing some consciousness, or whether another fit of seizing was coming on, he couldn't tell. All he knew was that he couldn't feel whether he was breathing.

"I truly am sorry," said Ash.

"One more false move out of you," said Caius, "and I'm sending you straight back to Devon. Got it?"

"Can't..." Swift snatched Brooke's hand. "Can't breathe."

Brooke dug into her medical bag and handed Caius a vial.

Caius snapped off its cap as she tore a syringe from its plastic. She quickly drew the medicine and injected it into Swift's arm.

"What's happening?" Ash backed away.

Swift cast out his hand and took hold of the cuff of Ash's trousers.

Caius rested his hand on Swift's shoulder. "Deep, slow breaths. You are breathing, see? In seizures, it just sometimes feels like you can't."

"Do we need to take him to a hospital?" Ash blotted his face.

"Not at this point," said Brooke. "But we will need to watch him." She glanced at Caius. "Why don't I take the first shift? I'm used to nights and am well-awake anyhow."

Caius drew Swift into his arms.

"Your leg—can you manage him?" asked Ash. "Can I help?"

Caius moved past him. "You've done plenty."

In this semi-consciousness, flashbacks struck Swift of being a small boy, of Caius carrying him up to his room. Even sedated, this was mortifying, being helpless and carried. And it was far more embarrassing that this was happening in front of Ash.

Despite the humiliation, though, Swift found he could relax into what was happening. He was in Caius' care in a way he hadn't been since they'd arrived. That felt good. And the way Caius was looking at him, he seemed apologetic. Maybe he now felt his negligence, his preoccupation with Brooke.

The next thing he knew, Swift was lying on his cot in the beach house, his body hot with blankets piled around him, his face cooled by a cloth in Brooke's hand.

21

Swift opened his eyes to find himself lying on his cot, to see Brooke watching him, her hand on his head, her thumb gently stroking his hair.

The room was still dark, but for a pale of dawn levitating from under the window.

"Where's Caius?" Swift whispered.

"Sleeping, I hope." Brooke clicked on a low lamp. "How are you feeling?"

The last time Swift had dropped unconscious with these fevers, it'd been a coma. This sleep seemed more induced by the shots Brooke had given him, and he found he could breathe, swallow, move normally.

Catching his face in a wall mirror opposite him, though, he hardly recognized himself. How shadowed his eyes looked, how gaunt his face.

The humiliation he'd felt last night struck anew, at anyone seeing him in this state of unwellness.

"You don't have to stay with me." He sat up.

She straightened his pillow and eased him to resting against it. "I want to stay."

"Do you?" asked Swift. "It seems you'd rather be up there with Caius."

A bit of the warmth left her face, and what replaced it looked like sorrow.

"I mean"—Swift glanced at his arm, sore from the injections—"you've done a lot for me. But I see why you're really here. And I see, truly, why Caius came, too."

She leaned her cheek against her hand. "It must be difficult for you, watching Caius take interest in somebody else."

She rested her fingers on his forehead.

"I think the fever might be leaving you."

Swift cringed back. "How can you stand to touch me like this?"

"There's no 'standing' about it. Seeing people sick rouses compassion in me. And seeing Caius' beloved brother unwell is enough to break my heart. When I say I want to take care of you, I mean it."

She set her hand on his shoulder.

"I promise you—you're the reason I'm here. Caius is a bonus."

"I'm not sure I'm Caius' 'beloved brother' anymore. I think I'm his nuisance more than anything."

Brooke drew back her hand. "Did you know that the first thing Caius and I ever talked about was you?"

Swift rested more closely into the pillow and watched her.

"Caius and I met when I presented to a class of his," said Brooke. "I could tell, by the way he was watching me, that he had more on his mind than nurse-doctor dynamics."

Swift eased the covers higher over his chest. "I don't like where this is going."

"Just listen." Brooke straightened. "After the class, Caius approached me and said—'I have a brother who would've loved your lecture, particularly the piece about a nurse's responsibility to tune into the patient's pain.' So I asked—'Oh? What kind of doctor is he? Or is he a medical student?' And Caius replied—'He's twelve.' I saw how special Caius was, to have a dear little brother on his mind. And I certainly understood how special you are. How close you two are."

"You talked to Caius' class about sensitivity to pain?"

Swift rested back more. "He never told me that."

"Doctors—the good ones—are lovely, and they're quite sensitive. But they're so overwhelmed, they often can't do much themselves for our patients' comfort. That's where we nurses come in."

"When I'm a doctor someday, I'm going to be the sort that does something about pain. I'm going to change things so sick and hurt people don't have to suffer so much."

Brooke gently smiled. "I believe you."

"I'm not so sure you should," said Swift. "Making it into the Practicum sometimes feels beyond impossible."

She studied him a moment.

"Keep in mind that the pathway to great places isn't always direct," she said. "To get where you're headed, some creative navigation might be called for. The accident you weathered and the challenges you're facing—I think they'll make you all the stronger when you reach your journey's end."

"I'll have to master more than twenty books," said Swift, "all as tough as that biochemistry text. There'll be some kind of difficult project. I'll have to sit through an interview with a doctor and observe and assist in rounds. Plus, they want an essay on my personal philosophy of medicine, which will have to be outstanding. And if I manage all that—I'll have only made it in. In the Practicum itself, I'll have to perform well, or they'll boot me."

He struggled to sit up higher.

"When I think of it all, it's like I'm back on that islet, seeing the shore and incapable of reaching it. It's like I'm watching Caius take that fall. It's like I'm seeing him in the water, and it seems he's not breathing."

"Swift." She rested her hand on his arm.

"I mean, would Dr. Keats even want me in the Practicum if he knew I didn't rescue Caius, but instead almost killed him?"

She placed her hand gently on his chest, alongside the cut, the way Caius usually did. "Try to slow down your breathing."

For the first time since Swift had met Brooke, it seemed like she was on his side, as much as she was allied with Caius.

Or—more accurately, it was like there simply weren't sides.

Swift closed his eyes. He let the vision of Caius bleeding into the sand fade.

"You've got a lot of trauma to recover from," said Brooke. "Even though you're healing, the shock of seeing your brother as you found him—and then caring for him and fighting to reach help—I can't imagine the despair you suffered that night." She tightened the blanket across him. "That's plenty for one lad to carry. So don't burden yourself by allowing the talk that you're giving me about almost killing Caius. That isn't what happened."

"I know." Swift found himself reaching for her hand. "I don't know why I go there sometimes."

She took his hand and held it warmly between both of hers.

22

When Swift again opened his eyes, Brooke was gone.

Caius was standing across the room, looking out the screen door at the sea. Beneath Swift's hand rested the Sunstone, just like it had when he'd been in the coma.

"Hey," Swift whispered.

Caius turned. Brightened. "Well, that's better." He came to standing beside Swift's cot. "I was beginning to entertain nightmares that this might end in another coma."

"Febrile seizures don't often go that way, do they?"

"Not often," said Caius. "But you'll find, as a doctor yourself someday, that when your own people are hurting, you'll feel most helpless. My knowledge of how trauma can go south—it's haunting. And while you slept, you again slipped into mumbling that mantra of yours, reciting the names of your favorite stars, speaking in Old Norse, in Celtic Akkadian, as you did in the coma."

"That delirium was likely from the shots that Brooke gave me."

"It might've been." Caius felt Swift's forehead. "Still. We doctors are cursed with anxiety."

"You're talking like you're already a doctor."

"I feel like one." Caius sat on Swift's cot. "Or that I soon will be one. You and Brooke are having some influence on me."

"Brooke?" Swift sat up a touch. "I thought she was pushing for you to back off."

Caius let a half-smile come. "She's only been like that when Mum's around." He opened the front of Swift's shirt. "Mum would be glad, you know, if I gave up medicine and took on something easier." He met Swift's eyes. "But Mum doesn't understand that the worst thing for me would be to give up on my dream. You and Brooke, though, seem to get it." He gently felt around Swift's healing cut.

Swift glanced beyond Caius, toward the old blue trunk. On its top rested *The Shepherd of the Stars*.

Swift tipped his chin at it. "You didn't hide that very well."

Caius let out a small laugh. "It was very wrong of me to take that from you." He closed Swift's shirt. "Can you forgive me?"

"I'm apparently the one who should apologize," said Swift. "You framed it like I'd cruelly lied to you."

"My wound from laying into you—it's salty enough. Let me off the hook, will you?"

"You weren't wrong," said Swift. "I did lie. Or I at least kept back a bit of the truth. I felt like I had to, though. I wasn't trying to be cruel."

"I don't think you were meaning to keep the book from me," said Caius. "To be straight, I think you were keeping it from Ash. Your hiding it from me was more collateral damage."

The fact that Caius could see straight into him like this—it was the best thing about being his brother. And the worst. Caius probably had seen all along that Swift had been acting deceitful.

"Where is Ash?" asked Swift.

"The house feels peaceful with him elsewhere, doesn't it? He retreated—again—to the maritime museum. After breakfast, he said he wanted to clear his head by walking there, then quickly left. I'm sure he was uncomfortable being in the same room with me, after what I said to him last night. I'm not as angry as I was, but it seems I really got to him."

"You wouldn't actually send Ash away, right? He is helping me. And I think I'm helping him."

"It's always going to be difficult for me to trust him, I think," said Caius. "And it seems you don't fully trust him either. You did want to hide that book from him, yes?"

"A part of me did." Swift toyed with the Sunstone. "I think Ash has it in him to be the caring person I once knew—to become a true friend again. In reading that book together, I felt we were finally connecting."

Caius raised his brow. "You don't think he's your true friend now?"

"He's getting there, I think," said Swift. "But when he came looking for me last night, we got into a slight argument. He called me selfish—but exploring that book together seemed to bring him around."

Caius held quiet a moment, as though working to master an upwelling anger.

"That lad is ungracious," he said. "He's clearly struggling to get past your old competition."

But was Caius not being ungracious? Was he not refusing to give Ash a chance to right himself?

Swift started to sit up higher, to argue the point.

Caius stopped him.

"I know—it upsets you that I can't warm to Ash. But I'm your brother, and so a little protective. That's just the way of things."

"You can't deny that Ash is helping me," said Swift. "I got further reading to him in *The Shepherd of the Stars* than I've gotten in any medical text. Caius—reading that, there's no block."

"Well, it's great that this is the case, because—I guess now is as good a time as any to tell you."

He more fully faced Swift.

"That curator, Octavian Krakau, called."

Swift shot to sitting straight.

"I see why you described him as shady," said Caius. "Ten seconds into our conversation, I had a good sense of his greed."

Swift clenched his fingers around the Star of Atlantis.

"What did he say?"

"Despite his best efforts, he failed at convincing the Welsh authorities that your Star of Atlantis relics should belong to his museum. The island we wrecked on, in Sterncastle Cove—it's outside every boundary." A small smile lit him. "I suppose you might say that it's pirate country."

A beam of sun brightened the window, brightened the whole room, as a weight seemed to vanish from Swift's chest.

It seemed something wonderful had just clicked into place, delivering a feeling of rightness. Of homeness.

He wondered whether this sense of things working out might be the feeling of destiny playing out its course.

"Most of the islets along the coast are incorporated," said Caius. "But not Sterncastle Cove. Whoever hid the Star of Atlantis did a bloody good job securing it to fall by rights to its finder. And its book and map, likewise, can't be traced to an origin that would let any institution or government claim them."

"Then—they're forever mine." Swift cradled the Sunstone.

"Unless you want to sell them," said Caius.

"I don't." Swift dropped to leaning against his pillow.

"You'll have to prepare yourself—they're worth quite a bit. And that Krakau guy is sure to make some sleazy pitch."

"It doesn't matter," said Swift. "I've made up my mind."

Caius studied him. "I can deal with him if you're too spent."

"I'll talk to him myself," said Swift.

"You sure you're up for that? You've slept restlessly. And Brooke's managed to get the fever out of you—but only in the last couple of hours."

"I just feel a little overworked is all," said Swift.

"If you want to go ahead to the museum," said Caius, "I'm fine with that. But it'll just be you and Ash."

"Why wouldn't you come with us?"

Warmth came into Caius' face. "Because today is the last day I can register for the fall term with my university in Bristol. Brooke and I plan to drive to their Haverfordwest campus and sign me up."

Swift jumped out of the cot and stood before him. "You're legit doing this?"

"Do you think it'll be good for your motivation if your brother's all the way in the drink with you?"

It was all Swift could do not to throw his arms around Caius.

Caius rose. "Get dressed. Brooke and I will drive you to the museum when you're ready. We'll take your bikes, and you and Ash can ride home if you feel up to it."

The memory flashed of riding his bike at twilight; of sitting at the precipice of the Wentletrap; of seeing the man with a lantern moving among the trees; of the curious lights brightening the canopy.

Maybe today held another chance for him to peer into the Wentletrap. If Ash wanted to spend the whole day at the museum with Octavian—which seemed likely—Swift could bike to the brink of the Wentletrap. Maybe he'd spy the cloaked wanderer again. Maybe he'd get a better look at the signs.

And it seemed even possible that he might cross paths with the fisherman. After all, on the night of the accident, when the fisherman had vanished from the beach, there was no place for him to go except into the Wentletrap.

But stealing a glimpse into the forest again might mean encountering those beasts. What if he had to face them again?

But here, in the broad light of day, the thought of their glowing eyes didn't trouble him. If Swift were to take a look inside the border of the forest beneath the strong sun that was rising and backlighting Caius—the coast seemed as safe as it always had been.

"If you start feeling unwell," said Caius, "I'll need to know that you'll call us. We've set up a mobile booster, so getting in touch with us won't be an issue."

"I'm sure I'll be fine," said Swift.

Caius looked at him sidelong. "After what happened last night—can I trust you to take it easy? If you feel a fever coming on, you need to let Ash know. And you must call me."

"I learned my lesson," said Swift.

Caius looked at him yet harder. "Can I trust you not to flush the medicine Brooke gives you?"

"Ash told you."

"He did," said Caius. "But he didn't have to. If you'd taken those meds, the seizure likely wouldn't have happened. No more tough guy, okay? No more bullheadedness."

"I wasn't trying to be a tough guy," said Swift. "The truth is —if it'd been you who gave me those capsules, I would've taken them. It was that Brooke gave them to me."

Caius sat back down.

Swift lowered his gaze. "It was that Brooke drew them out of your pocket like she did. Either those capsules were going into the loo, or my dinner was."

Caius drew him to sitting on the cot's edge.

"Look, we don't have to talk about her," said Swift, "I—"

"It's very normal, I think," said Caius, "for brothers, as close as we are, to feel a little jealous when someone else comes along. Who knows but that I might be a bit jealous of Ash? Maybe that's where part of my distrust is coming from. Though—I doubt it."

Swift studied his hands, remembering how warmly Brooke had held them. "I think I may have turned a corner with Brooke this morning."

Caius glanced at him. "Yeah?"

"She was very kind to me. She spoke of compassion. Of wanting to ease people's pain."

Caius tilted more to facing him. "I want you to like Brooke. The fact that you've struggled has been a bit hard for me. I don't want to be with someone you don't like."

"I like her." Swift shrugged. "Maybe I just don't like you being so close with anyone."

"I get that," said Caius. "But here you are, at all of fourteen —you're still a ways from understanding how deeply I feel for her."

Swift pulled away. "You really don't have to explain it."

"And I won't." Caius straightened. "Brooke and I think it's best if we cool things off. I'm sorry, actually, if we've freaked you lads out. What we've got going—it probably looks sappy from your point of view."

"That's an understatement. But—I really don't care anymore. I see how happy she makes you."

"Happy doesn't begin to describe it. It's like"—Caius opened his palms; studied his fingers—"it's like her heart is the most precious thing on Earth, and it's resting in my hands. I feel so lucky to have her. You'll understand this yourself one day."

"But trying to keep away from each other," said Swift, "that sounds awkward and artificial. I don't want to make you do that."

"It's all right," said Caius. "Forcing ourselves apart now—it'll just make things hotter when we're finally together."

"That's plenty." Swift shoved him off the cot.

23

Swift settled his suitcase onto his cot, beside where Ash was sitting.

He pulled off his T-shirt and tucked it in a corner of the case. He drew out a clean hoodie.

Ash glanced at the scar forming on Swift's chest. "Does that still hurt?"

"The pain is sharp," said Swift. "Mainly when I accidentally touch it."

"Are you glad the fisherman cut you?" asked Ash.

Swift gave him an odd look.

"I mean—it's a battle scar," said Ash. "And it seems sort of right that, if Caius came out of the accident marred, you would, too."

"Am I glad I got cut with a dirty knife and landed an infection that dropped me into a coma and almost killed me?" asked Swift. "No."

"I bet Caius is secretly glad. It probably seems like justice that your suffering sort of matches his." Ash picked up the Sunstone, lying next to Swift's suitcase. He held it up to the window. "It ties you two together in a way. Makes you even."

Swift watched him carefully. This was how Ash often

thought—in binary terms of deficit and payback. Never would he let an injury go unanswered.

"Caius hates that this happened to me." Swift pulled on the hoodie. "He isn't the sort who needs to get even."

Ash peered at the Sunstone through a gem lens Octavian had given him. "I can't believe this is actually yours."

Though the sun was now dampened by thick clouds, and though the room was just lamplit, the Sunstone captured the scarce light and held it, presenting a warm, gentle glow.

"Neither can I," said Swift.

"Though—I also can't understand why you don't want to sell it."

"Its worth is unfathomable," said Swift, "and has nothing to do with money."

"That makes no sense," said Ash. "What Octavian's willing to pay you for this—wouldn't that put you through med school? I know your family doesn't have as much money as mine does. Someone gave your father the *Regulus*, didn't they? Your father didn't buy his boat like my father did."

"If I make it into the Practicum—if I can make it through— I'll have scholarships to put me through med school."

Swift held out his hand for the Sunstone.

Ash gave it to him. "Octavian's going to be raving jealous. I'm glad you have to be the one to tell him you won't sell. I've only ever told him good news."

"I'm sure he was ecstatic when you told him you'd sell him your box." Swift closed the suitcase.

"That," said Ash, "and even this morning, I had some fun bringing him good news."

"What news?" Swift struggled with the suitcase's fasteners.

"About you finding *The Shepherd of the Stars*, of course."

"Hang on." Swift dropped the case, spilling everything. "You told Octavian?"

Ash stood. "While you were resting, I visited the museum. I thought Caius mentioned where I was."

"Yeah, but I didn't guess you'd tell him I found another relic."

Ash shrugged. "What's the problem? He'd already called to say everything belongs to you."

"But"—Swift knelt before the case—"I haven't reported *The Shepherd of the Stars* to the Welsh authorities. I was planning to call them this week—but I wasn't going to say a word to Octavian." He glanced at Ash. "Now Octavian will probably go after it."

"Oh." Ash shifted away. "I hadn't thought of that."

It was hard to believe. Ash might not be book smart, but he was bloody cunning.

"I guess I just wanted to tell him something positive," said Ash. "It felt considerate, seeing as how he was about to lose everything."

"He isn't 'losing' anything." Swift shoveled his clothes back into the case. "My relics never were his."

"But for a time, they weren't really yours either," said Ash.

"Why'd you even go to the museum earlier?" Swift lifted his case back onto the cot. "Didn't they display your box yesterday?"

"I didn't know whether you'd still be up for going." Ash shrugged. "And besides, I was bored. You were dead out, and Brooke and Caius were all over taking care of you. I needed something to do."

Swift lifted *The Shepherd of the Stars* off the trunk. Ash "needed something to do," so he'd gone straight to the person most ambitious to claim Swift's treasures. And he'd betrayed that Swift had found another one.

"Surely, the Welsh authorities will let you keep *The Shepherd of the Stars*," said Ash.

Swift, cradling the book, sank onto his cot. There were certainly no guarantees. They might judge it to be stolen property, seeing as Swift had taken it from the longboat.

Caius stepped through the kitchen doorway. "You lads ready?"

Swift didn't respond. Didn't look at him.

"What's up?" Caius glanced between Swift and Ash.

Swift set the book aside. "Nothing's up." He forced the fasteners on his suitcase to close.

"Not feeling feverish?" asked Caius.

"The medicine Brooke gave me is keeping me very cool," said Swift. "We're almost ready."

Caius cast Ash a serious look. "Promise you'll take good care of Swift today?"

"Of course." Ash offered his most charming smile.

It really was one of his most enchanting looks. It even seemed to relax Caius some.

"And you'll call me if he feels unwell?" asked Caius. "If that happens, you won't let him ride, yes?"

"I can call you myself," said Swift. "I already told you I would."

Caius backed up. "We'll be in the car."

Swift pulled his shoes out from under the cot.

Ash watched Caius leave, then knelt before Swift. "Look, it's me who messed up this time. I should've told you right away that I'd mentioned *The Shepherd of the Stars* to Octavian."

Swift glanced at him.

"I mean, I shouldn't have told Octavian in the first place." Ash glanced at *The Shepherd of the Stars*. "But seriously—you're going to get to keep this. If I'd doubted it, I would never have told Octavian. Right?"

Seeing Ash kneeling before him, his hand gently resting on Swift's knee, like a close brother, like a true friend—Swift found he couldn't stay upset.

Ash could be manipulative, without a doubt. But he could also be just thoughtless.

"I guess so," said Swift.

"I really do want you to keep *The Shepherd of the Stars*." Ash stood, holding it. "I'm dying to explore the rest, and I know you are, too. We're going to have so much fun looking through it alongside our other finds. And Octavian is chomping at the bit to see it. He'll certainly have plenty of insights."

"I'm not bringing that book with us," said Swift.

Ash looked stunned. "Why not? You have to report it, like

you said. And if we bring it, we can explore it using Octavian's artifact instruments. He has all sorts of lights and magnifiers and things."

Swift hesitated. "I don't know precisely why, but—I don't trust Octavian."

"If you don't know why, then you're just being paranoid. Octavian hasn't done anything untrustworthy, right?"

It was true that Octavian hadn't played dirty. So far. It was the Welsh authorities who'd instructed him to keep the *Star of Atlantis* book and map. But as possessive as he acted, he seemed capable of malice. Even Caius had picked up on his greed, and that was just from a phone call.

Ash held up *The Shepherd of the Stars*. "If we don't take this with us, we might never have another chance to compare it with my find. My relics and this book both speak to the culture of that Welsh clan. Do you not want to explore that a little?"

The point was sound. Even if Swift was permitted to keep *The Shepherd of the Stars*, he and Ash might never again get behind the scenes of this museum.

Ash handed *The Shepherd of the Stars* to Swift. "Octavian has no rights to this. If anything, it'll be like the Sunstone—you might get to keep it 'til they figure out what's to be done." He reached his hand to Swift.

Swift took it and let Ash guide him to his feet.

24

Caius pulled up to the door of the maritime museum. "Is this it? I can barely read that poor sign."

"It's nicer than it looks," said Swift, from the backseat.

"It doesn't seem much like a museum," said Brooke, "dark and holed up as it is."

"Oh, it's got wonderful displays," said Ash. "Octavian is a researcher more than anything—a specialist in rustic weapons and Welsh maritime history. And there's a big basement where he stores the artifacts he's investigating. He's let me see some of them."

"I suppose looks can be deceiving." Brooke climbed out with Ash and unhooked his bike, and Swift's.

Swift opened his back-seat door.

"Hey." Caius stopped him. "If you need to call me for any reason—do." He glanced at Ash, standing behind the car with Brooke. "I don't know what happened between you two this morning, and I see that you're not going to tell me."

Swift looked down at *The Shepherd of the Stars*, tight in his hands, for the moment.

"If he's upset you—"

"He hasn't." Swift forced a smile.

Caius held up his mobile and Brooke's, the small black signal boosters plugged into each.

"We'll be able to reach one another, all right?" Caius handed his own mobile to Swift. "I'm just a phone call away."

Swift smiled at Brooke, widening his door. "You won't hear from me. I'm glad to give you two the afternoon."

"We'll be back to the beach house by sunset, unless you call sooner." Brooke cupped his face the way Mum did. "And you will call us, if need be—yes? We're just a half-hour away."

"I took your medicine—I'll be perfectly fine." Swift glanced beyond her at the copse of tall, thin trees that marked the rim of the Wentletrap Forest. "When we're finished here, Ash and I might want to ride the coast, instead of going straight home."

Caius looked at Brooke.

She gave a small shrug. "The medicine's working. If it weren't, we would've seen another fever spike."

"Did you bring along water?" asked Caius. "Your first aid kit?"

Swift lifted his rucksack. "And a few hiking snacks."

Brooke climbed in beside Caius. "Come home by sunset in any case, all right?"

Swift nodded as he climbed out.

"Be honest with yourself about how you're doing." Caius took hold of Brooke's hand. Wove his fingers into hers. "And call us."

How they were gazing at each other—they certainly had more planned than registering Caius for the fall.

"Yeah, I'll call you." Swift backed away from the car and stood beside Ash. He handed Ash the mobile.

They together watched Caius and Brooke drive away.

Ash pocketed the mobile, then led Swift toward the museum. "Octavian said he stayed up all night researching the Star of Atlantis myth. He didn't tell me any of what he discovered. We decided to wait 'til you were with us. He said he'd come across so many insights, he might burst with the waiting!"

"I'm surprised he'd tell me anything." Swift shouldered his rucksack, soon to be heavy with his relics.

"Octavian's a great guy," said Ash. "You're the rightful owner of *The Star of Atlantis* book, the Sunstone, and the map."

He glanced at the book in Swift's hands.

"And probably *The Shepherd of the Stars*. As a professional, he should tell us all he knows about them. That's what he said, word for word."

"That's—really cool," said Swift.

As distrustful as he reflexively felt toward Octavian, the idea of learning his insights was appealing. If Octavian had research, maybe that was reason enough for Swift to not be so reserved. The more honest and upfront he was, the more he might learn.

"You have to stop thinking of Octavian as your opponent," said Ash. "I know you're competitive, and I know you don't like him. But your perception of him as a threat is hazing your judgement."

"Okay—first, I'm not being competitive. I would've given up everything if the authorities said I had to. And second, I don't dislike Octavian. I mean, I don't especially trust him. I just want to get this over with."

Ash rested his fingers on the door handle. "Just take the time to hear Octavian out. Who knows? Once you've listened to what he has to say, you might feel differently about whether to keep your finds."

Swift blocked the door. "Ash—I'm not selling them or donating them or consigning them or anything else."

"I get it," said Ash. "But just wait 'til you see Octavian at work. His appreciation for the Star of Atlantis myth is clear. Working with him, believe me, is fascinating. Course changing."

In Ash's eyes, Swift could glimpse the same subtle hunger that darkened Octavian's. For an instant, it seemed Ash wasn't just taken with Octavian's expertise, with his "appreciation" for the Star of Atlantis myth. Rather, it seemed Ash was allied with him. More than with Swift.

Ash smiled. "You ready?"

Swift moved aside for Ash to open the door.

"Mr. Emberly and Mr. Kingsley!" Octavian must have seen

them pull up. He was standing at the end of the stretching hall, waving.

"Come in, lads. Come in! What a day we're in for." He hurried to them, his eyes fixed on the book in Swift's hands. "I see you've brought your"—he licked his lips—"new find. Hurrah!"

Swift held the book tighter, a fear gripping him that Octavian might reach out with those fast arms and snap up the book.

"May I see my things?" asked Swift.

Octavian gestured to the great hall where above hung the whale bones. "I've laid your items beside Mr. Emberly's, as though on display. This will give you a slight idea of what your discoveries would look like, Mr. Kingsley, were you to place them in my care."

Swift clutched the Sunstone, heavy in his cargo pants pocket.

Octavian led them down the hall, past the cases of rustic weaponry. They seemed emptier than before.

"I think you'll find it quite grand to see your book and map displayed as they might be." Octavian glanced at Ash for a flicker of an instant before leading them in.

Swift followed him to the display—the only one in the room —at its dead center. There, a row of bright lights shone on an exhibition case, its domed covering glass tilted back.

On the right-hand end of the case lay Ash's treasure box with its papers. On its left-hand end rested *The Star of Atlantis* book, alongside its map.

Swift hurried to them. He reached for *The Star of Atlantis*.

"Ah! Ah!" Octavian jetted out his hands and stopped Swift's. "As long as these artifacts are under this roof, they shall be handled using gloves."

Swift took a pair from a box Octavian held.

"And if you'd be so kind." Octavian gestured at the book in Swift's hand.

Swift rested *The Shepherd of the Stars* on the display.

Octavian glanced at Swift's pocket, then lifted his brow.

Swift drew out the Sunstone and placed it on a blue cloth that seemed purposed to receive it.

The sharp lights beaming on the Sunstone set it to glowing as though inside it a pale fire were simmering.

"As I told Mr. Emberly this morning," said Octavian, "I've been conducting a very profitable examination of your discoveries. We wondered, knowing that, whether you'd consider consigning them to me for a few more days, perhaps a week to—"

"I'm taking them with me today." Swift stretched on his gloves.

The warmth vanished from Octavian, leaving him grim.

It was as though the smile he'd worn had been the metallic flash of a sunset lighting a bank of heavy clouds, and then fading, revealing the beauty as a mere illusion of light.

Ash, watching Swift, moved toward the end of the table, where his treasure box rested. "Want a look?"

Swift followed him to where the ancient-looking box and its aged papers were indeed laid out magnificently.

From the interior lid of the treasure box, the seven-pointed Celtic star gleamed. Before the box, etched on a gold label, scrolled the words:

Discovered by Ash Emberly, Devonshire's Boy Finder of Treasure.

"I must ask that you not touch Mr. Emberly's discoveries without my leave." Octavian moved closely beside Swift.

Swift studied the star on the box's lid. "That's exactly like what's drawn on my map. In my books."

"Indeed, it's a true Celtic Star," said Octavian. "This box belonged to the noble Atlantisean clan—those same people of enlightenment associated with your discoveries. The Celtic star, they adopted as their emblem."

Swift glanced at him. "Atlantisean?"

This was new information.

"Yes, the Atlantiseans were wanderers, pirates—people of no home and no name. Some said they were scoundrels, rogues. Others said they were heroes of legends, from Iceland, bringing knowledge and relief to folk along the coast. Because their origins are mysterious, they've come to be known as *Atlantiseans*."

Swift itched to scour *The Shepherd of the Stars* for the term.

Ash surveyed the papers from his box. "Did you find any more insights on these, as we hoped?"

"Not yet," said Octavian. "However they maintain great value. They're originals, it's clear."

"I've never come across the word *Atlantisean*," said Swift. "We've read of that clan only as *The Shepherds of the Stars*."

"The term 'Star Shepherds' does sometimes reference the whole clan. But it's more common to see it designating Cynfael Maddox, and sometimes his crew—those dauntless sojourners who once voyaged in the brave *Checkered Whelk*. A jolly band of rebels and do-gooders if ever there was one."

Swift leaned closely over Ash's parchments. He studied their lettering—faded and blurred. He couldn't help wondering if, seen through the Sunstone, hidden words would appear.

Swift glanced at Octavian. "Have these letters decomposed, or do you think they were written this way?"

"Time may have scuffed those letters," said Octavian. "I'm studying them digitally to see what I might make out. Mainly, they describe what the Atlantiseans did routinely. There are a few calendars of tides, along with schedules of fishing and growing seasons."

"Schedules." Ash rolled his eyes. "You're making them sound even more boring than they are. Let's get on with the plan to see what Swift's Sunstone might show."

The plan. Of course Ash had a plan. When Ash told Octavian about *The Shepherd of the Stars*, he must've also spilled that Swift had used the Sunstone—its distortion effect—to reveal text written in code.

"If you knew about that theory, why have you not tested it?" asked Swift. "Didn't you say before that you yourself have a Sunstone?"

"Not a navigational one."

Octavian glanced at the Star of Atlantis.

"You, Mr. Kingsley, are the sole known possessor of an authentic piece of Icelandic spar, which certainly once belonged to the Atlantiseans."

Ash seemed fidgety and pale with what must be keen anticipation to discover what the Sunstone might reveal on his box's documents.

"I'd appreciate it," said Octavian, "so very much, if you'd allow me a look through the Sunstone."

Though Swift instinctively bristled at the thought of Octavian's hands on the Star of Atlantis, he'd been generally professional. And having a knowledgeable curator take a look would certainly be advantageous for Ash's discovery.

Swift glanced at his Sunstone. "Please be careful."

The words, out, felt foolish. Of course a museum curator would be careful.

But Swift felt he needed to say something to assert his ownership of the Sunstone.

"Of course, Mr. Kingsley." Octavian visited the table's far end and gently lifted the Star of Atlantis.

Inside his large gloves, the Sunstone seemed to vanish, as though by sleight of hand he'd nicked it.

Swift shook his head, clearing the notion. Octavian was a specialist, with insights.

Octavian hurried to Ash's parchments. "If you'll kindly move out of the light." He not so gently shoved Swift aside.

Ash lifted a gem lens from the table and stood by Octavian.

Octavian drew out a metal scope apparatus bearing a light, which he adjusted. He held the Sunstone over one of the pages and peered at it through the scope.

Ash watched him for a few long minutes.

"Do you see anything unusual?" asked Ash. "Any hidden words? Secret codes?"

Octavian lowered the apparatus. "Not a jot."

"Can Swift look?" Ash glanced at him. "He's smart with this sort of thing."

Swift looked doubtfully at Ash. If Octavian wasn't seeing coded text revealed, he himself likely wouldn't.

"Yes," said Octavian, "however, I must be the one to hold the stone. If it were to be dropped onto these parchments by a clumsy hand—how devastating."

Swift grew a bit hot at Octavian implying he was careless. As frustrated as Octavian must be, though, he might take every passive-aggressive punch that he could. Swift would just have to ignore those jabs.

Swift studied Octavian's apparatus to find its lens adjustment. Its light.

Looking through, he found it to be excellent. The small lens showed the parchment magnified at a great strength, while leaving the clarity so intact that he could make out the individual filaments of the paper. The letters, through the scope, were vivid. And indeed, they appeared distorted by the Sunstone's facets.

And yet—they were no more than letters, weathered and dim.

Swift moved to a different page. "May I?"

Octavian sighed. "You may, though I don't believe you're in for any luck. The page you've just examined was the one I believed most likely to hold a code if one did exist."

Swift and Ash examined the papers one by one, Octavian less than patiently holding the Sunstone.

No hidden markings came into clarity. These records of daily life appeared to be just that—records.

Swift handed the apparatus back to Octavian.

"But you might still find something, by further examination," said Ash, to Octavian. "Right?" There was desperation in his voice, his deep wish manifesting that further insights were yet possible.

If it were so, his box and its papers would likely be worth more—a possibility Ash would certainly recognize.

Octavian put his eye to the scope, but his expression was not at all hopeful. He again carefully surveyed the page he'd deemed most promising, and then another.

He surfaced from the exploration bearing a sorrowful expression. "I'm sorry, Mr. Emberly."

Ash, staring down at the papers, looked like he'd just been told his hard-earned money was counterfeit.

Octavian patted Ash's shoulder. "We probably dreamed of the possibilities a little too much."

The somber expression on Ash shifted to anger as he looked up at Swift. "Your books hold letters that show up through the Sunstone." He thumbed at Octavian. "Shouldn't we show him?"

Swift, a bit stung by Ash's sudden harshness, felt like saying "no." He could just pack his relics, and he and Ash could look at them on their own later, after Ash had some time to cool off.

But that seemed cruel to Octavian, who—disturbing though he was—did harbor a genuine interest in the Star of Atlantis myth.

"Octavian, would you like to look first?" Swift lifted the Sunstone from the table and held it out.

Octavian snatched it. "Very kind of you, Mr. Kingsley." He hurried to the table's other end. "We'll first explore *The Star of Atlantis* and its map, then we'll move on to *The Shepherd of the Stars.*" He glanced back at Swift, following him. "Is there nothing I can do, Young Sir, to persuade you to leave these here? If you were to consign them for a week, even, they'd be flagged by a plaque scribed with your name."

"I've made up my—"

"You, too, could be distinguished before our patrons as a 'Boy Finder of Treasure.'" Octavian readied his apparatus. "And how much more you'd feel the accomplishment, were you to sell. Everywhere I released the news of my collection, your name would be spoken."

The grandiosity in Octavian's words struck Swift as rather sad. His museum, according to Justus' research, didn't have much notoriety, nor did it have the throngs of patrons Octavian was representing.

Octavian must have a good deal of money to court and bribe Swift and Ash as he had. His museum was a quaint place, finely focused on primal warfare and Welsh maritime history—which had pleased Justus, but that was all.

"Just think," said Octavian. "We could send these treasures

on traveling displays. People worldwide would marvel at the two lads from Devonshire—the Boy Finders of Treasure."

Octavian's description of the fame Swift might achieve was doing nothing but churning up nausea.

For no gem light, nor lovely display case, nor golden label could separate the joy of finding the Star of Atlantis from the bitterness that by it, he was responsible for mortally injuring Caius.

"I've honestly thought about it," said Swift, approaching his treasures. "I can't part with them."

"If you think they're worth more than what I've offered," said Octavian, "I could reappraise them."

Ash's eyes widened.

"They are worth more than what you've offered," said Swift. "More than money, even."

"Consider though, Swift," said Ash, nearing, his eyes hard fixed on the *Star of Atlantis* book and map. "Would you be capable of taking care of these like Octavian can?"

Swift ran his hand over his eyes. "Ash—"

"Yes, encourage him," said Octavian. "And I'll tell you what, Mr. Emberly. If you succeed in persuading your friend to sell these articles to me, I might arrange a sizable finder's fee for you."

Ash, his eyes glazing, stared at Swift.

Swift turned away and focused on his "articles," which were not articles, but a part of him.

Octavian advanced. "Kindly open *The Star of Atlantis*." He held his apparatus to his eye with one hand, while gripping the Sunstone in the other.

Ash stepped closer and peered over Swift's shoulder.

Swift opened *The Star of Atlantis* and explored with his gloved finger the markings lining the top of a page.

They were laid out exactly as in *The Shepherd of the Stars*.

Octavian held the Sunstone closer over the line of markings.

Through the internal facets of the Sunstone, the cryptic marks changed into the clear script of Celtic Akkadian.

"Look how the cyphers come to life!" said Octavian. "This indeed is a script. An old script."

Swift leaned closer. "That line reads—'Listen to the trees.'"

"Ah!" Octavian jumped like he'd been physically shocked. "The lad truly reads Celtic Akkadian—and with no study aids."

"I told you—he knows all sorts of languages." The anger on Ash seemed to be seeping out slowly, leaving him looking sapped.

"I admit, I somewhat doubted it," said Octavian. "Celtic Akkadian is so very rare that it's now almost an idiolect—with not even a handful of speakers."

"That's actually the reason I know it," said Swift. "My family discovered when I was very young that I was good at picking up languages. So they presented obscure ones for me to learn. It was kind of a joke among us. A parlor trick I'd perform for their friends."

Octavian turned the page. "This one, Mr. Kingsley. We shall read it together!"

The Sunstone showed the Celtic Akkadian cyphers in clarity.

Octavian grinned. "I believe this one reads—'Through the sky, trails stretch.'

"That word is 'starlight,' I think," said Swift. "It seems there's a tiny asterisk shape in one corner of that cypher. It delineates the 'sky' symbol as referencing something related to stars."

"Why"—Octavian stared at him—"what a genius we have here."

Swift glanced at the map resting alongside, the cryptic markings present on it, too. He drew it near.

Octavian held the stone over a line of strange markings winding around the edges of the map, just beneath the seafarer's oath.

Through the Sunstone, the strange text resolved into Celtic Akkadian. And word for word, concept for concept, the line of text matched the seafarer's oath.

Come hell. Come storm waters. Come the Kraken. I'll forsake all sound shores for the night-lighted passageways—untrodden reaches—for sun-brightened visions, for insights of stars.

The fact that the two strings of text matched was wonderful. By it, Swift could pick up on Celtic Akkadian words he'd never memorized.

Odd lines were also drawn inside the picture of the forest, starting at one edge and running straight across it, then folding back in on itself.

This pattern repeated and grew tighter and tighter as it crept up the map—a true mimic to the shape of a shell's wentletrap.

Finally, the line finished at a singular point, just left of the map's center.

Swift pointed at the markings. "I wonder if these are coded, too."

Ash leaned in as Octavian hovered the Sunstone over the place where the markings began.

Celtic Akkadian letters jumped out, clear as day.

Swift turned the map, following the string of text.

"Well, this is quite baffling," said Octavian. "Many of these cyphers, I don't know."

Swift studied the characters, the grouped concepts.

Most he could read, though a few were lost on him. What he could make out, over and over, was the word "shepherd," placed next to the concept of "starlight."

It struck as likely that this was indeed a map showing the way through the Wentletrap Forest, to where something signifi-cant to the Atlantiseans—to Cynfael Maddox—might rest. Likely, his tomb.

Octavian glanced at Swift. "How about you, Mr. Kingsley? Can you unriddle this?"

How odd, Swift thought, that he himself might read words— might interpret their layout—in a way a "renowned" historian seemed unable to. And it was striking that Octavian, still, after a whole night of study, seemed not to have picked up on the anachronism of the Cthulhu.

Perhaps he wasn't the great historian Ash believed him to be.

"Well?" asked Octavian. "Can't you translate any of it?"

Maybe it was Octavian's general aura of threat, or maybe it was the way he was watching Swift with an expression partly inquisitive and partly of that same sick hunger—that greed—Swift had noted at first glance, but something persuaded Swift to conceal what he saw.

"Again, 'starlight.'" Swift pointed to the one word he knew Octavian could recognize.

Octavian bent nearer to the map. "Can you read no others?"

Swift homed in on another word—one he'd never studied, but that appeared in the oath, alongside the English text. In correlating the two, he could deduce that this was the cypher for "insight."

"This one seems familiar." Swift glanced at Octavian. "Any guesses?"

Octavian spent a moment concentrating. "No—I haven't any idea. Even using my reference books, these would take some intensive study to decipher."

Swift focused on the oath, eyeing through the Sunstone the Celtic Akkadian cyphers he didn't know. By applying them together with the words he already knew, he could make out the gist of the text folding back and forth inside the drawn forest.

It read—

Deep nights yield insights...by storm waters sail true to the bone path of seas...night-lighted forests shine in star-brightened days...the shepherd of starlight remains...

And where the words terminated near the center of the map —at the pinnacle of the Wentletrap's crown—the Sunstone revealed a tiny star.

It wasn't the asterisk shape flagging a sky concept as "starlight."

It was an actual seven-pointed Celtic star.

Octavian merely glazed over the star with the Sunstone. He seemed not to have noticed its particular clearness.

"Come on, Swift," said Ash. "Can you not read more of it?"

Swift donned his best nonchalant expression. "If I had some study aides and a bit of time, maybe."

"Try again." Ash goaded him closer to the map.

Swift took the given time to ruminate on the enigmatic words, the descriptive concepts.

They seemed, in a way, to be giving guidance—actual directions, perhaps, laid out in a riddle.

'Deep nights yield insights' seemed abstract. But *'by storm waters'* and *'sail true to the bone path of seas'* both seemed to reference the Wentletrap Forest itself. For it lay along very stormy waters, and a wentletrap spiral—the interior structure of a shell—certainly could be called a "bone path of seas."

Though, that phrase also brought to mind the concept of a way to death—a bone path.

The key phrase, though, seemed to rest at its end, near the center of the map: *'the shepherd of starlight remains.'* That, placed alongside the Celtic star symbol, truly seemed to suggest that Cynfael Maddox had once dwelt in the Wentletrap Forest.

What might it mean to find his tomb? To discover what rested inside?

As compelled as Swift had been to seek the Star of Atlantis, a desperation struck a thousand times harder to explore the Wentletrap Forest. To solve its winding trails. To learn what rested at its heart.

"Well?" Ash nudged Swift.

Swift glanced up. "I can tell you that this speaks of starlight. If I were to guess"—he thought fast, Octavian and Ash leaning in—"I'd postulate that this is a sea shanty about starlight."

"Is that all?" Ash stepped back. "That's no more remarkable than farming schedules."

Octavian, from the peculiar gaze he was laying on Swift, seemed to be guessing it certainly wasn't all.

"What about those other markings?" asked Ash. "That

grouping, laid out in rows—there, in the lower right corner. Those seem important, the way they're strung out so straight, one right after another."

Octavian centered the Sunstone above the markings that, indeed, seemed laid out in a prominent way.

"The first one—I can read it," said Octavian.

"Valor is the gateway to destiny."

"That sounds worthless, like poetry," said Ash. "Isn't there anything else?"

"Indeed, yes." Octavian shifted his hungry gaze toward Ash. "Here lay numbers."

They were numbers, a slash dividing them into units or couplets, like a decimal point. They looked like longitude and latitude listings—navigational coordinates.

The fisherman had wanted Swift to hold tightly to the Sunstone—he'd actually instructed Swift to never let go of it.

And perhaps this was why.

Perhaps the fisherman had been guarding more treasures, their locations marked here.

Octavian muttered, "I must capture this."

It was likely that he, too, had reached the conclusion that here lay coordinates.

Swift couldn't deal with the idea of Octavian Krakau—threatening-seeming, possibly deceitful, maybe even fraudulent—capturing navigational coordinates from a map that was his, using a Sunstone that'd been entrusted to him alone; navigational coordinates that might lead to the tomb of the Cynfael Maddox, where God only knew what else waited.

"I'll take a picture." Ash pulled out the mobile Caius and Brooke had given them.

"Don't." Swift lowered Ash's hand. "The flash would be damaging."

"Try, lad," said Octavian, to Ash. "Snap the photograph straight through the Sunstone."

It was unfortunate that Octavian had realized the map probably held coordinates. But Octavian having a picture of them seemed disastrous.

Swift slid himself between Octavian and the map. "You instructed me to send you only one picture of these, to protect them from harm."

"This is too important." Octavian lowered the stone closer over the map. "Who knows but that the map's real purpose was to deliver its finder not to the Sunstone, but to where these numbers lead?" He glanced at *The Shepherd of the Stars*. "And we haven't even tapped what insights that complementary book might keep."

"It's my map," said Swift. "And I'm telling you—don't take any pictures."

Ash slipped the phone around Swift and snapped a picture. "Ash—I said don't."

"Relax, I didn't use the flash." Ash, his expression gone cold, glanced at Swift. "And besides, what gives you the right to decide who these secrets belong to?" He showed the picture to Octavian.

Swift went airless at those words. It felt like Ash had gut punched him.

His mind traced the moment of Ash catching him with *The Shepherd of the Stars*; of Ash accusing him of deceit, of refusing to listen, to understand.

Ash had come around. And at the time, it'd seemed like Ash was leaning away from his tendency to use Swift.

But the fact now dawning was incontrovertible. Ash had only come around once Swift had referred to the Sunstone and *The Shepherd of the Stars* as—"Our Sunstone. Our book."

Swift had feared that Ash, upon learning the secrets the book held, would abandon him. But seeing Ash cradling a mobile showing a picture he'd just stolen—a picture he was examining closely with Octavian—Swift realized how powerless he was.

There was nothing he could do to keep Ash from abandoning him.

Ash had already abandoned him.

"Damn worthless phone," said Octavian. "The picture is too blurred. I'll set up my documentation camera."

Ash toyed with the mobile. "Maybe adjusting the settings would help."

Swift faced the table. "I'm packing my things."

"Mr. Kingsley," said Octavian. "Seeing now, as you must, the worth of these relics—will you not sell them?" Gripping the Sunstone, he advanced, his big shoulders curving over Swift. "I implore you."

"I said 'no,' and I meant it." Swift folded his map.

Octavian walked past him toward the hallway. He dislodged a stop from beneath the large door leading to it and let it fall closed.

The clap of a deadbolt rang.

"Swift—be reasonable," said Ash. "He said he'd reappraise them for you."

It was still coming as a shock that Ash was pushing him as hard as Octavian was. Whatever "finder's fee" Octavian might give Ash—was that worth putting Swift through this degree of distress?

Swift stowed the map in his rucksack, along with his two books.

Octavian, clasping the Sunstone, moved to standing before him.

Swift stared up at him. "Please give me my Sunstone."

Octavian's face darkened into an expression it seemed built for.

Fury. Violence.

He seemed sufficiently angry to rip Swift's arms off and sufficiently calculating to make it look like an accident.

"You're going to leave the Sunstone with me," said Octavian, "along with everything else."

25

Swift reached for the Sunstone. Octavian held it away.

"You can't keep it," said Swift. "It's legally mine."

"Ah, but you've decided to entrust the Sunstone, along with everything, to my museum." Octavian shuffled a folded packet of papers from his pocket.

Swift sent Ash a pleading look, but Ash was refusing to meet his eyes.

Octavian glanced at Swift's rucksack on the floor, *The Shepherd of the Stars* tucked inside, along with *The Star of Atlantis* book and its map. "I'll have that."

"Ash." Swift tried to catch his eye. "Call Caius."

"Will I have to persuade you?" asked Octavian.

Ash still didn't move. Still wouldn't look at Swift.

"You should know that I'm very effective," said Octavian, "at getting what I want."

In the discord of Octavian's threats, Swift couldn't read Ash. Ash might be in shock, stunned by this change in Octavian. Or —it felt a little like Ash's immobility was a choice; like he was siding with Octavian.

"We'll tell the authorities."

Swift gave Ash a prompting nod.

"The police."

Ash didn't move.

His fingers, which had so deftly handled the mobile to steal the picture for Octavian, were now gripping it rigidly.

And Octavian seemed not at all daunted by Swift's refusal. He kept his eyes on the rucksack, as though deliberating how he might snatch it.

Despite his hulking size, though, despite those long arms and that resolute air, perhaps Octavian was all talk.

Swift couldn't imagine he'd take this so far as to actually rob them or hurt them.

Swift lifted his rucksack from the floor. He slipped it onto his shoulder.

Octavian watched him but didn't react.

"Hand over the Sunstone," said Swift. "If you don't, we'll call the police. You'd lose everything."

Octavian—cold, staring—said, "As I'll have your signature, the police won't believe you."

He seemed so confident, so doubtless that he could intimidate Swift.

The best way Swift could imagine—maybe the only way—to counter that boldness was to display equal confidence.

"I'm not signing anything." Swift held out his palm. "Give me my Sunstone, or I will report you."

Octavian narrowed his eyes. "Give me that rucksack, or I'll bloody you."

A red anger deepening on Octavian dismantled Swift's courage. Octavian was certainly too much for even Swift and Ash together to handle. And Ash didn't seem capable of handling anything.

"We're just lads," said Swift. "My brother is close by."

Ash finally roused enough to meet Swift's glance. He trained his eyes on the mobile. Dialed.

"Imagine what the police would do to you"—Swift took a step back, toward the closed door—"if you hurt us."

Octavian followed.

Ash checked the cord of the signal booster. Dialed again.

Swift eased back another step.

Octavian clenched his fist.

Octavian was going to hit him. He was really going to throw a punch.

Swift tried to turn, to put more distance between them, but found himself frozen—his eyes locked on Octavian lifting his fist.

"Octavian, stop." Ash moved between him and Swift.

Octavian met Ash's eyes. Something seemed to pass between them, some mutual understanding.

Ash looked back at Swift. He watched him for what seemed a long time.

The expression on Ash was not fear.

It was calculation.

He seemed to be weighing who to side with.

Finally, Ash faced Octavian. "You need to leave Swift alone."

Octavian looked down at him. "Get out of my way, lad."

Ash backed closer to Swift.

Octavian let fly a mean punch that narrowly missed Ash and sent the mobile coasting across the room.

"Run," yelled Ash. "Swift, run."

Swift unbolted and opened the door to the hallway leading out.

Ash tried to follow, but Octavian snatched him by the shirt.

"Run!" Ash's voice rasped, his collar tight on his throat.

There was no way Swift could run. He couldn't leave Ash.

Octavian tossed Ash aside and rushed Swift. He snatched for the strap of the rucksack but caught only air.

Ash took Octavian by an arm and yanked him back.

Octavian struck out again for the strap and missed, landing a hard punch instead to Swift's chest.

To his cut.

Pain blackened Swift's vision. He dropped flat on his rear inside the hallway.

Octavian seemed to relax a touch, as though pleased to see Swift so easily downed.

Ash tugged Octavian away from the door and slammed it.

"Get out, Swift," Ash hollered through the door. "Go!"

Swift pulled to his knees. He tried to stand but moving at all brought a sense of fire to the cut.

A snap rang from the door—the deadbolt engaging.

Swift looked around for an office, for workers—but there were none.

Cradling his chest, he struggled to stand. He heaved his weight against the door.

The effort was worthless.

Swift glanced toward the exit.

He could circle the building and look for another way in.

He clenched his shirt, holding it away from his skin, and managed a tripping walk down the corridor.

He opened the door and scanned the car park, the road.

There was not one car in sight—not along the road either way, nor any sound of a motor.

And there wouldn't be. This edge of Pembrokeshire was so scarcely populated, the chances of running into a passing car would be zilch.

Any patrons of the little museum would have to come from towns or hotels dozens of miles off. And the museum wasn't even open today.

The car park itself was dead empty, save for one red electric Volkswagen, its number plates reading "8TAVN," parked close to the building and plugged in.

It seemed Octavian was the only one working the museum.

It seemed Octavian might have planned this.

"Ash," Swift murmured. "I'm coming."

He walked as quickly as he could around one side of the building.

Near the back corner he found a metal door, below ground level like it led to the basement. It, too, was dead-bolted.

Walking the museum's full circuit showed Swift no other way in. But by the time he'd again reached the front, he could breathe a touch easier.

There, he paced, struggling to think what to do.

He could find something heavy—something that might break the handle on the door to the great hall.

Or—he could throw a rock through a window. Museums were often heavily armored, right? That might trigger a security alarm.

He set to searching for a rock big enough to break glass when the front door flew open.

From it, fled Ash.

"Go, go, go!" Ash ran for their bikes.

26

Swift raced after Ash. They hopped on their bikes and hauled off. Almost telepathically, they steered away from the road—on it, Octavian could catch them easily.

They biked around the museum, into the rough and uphill toward a winding trail that sped them down a steep slope toward the brink of the Wentletrap Forest.

Swift was great on his bike, and so was Ash, which was lucky. This was very rough terrain that could trip even a strong rider.

At the base of the hill, at the edge of the Wentletrap, they together braked and looked back up the rise.

There, Octavian appeared. "You'll regret crossing me, you filthy thief." He picked up a stone and hauled it straight at Swift.

Swift ducked as the stone struck a tree behind him, precisely at the height where his head had been.

"Quick"—Swift spun his bike—"into the trees."

His chest was burning sharply from his hard breathing, from sweat wetting him, from how his shirt was agitating his cut, but he didn't slow. Ash pumped his bike after him.

"Go on then, you miserable crook," Octavian shouted. "If

you won't give me what's mine, let the Wentletrap have you. It won't be the first time I've picked the bones of its kill!"

Swift rode yet harder, though he was having to steer one handed, the other hand clenching his clothes away from his chest. He slipped into an opening that led from the loose copse into a denser thicket.

"Hang on," Ash called. "Stop."

Swift glanced back. "We can't stop."

Ash braked. "We can't go into the Wentletrap."

Swift slowed to a stop. He glanced behind them, up the rise.

Octavian wasn't in sight, and there was a chance he'd given up.

But they couldn't depend on it. He might be coming around another way.

"We have to put some distance between us and Octavian," said Swift.

"I'm not going into that forest." Ash climbed off his bike. "And you"—he stood wide-eyed—"you look pale. Feverish. Like you did just before the seizure."

"It's the pain of the cut." Swift struggled to catch his breath as Ash walked his bike nearer. "Octavian hit it square." He studied Ash. "Did he hurt you?"

"I managed to fight him off." Ash watched him. "Why are you breathing like that? Can't you catch your breath?"

Swift's breathlessness seemed only partway incited by the sprint, by the pain of the cut. He needed a moment to deal with some disbelief, to struggle down waves of panic striking from what'd just happened.

Octavian Krakau had threatened and assaulted them. And the strike he'd landed on Swift's chest felt more than a byproduct of trying to reach the rucksack. Octavian knew the events from the night of Swift's accident. He was well-aware of the cut.

Swift cradled his chest. "That was brave, how you held him off."

Ash took Swift by the shoulders and studied his chest, as though looking for blood. "What am I supposed to do if you lose consciousness? There's no way I could help you. And then—what would I do?"

Of course Ash was concerned with what his own predicament would be if Swift slipped into delirium.

Swift glanced at Ash's pocket. "Did you get the mobile back?"

"Octavian wouldn't let me near it."

"Why didn't Caius answer when you called him?" asked Swift.

"I don't know. It just rang and rang." Ash pulled Swift's hand down from his chest. "Do you need to look at your cut? Did it open or something?"

"It's healed to the point that I don't think he could've ruptured it."

But the cut was deep, and the infection had trailed deeper still. Swift could feel by the intensity of the pain how much he had yet to heal.

"I can't believe he actually did that," muttered Ash, turning aside. "That he took it that far—"

His face was showing true shock. And yet, it sounded like he wasn't all that surprised.

Swift's mind retraced the moment, in the heat of Octavian's assault, when something unspoken seemed to have passed between Octavian and Ash. That moment really had seemed to hint of some sort of alliance.

Perhaps Ash had expected Octavian to try to take Swift's relics—though not by such force?

And the most unsettling moment, Swift found himself recognizing, was not when Octavian grew aggressive. Though startling, that only confirmed the vicious nature Swift always had sensed. What Swift found most disturbing was how easily Ash had teamed with Octavian to snap the picture of the map.

At this moment, though, Ash seemed genuinely afraid of Octavian. He kept glancing back up the rise, the look on him terror. If they had been in any sort of alliance, Ash might've broken it when he stepped in to defend Swift.

"Come on."

Swift eased his bike toward a slanted opening leading deeper into the trees.

"I know the Wentletrap seems like a foolish escape—but it's better than staying here. For all we know, Octavian might be closing in."

Ash followed in a hesitating way, onto a strip of ground that looked somewhat like a trail. Swift peddled ahead into a stretch planted thickly with undergrowth.

Ash slowed at entering the wilder patch.

And at a rustling in the distant brush, he fully stopped.

Swift, too, held up at the noise. It certainly could've been Octavian.

Or—could someone else be wandering through? The cloaked man. Or it might've been one of those creatures he'd seen last night.

After a moment, the wind died, and every sound in the Wentletrap shifted to silence.

Ash trained his eyes on Swift. "Trying the Wentletrap is a mad idea."

And, of course, he wasn't wrong. Every rush of wind, every creaking branch, every clatter of leaves struck as the carefully laid footfall of Octavian. Or of something even more dangerous.

Despite the Wentletrap's ghost stories, though, despite its confounding trails, Swift had to recognize that this forest hadn't been deadly to Cynfael Maddox. Rather, it'd been his refuge.

And at the heart of this forest, they might find something wonderful—likely a tomb, lush with secrets that Maddox had stowed. Or, at the very least, they might find some sort of shelter. There, they could regroup, and then navigate on.

"The Wentletrap is dangerous, for sure," said Swift, keeping his voice low out of an instinctual fear of provoking the approach of something he could not see. "But I think we can figure it out."

"It'd be smarter to skirt the forest south, then head east," said Ash, his eyes now heavy with tears. "We could look for a road, inland."

The idea was no good. The perimeter of the Wentletrap

was broken by streams and crevasses. If they hit a dead end, Octavian would find them easily.

He might even be expecting them to follow the forest's perimeter. He could be watching it, readying to head them off.

"I wish it were that easy," said Swift. "But the terrain breaks up inland. If we tried rounding the forest, Octavian would certainly sight us."

"Well what else can we do?" Ash blinked and tears fell. "There's no way we could navigate the Wentletrap."

But they could.

From the Star of Atlantis map, Swift had gathered a sound sense of the Wentletrap's structure. Though the map wasn't detailed, its principle was clear—the heart of the Wentletrap would be reached by tracing the illogical wrappings of trails that folded back onto themselves, like the interior chamber of a shell.

It was a counter-intuitive approach to navigating a forest. One's impulse was to try to cut through in a straight line. But by following the Wentletrap's secret structure, he truly felt he could find his way to its heart.

And he couldn't help wondering whether he was meant to.

"This forest is deadly," said Ash. "Our only shot is to keep to the outer rim for as long as we can. If we make it far enough south, we'd eventually reach your beach house, right?"

"We never could reach it," said Swift. "The land between here and the beach house is split with crags."

If they were successful in finding the center of the forest, they could use the same navigation strategy to keep moving east until they reached the Wentletrap's inland edge. There, they'd find villages and heavily used roads.

"But we're not certain to hit those crags," said Ash. "Maybe we'll get lucky and find a way past them."

"I know the terrain around the Wentletrap very well," said Swift. "There are four sharp ravines between here and the beach house. Without climbing gear, there's no way we could cross any of them, much less all of them. We have to get deep enough into the forest that Octavian can't track us."

"Going into the forest to lose Octavian is the same thing as getting lost ourselves," said Ash.

Swift struggled to think of what else he might say—what might coax Ash to follow him.

He could think of only one sure strategy to convince Ash to listen. He'd have to tell Ash what he'd discovered in *The Shepherd of the Stars*—that Cynfael Maddox's resting place, his tomb, might lay at the heart of the Wentletrap Forest.

Swift pressed back the idea.

Revealing that to Ash would mean admitting that he'd been deceitful. It'd mean showing Ash the map and confessing that he understood more than he'd let on. He'd have to tell Ash that the forest held lights—lights that'd shepherded him to safety once before. Lights that, if he were destined to dare this, might brighten again.

But revealing all this would annihilate every ounce of trust they'd established. Perhaps instead, he could convince Ash to simply listen to him, to follow his lead.

Ash was breathing rapidly, in a way Swift recognized from his own dealings with panic.

He had to calm Ash down. In a quieter state, Ash might tend more agreeable.

"I need you to listen to me," said Swift. "Together, I really believe we can manage this."

"I can't go into that forest with you." Ash glanced at Swift's chest. "Not when you might drop into a fit of seizing at any minute. You're as gray as those hanging mists. There has to be an easier way."

"I'm not dealing with any fever that would trigger a seizure."

An ache behind the cut felt deep enough that Swift feared he might've suffered a broken rib. And even if he hadn't, an internal contusion was possible. Either one meant heightening pain and diminishing stamina.

But there was no sign of a fever at this point. And the adrenaline coursing was certainly helping him strategize and think clearly.

"You don't have a clue about surviving this forest." Ash

moved his bike in front of Swift, fully facing him. "Here, people are known to have died. Don't pretend you aren't scared. I can see that you're panicking."

Of course he was panicking—he was near to hyperventilating. Though he honestly felt a surety about navigating the Wentletrap, he couldn't shake the dreadful feeling of being stalked by someone who'd hurt him. Someone who wanted to keep hurting him.

"If you'd been smart," said Ash, almost yelling, "you would've just given Octavian everything. If you'd done that, he wouldn't be after us."

Swift backed up his bike. "You can't think this is my fault."

But Octavian's intimidation, his threats, his bribery, probably made sense to Ash. Over the years, Swift had watched plenty of people give Ash what he wanted, by his cunning means of persuasion.

"And you're going to forever regret not taking the money he offered," said Ash.

"Just because Octavian wanted what's mine," said Swift, "just because he was willing to rob me—that doesn't mean I should've given anything up. In fact, it means I was right not to."

Ash was alternating between placing his panic-stricken gaze on the break in the trees where they'd come from, and on the deeps of the forest, darkening with clouds racing in from the sea.

Swift watched with him the deep shadows cutting between crooked old trees, the flashes of sunlight—fleeting, confounding, spearing through the canopy in shafts, and then vanishing.

Ash seemed torn, second by second, on which way to ride— whether to join with Swift or scurry back to Octavian.

"I've put up with your selfishness for a long time." Ash backed up his bike. "But now, your selfishness might actually kill us."

The words felt poisoned and called up a flash of heat that brought tears to Swift's eyes.

Ash got off his bike and angled it toward the gap in the trees where they'd come from; toward the rise, where Octavian had stood.

Swift couldn't let Ash go back up.

If they split up, Octavian would have no trouble dealing with each of them alone.

"Ash, wait."

"For what? You're determined to go into the Wentletrap, and I'm not stupid enough to follow suit."

"Bottom line—we need help," said Swift. "We need to reach Caius and Brooke. The police. On the Wentletrap's eastern border, we could."

"You think you can find your way not just into the Wentletrap, but back out of it as well?" Ash rolled his bike further away.

"Ash, think about it."

Swift followed him.

"The Wentletrap stretches forever north and south. But inland, the eastern edge isn't that far. There are towns and villages just beyond it."

Ash turned away from him.

Swift couldn't bear the sight—Ash drifting back into what was certainly peril.

"Ash. Stop." Swift took off his rucksack. "There's something I have to show you." He drew out the map and unfolded it. "This, I think, can guide us."

Ash faced him. "That map's hardly detailed. It won't be of any use."

"It isn't the only thing that can guide us." Swift drew out *The Shepherd of the Stars* and opened it to the Celtic Akkadian piece that spoke of the heart of the Wentletrap Forest.

Moving his finger along the hashes, Swift recalled how the Celtic Akkadian words had appeared through the Sunstone.

He translated for Ash the lines about the House of the Shepherd of the Stars.

"There's something at the center of this forest," said Swift. "From how this is phrased, I believe it's Maddox's tomb."

Ash's eyes widened.

"If we can find our way to it," said Swift, "we might be able to shelter there. We could see what it holds, and from there, we could navigate east and out."

Ash said nothing. But he was no longer checking the rise.

"I'm telling you," said Swift, "this is our best shot."

He told Ash what he'd seen in the canopy—lights, bearing writing—lights that guided like stars; lights that'd led him out of this forest once already. Lights that, it seemed, had been placed there to guide.

As Ash listened, his expression shifted from awestruck to agitated. His rapid breathing took on a new tone—less of panic and more gearing up for a fight.

"Let's follow the forest as I understand it." Swift closed the book. "Let's find those lights and see where they lead." He folded the map and stowed it along with *The Shepherd of the Stars*. "Let's do this together."

Ash's cheeks reddened. "Why can't you ever be honest with me?" He almost screamed the words. "How can I trust someone who never does anything but lie?"

Swift glanced up at the rise—still empty. "I felt what I discovered was a secret entrusted to my care."

"But no one's entrusted you with anything," said Ash. "All you did was steal a book."

"I don't expect you to exactly understand, but—"

"I understand perfectly," said Ash. "The fact is—you don't trust me."

Swift held quiet.

Ash's accusation sounded so certain. It seemed he might've suspected, for a while, that Swift had been feigning trust.

"All I've done," said Ash, "is to try to be a good friend and support."

"But that isn't exactly true, is it?" Swift met Ash's eyes. "If I don't trust you, is it not for good reasons? You snapped that picture of the map—stole that picture—after I asked you not to."

"I wouldn't have had to do it if you hadn't been acting so greedy," said Ash.

"That isn't at all what was going on," said Swift. "But at this point, it doesn't matter. We have to get someplace safe. And Ash

—just imagine—what if we were to find Cynfael Maddox's tomb?"

Though Ash still was tearful, the anger he'd vented seemed to have left him in a calmer state.

Swift faced the Wentletrap, its dark shades, the labyrinthine paths between trees.

He checked the rise, checked the corridors he could see. Though he picked up no sign of Octavian, he couldn't shake the sense that he might be close.

"If you can forgive me for keeping secrets from you," said Swift, "I can forgive you for taking that picture."

He pulled a water bottle from his rucksack and held it before Ash.

"Will you not explore with me where the map leads? Is it not possible that if Maddox's tomb waits in this forest, more Sunstones might be hidden there?"

Like a shaft of sun breaking through clouds, Ash's demeanor changed.

His eyes cleared, and into them slipped a brightness—like his thirst for adventure, which Swift loved so much, was dawning.

"Hey, I'm sorry about taking that picture," said Ash. "I shouldn't have done that. I see it now." He received the water bottle from Swift and opened it.

It'd seemed possible that Ash—at least a very small part of him—might actually care about Swift. That part appeared to have won out when he'd defended Swift from Octavian.

At this moment, though, watching this unwholesome ease come over Ash—this cooperation and friendliness that seemed only to visit when Swift harbored something Ash wanted—

Swift saw in him nothing but a puppeteer. A master manipulator.

"Can we not be friends?" asked Swift. "Can we never be friends?"

Ash took a drink. "We are friends." He tightened the bottle's cap and handed it back to Swift. "I'll show you by following you. Even into the Wentletrap Forest."

They were not friends. And Ash following him—this was not trust. He was seeing Swift just as a lead. There were more treasures—more Sunstones, perhaps—to be found, and Swift knew the way to them.

Despite how bitter the truth tasted, relief was striking that Ash was agreeing to follow. Making for the center of the Wentletrap, then on to its eastern side, was the best chance they had to reach help.

"The main path through the Wentletrap ought to bend in tight curves, back and forth," said Swift. "If we find the lit signs, it's possible they might even lead to the heart of the forest."

From the top of the rise, a snap rang, like a twig breaking underfoot.

Swift pushed off.

He glanced behind him, at Ash. "Are you with me?"

"Ride faster." Ash followed him under a tangle of dark trees. "I'll be right behind you."

27

hen Swift reached a fork in the pathway, he braked.

For the last half-hour, it seemed he and Ash had been following the Wentletrap's main, folding path.

Here, an opening peeled off to the left, while a brighter path continued before them, straight ahead.

The brighter way seemed more like the main path. But the opening on the left side was wider.

What he and Ash had been following, though—it hardly felt like a main path. It could easily be called just a looser part of the thicket, barely wide enough for their bikes to fit.

Swift studied the forking trail. A sea mist pressing inland made it tough to see more than a few yards around him.

Ash peered down the opening on the left. "That leads east, I'm pretty sure. It must be the main path."

"I don't think so," said Swift. "It seems like a branch."

This was exactly why the Wentletrap was known to trick hikers. New paths presented, and then openings coiled off those paths, twisting to nowhere.

Anything might lead to a dead end. And retracing one's steps was virtually impossible.

Ash glanced up at the canopy. "Where are your lit trees?"

Swift examined the boughs. "Maybe further in."

"I say we go left," said Ash. "Eastward. That way seems easier, and you're looking spent. And in pain."

The ache from Octavian's punch had been incrementally sharpening over the last hour. But Swift couldn't let it slow them. Making the most of the daylight was critical.

And though Ash seemed to be trying to mask his anxiety, Swift could read it. Ash was pale and breathing hard, and he kept checking behind them.

He had to be in some shock at having the foundation ripped out from under him—Octavian no longer his ally.

"This looks like a direct path to the forest's center," said Ash. "Why not take it?"

"Because the path leading to the center of the Wentletrap won't be direct," said Swift. "The shape of a wentletrap in a shell is a series of folds. It reaches the pinnacle gently, approaching it by curves. That's anything but direct."

"That's very little to go by." Ash rolled his bike in front of Swift's, angling his front tire toward the eastern path. "You don't have a clue which path would really be better, do you?"

"From my map, I feel that I'm gaining a sense of this forest. It seems to me like we should keep straight on."

"For all we know, Octavian understands this forest," said Ash. "You heard what he said about picking the bones of people the Wentletrap killed. Swift—I think he was serious."

A sound rose of leaves rustling.

Swift and Ash together faced the disturbance.

They held still as a wave of wind crested, then died.

Swift searched the trees again for any sign of lights but found nothing.

"I see lostness in your eyes," said Ash. "Fear and pain. I think I should take over making our decisions."

Swift's endurance was waning, it was true. "Yeah, I'm in pain. And afraid, but—"

"Look, who's always been better at getting us out of fixes?" asked Ash. "Me. And I say we should follow what actually looks like a trail, as this eastern path does."

Swift eased back a little. The undergrowth on the eastern path was clearer, with fewer downed branches.

And a case could be made, he had to admit, that the eastern path seemed to curve in the distance—a feature he could only see vaguely between blowing curtains of mist.

But many clear-seeming paths in the Wentletrap might turn out to be crooked, short corridors, angling off and dwindling to nothing.

"The Wentletrap is tricky, though," said Swift. "And you don't know it any better than I do."

"You aren't going to get far on a difficult path, looking as bad as you do."

Ash held out his hand.

"Why don't you let me carry your rucksack?"

"I'm fine." Swift clipped the front of his rucksack over his chest.

The move felt overly protective and deepened Swift's pain, adding a touch more pressure on the cut.

Ash, seeming to take the gesture as an affront, lowered his gaze to the ground.

From the way they'd come, a clear footfall landed.

Swift peered through the weave of branches and studied the corridors between trees.

A crack rang.

The forest went dark.

Swift opened his eyes to find himself lying on his back.

Above him, the high tops of branches netted the blue and white sky. A sharp pain was throbbing on his forehead.

Swift touched his face, where wetness was dripping into his eye.

He gazed up through a haze of blood to see standing over him—Octavian, holding a torn tree branch.

"Ash?" Swift glanced around.

Ash's bike was on the ground, but he was nowhere.

Maybe he'd panicked and run.

Panicked—and left Swift alone with Octavian, though?

Swift struggled to get to his feet. He felt the knot on his forehead.

It seemed not too severe, though blood was dripping steadily. And Octavian standing before him, gripping the branch, was certainly capable of inflicting more damage.

"You're a smart lad to keep your rucksack from that coward." Octavian raised the big branch with one hand. "And smart lad that you are, you're going to hand it over to me."

Swift studied the trees all around but still found no hint of which way Ash might've gone.

"What you carry is mine by rights, and I'll have it." Octavian, holding the heavy limb, drew closer.

Swift considered trying to rush off, but it was clear he'd have no hope of getting away. He was still half-blinded by pain, by blood, and even keeping his balance was proving a challenge.

Octavian swung the branch.

Swift ducked—barely dodged it.

"Don't toy with me, lad," said Octavian. "Take that bloody rucksack off."

Ash had thought it rational to give the rucksack to Octavian.

If Swift did give it up, would Octavian leave?

It seemed he probably would. If Swift gave up everything, Octavian could forge his signature. But even that seemed like a careless solution—one that would be easy for Swift to contest. If Octavian flat out stole everything now, he'd probably try to vanish.

Swift lifted his hand to the rucksack's latch on his chest.

But he found himself incapable of releasing it.

Sterncastle Cove had destroyed the *Strider*. Its sharp boulders had broken Caius' leg. The fever disease and coma had ripped the Earth from beneath Swift. He'd lost his connection with his med books, and his very ambition had been shaken.

Octavian drew a step nearer. "What's it going to be?"

Octavian standing hugely before him, wielding that massive branch, seemed an embodiment of all the forces that had, since the accident, sent Swift careening out of control.

Swift wiped blood out of his eye. "I'm not sacrificing what I've fought to gain." He held on to the straps of his rucksack.

"So be it." Octavian's face took on a resolute darkness.

A crunching sound lifted—leaf litter scattering.

And then came an ear-splitting snarl.

Octavian's gaze drifted to something behind Swift.

Swift eased around to find an animal standing in the thicket.

It was a dog.

No—a wolf.

A wolf lunging out of the thicket.

Octavian stumbled back, narrowly dodging its charge.

Swift leapt up and grabbed his bike.

Mounted it.

Took off.

He turned down what he believed to be the main path and rode hard. Balancing proved challenging, but he managed it and followed the weak trail toward a curve.

Riding the curve, he discovered that it doubled back.

He rode on until he reached a place well-shrouded by tree shoots. There, he slowed.

The wolf was in sight and standing unmoving, its gaze trained where Octavian seemed to have fled.

Octavian was out of sight but shouting, "Stay back, you bloody beast."

Swift remained still until Octavian's voice disappeared in the dampening mist.

All the while, the wolf, ears perked, remained sitting beside the limb Octavian had dropped.

The wolf was massive—a muscular gray and white creature with a coat showing casts of blue where the rare sunbeam glanced.

Swift had seen pictures and videos of wolves, but it was shocking how big a real one was. It was so broad in the head, so stocky, it seemed part bear—like something belonging in an Icelandic Norse nightmare.

The wolf peered back through the thicket, toward Swift.

Swift startled at the intelligence in its eyes. The cunning. The sharp stare of predation.

This had to be the animal he'd seen last night in the Wentle-trap. This, the animal that'd stalked him.

And wolves were known to hunt in packs.

Swift glanced around, his skin tingling with the notion of unseen wolves watching him.

He saw no others, but before this wolf appeared, Swift hadn't had any idea it was close.

Could Ash have seen the wolf? Maybe this was why he fled. Swift's stomach dropped at the thought of a wolf pack picking up Ash's scent.

It seemed unlikely, though, that Ash had been aware of the wolf. He'd vanished before Octavian had noticed it nearing.

The wolf stepped into the thicket, toward Swift.

Swift ever so slowly walked his bike past it.

The wolf barked.

Swift burst into flight along the narrow path, riding it as hard as his pain would allow, navigating haphazardly through a sheen of mist and blood.

28

Swift kept riding, kept following what seemed the Wentletrap's main path, though he had to go slowly, steeling himself against the pain in his chest, in his head.

His forehead had stopped bleeding, but its ache was fierce. And the bruise on his chest from Octavian's punch was throbbing deeply within, making him wonder if some serious damage had been done. He wanted to stop to look at it. To rest.

But he couldn't stop.

Ash was out here someplace. And so was that wolf.

The day was tending toward evening, and the mist was thickening. Come nightfall, who knew how many beasts would creep out and roam?

And night would bring a strong need for food and for more water than what he had left. Night would bring a cold for which their clothes were no match.

The trail was not clear—fallen branches and rough stretches kept forcing him off his bike for intervals.

At every break in the trees, he scanned for signs of Ash.

If Octavian caught Ash—if he hurt Ash—tears flashed into Swift's eyes at the thought of Ash in such danger.

And if Ash were hurt, Swift himself would feel it like the

agony he'd suffered over Caius—a brother imperiled by his own attachment to the Star of Atlantis, all over again.

But how Ash had vanished, right as Octavian appeared—it seemed strangely concerted.

Swift couldn't bring himself to entertain that Ash had anything to do with Octavian's assault. But if Ash had run, it meant he'd left Swift to fend for himself.

"Swift!"

It was Ash—calling distantly.

"Ash?" Swift eased his bike to a standstill.

"Where are you?" called Ash.

He didn't sound weak, as he might if he were hurt. The relief of the sound struck Swift as a shiver.

Swift climbed off his bike. "Can you see me?"

"No, I heard you, finally—your bike crushing leaves," said Ash. "Keep talking."

"Are you all right?" called Swift. "What happened to you?"

"Octavian, he…" Ash rode out of the mist from a side trail and braked.

Swift dropped his bike and ran to him. "I was so scared that something terrible happened to you."

"My God." Ash climbed off his bike. "Your head."

"It isn't too bad, I think. It's stopped bleeding." Swift rubbed his sleeve across his cheek—stiff with a coat of dried blood. "Where'd you go? It was like you just disappeared."

"Octavian yanked me off my bike and spilled me down a hill. Then he must've gone after you."

Swift sat quietly a moment. That wasn't at all how he remembered Octavian's appearance.

He remembered hearing a disturbance in the forest. He remembered looking at Ash—Ash, staring at the ground—and then there'd been a burst of pain.

But maybe his memory was off. He had taken a blow to the head.

Ash showed Swift his trousers, mud slicked. "I slipped down a hill, you see. Then I lost all sense of direction. But—that growling. It guided me back to where we were divided. I waited until that wolf cleared out, then found my bike. By then, you were gone."

"I think that's the animal I saw in the night," said Swift. "There's a whole pack. And it'll be dark in a matter of hours. We need to move on."

"I'm all for that," said Ash. "Which way?"

Swift studied him. "Are you saying you want me to decide?"

"I'm completely lost," said Ash. "Do you have a sense of the trail?"

Swift pointed ahead. "This is the same path we were following earlier. It looks vague, I know. But I think we should keep trying to follow it." He pulled out a dwindling bottle of water and gave it to Ash. "It's been unfolding consistently, like the trail on my map."

"You've still got your rucksack." Ash finished the water. "Octavian didn't get at any of your things?"

"If that wolf hadn't appeared, he would've." Swift climbed onto his bike.

Up ahead, high in the canopy of tall oaks, from within a sliver in the mist—something ignited to glowing.

It shone very low, like a firefly's chemical luminance obscured by a leaf.

"I wonder if Octavian's still out here," said Ash, glancing around.

Swift studied the brightness against the deepening blue sky and the darkness of trees.

"If Octavian finds us again," said Ash, "you'd be smart to just hand everything over."

The light in the tree, shining 30 feet up or so, was exactly what Swift had seen during the night.

When the wind shredded the mist, Swift could make out a shape imprinted. It was the Celtic Akkadian cypher for "shepherd."

At seeing this sign shining pale against the pearled blue of the twilit mist, the whole Wentletrap Forest felt like a solution Swift had been waiting for.

"What's wrong?" asked Ash.

"There's a light," said Swift. "A light in the trees." He backed up his bike and pointed along Ash's sightline.

"Those two oaks whose branches meet overhead—follow the right-hand one down, about a third of the way. The light—it's like seeing a setting dawn star—pale, but clear."

"Wait—yes." Ash straightened. "There is something."

"I saw it ignite." Swift biked toward it. "Something—or someone—just set it to glowing."

During the night, these signs had led him out of the forest. He couldn't help but wonder if whoever was lighting them now wanted him to find his way in.

Ash followed. "What's that symbol on it?"

Swift stopped at the base of the oak whose bough held the light. "It's Celtic Akkadian. It means 'shepherd.'"

On a tree in the distance, another light flared.

Swift led Ash toward it.

The pain in his chest, though still strong, troubled Swift little as he keyed in on the forest's lights. He couldn't even feel a proper fear over the wolf, nor even Octavian, for the joy of sensing that answers might be near at hand.

Ash eased alongside Swift as they stopped before the second light. "What's that one say?"

"It's a variation of the same word," said Swift. "It means, *lead shepherd.*' And look—there's another."

Swift set to speed off, but Ash grabbed the back of his bike.

Swift glanced over his shoulder. "What?"

Ash stared up at the light looming. "Isn't this a little unsettling?"

Unsettling, it was not. There were Celtic Akkadian symbols hanging inside the Wentletrap Forest; Celtic Akkadian symbols that were also written in *The Shepherd of the Stars.*

Someone had to have hung these symbols—someone had to be lighting them. These symbols, found inside a book belonging to the fisherman, had guided Swift.

They were odd, certainly. But thrilling.

"It feels like we're meant to follow these lights," said Swift. "Like someone wants us to."

"Exactly," said Ash. "I can't shake the feeling that we're being baited."

Swift glanced around at the tangle of forest, heavy with mist, its vast size palpable by the pressure of its silence.

"Or guided." Swift tugged his bike away from Ash. "Whoever placed these lights knows the Star of Atlantis myth. Cynfael Maddox was a renaissance maker. A helper. A teacher. Any remnant of that clan might be the same sort of wonderful."

He rode on toward the brightening sign.

Ash didn't follow. "Or they could be knife-wielding fishermen and thieves."

"How can you not want to see where the lights lead?" Swift called back. "They could mean rescue."

"Or they could mean a trap," Ash hollered. "Will you just wait a minute?"

Swift wheeled toward him and stopped.

"We need to think this through." Ash got off his bike. "Has it not occurred to you that Octavian might've hung these?"

"I honestly don't think he's capable of pulling off something like that," said Swift. "But it's true that Octavian might still be out here. And it's going to be dark soon. And those wolves could be anywhere."

Ash climbed back onto his bike.

"It's a risk, yes. But one worth taking." Swift pushed off.

Ash followed, though not closely, though slowing, though even stopping at times.

A new light presented itself after almost every bend in the trail, the tight folds now coming at quicker intervals.

Light by light, Swift coaxed Ash on along tenuous tracks that carried them over brooks and through patches of brush.

The trail soon narrowed so drastically, they had to abandon their bikes.

"It seems we're being driven to no place," said Ash.

Swift held back a tree branch for him. "Wherever the signs are leading—we have to be close."

"The forest is so thick here," said Ash. "The fog's worsening. And your head's bleeding again."

He held up.

"Don't you think we should stop?"

"Why are you challenging me so much now?" asked Swift. "Are you not at least a little relieved at the thought of finding the center of this forest? Once we reach it, we'll have proven that our navigation technique works. We can use the same strategy to find our way east through the forest and out."

Ash didn't respond. He seemed to be listening.

Swift glanced around. "Are you hearing something?"

"No, I'm just...I'm afraid Octavian is following."

"Come on, then," said Swift. "We can't have far to go."

Ash and Swift together pushed back the spindly limbs of saplings as they moved deeper into the tight growth.

"If this thickens to the point where we can't move through," said Ash, "we're royally screwed."

"No, if we needed to"—Swift turned—"we could just... follow the lights back—"

But searching the trees behind them, he could find no lights.

He studied a taller oak, where he was certain one of the lit signs had hung.

But there was nothing.

"They must shine just one way," said Swift.

"That means for sure someone's baiting us." Ash sank into a crouch. "Someone hung those to get people lost, and you were stupid enough to take the bait, and I was stupid enough to follow you."

"At this point, we have no choice but to follow where the lights lead." Swift pulled Ash back to standing. "We might find a place to take shelter, and—who knows what else?"

"I hate how this is narrowing." Despite all his resistance, Ash was following. "It's making me claustrophobic. This feels like winding into the funnel of a huntsman spider's trap."

Swift squeezed between two trees and into a bank of weeds. "Just a little further." He ducked under a thicket of stiff juniper branches.

The way everything was tightening—tightening to what felt like trails created by animals; tightening until he couldn't move

without picking up scratches; tightening like the pinnacle of a
wentletrap shell—they had to be very close.

The juniper thicket ended abruptly at a straight row of
cypress trees, making a sort of natural wall.

Swift eased through two trees set wide enough that he could
just fit.

Upon reaching its other side, he froze.

Ash struggled through behind him.

There, he stilled as though in a state of shock. "Whoa."

29

Before Swift and Ash, there stretched a glade of tall autumn wildflowers wrapping a field of mown grass.

And at its center rested a bright garden, inside of which nestled the oddest house Swift had ever seen.

Although, "house" didn't capture it. "Cottage" would've been closer, and "storybook cottage" more fitting yet.

The walls weren't made from wood, nor stone, nor brick, nor anything else recognizable. If anything familiar, it might've been stucco or plaster—but stucco or plaster applied with a cake decorating pouch.

There was nothing straight, nothing plumb about the structure. The walls, the corners, the roofline swirled in pleasing ways like waves heaving. The windows peaked like the tips on whipped cream. It seemed faeries or hobbits or wizards had cobbled this house.

The walls were a warm tone between bright honey and sand. The door was a rich, sea-toned turquoise.

Though the mist still hung thickly, the sun was cutting through in shafts, lighting moisture drops clinging to the grass, to the blooming garden, brightening everything like a field of fair stars.

And at the center of the garden, in a beach lounger, a man sat, reading.

Ash pulled Swift to crouching behind a cluster of wildflowers. "Is that your fisherman?"

Swift peered through the lanky stalks at the man. He was more broad-shouldered than the fisherman. Not as tall.

"I don't think so," said Swift.

He was wearing a hooded cloak—just like the man Swift had glimpsed wandering the Wentletrap by lantern light.

There was something majestic about him, detectable from a mere glance. His eyes were pale green, lending him the calm of a silence of woods. His face was shadowed with a day's thickening of a black beard, and his hair—thick, curling tousles—was not unlike Swift's. Except its jet black and silver made it seem purposed to hold the circlet of a crown.

"I think it's the man I saw last night," whispered Swift.

"He looks awfully powerful," said Ash. "Like a king from the legends we've read."

Swift, ever before, had pictured Neptune as an oldish man, white-bearded and fierce. At this moment, he adapted his vision of a seaborne god to match the appearance of this man. As serious as the kingly man's countenance was, a gentleness radiated from him, like light shining from a Celtic Akkadian letter. A Sunstone.

And his large eyes held something timeless and wise. He seemed capable of great deeds in battle—but the softness in his look betrayed a stronger readiness to heal than to hurt. It was like he equally knew how to command a crew and gently lead a child.

"A king of old," Swift whispered back. "He does seem like that."

"I don't like him," said Ash. "He looks stern. Maybe cross. Cross and perhaps hiding a knife in that weird cloak he's wearing."

"I don't think he looks cross," said Swift.

Ash crept back. "For us to trespass here—Swift—we can't. The Wentletrap is rumored to hold all kinds of terrible things.

What if that man is one of them? My instincts are telling me we should get out of here."

The *Star of Atlantis* promised a destiny to its finder. And Swift's pursuit of those myths had led him, in a winding path, here.

"We're cold," said Swift. "We're out of water. We've been knocked around." He turned his gaze onto the kind-looking man. "He'll help us. He's got to."

Ash held Swift's arm. "You'd trust a weirdo who wanders around at night and talks to trees more than you'd trust my instincts?"

"Even if he wants nothing to do with us, he must have a phone. I think he'd at least let us make a call."

Ash's gaze fell to Swift's chest. "Are you not remembering the last time you snuck up on somebody in these wilds?" He studied the peaceful man suspiciously. "Even if that isn't your fisherman, he might be just as cracked."

Swift pulled away from Ash. "You trusted Octavian, who was creepy as all Hell. Why couldn't you give the benefit of the doubt to a guy reading quietly in a garden?"

Ash glanced back into the woods. "We should wait until dark. Maybe he'll leave again. Then we could check out this place without him around."

"Bottom line," said Swift. "We must call the police. We must reach Caius. I'm going to talk to that man." He stood. "Any decent person would help us."

Swift moved through the meadow, Ash following at some distance.

When Swift reached the lawn, the man looked up. He laid aside his book.

He appeared to remain calm. Even friendly, perhaps, though marked by some wonder, and not a small bit of shock— likely from seeing the blood on Swift.

Swift stopped at the edge of his garden. "I'm sorry to bother you—but we need help."

"Chance had it that you'd come today," said the man.

Ash moved closely behind Swift. "See? He's senseless. He won't be any help to us."

Swift glanced at the book the man had laid aside.

It was a textbook. Astronomy.

Just being in the presence of the man, standing in his sight, felt like a lightening of a load.

The ache in Swift's chest from Octavian's punch was singing out as a deep throb, and he found himself wanting to run to the man as a boy might rush to a parent, for comfort in pain.

The man—an astronomer, maybe—moved to the blue door of his house. "You've wound through the Wentletrap and so could use a bit of water." He opened the door. "Would you like to come in, or shall I bring it to you?"

The way he spoke felt timeless. He seemed to foster a courtesy of a bygone era—a skill of reading others and responding well. He probably could sense the hesitation in Ash. And maybe he sensed the awe in Swift.

Swift found himself wholly willing to put himself in this man's care. Wanting to.

Ash gripped Swift's shirt, holding him back.

"I see that you're hurt," said the astronomer. "I can help you."

Swift glanced at Ash. "We could be on the phone with Caius and Brooke in a matter of minutes."

"Or, in a matter of minutes, we could both be cut open."

Swift called to the man, "What we really need is a phone."

The man gestured inside. "I have one, but it's old. Tied to the wall."

Swift offered Ash an encouraging look.

"I'm telling you," said Ash, "we should trust my instincts—not him."

But the thought of speaking to Caius, to the police—the idea of finally being in a warm place won out.

Swift trekked through the garden toward the astronomer and his curious house.

30

S wift stepped through the doorway of the astronomer's strange house.

Ash closely followed him.

The place was cool and spacious—quite large. Though, it looked less like a home and more an office.

Along one wall stood tall display cases, lit and holding specimens of rocks. Crystals. Fossils. On a desk sprawled an elaborate bank of computers. And at every window perched a telescope, peering high through the glass and seeming to stand in a sacred silence, awaiting the onset of night.

"What are all those computers for?" asked Ash, his wide eyes tracing the room.

"Astronomy, mainly," said the man. "And astrophysics."

"You're a scientist, then," said Swift.

The man gestured to a wall where a cluster of framed certificates hung.

They showed doctoral degrees from six universities.

"More than anything," said the man, "I'm a teacher."

A teacher.

At the heart of the Wentletrap Forest, Swift had discovered a teacher.

"Seems he's more than a teacher," whispered Ash, pointing through an arched doorway, at a gently lit adjoining room.

Swift peered with him toward it.

The room was lined with more display cases, tables, and shelves, all crowded and shining with glazed pottery and jewelry, with the polished facets of colossal quartz crystals.

Statues of stone and metal stood among ornate boxes. Some of the statues were clad in what looked like ancient suits of armor, others in time-worn clothes.

Ash shifted his wide eyes onto Swift.

The expression on him was hunger. Greed.

"Don't touch anything," said Swift.

The admonishment had come out in a big brotherly way, like he were trying to mimic Caius.

But Swift couldn't help saying something. He could only imagine what Ash might dream up in this place; what he might try, confronted with this degree of opportunity.

Ash cast him a dismissive look. "You're not the only one who knows how to handle treasures."

"Those are indeed treasures," said the astronomer, holding his gaze very watchfully over Ash, looming nearer to the doorway. "They're memories."

"Not yours, though," said Ash. "They couldn't be. Look at those clothes, and that jewelry—it's all clearly old, like what might be in a museum. That suit of armor, for instance. It looks like it's from the Middle Ages. Is it? And those statues—how they're tarnished—are they made of real silver?"

"Why don't you lads sit down?" The astronomer gestured to a ring of couches wrapping the middle of the main space, circling a hearth that, though unlit, smelled of newly burnt wood.

Upon sitting, Swift's muscles, head to toe, tingled with relief. He didn't realize how spent he was until now, upon finally allowing himself to rest.

"May I take a look at your head?" the astronomer asked Swift.

Swift touched the bump, which was receding, though

slightly bleeding. "I think I'm all right." He glanced down at his bloodied clothes. "Though—I must look awful."

The astronomer stepped out of the room a moment, then returned with a damp rag draped over his wrist. He held a pitcher of water and a stack of cups.

The water pitcher and cups, he handed to Ash. "Help yourself."

Ash held the pitcher up to the light. "You didn't just draw this from some creek, did you?"

"Ash, I'm sure it's fine," said Swift.

"May I?" The astronomer took the damp cloth in hand and sat down beside Swift.

Swift nodded.

The astronomer gently washed Swift's face, where blood had dried. The soft motions he used, the gentle pressure, how delicate he was around Swift's eyes, the care he took avoiding any place that might be tender—it reminded Swift of being a small child under the care of Caius, tenderly looking after him following some fall.

And he found himself feeling toward the astronomer an awe, a trust, not unlike what he felt for Caius.

Like Caius, the astronomer seemed not at all appalled by the task of tending his wound.

Nor did his face carry any trace of judgment or impatience.

Rather, he took his time, successfully staunching the cut's seeping, and seeming to want to see Swift comfortable, as well as clean.

The ease of how fluidly Swift was slipping into this state of assurance surprised him.

But he welcomed it. For it was delivering a calm—a sense of coming home, as though he really had been destined to arrive here.

The astronomer gave the cut on Swift's head a final look before handing Swift the rag. "I'll let you do what you can for your clothes."

Throughout Swift's tending, Ash had kept his eyes locked on the astronomer.

He looked a touch less distrustful, but now seemed to simply have no idea what to think of him.

The astronomer, in turn, appeared to be appraising both Swift and Ash. But he seemed little concerned—like having two lost lads turn up at this place was unsurprising. Like having to sponge blood off someone in the middle of the Wentletrap Forest wasn't any shock.

Swift dabbed at the front of his hoodie with the rag, but the effort was wasted. He managed nothing more than smearing the blood into unpleasant dark stains.

He gave up on it and instead scrubbed the back of his neck where it itched, where blood had dried.

The astronomer poured a glass of water and handed it to Swift.

"I can't believe we actually found someone inside this freakish forest," said Ash.

"I'm pleased you did," said the astronomer. "Can you tell me what happened to you?"

"We were at a museum," said Swift, "where some artifacts that we'd found were being studied."

"So, you're treasure hunters," said the astronomer.

"We need to call the police," said Swift. "The museum curator got after us and tried to take everything."

"The museum on the northwestern edge of the coast?" The astronomer leaned back as though he had no doubt. "You're speaking of Octavian Krakau."

"That's him." Swift set aside his glass.

"You know Octavian?" asked Ash.

"Too well." From a side table, the astronomer lifted a phone that looked ancient, wrapped as it was in cords, bearing a round face and dial. "He's one of the most avaricious people I've come across, which is saying something." He stood. "Call whomever you'd like. I'll do my part by getting chance on the case." He stood and moved to an open window.

"What could he possibly mean, 'get chance on the case?'" whispered Ash.

The astronomer leaned out the window and whistled.

"So I'll give you that you were right about the phone," said Ash. "But I was right that he's mental."

Swift studied the phone. "Help me figure out how to use this."

"My grandmum once had a phone like this." Ash lifted the receiver and handed it to Swift. "What's the number?"

Swift spoke the number as Ash dialed.

"It's ringing," said Swift.

But it was only ringing.

Swift left Caius a voicemail—that they were in some trouble but okay, and that they'd try to call again.

"Why wouldn't Caius and Brooke be picking up?" asked Swift. "What if something's happened to them?"

Ash scoffed. "Did you not see what Brooke was wearing? Just that tiny sundress. Man, if I had her alone under any circumstances—"

"The police," said Swift. "Call the police."

Ash dialed.

They picked up after the first ring.

Swift closed his eyes, relief striking.

He told the officer exactly what'd happened. He told his name and Ash's, along with their parents' names. He recounted the attack in the museum and in the forest. His Sunstone, he reported stolen. He described their failed attempts to reach Caius.

"Where are you?" asked the officer.

"We're in a house, in the middle of the Wentletrap Forest— if you can believe it," said Swift.

"You'll be fine there." A smile seemed to brighten the officer's voice. "Stay put until we can get someone to you. Don't leave that house. We'll keep trying to reach your brother."

Swift hung up. "They seemed to know this place."

Ash studied the arched doorway, leading to the shining room. "Why would the police know this place?"

Swift shrugged. "We're to stay here."

Ash glanced at the astronomer—still gazing out the front

window, whistling. "That head case of yours looks well-distracted. I'm going to have a look around."

"You can't just go wandering around someone else's house," Swift whispered. "Just ask him to show you. I bet he would."

Ash cast Swift a doubtful look as he stood and faced the room, sparkling with what the astronomer had called "memories."

"Ash," Swift stood. "Don't—"

The front door swung and struck the wall.

In blew a frigid wind—the onset of twilight.

Looming in the doorway, against a backdrop of steely mist, stood a tall man with ghostly pale eyes.

Swift gripped Ash's arm. "It's him," he whispered. "It's the fisherman."

31

*E*veryone had cast doubt on Swift's story of the fisherman, at times making Swift himself skeptical about what he'd seen.

And now, it seemed the fisherman had rambled not out of the Wentletrap, but out of Swift's dreams.

Or his nightmares.

Memories rushed of the terrible night of the *Strider's* wreck in Sterncastle Cove—the heaviness of the longboat; the fisherman's elusive, crazed talk as Swift tried to explain what'd happened—that Caius was bleeding out; the fisherman—the very man now standing in the doorway before him—jolting awake and slashing Swift with a dagger.

Swift held on to his chest as the fisherman moved into the room.

He looked just as fierce as Swift remembered—like a soldier relieved prematurely from battle. It seemed he might slide out his blade and slash the astronomer.

"Sir," said Swift, to the astronomer. "He—"

"Chance." The astronomer, arms folded, stood before the fisherman. "I suppose that you'll tell me I owe you a gold piece."

"That, you do." The fisherman gestured at Swift. "There he is."

"What you do mean, 'there he is?'" asked Ash. "It's not like you knew we were coming."

The fisherman turned his gaze onto Ash. "Though—I can't tell you a thing about this other one."

"My name's Ash Emberly." Ash stepped to him boldly—though it was clear he was struggling to conceal his intimidation at the man's wildness, at his cutting blue eyes, at the high-cheek-boned face that made him seem somewhat skeletal.

"Have you not seen me on the news?" asked Ash. "I'm the *Boy Finder of Treasure from Devonshire.*"

The fisherman and astronomer glanced at each other.

A shared familiarity made them seem like brothers-in-arms, or even true brothers—though they looked nothing alike. The fisherman was a head taller than the astronomer, and the fisherman's thick pale hair was knotted over his head in rows, as Swift remembered. The astronomer's eyes were soft-seeming, whereas the fisherman's eyes—sharp and icy—were ghoulish.

"We've met before," said the fisherman, watching Swift.

Looking into the fisherman's eyes was like looking into the face of a quick death—the pale blue mist of waters that drag. A sunlit airlessness.

And yet Swift felt no fear. The sight of the fisherman, though riddled with endings, with memories of pain, though mist-shrouded and dire, brought a sense—like a battle-worthy ship—of steadiness. Of bearings found.

"Yes," Swift returned. "On the beach beyond Sterncastle Cove."

The fisherman closed in. "I caused you an injury that night."

Despite that this fisherman was the very man who'd cut him, despite that the astronomer was starkly mysterious, in their company, Swift felt at peace.

Being in this strange house, in the heart of these perilous woods, was like finding oneself in the center of a storm—in its eye, with water and wind churning in chaos, but distantly.

It was like he'd stumbled across members of his own family, before now unknown.

"It wasn't your fault," said Swift. "You were my salvation. And my brother's."

Speaking these words of thanks to the fisherman, of acknowledgement, was sheer relief. And it was refreshing to talk with him so directly, after how dreamy and twisting their last conversation had been.

"It pains me that you've suffered," said the fisherman.

"I hope I can free you of that," said Swift. "Truly, I feel nothing toward you but gratitude."

The fisherman advanced and stood before Swift. He took hold of Swift's jaw, gently, and tilted back his head.

Though the fisherman's appearance was terrifying—Swift couldn't help wondering if he still carried a dagger, he found himself again welcoming the man's help.

"Your eyes hold the look of one who's peered into the very face of death," said the fisherman.

And though the fisherman looked young, peering into his eyes felt like looking into the ages; like glimpsing a soul weathered by many centuries of dark nights.

"As do yours," said Swift.

The fisherman pulled a rag off his belt and wiped from Swift's neck a missed line of dried blood.

The fisherman's tending was rougher than the astronomer's had been. In the fisherman's hands, Swift felt like a sculpture undergoing an artist's incisive treatment.

"Swift almost died from that cut," said Ash, from behind the fisherman. "Why didn't you go with him in your longboat? Why didn't you see him safe?"

"My master called," said the fisherman, not looking at Ash. He studied the knot on Swift's head but left it untouched.

The astronomer approached, watching as the fisherman cleaned a last trace of dried blood from Swift's cheek.

"Chance injured you," said the astronomer, "but I can attest that the hurt laid was not deliberate."

Chance. The fisherman's name was Chance.

"He seemed to know I'd find help," said Swift, closely watching Chance.

Chance appeared to be feeling, to some degree, the suffering he was noting in Swift.

It was like they shared an understanding of what it was to be broken.

"It's true that I summoned him away," said the astronomer. "We had to leave the shire quickly, but we first called in your distress. Not long after, the police notified us that you'd been picked up by a ship."

"He's in pain." Chance glanced at the astronomer. "Can you get him some ice?"

The astronomer left and returned a moment later with a dripping bag wrapped in a dishtowel.

"Swift is in pain," said Ash, "because he just got punched in the very place where you cut him on the night that he all but killed his brother."

Chance looked gently at Swift. "May I see the damage?"

With the question came a warmth of companionship.

Having both Chance and the astronomer standing near, tuning into his pain—Swift felt he was being assessed by comrades following a battle.

Swift pulled off his hoodie and unbuttoned his shirt underneath.

Chance looked closely at Swift's cut. He gently touched the skin on either side. "This will heal, in slow time. But the night you received this, a fiercer blow struck. And deeply. Do you know of what I speak?"

Chance seemed to have the terrible night branded in his memory as blackly as Swift did. It was as though he understood not just what'd happened physically to Swift, but Swift's state of mind. For Chance's words recalled the feeling of isolation, of despair; of realizing that Caius might die—that he himself might, too.

"I faced death that night," said Swift.

"And you'll look again on death," said Chance, "before the ending of things." He rested the ice pack on precisely the most tender place along Swift's cut. "Before the beginning."

"Octavian Krakau—the curator of the museum on the coast," said Swift. "He took the Sunstone."

Chance's gaze fell distant. He secured Swift's hand on the ice and backed off.

The silence in the room broke beneath the blaring of a high howl.

Ash rushed to a window. "It's that wolf!" He raced to the door and shut it. "We saw that thing in the forest."

With a boom—a force struck the door.

Another blow forced the door open, and through it bounded the wolf, silver-coated and pale-eyed.

Ash slunk to a side wall.

Swift, all but frozen with fear, managed only to ease a step closer to Chance.

The wolf leapt over the couch toward Swift.

Chance caught the scruff of the wolf's neck mid-air and led her down to sitting beside him.

Her head reached Chance's waist and was twice as broad as his hand, resting atop it.

Chance took hold of Swift's rigid hand. He brought it to the wolf's snout.

Swift fought a reflex to pull back.

Chance kept him steady. "Let her smell. Let her taste."

The wolf snuffled Swift's hand. Licked his fingers and wrist.

"There, now," said Chance. "You've been kissed by a Sea Wolf. You've a friend for life in this lass—our Fortuna."

"Fortuna." Though Swift couldn't shake the fear of her, he found himself easing closer for the sake of her beauty. Her magnificent size. Her silver eyes, seeming lit. "A Sea Wolf?"

He'd heard of Sea Wolves, but only in Old Norse tales. He'd never imagined they might actually exist.

Swift stroked her husky neck, his touch collapsing her to lying down at his feet.

From outside, a chorus of howls rang.

Fortuna answered but didn't rise. She kicked at her ear where she apparently wanted Swift to scratch.

In an instant, the house transformed from a rather still space to a torrent of wolf puppies—eight at least—racing in a floppy-eared run, heading fast to Fortuna.

Swift crouched before a tumble of three puppies squirming at his feet.

They were small, the tops of their heads hardly reaching half the height of Fortuna's legs. Their beating tails stood short and alert, and their silky ears drooped.

Swift stroked the silver blue of them, mottled with white. He looked into their eyes at the brightness of what had to be the source of the beasty lights he'd seen in the forest.

"Do they belong to you?" Swift asked Chance.

"They belong to the Wentletrap." Chance glanced at Ash. "Care to be introduced?"

From his wall, Ash, seeming terrified of a growling wolf puppy bouncing his way, shook his head.

Ash's dislike of the wolves appeared mutual. Fortuna, watching him, set her ears back defensively, as though waiting for some aggression from him.

The astronomer and Chance moved to the door.

Chance whistled, and Fortuna wound after them, her puppies in tow.

"See where she's driven Octavian," said the astronomer. "Take back what belongs to Swift."

Chance and Fortuna ran into the mist, trailed by a din of wolves howling.

32

When Chance and the Sea Wolves were far gone, Swift approached Ash at the door.

They together peered out at the fisherman and his pack, disappearing into the trees.

Watching them leave, Ash straightened. He seemed to feel bolder, like he thought dealing with just the strange astronomer was no challenge.

To Swift, though, the astronomer, with his regal nature, seemed more powerful than either Chance or his Sea Wolves. The astronomer's strength seemed of a cooler kind, and yet more formidable. And Chance clearly answered to him.

"Chance won't try to take Octavian on, will he?" asked Ash. "He's bloody stupid if he thinks he could."

"There's no need to worry over Chance," said the astronomer.

"Octavian deals in rustic weapons," said Ash, staring out the door. "And he knows how to use them."

The astronomer closed the door. "Sit down if you will. Drink more water."

"Chance." Swift followed the astronomer to the couch. "Who is he?"

"He's called Chance Merriweather." The astronomer sat. "Will you not rest?"

"Chance...Merriweather," Swift mumbled.

Chance Merriweather. As in—named for the first mate on the legendary *Checkered Whelk*—the ship guided by the dashing crew that robbed from rich tyrants and shared treasures of knowledge and wealth with the poor; the ship whose crew—hundreds of years ago—stole and stowed the Star of Atlantis.

"And what"—Swift stared at the astronomer—"what are you called?"

The astronomer rested his arms on the cushions behind him. "My friends call me Cynfael Maddox."

Swift felt for the couch behind him and dropped onto it.

Ash, his brow quirked, stared at the astronomer. "And what does your therapist call you?"

Swift pulled Ash to sitting beside him.

"It's all right," said Cynfael.

Cynfael Maddox.

A man carrying the name of the *Checkered Whelk's* Captain.

"I see you lads know the Star of Atlantis legends," said Cynfael Maddox. "It would be a bit of a shock, I imagine, meeting two chaps named for the fellows in those myths." He focused on Swift. "Two chaps embracing the legacy of the Shepherd of the Stars."

Swift gripped the strap of his rucksack, resting on the floor; the rucksack bearing the very books that held myths the astronomer—Cynfael—had named.

"It would seem we don't know the legends like you do," said Swift.

Ash narrowed his eyes at Cynfael. "How exactly is it that you know so much? I mean, everyone knows generally of the Star of Atlantis. But it took Swift and me months of research, and some luck, to come across Sterncastle Cove and the *Checkered Whelk* and the Shepherd of the Stars and all that."

"Luck," said Cynfael. "No. There's no such thing. What you're calling luck, I call the fruits of intentionality. Although I wouldn't argue so much if you'd named your achievement 'destiny.'"

He leaned back, as comfortably, as casually, as if it were an everyday thing—speaking with two lads who closely understood the Star of Atlantis.

It seemed he really had been expecting them.

"You believe in destiny?" asked Swift.

"We, all of us, are quite connected," said Cynfael. "Connected to one another, connected by worlds. Across vast distances. Through ages. Connected, as we are, certain things are bound to unfold."

"Connected," Swift echoed.

"You don't seem connected to much," said Ash, staring at Cynfael as though watching him for signs of malice. "We're all but marooned here, in this labyrinthine forest, known to be deadly."

Swift couldn't tell whether this defensiveness on Ash was born of fear—fear from the wolf, from Octavian's attack, fear from feeling isolated—or if it was a growing excitement as thoughts were blooming about how he might get his hands on what treasures Cynfael kept.

"Ash, is it?" Cynfael glanced out the windows at the trees rocking in their blanket of mist. "You've reached a steady place. For I own the Wentletrap Forest. And I mean to protect it from marauders, from destroyers seeking to profit, stripping this ancient woodland of more than the fair and free share of its bounty."

"You can't claim this forest is safe," said Ash. "Swift and I were dead lost." He glanced around. "Anything could happen here, and no one would know."

"Even in desolation," said Cynfael, "sources of help are abundant and near to us." He rested his gaze on Swift. "Even confounded inside the Wentletrap, my young friend, you were never lost."

"If you own all this," said Ash, "it seems a bit of a waste not to make the most of it. The Wentletrap's only made of trees, after all."

He stood from the couch and moved to Cynfael's cases of natural wonders—gemstones, minerals, and fossils.

"Ash, come back," said Swift. "Cynfael hasn't invited us to look at his things."

"Cynfael." Ash shook his head. "A guy holding ground in a dangerous forest where people are known to have died." He faced Cynfael. "Does owning this forest make you responsible for that?"

"Why are you being so coarse?" Swift asked.

Ash, ignoring him, went on with his perusal of the lit cases.

Cynfael, though he seemed to be keeping an eye on Ash, didn't appear affronted by his rudeness, nor concerned with his unflagging interest in the lit cases.

"It was you, wasn't it, who placed those bright signs in the trees?" Swift asked Cynfael.

"Indeed."

"Had it not been for those," said Swift, "we might not have made it here."

Cynfael looked at Swift with a measure of surprise. "You sell yourself short, Swift Starbearer."

Ash huffed. "That's not his name."

He stood from crouching before a case of tarnished necklaces.

"Swift carries the plain name of Kingsley."

"Live long enough," said Cynfael, "and you'll accrete names, the way corals make an empire of sea-buried ships."

"*Devonshire's Boy Finder of Treasure* is better," Ash muttered.

"Those bright signs," said Swift, "signs pointing to the house of the Shepherd of the Stars—is that how you yourself track your way through the Wentletrap?"

Cynfael gazed out the window to the west, toward an eye-catching silver sunset.

"I know the Wentletrap as well as I know the North Atlantic. Its deep shadows, its close growth, its pockets of starlight revealed when the winds deliver their mists back to the sea. The Wentletrap is as much a home to us as this very house."

He met Swift's eyes. "Chance sets those symbols to light when we're expecting company."

Ash cast Cynfael a disparaging look.

"Are you two some sort of Reconstructionist actors? A theatre troupe?"

He came back to the couches and stood behind Swift.

"The next thing he'll tell us is that he knows Griselda Jib and Bones Cooper."

Cynfael, though he said nothing, bore an expression that seemed to confirm some familiarity.

Swift caught Ash's glance and a minor eye roll.

Ash's doubt, though manifesting in disrespect to the person now sheltering them, was understandable.

Swift himself couldn't make heads nor tails of this man, this astronomer going by the name of Cynfael Maddox, sitting in an unbelievable house in the middle of a fantastical forest, the low sunlight spinning now through its trees, casting through plentiful windows shafts of light that set to shimmering walls of cases holding relics and gems Swift could label as none other than "treasure."

Could the astronomer, to some degree, think of himself as the actual Cynfael Maddox—Captain of the *Checkered Whelk*? The leader of mages? The Robin Hood of Welsh Waters? Teacher of thousands? The bane of the powerful, of kings?

But after a moment of concentrating on Cynfael, of trying to read him, Swift found he had to draw away his gaze. It wasn't just that Cynfael seemed impossible to decipher, though that was true. A low burn was igniting in his cut.

Swift clutched the front of his shirt to keep the fabric from touching the tender skin.

"You're yet in pain," said Cynfael.

"When the police arrive to collect us," said Ash, "we should tell them we've found the person who did all that damage to you."

"Lay off him, all right?" Swift, cradling his chest, met Cynfael's eyes. "I'm not going to make any trouble for Chance."

Cynfael sat forward. "It does seem like you're in a good deal of pain. How can I help?"

"The cut wasn't done healing," said Swift. "It isn't ruptured, but Octavian did me no favors."

"It's painful to watch him like that, isn't it?" Ash came around the couch and stood before Swift. "He still drops into fevers from an infection the cut gave him. A fever's probably coming on now."

Swift glanced down at his chest. "As bad as this is, I didn't catch the worst of it that night. My brother broke his leg—almost lost his leg. Almost died. And the boat we wrecked in—the *Star Strider*. She's done for."

"Where is she?" asked Cynfael.

"Tied up by our dock. She's practically swamped. Barnacles are taking hold, and anytime I go out there, I find her choked with seaweed. I fear every storm—that whatever's coming might sink her."

Cynfael poured Swift more water. "And what of her bones?"

"Her skeleton is nearly intact," said Swift. "But it feels like any hard wave might crush her."

"You've had a strange day, heavy with pain and fear," said Cynfael. "Now might not be the best time to assess such matters."

"You're starting to go pale again," said Ash, staring at Swift.

"A fever probably is coming." Swift pointed at his rucksack. "I have medicine."

Cynfael handed him the rucksack.

"He can barely do anything like he used to," said Ash.

Swift glanced at him. "That's not entirely true."

"But it is." Ash glanced at Cynfael. "I mean, Swift is aiming to work his way into this Practicum, for young students wanting to study medicine. But he can't read a word of any medical text. Not that that's a surprise. Anyone would struggle to read such graphic stuff after they'd caused an accident that almost killed someone."

Swift's hands shook as he opened the medicine bottle.

"You wish to study medicine?" asked Cynfael, glancing at the biochemistry text in Swift's rucksack. "That's a bit of a surprise."

Ash gave him an odd look. "Why?"

Swift, though, couldn't dwell on the question. *The Shepherd of the Stars*, too, was peeking from the rucksack. *The Shepherd of the Stars*, which he'd taken from Chance's boat. Or—more accurately—which he'd stolen.

And *The Star of Atlantis*—the fact that it held handwriting alike to what was scrawled in *The Shepherd of the Stars*—it seemed to suggest that here, right before him, sat the real owner of both books.

And it might be that their owner would want the books back.

The thought of losing the books was more painful than the ache of the cut.

And yet—though Swift never could stomach the thought of Octavian's hands on these books, Cynfael's hands seemed a fitting place for them.

Swift pulled out *The Star of Atlantis*. "You know this well, I'd guess."

Cynfael received the book. "And how many long years have passed since I watched its ink dry."

Ash scoffed. "You can't expect us to believe that you saw that book written. Or—you're not claiming to have written it yourself, are you?"

Swift pulled out *The Shepherd of the Stars*.

"Well." Cynfael's eyes brightened. "When you hinted at your knowledge of the Shepherd of the Stars, why—you must've read all about him yourself."

"Using the Sunstone," said Swift.

"A scholar already, then!" Cynfael opened the book. "A student of languages, of Celtic Akkadian?"

"He doesn't know that one as well as some others," said Ash. "Didn't you say, Swift, that you only dabble, amateur-like, in it?"

"I don't think I ever—"

"Chance believed you to be clever"—Cynfael cast a bright

look Swift's way—"but I suspect he hasn't seen the half of it. We hoped you were the one to have taken this from the longboat."

"When did you say the police would arrive?" asked Ash.

Swift found he couldn't take his eyes off Cynfael.

From Cynfael's comment about watching the ink dry in *The Star of Atlantis*—from the honesty on his face, Swift found himself judging it as plausible. At least, Cynfael believed it. Maybe Cynfael was the last in the long line of authors Swift had imagined.

"Did you actually write *The Star of Atlantis? The Shepherd of the Stars?*" asked Swift. "Or—parts of them?"

"It was Chance and I both who put pen to these pages," said Cynfael. "He aimed to capture the spirit of our many voyages—both on these Celtic Seas and on seas yet more magnificent. I added the bits about navigation. Not to mention the science notes."

Swift flipped back to a well-loved page, near the beginning of *The Star of Atlantis*. "Chance wrote the shanty, then?"

Cynfael, without placing his gaze on the page, whistled the shanty. Note for note.

And how beautiful was the sound. Swift didn't realize until this moment—that was the tune Cynfael had used to summon Chance from the forest.

Cynfael turned the books over, appraising their condition, perhaps. Maybe judging some lack of care on Swift's part.

"Chance will be pleased," said Cynfael, "to know his old books have survived."

His old books. Chance's books.

Chance certainly would want to keep them.

Swift had already been stripped of his Sunstone, the absence of which felt like a hole punched right through him. It would be excruciating, parting from these.

But if Cynfael and Chance wanted the books, the map, of course he'd hand them over.

"I suppose," said Swift, trying his best to dampen any emotion in his voice, "that Chance will be glad to have them back."

"Now hang on." Ash dropped to sitting by him. "You can't agree that your books belong to these two. Didn't you buy *The Star of Atlantis*, with your own money, in Exeter?"

"If Chance wrote these books," said Swift, "I'm not keeping them."

"But"—Ash glanced at Cynfael—"how could he have? *The Star of Atlantis* is hundreds of years old."

"Or made to look that way," said Cynfael. "Chance is an artist, at heart. He's aimed to create pieces as true as possible to the actual myth—now many hundreds of years old."

Made to look old.

Swift smiled to himself at the sense of a wound finally seaming—at the feeling of closure to the question of the Cthulhu, that monster so troubling.

"Those books belong in a museum"—Ash straightened, his eyes sharp on Swift—"which you've flat out refused. And yet, here you are, willing to give them to perfect strangers, who"—he glanced at Cynfael—"no offense, might be less than sane."

Swift couldn't meet Ash's eyes.

Ash certainly had wanted Swift to give everything to Octavian. In this moment of stillness, having reached a place of safety, of calm, Swift couldn't help recognizing why.

Octavian had promised Ash a "finder's fee." By refusing Octavian, Swift had probably also denied Ash a weighty reward. A reward for which Ash would resent him until he claimed payback.

"If you're not going to keep those," said Ash, "they ought to be entrusted to someone responsible."

Swift glanced toward the lamplit doorway where treasures —well-cared for—reposed.

"It seems I would be entrusting them to someone responsible." He met Cynfael's eyes. "I can see that these belong in your house. In the House of the Shepherd of the Stars."

Cynfael leaned in. "They belong to you." He slid the books back into Swift's rucksack. "As does The Star of Atlantis, unfortunate, though it is, that you've been parted from it."

Ash rose and stepped away as though throwing a quiet fit.

Swift relaxed back. He glanced at the books, at their silver titles shining from inside his rucksack—as though the ink had been forged of iridium.

And within, they held science notes written by Cynfael's own hand.

Though it was, of course, impossible that this man sitting before him was the actual Cynfael Maddox, Swift found himself feeling that he was every bit as great.

Swift gazed at Cynfael. "Are you, somehow, like the old Captain Maddox, a Shepherd of the Stars?"

"After long years, a person becomes many things," said Cynfael. "From all that makes me who I am—yes, I like to think that I am a Star Shepherd."

Watching him, Swift still couldn't shake the impression that a circlet of silver belonged on his head.

33

Swift ran his fingers over his two books, gifted to him by Cynfael. "I promise to take care of them."

"I believe that you will," Cynfael went to the hearth and adjusted its logs. "You deciphered the Celtic Akkadian text. That's no trifle." He lit the kindling and coaxed it to blaze. "I expect you'll come to appreciate, more and more, what those books hold."

The warmth from the fire was heavenly. But the warmth reaching Swift most deeply seemed not to be coming from the fire, but from Cynfael, standing before the embers and feeding the golden flame oak leaves and twigs given by the Wentletrap's ancient trees.

"How about that?" Ash, standing behind the couch, behind Swift, slugged him in the arm. Too hard. "Swift can read freaking Celtic Akkadian in these books, but hardly a word of that biochemistry one."

Cynfael watched Ash. "Now that is odd."

"In the past, I've read some of my brother's medical texts," said Swift. "My brother, Caius, is on his way to becoming a doctor. If I can master this biochemistry text, and some others, I might earn a place in this incredible Practicum in Somerset. It would let me start reading medicine early, and I could win a seat in a great university—one I might not get into otherwise."

"You sound like a most motivated student," said Cynfael.

"Ash is right, though," said Swift. "Since the accident, I've barely managed to read a word of medicine."

Cynfael glanced at Swift's biochemistry text. "May I see?"

Swift lifted the book out of his rucksack and handed it to Cynfael.

"I've taught students your age before," said Cynfael, opening the book.

"My age." Swift rested his eyes on Cynfael, on the masterful way he was appraising the book.

"Ay, though perhaps not with your capabilities." Cynfael held the biochemistry text before Swift. "Would you like to try reading a page or two to me?"

Swift went dizzy with pleasure at the thought of sitting side-by-side with Cynfael; of Cynfael teaching him and he working hard for him; of having Cynfael's gentle attentiveness directed at him.

But at the same time, if he did open himself to the help, Cynfael would no longer see a student with "capabilities." He'd see only a damaged lad, struggling. But as unpredictable as was everything in the Wentletrap Forest—Cynfael himself seemed the most unfathomable of all. Showing him honestly how deeply this problem ran—despite how mortifying that would be to reveal—it seemed worth the risk.

"I can try." Swift took the text. "Though I'm afraid all you'll see is that reading is difficult for me."

"But that's not quite true, is it?" Cynfael glanced at Swift's other books.

"It is true," said Ash. "But no one could blame Swift for struggling to read medical rubbish, to study injuries and pain after they'd seen what Swift's seen. After they'd done what he's done."

Cynfael watched Ash. "You're a sly lad. Very sly."

Ash looked pleased. "I like to think so."

Cynfael trained his gaze on Swift. "If you let me see you

read, I might gather an idea of the source of your trouble. Shall we learn what I might observe?"

Swift thumbed to the first chapter of the biochemistry text—to a section on nucleic acid.

Ash leaned in. "Go on, Swift. You can do it. Prove your brother wrong. Broken as he is, what if you did manage to press on? You might overtake him. Wouldn't that be something?"

Swift and managed to draw out the first line. He started on the second, but paused.

"You're doing great," said Ash. "If Caius were to limp in right now, he'd be wowed."

Swift tried again but could hardly get a single word out of his mouth.

And looking at the sentences strung together—they struck as senseless.

"It may not seem like it"—Ash glanced at Cynfael—"but this lad's bloody brilliant. He saved his brother's life when they wrecked. It was a good thing he'd read some medical texts by then. Otherwise—who knows? He might've been convicted of manslaughter."

The fever igniting from the exertion of their ride, or panic from the images Ash was conjuring, or maybe the tension from having been in a fight, from having run from Octavian and the Sea Wolf—something inside Swift was reaching a breaking point, making his hands shake and quickening his heart.

Cynfael watched Swift. "Keep on."

Swift laid his finger, trembling, on the page.

He managed to push his way through the second sentence, but in the third, he got no further than the first word—hemoglobin. And it came out—"hobgoblin." He closed the book.

"Maybe we should give him a break?" Ash glanced at Cynfael. "I'd love to hear what you know about that book Swift swiped from the longboat. Swift would, too, I'm sure. If you and that Chance guy wrote *The Shepherd of the Stars*—if you two really can write Celtic Akkadian in code, you must be a master of languages, like Swift. Even better than Swift. We'd be desperate to know what else you've written about, using those secret symbols."

Cynfael started to speak, but—

"Maddox and Merriweather—the old pirates you guys are pretending to be"—Ash leaned between Swift and Cynfael; rested his elbows on the back of the couch—"do you know a lot about them? I mean, legend has it that they guarded many treasures. Would you say that's true?"

Although Swift certainly wanted to know Cynfael's thoughts on the Star of Atlantis myth, Ash pressing him like this was disrespectful. Ash clearly had no interest in Cynfael or Chance—he just wanted access to what they knew; to what they had.

Swift felt it keenly, for this was exactly how Ash treated him.

A wave of protectiveness striking, at watching it happen to Cynfael, brought Swift edging closer to him.

Ash glanced around the house. "Legend has it there were more treasures, like the Sunstone, kept by the Atlantiseans. Do you think there are more Sunstones? I can't help but hope so. As *Devonshire's Boy Finder of Treasure*, I'd love any leads you could share."

"Well," Cynfael shifted, "I really can't—"

"Or perhaps you're hoarding relics here that are even better."

Ash, wide-eyed, glanced behind them, toward the lamplit room.

"Are you?"

Swift said, "Ash, leave it—"

"I mean," said Ash, "the real Cynfael Maddox, and the real Chance Merriweather—they stole all kinds of things. I've wondered whether the 'Star of Atlantis' doesn't refer to more treasures than just Sunstones." He narrowed his eyes at Cynfael. "What do you think?"

"Ash," said Swift, adopting a stern tone belonging to Caius. "Cool it, okay?"

Cynfael seemed to collect his calm as quickly as Ash had

disrupted it. "You lads have some claim on the Star of Atlantis, I'd say"—he offered a kind glance to both Swift and Ash—"considering how hard you've worked to learn its legends."

"That's just how I see it," said Ash. "So—can you tell us anything?"

Cynfael leaned in. "What do you know about the seven-pointed star of Celtic myths?"

Swift picked up his *Star of Atlantis* book. He held it inside a beam of failing twilight, making the star on its cover shimmer.

"Seven-pointed stars represent what the ancient Celts defined as foundational elements," said Cynfael.

"I can recite those." Ash leaned over the book and pointed to the star's pinnacles. "The moon...wind...next is enchantment...the sea...then spirit, I think...forests...and the sun." He stood back as though expecting applause. "It's banking knowledge like this that helped me find my incredible treasure."

Swift cast him a look. "You do realize that Cynfael is an expert in these myths."

"You've rattled them off right," said Cynfael. "What you call 'spirit,' though, I'd call 'connectivity.' There are forces that draw us together, alongside forces that tear us apart. And speaking of treasures"—Cynfael looked directly at Ash—"I have a task for you. Or more, it's a puzzle."

"Oh, marvelous!" said Ash. "I'm great at puzzles. If I'd have studied Celtic Akkadian—who knows? I might've been the one to figure out your book's code."

Cynfael angled toward the lamplit room, its arched doorway aglow with the silver of the setting sun, its rays glancing off suits of armor, off crystals. "In that room, I keep some most valuable relics, collected over...well, over a very long span of time. Wander around in there, and take a good look."

"Seriously?" Ash stepped back toward the room.

"See if you can identify the most ancient artifact," said Cynfael. "A hint—it isn't what you first might think."

"Can I touch things?" asked Ash.

Swift faced him. "Can you not just look?"

"I'm not concerned," said Cynfael. "After all, you're *Devon-*

shire's Boy Finder of Treasure. From one treasure hound to another—surely I can count on you to handle my things delicately."

"Man, oh man, yes." Ash raced to the glowing room and clung to its arched doorway. "Swift, if you need anything, I'll just be—" he pointed inside.

"On with you, then," said Cynfael.

Ash hurried out of sight.

His disappearance brought a wash of relief, like a dying down of storm wind.

This release at Ash's departure was familiar to Swift. In the past, Swift had chalked it up to overstimulation—a simple effect of being around an intense person.

But this change of pressure, Swift felt with more clarity—maybe from seeing his own liberation reflected in Cynfael. It was an escape from Ash's questioning. His cynicism. His accusations.

Cynfael glanced at the biochemistry book. "Shall we try again?"

Swift rested his hand on the book. "Trying again may not help. I don't know why I can't do this. My cut's hurting. So is my head. Maybe they're distracting me."

"Something is distracting you, certainly," said Cynfael.

Swift slid the text onto the coffee table. "My brother has thought that the Star of Atlantis and all its legends have driven off my focus." He drew from his rucksack the map. "But how could they? These are wonder filled."

He unfolded it.

"What a sight for sore eyes." Cynfael straightened it.

"You really created all this?" asked Swift.

"Ay, along with Chance. The drawings of the sea creatures were the work of another friend of ours." He met Swift's gaze. "A friend by the name of Bones Cooper."

Swift jolted at that.

"Bones is an excellent artist, though not as strong as Chance I think. Chance, you see, is sensitive—damaged by the conflict, the cruelty he's seen. He uses artistry as a tool for handling that pain."

Swift trailed his finger along the map, following the excellent artwork.

He landed where the ordered text lay—the coded Celtic Akkadian symbols he knew to be coordinates.

"Who did these?"

Cynfael glanced at him. "Did you read them?"

"Yes, along with Octavian, unfortunately. I know this line crossing the top reads—*Valor is the gateway to destiny*. I know that these lines include numbers. Coordinates, it seems. But I barely got a look and can hardly recall what I saw. Ash believes they name the locations of other treasures."

"They do," said Cynfael, a look of satisfaction, of deep joy brightening his eyes.

Swift felt his own eyes widen.

Cynfael rested his gaze on Swift. "These are longitudinal, latitudinal notations corresponding with the finest stargazing points in Pembrokeshire."

Swift leaned back, a deep-seated tension in his body dissolving.

This great man—Cynfael Maddox—valued stargazing, astronomy, science, and wisdom above what was merely of material worth.

Swift couldn't draw his gaze off Cynfael. "That might be the most wonderful thing I've ever heard."

"I hoped you'd think so," said Cynfael.

"Hey, Maddox." Ash appeared in the arched doorway, holding up a tattered cloak that looked like it'd been through a fire. "Is everything here authentic? Some seem theatrical, like costumes."

Though Ash was speaking to Cynfael, his gaze was fixed on the map in Swift's hands.

"All is authentic," said Cynfael.

Ash lingered in the doorway, as though wanting to hear what Cynfael and Swift were talking about.

"And I'll tell you what," said Cynfael, to Ash. "If you indeed guess the oldest thing in there, I'll let you keep it."

"God—really?" asked Ash.

"Go," said Cynfael. "Plan your guess."

Ash disappeared.

Swift focused again on the map, on the coordinates. "The stars are stunning in Wales, even on hazy nights. How beautiful they must shine from points you'd identify as the finest."

"I'm not sure how one can live in Pembrokeshire and not fall in love with the stars," said Cynfael.

"I've always been drawn to stars, too," said Swift.

"Indeed?" Cynfael watched Swift with a knowing expression.

"I feel there's a depth of meaning to them," said Swift, "these lights that peer down on us, these suns."

He gazed more closely at the coordinates.

"Stars and legends and venturing into the unknown—I'm not sure how Caius can call these distractions. More than anything, they're enlivening."

"Caius—your brother," said Cynfael, "is he the one looking after you here?"

"The idea was that he'd look after me," said Swift. "He means to—but the truth is, I don't think that he can."

Swift startled at hearing himself articulate this problem so plainly.

It felt partly relieving to tell Cynfael, this unexpected sympathetic listener, that Caius was failing him. But it also felt treacherous.

Caius wanted to help. He was trying.

"I've lately lost track of Caius," said Swift. "Or maybe he's lost track of me. I thought he understood these legends as I do. Legends, I've always felt, steady us. Sometimes it seems the problem is too much reality. Maybe it's reality that sinks us."

"But more wonderful than legends, even"—Cynfael stood and went to a bookcase—"is reality."

He drew a book from his shelf and set it before Swift.

It was an anatomy text.

"For on what else could the magnificent trees of the Wentletrap grow but the plain soil of Earth?" asked Cynfael. "It's their grounded nature that lets them sail in high winds, beneath stars."

Swift opened the anatomy text.

"I'm no student of medicine," said Cynfael, "but I have a fine library, which I've read through to completion. And I do understand that the human body is no less wonderful than any treasure a coastal cave might keep."

"So—you've read anatomy?" asked Swift.

"Some years ago."

"But you're an astronomer," said Swift. "What would a star scientist want with an anatomy book?"

Cynfael studied Swift. "Much, it would seem." He sat down opposite him. "You and I are quite alike in that many of the sciences fascinate us. For in such a book as that which you hold, we read about cells—each comprised of complex microstructures carrying out tasks with intention. Structures sharing the chemistry of stars."

Cynfael flipped to a picture of human musculature.

"The tendons, the tissues, all connected, all carrying out tasks with deliberation."

He flipped again.

"And there—the brain—keeper of meaning and memory and will. The mind—is it not the treasure store of the strategist, a trove whose mysteries, even now, we've not tapped?"

He flipped on.

"There—blood to nourish us. Bones to lend form." He stopped at a cardiovascular diagram. "A heart that persists, despite all, sending energy thrashing, the ultimate coursing of waves. All that's mystical, magical, grounding—you deal in when you deal in anatomy."

In the silence that followed, Swift realized his own heart was calming, his trembling easing.

"But I'm speaking to you nothing which is new," said Cynfael. "In caring for your brother on your darkest night, you were stirred by more forces than simple medical knowledge, I think."

"I was terrified for Caius," said Swift. "I couldn't stand to see him in such pain. I wanted to understand what was happening and intervene. I wanted to fix what I'd done, though I hardly knew what to make of his injuries. Still, I was determined to help him."

"In you, I see a lad stirred by purpose. Full of resolve." Cynfael held Swift's glance. "A lad of compassion and gentleness. And so, harnessing what you'd managed to learn of these grounding realities, driven by your tenacity, your decisiveness, you delivered Caius his life back."

Swift, staring at Cynfael, found himself set wholly at ease by his words—framing that darkest night, it seemed, more truly than he himself ever had managed.

For the first time since the accident, Swift felt he'd handled things well. For the first time, he felt that he wasn't to blame for what happened to Caius. To the *Strider*. To himself.

For the first time, he could see that he'd done his best.

Breathing steadily, his heart gentled, he felt like a small lad listening to a trusted brother saying—"Everything's going to be okay."

Swift squared the anatomy book before him. "Can I try this again?"

Cynfael rested back. "Read."

Swift stared at the page of tight text, the words seeming to jumble together until they were as overstimulating as Ash.

"But—I don't even know how to approach this," said Swift. "Or at least not without some support."

"Is that so?" asked Cynfael.

"Caius normally places his hand on my shoulder. Or Ash— he cheers me on, like you heard. He encourages me, reinforcing my effort when I make any headway."

"I've seen exactly what Ash does," said Cynfael.

"Can you set your hand on my shoulder, or say encouraging words to me?"

Swift glanced at him.

"Or maybe both?"

"I'm not doing either of those things," said Cynfael. "You say you want to read medicine, and that's well enough. But in doing so, you'll be achieving strides all on your own."

"But that's the problem," said Swift. "I can't do it on my own."

"Did you not read *The Shepherd of the Stars* on your own?"

"Yes, but that's different. I love that book. It's about myths and sea histories and treasures and the ways of the *Checkered Whelk*—your book."

"Do you not love medicine?"

"I do," said Swift. "I love it. It's just—"

"Then read," said Cynfael. "If you can. And don't stop until you've made it a full page. I won't rush you. I won't interrupt you. I'll only be listening."

Swift suffered a painful lash of isolation. Caius and Ash—to some extent—were at least trying to help him. Why would Cynfael seem only interested in challenging him? Why had he stated outright the awful possibility that Swift might fail?

"What if I can't do it?" asked Swift.

"Then you'll know the truth and can alter your course. As you grow, you'll come to see that there's no sense in wasting your precious time harboring illusions."

"But—what then?" asked Swift.

"Then you and I shall have little left to do with one another on this matter."

"So that's it?" asked Swift. "If I can't read this—right now— you're giving up on me? Even though you say you're a teacher, you're just resolving already that I can't do it?"

"I never said you can't do it," said Cynfael. "Shall we find out?"

"You're not getting it," said Swift. "My whole problem is that I don't know how to read this on my own."

"No," said Cynfael. "Your problem is that you aren't willing to try on your own, as I'm asking. Understand—I can help a student take in new knowledge, and with that knowledge render magnificent feats. I can't, however, help a student be willing."

Swift held himself quiet a moment.

He'd never thought of his struggle in terms of willingness. Had he never been willing to trust himself to read, to try without depending on supports? It really seemed that without supports, he'd get nowhere.

But what if that wasn't true? What if Cynfael was right?

What if the problem wasn't that he'd lost the skill, but that he'd never properly tried?

"Are you willing to try on your own?" Cynfael watched him, a keen look of expectation on his face.

Beneath Cynfael's gaze, a deep insight grew clear.

Whenever Swift had picked up a medical text, he'd never really felt he had permission to engage with it. Or it was as though, if he did, he'd be paining someone—causing Caius to feel resentment or Ash to feel outdone.

Cynfael brightened, as though perceiving what was dawning.

Swift was glad to be with Cynfael, such a caring soul, as an agonizing certainty came to light.

For the fact was—whether he succeeded at reading medicine, at the Practicum, the separation between himself and Caius would probably expand. And Ash might choose to abandon him, no matter what.

All this time, he'd been snatching at supports no more stable than sand. He'd been grasping at things already lost.

It seemed Cynfael might be right, then. The only thing Swift could control was whether he himself wanted this, and how badly—for himself and for his own reasons. Not for Caius or Justus or Ash. Not in spite of them. But because—

"Swift?" Cynfael captured his glance. "Are we doing this?"

"Because I love medicine," Swift murmured.

And because he loved the great feats he imagined accomplishing with it. Helping people the way he'd helped Caius. Tending to the suffering of others, to pain, as Brooke did. Healing the whole person, like Dr. Keats could. Transcending the practice of medicine, striving to innovate, like his own great-grandfather.

Swift widened the anatomy book.

Cynfael leaned back again, not looking at Swift, but gazing at the fragrant, stony hearth and its steady blaze.

Swift read the first line from the anatomy book fluidly. He followed it by reading the entire first paragraph. The next three paragraphs flowed more quickly yet.

Swift spoke the final word on the page.

He closed the book. Looked up at Cynfael. "Whoa."

"And there you have it." Cynfael shifted his gaze onto Swift. "You haven't lost anything."

Swift stared at him. "How'd you do that?"

Cynfael brightened. "I did nothing, Swift. You did."

34

A hard knock rang at the door, making Swift jump.
Swift and Cynfael together stood.

It had to be the police.

Swift called over his shoulder. "Ash, the police have come."
Glancing at Cynfael, he picked up his rucksack. "I hate to leave
you, to leave this place. Could I come back to see you?"

Cynfael guided Swift to the door. "Anytime. Chance will
keep the lights in the trees shining for you."

"But—will that not lead others here?" asked Swift. "You said
that you keep this place secret."

"The Wentletrap is too treacherous to attract wanderers.
And no one uninvited would have a sense of what our signs
mean. Even Octavian Krakau, who's tried plundering us more
than once, finds it too confounding."

Cynfael opened the front door.

On the threshold, wet with mist and looking wild with
distress, stood Caius. Swift threw his arms around his brother.

It was rare in their family to show physical affection. But
Swift couldn't help himself. Caius, standing before him, meant
the safety of home.

Caius seemed equally unable to resist the embrace. After a

345

moment, he held Swift before him. "God—your face." He studied the blood staining Swift's shirt. "Let me see you."

"I'm fine." Swift held still for Caius to look at the knot on his forehead. "Better than fine, actually." He glanced at Cynfael.

Cynfael held open the door. "Come in, lad."

Caius limped in. "I can't thank you enough for seeing him safe." He glanced around. "Where's Ash?"

Swift glanced over his shoulder, at the lamplit room of relics, where it sounded like Ash was sliding open one of the display cases. "He's looking at some of Cynfael's things."

"Cynfael." Caius stared at him.

Cynfael guided Caius to the couch. "Ease your body and your mind. Your brother is all right. And he'll no doubt grow stronger in the days to come."

Caius looked so wearied, and no wonder—he must've had an intense trek, struggling through the Wentletrap in his rigid walking cast. But even more than seeming in pain, he looked pale with anguish.

Maybe Caius would be angry with him, as Ash had been, for not just giving up everything to Octavian.

If he had, all this danger might've been avoided.

Would Caius, like Ash, consider Swift selfish?

But from the relieved way Caius was appraising him, it seemed the comfort of their having found one another might displace any anger.

Caius gestured for Swift to sit by him. "Tell me everything."

Swift gently laid out what'd happened at the museum to drive them into the Wentletrap Forest. He told Caius of their trek through the forest—told him of Octavian and his threats and his tree branch.

"Let me see your chest," said Caius.

"Don't worry about that now." Though Swift was still having to hold his shirt away from his skin, he couldn't give the cut nor the blow to his head a second of concern. Not when he was burning to tell Caius of the success he'd had reading with Cynfael. "I think the punch left nothing more than a bruise."

Caius drifted against the back of the couch, as though in some shock. "This is twice, now, I've let you down."

"No—you found me," said Swift. "How exactly did you find me?"

Cynfael poured Caius a cup of water. "My guess is the police sent you our way."

"They did." Caius gave Cynfael a grateful glance as he took the cup.

"Hey Maddox." Ash ambled into the doorway and leaned against the jamb. "I think I solved your puzzle."

"How did the police even reach you?" Swift asked Caius. "Your phone—why didn't it work?"

Caius rubbed at the back of his neck. "Brooke and I passed a little hotel, on a river. They had a pub right on the water. So we stopped and had some wine. My phone, you see—it fell into the water, and—"

"How'd it fall into the water?" Ash, folding his arms, was grinning.

Caius held still a moment. "It just fell." He placed his gaze again on Swift. "With the phone gone, a terrible fear struck. It was that horrible feeling we both suffered in Sterncastle Cove— the sense of being dangerously divided from one another."

"Take heart," said Cynfael, watching Caius in a pleased way, as though reading his character and liking what he saw. "Your brother is safe."

"And that would be thanks to you." Caius shed barely a glance at Cynfael, as though he were ashamed of himself. "The instant that phone went into the river, we left. We didn't even try fishing it out. We just came. We checked quickly at home. Brooke stayed there, in case you and Ash came back, while I went to the museum." A look of panic crossed Caius' face. "When I arrived, the place was in chaos. Flashing lights. Police cars. The whole place taped off. I told them who I was, and they gave me a motorbike and pointed out the trail you must've followed. The police said I'd find lights in the trees—lights glowing in the mist. I saw them and followed. I rode as far as I could, then I dropped the motorbike and kept going on foot. I found a fresh trail through the trees—your trail, it seemed. That led me to this place." He looked around. "This unbelievable place."

Ash came to standing behind them. "I hope your finding us doesn't mean we have to go. I've seen why Cynfael keeps this house a secret. You won't believe what he's got back there."

"What did the police say about Octavian?" Swift asked Caius.

"They think Octavian is on the run. With the Sunstone, I'm afraid, and quite a few stolen relics." Caius glanced at Ash. "I'm sorry, but your box was among what he took."

"That's"—Ash flinched—"that's not possible."

"Even his house has been vacated," said Caius. "The police believe it was emptied a few days ago. It seems like he schemed this getaway." His hands twitched as he spoke.

"You've got it wrong." Ash stumbled back a step. "Octavian said he wanted to see me tomorrow."

"Ash, think it through," said Swift. "There's no way he wanted to see you tomorrow. And the police couldn't be mistaken."

"Then they have to be lying," said Ash. "Octavian wouldn't have gone on the run like that."

"But he has," said Caius, the expression on his face tender as he watched Ash.

This was the first time since they'd arrived in Pembrokeshire that Caius had offered Ash any hint of compassion. It was a relief, at least, that it seemed Caius wouldn't blame Ash for any of this.

"The important thing is that we're all safe," said Swift.

Ash caught Cynfael's glance. "I figured out your puzzle. Don't you care? It wasn't even very hard."

Caius felt Swift's cheeks. "You're cool at least. After a day like this, I thought I'd find you ill." He glanced at Swift's hand, still holding his shirt away from his chest. "When we get home, I'll clean your cut and take a good look." He poured more water into his glass and handed it to Swift.

"Cynfael," said Swift, "he's a great teacher." He slid the

anatomy text toward Caius. "With him, I read a whole page. And fast—like I could before our accident."

Caius glanced at Cynfael. "You saw him read a medical text?"

"Doesn't anyone want to know my solution to Cynfael's puzzle?" Ash focused on Caius. "Cynfael set me on an interesting scavenger hunt, which I've finished."

Cynfael, though he'd been very patient with Ash, seemed to be working hard to remain so.

"Your answer, then."

"I was to find the oldest thing in that room." Ash, his hands behind his back, eased closer to them. "And I believe that I have." He seemed to be struggling to conceal a grin.

"Well?" asked Cynfael.

Ash held out a silver dagger, its hilt shaped like a mermaid, diamonds lighting her eyes.

A dagger that gleamed, as though moonlit, in the gray twilight shafting through the windows.

It was the fisherman's dagger. The dagger that'd drawn the cut on Swift's chest.

Swift stood.

Caius, watching Swift, stood, too.

Cynfael hurried to Ash. "Give it here, lad."

"I know it's old"—Ash held it away from Cynfael—"because I recognized it, from Swift's description, as probably the meteorite-forged blade that Chance used to cut him." He laughed. "And—the look on your face, Swift—I see I was right!"

Cynfael held his hand open for the dagger.

"I thought to myself—what's older than a meteorite? Nothing." Ash placed the dagger in Cynfael's hand. "Am I right?"

Caius stared at Cynfael. "The fisherman." He glanced at Swift. "Is he...?"

Swift shook his head.

"Though, we should lend you fair warning." Cynfael quickly shrouded the dagger in a drawer. "Chance—Swift's fisherman—does live here, too. He and I are as brothers. Upon learning what happened today, I sent him to look for Octavian."

"Do you know Octavian?" asked Caius.

"A canker in the world if ever there was one," said Cynfael. "But Chance, I assure you, is trustworthy."

Caius glanced at Swift's chest.

"Troubled," said Cynfael, "but trustworthy."

Caius, his hands shaky, eased Swift to sitting back down. "Take it easy, all right?" He approached Ash. "You believed that was the dagger that cut Swift—and yet you brought it out?"

Ash shrugged. "Cynfael told me to find the oldest thing." He looked at Cynfael. "I mean—was I wrong?"

Cynfael pointed through the arched doorway. "The black jar, on the entryway table—bring it to me."

"That jar of marbles?" Ash collected it and brought it to Cynfael. "Those can't be old—I mean, not older than a blade forged from a meteorite."

Cynfael received the jar and lifted out one of its small, gunmetal-gray balls. "The dagger was forged from meteorite metal, yes—in the twelfth century. As old as it is, though, these 'marbles' are far older. This metal—also not of this Earth—was used for wide-scale combat, in the fifth century."

"Back when they used to throw rocks at each other?" asked Ash. "Those marbles couldn't have been very powerful."

"These aren't marbles," said Cynfael. "They're the makings of a bomb."

Caius glanced from the small sphere to Cynfael. "Are they dangerous?"

"Not in themselves." Cynfael handed it to him. "They're what one might call ammunition. Without a detonator, they're completely benign. Worthless, really, except to a collector."

Caius placed it back inside the jar.

"There's no way you're right," said Ash. "I mean—people living more than a thousand years ago would've been too primitive to construct a bomb."

"Primitive," said Cynfael. "Not in the least."

Ash's expression darkened, as it did often when he grew upset.

He'd been wrong, which he hated. And he'd probably been counting on getting to keep Chance's meteor-made dagger.

"Those marbles don't seem so old to me," said Ash. "And they don't look at all dangerous."

"Things that might seem benign," said Cynfael, studying Ash, "can be quite deadly."

Ash returned the appraisal. "You mean like a fisherman?"

A paleness of fury, it seemed, took Caius. He crossed his arms, clearly struggling to contain it.

Cynfael rested his gaze on Caius. "You and I must speak, in privacy." He glanced at Swift. At Ash. "Ramble about in my relic room. Just beyond it, you'll find the kitchen. Help yourself to anything you like."

Why would Cynfael want to speak to Caius in privacy? It seemed anything he had to say, he could say to them together.

Caius glanced at Swift. "Go on."

35

Swift followed Ash into Cynfael's room of relics. He settled at a small table just inside the arched doorway.

From here, he could hear Caius and Cynfael speaking, barely.

Leaning ever so slightly, keeping in the room's shadow, he could see them, too.

They were settling beside one another on the couch—Caius watching Cynfael closely, Cynfael bearing a grave expression.

If they glanced this way, Swift would need to seem absorbed in something. He drew his map and two legend books from his rucksack. He unfolded the map before him on the small table.

But it wasn't too difficult to make his perusal seem genuine. His eye was drawn to the line of coordinates, cryptic and partial without the clarity lent by the Star of Atlantis. He studied the first set of coordinates—worked to recall the characters as they'd looked through the stone.

Ash spent a moment investigating a bowl of what looked like semi-precious gems before stepping into the kitchen.

"Are all these merits yours?" Caius asked Cynfael.

Swift peered in to see Caius standing from the couch.

Cynfael joined him at the wall of credentials.

"I'm a teacher by trade," replied Cynfael. "Though, I've dabbled in many sciences."

Swift recalled the passage he'd read with Ash in *The Shepherd of the Stars*—a passage speaking of the original Cynfael Maddox as a teacher.

He flipped to it and read—

People encountering the spirit of Cynfael Maddox, over centuries, often reported that they felt a sense of destiny, a great wisdom imparted. Many think of him as a true renaissance man—a magnificent teacher with endless ideas and knowledge. And some in his company were known to be gifted with foresight.

The man standing with Caius couldn't be the actual Cynfael Maddox. Of course not. But it was thrilling how alike Cynfael—a great teacher—was to the Captain inhabiting legends.

"He's got scones." Ash, his mouth full, appeared at the kitchen doorway. "Want any?"

Swift shook his head.

Ash moved to the far end of the room—to a corner with fewer displays.

He stood before a line of trunks set beside stacks of loose-leaf papers and folders.

Swift lifted a small magnifying glass from a bowl of trinkets resting on the center of his table.

He straightened the map before him and studied it through the glass.

He could recall a few bits of how the first line of coordinates had appeared—enough to deduce that they were referencing a point within the map. He followed the longitudinal markings scaling the map's edge.

It seemed the first coordinate set pointed to a place within the lower left quadrant, where the coast met the forest.

At the center of that quadrant, an interesting feature was

drawn—a hill rising quite a bit higher than the surrounding land.

And on it was marked a small spiral of hashes.

He'd noticed the feature before but had never paid it much mind. The whole map was drawn with so many artistic details, he'd thought this was a mere decoration—a semblance of a seashell.

Perhaps, though, it marked the winding way up to a pinnacle—one of Cynfael's stargazing heights.

"Some of my merits are honorary," said Cynfael, to Caius. "Some are well-earned."

"They all must be well-earned," said Caius. "Universities don't loosely distribute honorary degrees. What did you teach?"

"I'm an astronomer and physicist more than anything. One might call me a seafarer, too. I've done well enough to enjoy an early retirement—I now own and care for this forest. And since I've let go of formal employment, I find myself a scientist jack of all trades. I consult when my friends in the science community seek collaboration. I work mainly with other astronomers, engineers, and physicists."

"How have you had time to manage all this?" asked Caius. "You can't be but a decade older than me."

"I might be a bit older than I look," said Cynfael, a smile brightening his voice. "And I guess you could say—I began my career at an early age."

"Then you have something in common with Swift," said Caius. "He's aiming to start soon in his medical studies."

"Young Swift, with his interest in medicine," said Cynfael, "he's reminded me of my own love for the field. I have no experience there, although Chance does. Field experience, that is. Military."

"Whatever your accomplishments," said Caius, "among them is what you did this day, keeping those lads safe. I can't tell you how terrified I was. My hands, you see—they're still shaking."

"Swift is lucky to have someone like you to care for him."

"He needs more than care." Caius' words sounded pained.

Swift leaned back ever so slightly to catch a better view through the doorway.

Cynfael was guiding Caius again to the couch.

"Swift needs healing," said Caius.

"I surmise," said Cynfael, "that he isn't the only one."

"Here I am, aiming to train to be a doctor." Caius glanced up at Cynfael. "Yet I can't even look after my own brother. But —why am I telling you this? I don't need to bother you with my troubles."

Cynfael relaxed back, offering Caius the same generous attentiveness he'd offered Swift. "Sometimes we demand too much of ourselves. Would you say you yourself have some recovering to do?"

"Sure," said Caius, adjusting his walking cast so no weight was on it. "But it's more complicated than that. I feel like a father to that lad. But it seems the last thing he needs is a father."

"It's clear you've invested much in young Swift," said Cynfael, "to his benefit."

"It pains me to admit it," said Caius, "but I'm doubting I'm the person he needs anymore."

Swift wanted to rush in and say of course Caius was the person he needed.

But Swift himself had admitted this same difficulty to Cynfael. For although Caius was genuinely trying to help, in truth, he wasn't just on the brink of pulling away from Swift. Caius had already pulled away.

Coming to Wales together hadn't changed anything. It hadn't kept Caius close, as Swift imagined it might. It hadn't fixed anything. It'd only prolonged the illusion that nothing between them had changed.

"What Swift needs a teacher," said Caius. "A great one. And he needs a true friend. Since the accident, I've been neither of those things to him."

"The poor lad believes that he has a true friend," said Cynfael.

Caius shared a moment of what looked like mutual understanding with Cynfael.

"Swift, you have to come see this," called Ash, from the far end of the room.

Cynfael and Caius both glanced back toward the doorway.

Swift ducked out of their sightline.

"Cynfael's got whole trunks of old parchments," said Ash. "They look just like what came from my box."

Cynfael spoke on to Caius, but his voice trailed off, too low for Swift to hear.

Caius, too, now was whispering.

Ash approached Swift. "What are you doing?"

Swift glanced at the map. "I was...seeing if I could trace our path through the forest."

Ash angled the map toward himself. "Cynfael spoke to you about this, didn't he?"

Caius' voice sounded from the other room. "My father will, of course, want to meet you."

"Naturally," said Cynfael. "I've taught many students, but never have I taught from medical texts. Perhaps he'd rather Swift be paired with someone more knowledgeable of his chosen field."

Swift's heart quickened. Caius was arranging for Cynfael to teach him. He glanced up at Ash, wondering if he were listening to this.

Ash set his fingers beside the Celtic Akkadian coordinates. "Did Cynfael tell you what these are?"

"Insight on the medical field, we can contribute," said Caius. "I'm afraid Swift has endured a steady regimen of it since he was born. What he needs is structure for learning. And challenges. From the way Swift described how you've already helped him, I think our father will be pleased."

Ash appeared not to be listening to the talk. He was staring down at Swift in an expectant way.

"You're not keeping more secrets, are you?" asked Ash. "What did Cynfael tell you about the map? It seemed like you two were talking over these markings, laid out in rows."

Cynfael had kept his voice very low when speaking of the coordinates. This information, he might have intended to share exclusively with Swift.

Ash lifted his brow. "Why aren't you answering me?"

Swift felt the flash of anxiety Ash certainly had intended to deal him.

This was a familiar pressure, and one he'd caved beneath time after time.

What could he say that would appease Ash while concealing the truth of what Cynfael had revealed?

But lying didn't feel right.

It felt nauseating, in fact—a petty continuation of a game he wanted out of.

And really, what would it matter if he told Ash what Cynfael had shared? A list of stargazing locations wouldn't impress him.

"He did tell me what those are," said Swift.

"Are they coordinates, like Octavian thought?" asked Ash.

"Yes, but I doubt you'll find them interesting."

Ash narrowed his eyes. "Try me."

"They're the locations of Pembrokeshire's best stargazing points," said Swift. "I got a good look at the first set of coordinates through the Sunstone, and I think I remember them—though I can't be sure. I wish we had the Sunstone so I could translate them."

"Why didn't Cynfael translate them for you?" asked Ash. "If he's as smart as he seems to think he is—if he and Chance really did make this map, shouldn't he have?"

"I didn't ask him to," said Swift. "And anyway, I believe I located the first one." He pointed to the spiral of hash marks in the lower left quadrant. "If this indicates a rise, it'd certainly be a great place for stargazing."

Ash, studying the map, seemed smug, as though he were figuring something out.

"Stargazing."

"I'd love to hike to that point," said Swift.

Ash set his finger beside the point and traced it to the latitude and longitude coordinates ticked on the map's edges. "Me too." He jotted the coordinates on a pocket notebook and tucked it away. "Why don't we make a camping trip out of this? A studying trip."

The notion struck Swift like a flash of warm, gentle wind. How the Welsh night must blaze in that place, stars shining horizon to horizon.

The thought of being in such a place with Caius and Brooke, of studying in such a place with Cynfael, was thrilling.

But the thought of Ash with them there—it brought a sense of weariness.

"Caius likely won't let me out of his sight again," said Swift. "And I doubt Brooke would want to camp."

Ash shrugged. "You're probably right." He went back to the trunk and again set to perusing it.

For some long minutes, Swift could hear nothing of Caius' conversation with Cynfael, but only the rustle of the papers Ash was dragging out.

"And those lights," said Caius, finally in an audible voice. "How would Swift have found you without them? The fact that you're even here, that there was someone in this forest to receive my brother—I'm so grateful to you. And your willingness to take him on as a student—I feel indebted."

"Indebted, you're most certainly not."

"That's kind, but"—Caius lowered his voice—"I feel you need to know what you're in for. It's possible that even a great teacher might make no significant difference to Swift's progress."

Though the words had been all but whispered, they struck Swift like a punch to the gut. He let his head tip against the wall.

Caius described to Cynfael, in medical detail, what Swift had suffered. The coma. The deep trauma from the knife cut. The relapsing fever disease. The possibility of lasting impairment.

"There's a good chance Swift is swamped," said Caius. "And I fear he may never be able to see it."

Swift had suspected that Caius viewed him this way.

But to hear him speak of it—the pain was so strong, he felt paralyzed.

"Perhaps his determination will serve him," said Cynfael. "Especially in light of—"

It seemed Cynfael was trying to discern whether Swift and Ash might hear.

For this second, Swift was glad Ash was making a ruckus of the trunk and its papers.

"—in light of the concern I shared," said Cynfael, his voice very low. "I observed how Swift processes text—he manages wonderfully. He reads rapidly. He wraps his mind around concepts with the speed of a striking snake. As sharp as he is, he's sensitive. The obstacle at hand is what I fear might prove fatal to his ambitions."

What obstacle? What concern had Cynfael shared with Caius?

"Swift needs rescue," said Caius. "I should've acted on my instincts and not let this carry on for so long."

"Rescue isn't at all what's needed," said Cynfael. "Young Swift is full of potential energy. You were absolutely right when you said Swift needs challenges."

Swift tried to focus on Caius and Cynfael, but Ash was now calling out with gusto a play-by-play account of what he was pulling from the trunk.

All Swift could clearly pick up from Cynfael was the phrase —"throws guilt and painful reminders."

Swift peered through the doorway at Caius and Cynfael.

Something seemed to be passing between them—a certainty dawning. A mutual recognition.

Cynfael said—"not brain damage. An emotional problem, rather. Panic. It isn't the medical books."

Ash scurried to Swift's side. "Mind if I borrow this?" He slipped the map out from under Swift's hand and ran with it to the other end of the room.

Swift watched Ash race away with what was his.

The gesture—seemingly innocent and careless—highlighted an element of Ash's character which appeared set.

Anything belonging to Swift, Ash would take.

There was no friendship here.

No reciprocated respect.

Throws guilt and painful reminders.

Cynfael and Caius had to have been talking about Ash, for that small phrase rang true of him. Since the day Swift had woken from the coma, Ash had regularly brought up the accident.

As concretely as Swift had realized that Caius had already left him, he sighted in clarity another terrible truth.

Ash's friendship, which Swift had been hoping to nurture to health, had never been alive in the first place. Since the accident, Ash had done little besides throw guilt and painful reminders Swift's way.

But why?

Ash, from where he sat, glanced up at Swift and smiled. It was an innocent expression. Careless.

But nothing about Ash was innocent or careless.

Ash was smart and cunning. Intentional and calculating. Creative and successful at getting whatever he wanted.

Suddenly, like a film of haze peeled back, Swift could see Ash objectively—Ash kneeling, his hands on Swift's map.

The change in perspective was as stark as a shifting of sunlight—a darkness resolving to dawn.

A dizzying feeling struck, like keeping one's stance on a ship deck when the sails tilt with a shifting of winds.

For Swift was realizing—Ash had been aiming to keep him in the state of low panic he'd suffered since the accident.

And Ash was succeeding.

"An emotional problem," Cynfael had said. *"It isn't the medical books."*

And the problem wasn't the medical books. In this very hour, Swift had comprehended Cynfael's anatomy text.

And he'd done it after Cynfael had chased Ash from the room, relieving Swift of the pressure of his condemnations.

The clarity, the surety, of the insight brought Swift to his feet.

His whole problem with focusing, with struggling to recover —it wasn't the coma or the fever disease.

It was Ash.

Gazing at Ash brought a flashing of painful memories—Ash reopening Swift's trauma of having to leave Caius on the beach; Ash on the cliff overlooking the Wentletrap, casting guilt at Swift and manipulating an apology out of him; Ash making Swift feel like he himself was in the wrong, over and over; Ash arguing that his emotional pain was greater than Swift's—that Ash's own trials excused him from everything.

"Hey, come and look at this with me," Ash called.

Swift couldn't move.

He could only stare at Ash.

"Swift needs rescue," Caius had said.

A part of him wished Caius would rescue him. Caius, who'd seen, for such a long time, Ash's true nature. If Caius would storm in and handle this, Swift would be free of Ash, free of his oppression.

But—would he be free? If Caius or Cynfael confronted Ash, he'd just cast excuses and plead with Swift to side with him— and for good reason. Swift had done nothing but defend Ash.

The only way to escape Ash would be to stand up to him.

Ash again looked up from the parchments, the map. "Don't you want to see this?"

Swift drifted to him. Stood over him.

"I'm wondering," said Ash, focusing on the map, "whether any of the map's partial Celtic Akkadian letters match anything I might find on these records. If so, the Sunstone might reveal secrets written here." He pressed one of the parchments into Swift's hand. "Can you read the language on that? Let's see if there's any hint of where other treasures might be."

That was all Ash cared about—leads to other treasures.

Panic constricted Swift. Panic over being for so long under the power of someone who cared nothing for him. Someone who wanted only to use him.

Edric had once pegged Ash as narcissistic, which had seemed ungenerous. But Edric might not have been far off.

Ash seemed incapable of seeing anything beyond himself.

"Well, can you read that?" asked Ash. "What language do you think it's written in?"

Ash's exaggerated fury at Swift for concealing *The Shepherd of the Stars* now made perfect sense. Ash had thought the book could lead him to other treasures, perhaps even to Sunstones.

"This parchment seems very old." Swift worked to keep his voice calm.

"Is the language one you understand?" asked Ash.

Swift studied the writing a moment, buying himself time to think, to figure out how to handle this.

"It's a dialect of Icelandic," said Swift. "This seems to hold the same sort of information as the papers in the box you discovered. This page is about crops."

Ash swiped the parchment from Swift. "Do you see any hints of a code?"

Swift lowered into a crouch, next to his map. "Everything there is related to agriculture." He eased the map closer to him.

"The fact that Cynfael has these," said Ash, pulling the map away from Swift, "the fact that they've been preserved here rather than stuck in some box and abandoned—I bet they hold more than farming notes."

"Maybe, like what your box held," said Swift, "these parchments hold value just as they are."

They both looked up at the sound of Caius and Cynfael laughing together.

"I can't get over how that bozo named himself for Cynfael Maddox," said Ash. "And then that daft friend of his—Merriweather—followed suit."

"A lot of guys in Wales might be called 'Cynfael,'" said Swift. "And 'Maddox' or 'Merriweather'—those aren't such uncommon last names."

"They're one kind of unstable if they think it's clever to have taken on names from legends," said Ash. "They're an entirely different kind of insane, though, if they actually believe they're a part of those legends."

Swift could feel what Ash was doing. It was as though, by this fresh clarity, he'd acquired a new language and could interpret Ash's behavior for what it really was.

Ash was manipulating Swift to dislike Cynfael and Chance. To distrust them.

"When the police arrive, I think we should tell them what we've found here." Ash glanced through the doorway. "Or—let's pack up some of this stuff. Did you bring your rucksack in here? We could take a few things and have them appraised."

Swift sat back on his heels. "You're not actually thinking of stealing from them—right?"

Ash surveyed the room. "You know how strongly I feel about the importance of preserving things."

Of course—preserving things for his own purposes.

"Now that we two treasure hunters know about this house," said Ash, "now that we know that the people living here are unsound—we have to do something about it."

"Cynfael and Chance aren't unsound," said Swift. "And we're not going to steal from them."

"Go get your rucksack," said Ash. "Help me gather some of this up. Or—don't tell me you actually trust them."

"I absolutely trust them," said Swift. "And I'm not stealing from them."

"Swift, listen." Ash placed the parchment on a stack he'd created. "If 'Cynfael' and 'Chance' really think of themselves as 'Atlantiseans,' that might mean they stole all this. Didn't the whole crew of the *Checkered Whelk* have a history of kleptomania? We bear a responsibility to bring this to the authorities."

"We have zero reason to think Cynfael and Chance have stolen anything," said Swift. "Would Cynfael have let us call the police if he were afraid of them, or if he were hiding anything?"

Ash shrugged. "People hoard all kinds of contraband. And this house is guarded by layers and layers of danger. That's suspicious."

And Ash would know, certainly, how someone would think,

how someone would act, if they had stolen something. He himself had a history of kleptomania.

Ash grinned. "And who knows but that these parchments really might lead to more treasures? Here, they're just wasting away."

Inside Swift, energy was percolating—energy rising to stop Ash from this recklessness, to call him out.

But he could find no words. It was like a wound—deeper than the cut—was singing out a pain that was keeping him petrified.

"Cynfael and Chance aren't dishonest," was all Swift could manage to say.

"That's only what you want to believe." Ash held up the map. "Cynfael claimed he and Chance drew this and wrote the books you found. That's codswallop." He cast Swift a look. "Right?"

It was a look tuned to program Swift—to threaten judgment if he didn't cave to Ash's perception.

"They're trustworthy," said Swift, resolutely. "More than most."

Ash seemed shocked that Swift wasn't agreeing; that he wasn't falling into line.

Ash straightened. "Tell me that you don't believe them." He cast another look of criticism at Swift. "Tell me that you aren't as loony as they are. Tell me by bringing me your rucksack."

That was a direct order. And it carried a threat of consequence if Swift didn't carry it out.

This clarity striking was marvelous. It was as though Swift could perceive two paths stretching before him—one of following right after Ash's glaring leadership, the other one winding away into dimness.

The path following Ash was worn and easy. Familiar.

The other path—wholly separate and true to himself—was dark-seeming and wild.

The comfort of Ash's path was mainly what had compelled Swift to believe that he needed Ash, that Ash offered stability.

But on that path, Swift wasn't stable. He was only within Ash's control.

And with the ease of Ash's path—with its sunlight and openness—came a dismissal of who Swift himself was; a disbelief that he had any strength of his own.

To follow after Ash was to sacrifice his own pursuits for the sake of whatever Ash wanted.

And Ash wanted treasure. Fame. Power.

He didn't care whether Swift found his way into medicine. He didn't even care whether Swift reached a place of healing. And yet—the thought of dividing himself from Ash was terrifying.

The Wentletrap had been terrifying, though. And Swift had navigated it.

He hadn't needed to lean on Ash's bravery. He hadn't needed Ash to guide him. He'd found his way to safety without Ash. In spite of Ash.

"I believe Cynfael is genuine." Swift, picturing the bleak trail, the blind trail, pushed to standing. "After just one hour with him, I saw my capabilities."

"If you trust that nutcase, he'll just disappoint you." Ash stood, too, clutching Swift's map in one hand and a parchment in the other. "Because he's lying. Say it, Swift. Say that Cynfael and Chance are liars."

Swift slipped his map from Ash's hand.

Ash watched the map leave him, but he didn't resist—he seemed too surprised at Swift's assertiveness.

"Maybe Cynfael and Chance are trying to preserve the culture of the Atlantiseans," said Swift. "Maybe they're actually part of the clan. I don't care one way or the other. They're good people. And I trust them."

Ash cast a look at Swift that seemed like compassion. "After all you've been through, it's no surprise you'd struggle to know who you can trust."

"I have struggled to know who I can trust," said Swift. "But I think I'm figuring it out."

Ash visibly swallowed. His eyes were fixed on Swift, and yet he seemed to be seeing nothing.

He looked like he was rifling through his store of emotional arsenal, trying to locate something he could lob at Swift, to gain back control.

"Ash." Swift held his gaze. "You can stop. I can see what you're doing."

The lostness on Ash shifted to anger. "And what, exactly, do you think I'm doing?"

Seeing Ash angry—angry at him—and feeling no obligation to appease him was like drawing a deep breath after surfacing from a long dive.

"You're not here to help me." Swift folded his map. "And that's okay. I'm not upset with you for not being honest with me. I understand, I think, what you're after. And why."

Ash backed away from him. "I'm not after anything."

"But you are," said Swift. "You came to Wales with me hoping you'd find leads to more treasures. To some degree, I wish you had been the one to find the Star of Atlantis."

"I don't care about your stupid Star of Atlantis."

"I know you don't," said Swift. "Because it's mine. You're only interested in things that are yours—treasures that can be yours, to deliver the fame that you're after."

Ash's face darkened to a deep red.

"You can let go of that drive, though," said Swift. "You have nothing to prove. Not to anyone. Your father is so proud of you."

Two streams of tears raced down Ash's face.

"My father," said Swift, "even, is proud of you."

Ash cast down the parchment. "But my mother isn't." The words came in almost a scream.

Swift eased nearer to him. "Let's talk this through, all right?"

Cynfael and Caius appeared in the doorway.

Ash struck the tears off his face. "You can have your stupid books and your Sunstone and your glory."

"Forget all that," Swift rested his hand on Ash's shoulder. "I want to help you."

Ash cast Swift's hand off him. "Right, because you're better than me in every way. You're always the one reaching down to pull me up."

He stormed to the door and tried to bulldoze his way between Caius and Cynfael.

"Whoa, lad," Caius caught him. "What's the problem?"

Ash stepped up in Caius' face.

"Right now, you're my problem. Get out of my way, or I'll move you."

"I'm not going anywhere," said Caius. "And neither are you until you let me in on what's happened."

Cynfael stepped closer behind Caius. "Whatever it is—let us help."

Ash faced Swift. "Want to know what she said to me on the morning she left? 'Be like Swift,' my mum said. 'He's how I hope you'll turn out.'" Ash blinked away tears. "'Be like Swift, and you'll be all right.'"

"Your mum loves you," said Swift. "She's troubled—give her that. Forgive her—you'll see she still loves you. She's your mum."

"She was my mum," said Ash. "Just like you were my friend." He faced Caius. "Move."

Swift closed in. "I always will be here." He couldn't stop his own tears from welling—the feeling of Ash leaving him was sheer grief. "If you need me—I'm here."

Caius offered Ash a gentle look. "Let's call your father."

Ash stepped to standing a mere inch from Caius. "I said—move."

"I can't let you just wander off," said Caius. "You realize I'm responsible for you, yes?"

In a flash, Ash cocked his arm and threw a punch to Caius' cheek, so hard he stumbled back into Cynfael.

Ash slipped past them, staring at Caius as he moved to the door. "Don't you dare follow me."

<h1 style="text-align:center">36</h1>

Swift dropped to sitting on a log beside the blazing campfire. The night was overcast, so black that beyond the firelight, he couldn't even see the white flashes of waves breaking in the bay.

Brooke sat down gently beside him. She rested her hand on his back. Caius, holding an ice pack to his face, sat at Swift's other side.

"It's important that you know," said Caius. "You did nothing wrong."

Swift stared at the chaotic flames. He knew, rationally, that he'd done nothing wrong. This was the first time, though, that he'd stood up to Ash. Every bit of it struck as wrong.

"I failed him," said Swift.

Brooke leaned in. "He failed you."

And that was true.

Swift felt severed, now, from the friendship he'd believed was his deepest. Sitting here, divided from Ash, he could finally breathe.

But it felt like free-falling.

"Ash never was with you," said Caius. "You did right by letting him know you were on to him."

"I think I've known it for a long time."

Swift pressed his fingers against his eyelids.

"Something's been pulling him further and further away. But I thought I could stop it. I thought I could bring him back to the surface, back to where he could breathe."

Caius pulled Swift into a rare hug—let Swift bury his face in his chest.

"I ache that he's so hurt," said Swift. "I ache that I can't do anything about it."

"But you did do something about it," said Brooke. "You set a boundary with Ash, which he needed. I know—this separation is an agony worse than any cut. But it might be the onset of healing, for you both."

She was right. As painful as this wound was, it felt clean.

Swift sat up, away from Caius.

"There's always hope for restoration," said Caius.

Swift glanced at him. "Do you really think it's possible that Ash will ever heal from his Mum leaving him?"

"I hope so," said Caius. "But it's clear he won't be healed by your hands. His father will know how to help him. And he'll be with his father soon."

And that was some comfort. Shortly after Ash had bolted, the police had arrived. They contacted Mr. Emberly, then left quickly to look for Ash, and to connect with Chance.

The police believed Ash's trail would be easy to follow, and they'd arranged for a boat to carry him back to Devon tonight.

"And with Ash gone," said Brooke, "you can focus on mending yourself."

"If I'd managed things differently when he first came to me," said Swift, "if I'd set a boundary then—maybe he wouldn't have taken things this far. Maybe we'd have figured out how to be true friends."

Caius set his hand on Swift's shoulder. "True friendship with him never was likely. Keep in mind..."

But something caught his eye. Something in the distance, beyond the fire.

"What in Valhalla?" Caius stood.

From the north, slowly nearing, came a shining set of silver eyes.

Fortuna's eyes.

Eyes as bright as the Welsh stars, now cloaked.

More eyes appeared, drifting just beyond the light of the fire.

"It's dogs." Brooke stood, too. "It's a pack of wild dogs."

"Brooke," said Caius, "Swift. Get behind me."

Swift stood.

The Sea Wolf jumped a log and rounded the fire.

Caius snatched Brooke back. Tugged Swift close.

"It's all right." Swift reached around Caius to let the Sea Wolf sniff his hand. "This is Fortuna."

She dropped to her belly before him.

"She's Chance and Cynfael's Sea Wolf," said Swift, kneeling.

"They have a wolf?" Brooke peered out from behind Caius. "I get that they're eccentric, but—a wolf?"

Swift glanced around. "Many wolves, actually. Those eyes shining over there belong to Fortuna's puppies. They were bold enough when Ash and I were with Cynfael and Chance, but here they look frightened. I don't think they'll come close to the fire."

Swift reached to Caius and Brooke. "Let me give her your hands. This is how Chance introduced her to me. I think she won't be aggressive."

"You think—" said Caius.

Swift opened his palm. "Chance says that Sea Wolves attach to people for life."

"Sea Wolves." Caius slowly placed his hand in Swift's. "You realize you might be treating another complex fracture in a moment?"

Swift guided Caius' fingers to Fortuna's mouth.

She licked his fingers. Sniffed his palm.

Caius ran his hand across her huge head. Fortuna turned her eyes onto Brooke.

Brooke crouched before her.

Swift took Brooke's hand and presented it.

"She's terrifying," said Brooke, as Fortuna licked her fingers. "Beautiful, though."

Fortuna forced her head beneath Brooke's hand.

"Chance took her out with him, looking for Octavian, for Ash," said Swift. "Her being here might mean the police found them."

Caius fed the fire, brightening it.

Swift could hardly bear to look at Caius' face, at his swollen cheek.

Swift sat down again beside Brooke, but moved wrong and winced at his agitated cut, still aching from Octavian's punch.

Caius handed Brooke his ice pack and sat beside Swift. "Let's have a look at your chest."

Brooke drew Swift's penlight from his rucksack.

Swift eased off his hoodie and unbuttoned his shirt.

Caius rested his hands on Swift's shoulders as he carefully looked at the healing red line. "From the force of the strike you described, I worried he might've cracked your ribs. But it doesn't look like it." Caius held the ice pack to Swift's chest.

"Does anything else hurt?" Brooke held Swift's cheek. "We ought to go in soon and let you rest."

"Rest is the last thing I want." Swift brought down her hand and held it. "I feel hollowed. No rest will fix that. Imagining that Ash was here for me—I think that was helping me. Without him—"

"Without him, you're going to do just fine." Caius situated Swift's hand to hold the ice pack. "Cynfael is a masterful teacher. And that odd friend of his—Chance—Cynfael says he does have some medical training. I like the thought of your ambition in their hands. Brooke and I, too, will of course help you."

The words, though kind, rang illusory.

Swift let them go without even trying to believe them.

Because Cynfael was right.

Swift would succeed at making it into the Practicum on his own, or he'd fail.

From here on, there was nothing Brooke and Caius could do for him.

"Cynfael knows where the stars shine the brightest in Pembrokeshire," said Swift. "Just before we left his house, he told me we could visit those places. Study there."

"Cynfael's certainly your kind of teacher," said Caius.

"As much as I like Cynfael, from how you both describe him," said Brooke, "I have to acknowledge that we barely know him. Justus will certainly want to vet him, right?"

"He already has," said Caius. "While Swift was giving his report to the police, I contacted Justus. We checked the references Cynfael offered. One is even a professor at my university. Everyone said Cynfael would be a dream of a teacher to a student with a drive for greatness. Though they all warned us— he's challenging."

"Cynfael might be an accomplished teacher." Swift wrapped his arm around Fortuna, settling closer to him. "But can he teach me?" He captured Caius' glance. "I heard you telling him about the coma. You said I was 'swamped.'"

"I'm ashamed to admit it," said Caius, "but I was blind to how severely Ash was affecting you. I credited your difficulty with reading mainly to the coma. To the fever disease and the trauma. Cynfael saw—in a split second—how badly Ash was distorting your focus. Once he guided me to face that, I realized how far Ash had pulled the wool over my eyes, too."

Swift glanced at Brooke. "And what about you? Do you think I can do it?"

"I do—but that matters little." She cast him an honest look. "What do you think?"

Swift glanced at his rucksack on the sand at Caius' feet, his books spilling out of it. "Would you hand me Cynfael's anatomy text?"

Caius cast him a half-smile. "I was hoping you'd ask."

37

Swift, hiking alone to the prominence in the Wentletrap, could hardly sense the earth beneath his feet. He'd spent two full days studying medical texts, and this morning—before Caius even had breakfast made—Swift completed a chapter in a wonderful astronomy text Cynfael had given him.

Ash's departure, though still tainted with grief, had lightened the atmosphere in the beach house. A tension seemed to have lifted from Swift's body, even.

He could realize, now, that he'd been holding himself in a perpetual cringe, as though anticipating the next moment when Ash would throw an emotional punch, casting guilt or blame at him, asserting control.

Swift had, several times, asked to call Ash—just to be sure he'd made it safely home. Caius, though, had discouraged it. The police would see to Ash, he'd said. Plus, he was sure Mr. Emberly would come to Wales to collect Ash.

Brooke had agreed—it'd be better to leave them alone for now. As well-meaning as Swift's call would be, it might complicate any progress Mr. Emberly was making with Ash.

Walking the Wentletrap now, Swift felt a sense of momentum, as though each step he took was forward progress toward excelling at the books Cynfael was helping him master.

Every day since he'd met Cynfael, Swift had trekked into the Wentletrap, Fortuna often by his side, and sometimes with Chance.

Twisting into its maze with deliberation, learning its secrets, was exhilarating.

Though, when he lingered in the woodland past nightfall, he'd ache for the loss of his Sunstone.

This evening was a clear one, and the Wentletrap Forest was glowing underneath a strong sun, its slanted beams turning autumn's leaves, spiraling down, into gold.

Cynfael and Chance were planning to join Swift, come sundown, at the prominence keyed on the *Star of Atlantis* map —the first set of coordinates, which turned out to be Cynfael's very favorite stargazing location.

Swift found his eyes drawn to the canopy, to search out Chance's lights, for assurance that he was on the right path. But Chance had set no lights in this part of the forest.

Rather, he'd drawn a map just for Swift—a gorgeous map— for finding his way to the prominence.

The silence of the woods broke with a rustling of branches.

Swift, listening, stopped. "Cynfael, is that you?"

No response.

"Chance?" Swift called.

But the noise likely wasn't them.

Swift had timed his walk to reach the prominence early, so he could spend a few hours alone with his books—all his books.

His rucksack was deliciously weighted with the *Star of Atlantis* book and map, *The Shepherd of the Stars*, Cynfael's anatomy and astronomy texts, plus hiking gear—water and bars, his first aid kit.

A cluster of saplings shook.

Swift stopped.

The underbrush split, and out bounded Fortuna.

Swift stumbled back at the Sea Wolf jumping at him. She knocked him flat and with her great paws, held him down.

Swift scruffed her head, then twisted out from beneath her. "I was looking for some solitude."

He glanced at the underbrush.

"But I bet you were, too. Where are those wolf pups of yours? Had to get away from them nipping you all over, I bet."

He picked up a piece of a broken tree branch and cast it as far down the trail as he could.

Fortuna raced after it, then hurried back a moment later, hauling it.

"You probably know where I'm going," said Swift. "I bet you've visited all Cynfael's favorite places."

She glanced at him as she trotted alongside, promenading the branch she'd won.

Having Fortuna near was soothing. It seemed her pure friendship was part of the medicine that might heal the void Ash had left.

After turning a few bends, Swift sighted the prominence rising out of the trees. He tucked away his map, following Fortuna instead—for her eyes were fixed on the rocky rise.

"You think your master's up there? Well, he isn't yet. But he's coming."

Fortuna took off along the trail, then cut right onto an elevated fork. They together wound up a steep path, tight with boulders.

Swift climbed onto the highest shelf and rounded a slight bend that led to the wide, open air.

There, he discovered the summit of the prominence to be very broad. It was stacked with angular boulders and curious rock formations. Come nightfall, it seemed the place would feel extraterrestrial.

From this height, he could see the Wentletrap stretching for miles to the north, south, and east. And to the west, the Celtic Sea swayed in Coracle Bay and shimmered in an unbroken stretch of blue to the horizon, where the sun was gilding molten bars on the tops of low clouds.

Fortuna trotted to the eastern end of the prominence, near

to where they'd come up. There, she slipped between a couple of closely set boulders.

Swift followed her.

She seemed deeply purposeful as she wound down a steep ravine, like she anticipated something wonderful waiting.

Swift kept right behind her, shimmying among rocks that narrowed to almost the mere width of his body. When he reached the trail's base and turned a final bend, he found himself inside a cool enclosure, mostly open to the sky and shielded on all sides by the ravine's walls.

Fortuna was standing at the inner wall of the rock column, scratching at a pile of mud at its base.

Higher up, there was a cleft—it seemed runoff from the autumn rains had spackled it almost solid.

Swift studied the split, the dried mud that Fortuna was effectively loosening.

He slid his hand into the opening and discovered a cool, slight wind. "A cave."

Cynfael had never spoken of a cave beneath the prominence.

Swift helped Fortuna dig. Together, it took them just minutes to clear enough sediment that they could slip through.

Fortuna eased inside first, hardly giving Swift time to pull his penlight from his rucksack before racing around an interior bend and down a rocky declination.

Swift tried to keep up, but had to make his way slowly. He could stand to his full height, but the cave floor seemed a bit touchy with loose gravel, and there were several points where the ground dropped sharply away to the left or the right. Sometimes both.

After a few turns, Swift reached a broader stretch—the cave's base, it seemed.

The sound of Fortuna snuffling, of metal scraping stone, guided Swift around a bend, toward a doorway cut in the rock wall.

Beyond the doorway stretched a wide cavern, three times Swift's height and about the whole footprint of the beach house.

Small rooms branched off from the main space, but they seemed terminal rather than passageways.

The silver light from the setting sun streamed from most of the rooms, defining their southwestern orientation.

The windows were cleverly chiseled, following the shapes of the boulders and stones. From the outside, those openings would probably look like natural fissures.

Furniture pieces, hewn from the walls or cobbled of boulders and wood planks, stood here and there—benches and shelves, some holding books, most of them physics texts. From one wall jetted a table with clay dishes, stacked.

Fortuna was crawling at the edge of the room, licking a metal dog food bowl, pushing it toward Swift.

"I guess this is your master's place," said Swift. "I wonder if he'll mind that I came here on my own."

Fortuna, whining, led Swift to one of the cubby rooms where stood a cabinet with a hook lock.

Inside, Swift found cans of dog food, stacked.

He opened one and emptied it into Fortuna's bowl. "I guess Cynfael will see that I'm here under your command."

Fortuna finished the food, licked the bowl clean, then lay down.

"What a great place to study." Swift moved to the stone table, enchanting beneath a beam of sunset.

He opened his rucksack and pulled out his maps and books, along with a mobile—one of two Caius had borrowed from the police to replace those they'd lost.

He sent Caius a quick text, letting him know he'd reached the prominence and had found an incredible cave. *I can't imagine a better place to study*, he typed.

He laid the phone aside and opened the anatomy text. He settled down and picked up where he left off—at a section on the skeletal system. He lost himself reading, watching the page grow dim with the twilight's tide shifting to deep evening.

Fortuna came to sitting beside him. She heavily pressed her warm body against his legs as he read, until he followed her prompting and set to stroking her head.

He eventually had to read by his penlight but didn't look up again until Fortuna stood.

"Whoa."

The room around him was pure darkness.

Swift flipped through the chunk of pages he'd read—more than a hundred.

He checked the phone for any text from Caius, but its signal had been fading in and out. A notification suggested Caius had texted back, but here inside the cave, the message wasn't making it through.

Fortuna crept to the entryway, as though she sensed someone coming.

"I'll bet Cynfael intended for us to spend the night in here, rather than camp up on the prominence," said Swift. "I wonder whether we'll use this place often to study."

He packed his anatomy and astronomy texts in his rucksack, alongside his hiking supplies. He slid in the mobile, but he didn't bother packing his two legend books or the maps. Leaving those behind would make a less cumbersome load for climbing back up the ravine. And in the cave, they'd certainly be protected from any weather.

He slipped out through the narrow opening, Fortuna following.

Using his penlight, he guided their climb back to the pinnacle, though Fortuna seemed not to need it, navigating as she apparently could by feel and smell.

Rising to the top of the night-shining prominence was an entrance into a world of stars. The Milky Way ascending in the east almost looked like a sunrise.

Swift had witnessed the stars lighting the Welsh night plenty from his father's ship. But never had he seen the Welsh atmosphere from a height like this, its stars shimmering in the mist winding through the Wentletrap's tree spires and strongly reflected in the great expanse of the Celtic Sea to the west.

Swift, spellbound by the luminous sky, sat down at the center of the prominence.

From this place, the stars seemed more than stars. They

seemed larger, closer, and even a touch warmer. It seemed the stars, from here, could be perceived as the creatures they actually were.

Suns. Suns with atmospheres and cores. Suns with coronas and projections. Suns that flared and convected. Suns keeping gravity fields, some entertaining ringing planets in their courts.

Fortuna lay down beside Swift. She, too, seemed captivated by the arcing Milky Way, flopping onto her side as she was, letting her gaze fix on the sky.

Swift rubbed her belly a moment, then pulled out the anatomy text and his penlight.

He read to the chorus of wind currents sweeping the trees. He read to the starlight, shivering him with goosebumps each time he glanced up. He read to the distant cadence of breakers rhythmically flashing.

The night slipped into its colder hours, and Cynfael and Chance still didn't appear.

But Chance had said something about the great fishing he anticipated today. Maybe he was just late in wrapping up his work. Cynfael might be helping him.

A kindling pile rested on one side of the prominence, and a charred divot in the stones showed a space obviously purposed to hold a campfire.

If it got too chilly, it would be wise to go back down into the cave. But now that he was under the charm of Cynfael's stars, Swift couldn't bring himself to leave them.

Beneath Fortuna's supervisory gaze, Swift located a wood pile and carried to the stone divot an armload of kindling and two heavy logs. He built the framework of his fire and drew a match from his rucksack.

The wood had been stacked in a good place, under an overhang and well out of the elements, for the fire sprang to life at once, wrapping itself around the body of the logs and roaring over the kindling.

After only a moment, Swift grew warm enough to again focus on reading.

He brought out his anatomy text and launched into a new

chapter, on the chemical activity in neurons. He read on by the light of the fire and, at every turning of a page, let himself be dazzled by stars.

As he neared a chapter's end, Fortuna lifted her chin off her paws. Her eyes seemed to fix on the stretch of the Wentletrap dividing the prominence from the coast.

Swift closed his book and peered down with her into the dark trees. "Do you sense your master?"

Fortuna got to her feet.

Swift stroked her. "Are you hearing something?"

Beneath Swift's hand, her muscles stiffened.

Swift eased away from her, giving her a bit of space. She knew him and liked him, but for all that, she was a Sea Wolf who lived in these wilds.

Fortuna uttered a low, whispered growl.

A tingling of adrenaline brought Swift to standing.

Fortuna glanced at him, licked his hand, then again faced the west.

Swift ventured close to the edge of the prominence. "Cynfael?" he called. "Chance?"

He startled at Fortuna biting his ankle.

"Ow—hey." He shook her off. "What was that for?"

He tried to move again to the precipice, but she wouldn't have it. She nipped the cuff of his trousers and pulled him back to the fire.

What could she possibly have heard? Maybe she'd caught wind of an animal. This could be a Sea Wolf's response to encountering something outside the pack—the way a tame dog might bark fiercely at an unfamiliar person.

"We're okay," said Swift. "Are you smelling a fox or something? Sit down."

She consented to sit on the rock he touched, but she didn't take her eyes off the western forest.

Together, they watched the trees gently sway, as hackles on the back of Fortuna's neck rose.

Swift wanted to stroke her, to reassure her—but the tame part of her seemed to be dissipating, leaving just the wild wolf.

Even at their first meeting, when she'd been nothing but a pair of silver eyes glowing among dense trees, she hadn't cast this deadly sense of resolve, to go after something. To kill.

A sound lifted from the forest. Voices, maybe.

But with the moving of the wind, with the distant waves rushing, Swift couldn't quite discern what it was.

The sound strengthened into what seemed like a shout.

Fortuna ripped a snarl that shredded the air and took the strength from Swift's legs, sinking him to a crouch.

She tore to the path leading down toward the forest.

The underbrush swayed. Leaves rustled, and twigs snapped.

And then all fell silent but for a cadence of breakers.

38

Swift steadied himself against a boulder. The fierceness of Fortuna's snarl, he couldn't shake—he was struggling to wrangle his breathing back under control.

After a few moments, though, enough of the panic dissipated to let him stand.

He crept to the edge of the prominence and strained to see into the dark forest.

He could pick up no movement. No voices. No sign of Fortuna.

Going to the cave again seemed prudent. But he should probably wait here. If Cynfael and Chance were on their way, Swift could climb down and meet them. They'd want to know Fortuna had taken off like that.

But it didn't seem they were anyplace close. It was hours beyond when they said they'd arrive.

Swift's mobile was showing a stronger signal—though Caius' message still hadn't come through. He tried sending another text, letting Caius know Chance and Cynfael hadn't made it to the prominence. But the signal dropped before Swift could be sure it sent. He stowed his phone in his rucksack.

By knowing Cynfael and Chance served as stewards of the

385

great Wentletrap Forest, Swift's fright over this wilderness had diminished.

With the leading lights they'd placed in its canopy, from walking its wild trails with them as guides, even Caius had grown unafraid.

But standing on this surreal, rocky expanse, Fortuna's growl still thrumming in his chest, Swift found himself entertaining that the more frightening tales of the Wentletrap held some truth.

Bodies had been found in this forest. Sightings of spirits were rumored. Though some accounts might be explained by Fortuna and other animals, by nature's harshness, not all could.

"Swift," a voice whispered.

Swift spun toward where the prominence opened onto the trail winding down to the forest.

"Cynfael?" Swift peered through the fire—spitting sparks in a gust of wind. "Chance?"

"I don't think they're coming."

Stumbling up from the dark rise and into the shatters of fire-light came Ash.

He seemed unsteady.

One side of his face was darkened with blood.

Swift ran to him. "Oh, my God." He guided Ash close to the firelight. "What happened?"

"Running—I tripped," said Ash.

Perhaps it was Ash that Fortuna had scented. When she'd first met him, she'd seemed to pick up on her master's distrust of him.

"Here, sit." Swift eased Ash down onto a boulder.

"Can't." Ash shoved Swift away and kept on his feet. "I have to run. We have to run."

Ash seemed unable to focus, and he was struggling to keep his balance.

Swift swept the penlight from his pocket and shone it in Ash's eyes.

One of his pupils was dilated.

"I think you have a concussion," said Swift. "When did—"

Fortuna's growl pierced from the forest.

And then a yelp—a wolf's pained whine.

And then nothing.

The terror of the sound, of the silence, held Swift and Ash together stone still.

"I know a way back that won't cross him," Ash finally whispered, blood from his forehead dripping off his chin.

"Who?" Swift tried again to lead Ash to sit.

"The coast," said Ash, pointing inland as Swift seated him. "We should head for the coast."

"I'm going to try and stop this bleeding," said Swift. "Can you tell me exactly what happened? What are you doing still in Wales?" He pulled out his first aid kit. "Why aren't you with your father?"

"I ran off," said Ash. "And you would've run, too. Don't pretend otherwise. I know you aren't as brave as you put on."

Swift glanced down at the forest. Listened for any more sounds.

He heard only an uptick of wind.

He blotted Ash's head with a bit of cotton.

"I ran into danger, not from it," said Ash. "I wanted my box back."

"Your box?" With Ash rambling like this, the concussion seemed significant. He needed help.

"I see why the old Maddox and Merriweather stole back their Sunstone from that king," said Ash. "He was keeping them at a disadvantage. I wasn't about to let Octavian do that to me."

Swift tried holding the cotton to the cut, but the bleeding couldn't be checked.

"This will need stitches." Swift took out his phone and tried to call Caius, but the signal wouldn't catch.

He sent another text.

"Caius is bound to get one of those." Swift laid aside his phone.

He cleaned Ash's cut as well as he could, dried it, and did his best to make a tight dressing using butterfly bandages, gauze, and tape.

"That'll have to do." Swift crouched before Ash. "Can you not tell me what happened to you?"

Ash, smiling some, stared into the distance. "My mum—she would've loved to see me with my box. And with the Star of Atlantis." Tears welled. "But he lied." His eyes closed. He fell back.

Swift caught him.

Ash roused. "What are we still doing here?" He glanced around, smearing the blood on his cheek with the back of his hand. "We have to run."

"Run from what?"

Ash focused behind Swift and pointed. "Him."

Up from the trail leading to the forest climbed Octavian Krakau.

Swift pulled Ash to his feet. He placed himself closely in front of Ash.

"Mr. Kingsley," said Octavian, nearing. "You're just where Mr. Emberly predicted you'd be."

Swift glanced at Ash. "What have you done?"

"Neither of you has any right to be mad at me." Ash snatched up Swift's phone. "I'm calling my father."

"The police are on their way," said Swift, as Octavian neared. "They'll be here any minute."

Octavian plucked the phone from Ash's hand. "You've no chance of reaching anyone this deep in the Wentletrap."

"You're the thing in the woods that Fortuna scented," said Swift. "When she comes back, you'll be sorry you ever laid eyes on us."

"Fortuna won't be coming back." Octavian flexed his fingers. "Leastways not anytime soon."

Ash tapped Swift's shoulder. "Thanks for letting me spend the night. Sorry, but I can't keep my eyes open." He slunk down onto a boulder. "Say goodnight to Caius and Brooke for me." He slipped off.

Swift jerked him to his feet. "You stand up, and you keep standing. Got it?"

Ash nodded, resting his knee on the boulder. Though still unsteady, he seemed a bit more awake.

Swift faced Octavian. "Stay away from us."

Octavian glanced at Swift's rucksack.

Swift jumped for the rucksack and pulled it out of Octavian's reach.

The action was reflexive—he'd forgotten that the *Star of Atlantis* map and its books were inside the cave.

Octavian might not know about the cave. He was too broad, probably, to fit through its entryway.

"Those bloody books and that map," said Octavian. "Are they worth dying for?"

The best defense—the only defense—Swift could come up with was to stall.

"The books and map"—Swift steadied Ash, who'd slipped to kneeling—"are they worth killing for?"

"Look, Swift." Ash gazed up at him. "I thought we were friends. Octavian and me—we've been coming up here every night, but you stood us up." Laughing lightly, he rested against the boulder. "I didn't know he'd get after us like this. I thought it'd just be you."

Swift stared at Octavian.

"Did you do this to Ash?"

"Hand over those relics, or I'll do worse to you."

The coldness in Octavian's eyes was a match to Fortuna's. It petrified Swift.

"Not going to cooperate?" Octavian yanked Swift into a tight hold, his fast arms snaking around Swift's chest.

The pressure on the cut was agony, but Swift managed to kick his rucksack out of Octavian's reach.

Octavian strained to reach into his own pocket. It was like he was aiming to draw something out—a knife, or—Swift couldn't bear to imagine what.

He twisted to keep Octavian's hand restrained.

"The rucksack—take it," Octavian shouted to Ash. "Like I said—you help me, I'll help you."

Ash got to his feet. "I don't believe anything you say

anymore." He touched the coarse bandage on his head. "I told you where he'd be, but look what you've done."

He walked to standing before them.

"From now on, I'm on Swift's side." Ash patted Swift's hand, clawing at Octavian's arm tightening on his throat.

"Ash," Swift rasped. "Help me."

But that'd been the end of Ash's stab at maintaining consciousness. He dropped like a stone and lay unmoving, face-down by the fire.

Swift judged the distance to the edge of the prominence. If he could cast his rucksack into the forest, Octavian might go after it. If he did, Swift could make sure Ash was breathing. He might have time to move Ash down the ravine. They could hide in the forest.

Swift reached, hooking the rucksack's strap with one finger. He gripped it and cast it toward the drop.

Octavian let go of him. He snagged the rucksack in midair.

Swift rushed to Ash. He turned him over and felt his chest.

Ash was breathing, but no shaking could wake him.

Octavian peered into the rucksack. He turned it upside down, emptying it of its textbooks, its water and snacks.

Swift dragged Ash to the ravine's mouth.

Octavian shifted his gaze onto Swift. "Where are my relics?"

Swift pulled Ash a step down the ravine.

Octavian rushed to him and seized the front of Swift's hoodie, jerking him away from Ash and scraping his cut. "Where?"

The pain in Swift's chest called up a flash of excruciating memories—visions of the night he'd fled this coast, straining to reach the open ocean and help.

The pain, though crippling, delivered a gush of the same determination that'd sparked on that darkest night—a resolve to survive. To see that his brother survived.

Swift threw a punch, landing a brutal hit to Octavian's chin.

Octavian cast him to the ground.

Swift, for a moment, couldn't move. His knuckles smarted as

though sprained, and it shocked him that the impulse to hit Octavian had come with such force.

Octavian wiped blood off his mouth. He reached into his pocket.

Swift couldn't judge whether telling him where the books were or keeping him guessing would deliver the better chance of escape.

But he could do neither. He couldn't speak for the pain in his chest.

From his pocket, Octavian drew a bamboo pipe.

It was one Swift remembered from the museum's display of rustic weapons. Beside it had hung a cluster of feathered darts and vials of poisons, labeled with their effects. *Neural disruption. Septic infection. Paralysis. Death.*

Octavian dropped into the pipe a feathered dart tipped with a needle a good inch long. "If you won't tell me now where you've stashed what's mine, I wager that you'll tell me later."

Swift crawled away from him.

Octavian shot the dart, landing it in the side of Swift's neck. A chemical taste filled his mouth.

He eased out the dart and cast it into the fire.

Octavian stood still, watching, it seemed, for Swift to fall unconscious.

Though off kilter, Swift wasn't weakening. In fact, the pain of the cut was fading, and he could probably stand. Maybe he'd gotten the dart out before it could deliver much poison.

He pushed to his feet.

Finding himself steady, he ran at Octavian. Shoved him back.

The move seemed to catch Octavian off guard, and he stumbled, tripping on an unsteady rock and falling backwards.

Swift raced to Ash and knelt before him.

Octavian was trying to rise, but he was moving slowly, holding the back of his head.

Swift dragged Ash down the ravine.

The trip to its bottom roused Ash, and by the time Swift

was pulling him into the underbrush, Ash was fighting to get free.

Swift let go of him, giving him a moment to sit up and look around.

"I don't think we're supposed to be here," said Ash. "Didn't Brooke tell us to go to bed?"

From the top of the precipice came the sound of shoes scraping on gravel—Octavian rising to his feet, it seemed. Maybe coming.

Swift crouched before Ash. "Brooke did say that," he slid his shoulders beneath Ash's arm and pulled him to his feet.

Upon rising, a bout of slight dizziness struck. But Swift's strength was still sound, and it seemed Ash could manage, with help, to stay upright.

"We must be very quiet," Swift whispered, "or she'll catch us."

He wrapped his arm around Ash's waist, steadying him as they slipped into the forest, moving tree to tree.

Keeping in motion seemed to be holding at bay the effects of whatever drug the dart had been laced with, but Swift was wearing out quickly. He'd have to stop soon.

"You might as well give up," Octavian hollered. "You're like a pierced hart leaving blood in your wake."

Swift tried to move faster, but his feet were growing clumsy and catching on roots. The drug would probably soon overwhelm him.

A weak, shrill sound pealed.

It was a dog's whimper. A wolf's.

Swift focused on the sound and kept on, leaning against trees for support. Ash seemed barely conscious, but he was still managing to walk, to follow Swift's lead.

Finally, moonlight glancing from Fortuna's silver coat showed Swift a small open glade. She was lying between two cloaked figures stretched flat on their backs.

"No," Swift whispered. "Oh no."

He placed Ash gently on the ground, easing his head to rest on its uninjured side.

He knelt over Cynfael. Shook him.

Cynfael blinked his eyes open but seemed unable to move.

Swift crawled to Chance and found him awake and turning onto his side.

Fortuna moved to Chance and did what she could for him, licking his chin.

Chance grabbed her scruff and let her haul him to sitting.

Fortuna faced the eastern trees. A low growl escaped her.

Chance stared with her into the thicket.

Swift tried to stand but his strength gave out.

Chance eased Swift to lying on his back. Patted his shoulder.

Swift understood the command in it. Stay where you are. Lie still.

Through a dozy haze, Swift watched Chance help Cynfael to his feet.

"Where are you, thief?" yelled Octavian.

Out of a line of trees, he surfaced, holding a torch.

From behind Octavian, two shadows crept—Chance and Cynfael, rounding him. And between them walked the dark form of the Sea Wolf.

As though watching a slow-motion film, Swift caught sight of Fortuna leaping, her silhouette dampening the moony trees.

Fortuna, taking Octavian by the shoulder, her jaws clenching.

The night pealing with Fortuna's blood-curdling growl, with Octavian hollering.

Chance, knocking Octavian to the ground.

Fortuna standing over him, her cold stare piercing his, saliva from her snarl dripping onto his cheek.

Every move Octavian made was repaid with a bite to his ears.

Chance drew from Octavian's pocket a dart and with it pierced him.

Cynfael stood away from them and came to kneeling before Swift.

Starlight seemed to swarm Cynfael as he lowered his hood. Moonlight brightened his face as he lifted Swift into his arms.

39

Swift sensed coolness on his forehead. Behind his eyelids, light seemed to swell.

A memory surfaced of being inside the coma, of waking slowly, being never quite able to open his eyes.

He grew sensible, after a moment, to the warmth of the place he was in.

The stillness of the air told him he was indoors. But a hint of earth, a damp smell of stone, lingered here.

Voices were speaking. Low voices.

Voices speaking in Old Norse.

"I've seen young Swift's path."

Through the dark beauty of the ancient accent, Swift could recognize the voice as belonging to Chance.

"We know his destiny," said Chance, in the old, dashing language. "Medicine? It's too far off course. A winding distraction."

"But when is the way straight?" asked Cynfael, speaking, too, in Old Norse. "You've seen what Swift might one day achieve. May it be. But we don't know the path he'll forge. Swift himself has a hand in his destiny."

"In our destiny," said Chance. "The lad's choices will determine our winds."

"Ay," said Cynfael.

"And he's been delivered to us," said Chance. "My book. My map. They came into his hands, just like I saw. As did the Star of Atlantis."

How had Chance seen his book, his map, and the Star of Atlantis falling into Swift's hands?

Swift tried to open his eyes, to move. He managed nothing but bending his fingers.

His fingertips glanced off something cold resting by his leg.

A stone, rhombus shaped. His Sunstone.

"Might we not, now, serve as guides?" asked Chance, still in Old Norse.

"Guides, we shall be," Cynfael returned.

"Then," said Chance, "we must tell him everything."

"You have merely foresight," said Cynfael. "You have no power over future events."

"But Swift will have much to do with the unity that's been seen by so many with foresight," said Chance. "May we not shape that?"

"If you try to govern Swift," said Cynfael, "you'll see your dreams fade to nothing. And we shall be forever marooned. No, Swift's choices belong to him. This is his path to walk; his destiny to achieve."

Swift tried to ask them of what they could possibly be talking. His path. His destiny. And dreams fading to nothing.

But the effort was futile—exactly like trying and failing to rouse from the coma.

Cynfael spoke on. "I'm burning to see what this lad wants. What he might manage."

Swift forced a deep breath. He tried to move and found that he could, barely.

"There, now," said Chance. "Look. I think he's waking."

Swift struggled to open his eyes.

"Take your time," said Cynfael, no longer in Old Norse.

A rush of terrible recollections swarmed—Octavian advancing onto the prominence. Fortuna crying. An anguish of panic. Octavian's strangling arms. Ash stumbling near, blood on his face.

"Ash." Swift fully opened his eyes.

The ceiling above him was stone. He was lying on a slab—the table inside Cynfael's cave. Cynfael and Chance were standing on either side of him.

Swift tried to sit up.

Chance pressed his shoulder down. "Your head may not be clear for some time."

Swift realized a cloak was draped over him—Cynfael's.

He gathered a handful of its cloth. "Ash was out of his mind, his head bleeding. I couldn't keep him awake."

"Our friend, Ash, is riding the Coast Guard's boat," said Chance. "He's on his way to Devonshire."

"How is it he was still in the Wentletrap?" asked Swift. "Did the police never find him?"

"They followed his trail to a dock where he'd taken a boat with Octavian," said Chance. "They focused the search on the water. On nearer islands. But Octavian and Ash managed to make it back to the coast." He glanced at Cynfael. "To hide so well, the police believe they had help."

Swift struggled to press back a draw toward unconsciousness. The taste of the drug lingered, and the heat of a fever was tacitly strengthening.

His gaze dropped, landing on the metal bowl on the floor. Fortuna's bowl.

The sight of it pricked him as a clear memory flashed—Fortuna's snarl, her yelp.

Her silence.

He'd seen her awake in the forest, but she'd clearly been drugged along with the rest of them. Who knew what effect that chemical might have on wolves?

"Fortuna." Swift could hardly meet Cynfael's eyes for fear of what grief they might hold.

Chance snapped, and up from the floor at the table's end, Fortuna stood.

Relief washed over Swift as a chill.

He reached for the Sea Wolf.

Fortuna came near and pressed her head beneath his palm.

"What did Octavian do to her?"

Swift looked from Chance to Cynfael.

"To you?"

"We got the same treatment you did, though a bit earlier." Cynfael removed a cold cloth resting on Swift's head and placed it in a bowl of water fragrant with mint. "Chance and I had business in the forest. Octavian claimed first me, then Chance, with his darts. And then, finally, Fortuna."

"Is Octavian still out there?"

Swift lifted the Sunstone from beneath the cloak.

"How is it I have this?"

"The boat that holds Ash and his father also holds Octavian, who was found carrying the Sunstone," said Cynfael. "This justice is due. His viciousness is part of a long line of treachery troubling this coast."

A weariness, deep and gray, passing over Cynfael's face made it seem he was referencing a pestilence that'd affected the coast—that he'd dealt with—for centuries.

At the notion, Swift's imagination woke.

Watching his two friends, he found he could picture them as the true Chance Merriweather. The true Cynfael Maddox.

And how odd it seemed that, though the notion was impossible, it didn't feel far-fetched.

Swift recalled the words from *The Shepherd of the Stars*, describing Cynfael Maddox—

People encountering the spirit of Cynfael Maddox, over centuries, often reported that they felt a sense of destiny, a great wisdom imparted.

Bearing a destiny, tasting wisdom within reach—this precisely described how Swift saw himself, close in their company.

"How long has this treachery troubled the coast?" Swift asked.

Cynfael watched him gently.

"Since before you were born."

"I couldn't believe it when I saw Octavian climbing onto the prominence," said Swift. "I'd actually wondered if the Wentletrap—having killed so many—might've taken him, too."

"Not one soul has the Wentletrap claimed," said Chance. "Not in centuries."

"But all my life, I've heard stories of people lost in the Wentletrap," said Swift. "Dying in the Wentletrap."

"Rumors and tall tales," said Chance.

"From time to time, people slip into the Wentletrap," said Cynfael, "trying to escape the police. Using keen physics tricks, with lights and with mirrors and sound, we've taken on the duty of spinning them to a place where they can be caught."

"So—you work with the police," said Swift. "That's why they seemed to know you so well."

"Lost hikers, by the same tricks, are rapidly turned out of the forest," said Cynfael.

"Octavian must've found Ash after he ran from us," said Swift.

"Or Ash found Octavian," said Chance. "They're both consumed with a hunger we've seen time after time—a hunger that drives terrible deeds." He glanced at Cynfael. "If only they could see with our view, they'd realize the worthlessness of that course."

The way Chance was speaking—and the way he'd spoken of destiny—it was like he and Cynfael really believed they had some special access to knowledge.

Swift held the Star of Atlantis up to a lit lantern hanging on the wall. "Sunstones are said to reveal not just the course of a ship, but of a person." He rested his gaze on Cynfael. "Do you think a course—a destiny—waits for me?"

"We all have a destiny," said Cynfael. "For destiny is simply our crowning achievements—the pinnacles of the actions, decisions, and failures that weave all together, culminating in one's legacy."

"That might generally be true," said Swift, "but holding the

Star of Atlantis—it feels like destiny means something particular for me."

He watched them carefully.

"And as I was waking, I heard you saying that you'd seen my destiny. Do you think you know what I'm fated for?"

Chance turned his gaze onto Cynfael.

In Old Norse, he said, "We must answer him."

After a moment of thoughtfulness, Cynfael replied, "Keep it simple."

Chance eased closer to Swift. "Fated, you're not. For no one is bound to any one course. Many paths wait. But I've seen some of your choices unfold, lad. And of your legacy—your destiny— I've dreamed."

"What you're meaning to say is—you've imagined what choices I might make," said Swift. "Right?"

Chance held his gaze. "Every night, before my eyes, dreams play out key events of our time. In some dreams, I relive my most cherished memories. Some dreams are dreadful—a revisitation of hellish days that I'd like to forget."

"So—you remember your dreams," said Swift. "Don't a lot of people dream vividly like that?"

"Sometimes, lad, I dream of happenings yet to be," said Chance, his expression disturbingly sincere. "I dream of lands ridden with death. I see magnificent deeds done. I'm a steward of these sights."

He lifted Swift's two books—*The Star of Atlantis* and *The Shepherd of the Stars*.

"Some of my visions, I've written, in the language revealed by your stone."

"You can't be claiming to have actually seen the future, though," said Swift.

"Where we come from, some people are born having foresight," said Cynfael. "Foresight, meaning fairly accurate moments of clarity that hint of future events. Chance is one of them." He lifted his brow. "Do you find that hard to believe?"

Of course it was hard to believe. And yet Swift couldn't help wishing that it might be true—that they knew his destiny.

"I find it hard to accept that you buy it," said Swift, studying Cynfael. "You—a scientist."

"As a scientist, I hope to one day understand the phenomenon," said Cynfael. "I've seen Chance's visions come to light many times. In fact, I'm looking at one of his visions right now."

Swift rested his gaze on Chance. "What, exactly, have you seen?"

Cynfael met Chance's eyes. "Go easy."

Chance rested his hand on Fortuna's head. "Years ago, a dream visited me—the most vibrant I've known. I saw books I'd written, a map that I'd drawn, in the hands of a lad—I saw you."

"You dreamed of me before we ever met?" asked Swift.

"Ay," said Chance. "I saw you and a young man sailing into Sterncastle Cove. I saw you tumbled onto its shores, bearing the Star of Atlantis. I've had visions of you older, too. Grown. I had no doubt you'd survive Sterncastle Cove; that my longboat would deliver you. And I've seen you do great things. I've seen—"

Cynfael lifted his hand. Chance quieted.

The revelation, despite its impossibility, brought Swift a deep sense of elation—a confidence that he could do magnificent things. For no matter what truth rested in their claims, Chance and Cynfael seemed to think he had a great legacy to live out. It made him feel like a fledged falcon—leaping off a cliff for his first flight and discovering, as he only ever had dreamed, that he really could coast airborne.

"These visions, or dreams—how common are they where you come from?" asked Swift.

"It's a rare gift," said Cynfael. "It visits but a few within each generation."

"And—where exactly do you come from?" asked Swift. "I heard you speaking in Old Norse. Fluently."

Cynfael and Chance held one another's gaze.

Finally, Cynfael broke away.

"We come from Iceland."

"I wish my destiny were certain," said Swift. "I feel meant to earn a place reading medicine with Dr. Jairo Keats. Does having foresight mean you know whether I'll actually make it?"

"I have clarity on but few of your steps," said Chance. "Your path must be your own to fashion."

Cynfael offered Chance a nod of what seemed like approval. "As much, and as little, as we understand destiny, we perceive that you're meant to be closely connected with us. You've taken the steps Chance has seen to bring us together. And he knows that your legacy shall be great."

"But how can I know what I should do next?" asked Swift. "If I do have a destiny, a great legacy—what if I make the wrong choices and mess it up?"

"You shall advance in the same way you've been moving," said Cynfael. "You found our book, our map, our Star of Atlantis. Be true to your heart, and you shall create your legacy. And from it we might restore bonds that long have been lost."

The way Cynfael was eyeing Swift—it was like he was watching over a prince on the brink of inheriting a kingdom.

"I've made plenty of mistakes," Swift said, "and I'm bound to make more."

"Our mistakes become part of our legacy," said Chance. "You just keep on. Keep pressing. Keep following your heart."

"It might've been happenstance that I came your way," said Swift. "I, who've created not a small load of trouble for you."

"Is it so foolish, though?" asked Cynfael. "Don't all great friendships seem to stem from a force higher? A mighty purpose."

Swift rested beneath their gazes as they watched him with what looked like great expectation.

Staying true to his heart—for better or worse—his course would certainly be medicine.

"Working with Dr. Keats," said Swift, "I can't think of any stronger purpose I could seek."

"A strong purpose." Cynfael drew the cloth from the bowl of fragrant water and rang it out. "Though, a trying one."

The stone slab beneath Swift's body seemed to grow colder at Cynfael's words, for his expression was grave. And for good reason. Despite any visions of destiny, Cynfael had made it clear to Swift that he'd be succeeding or failing alone.

"Trying for the Practicum is something I must do," said Swift. "Even though I'm as alone as I've feared—Caius, pulling away as he has. Ash having betrayed me."

Cynfael rested the freshly cooled cloth on Swift's forehead. "We, none of us, are alone. In striving toward medicine, though, you're right that you'll work by your own strength."

Cynfael's words conjured the feeling of being isolated in Chance's terribly heavy longboat—wholly responsible for his own survival, having no one to take over, even though he was wounded.

And yet. Swift had oared Chance's longboat. He'd taken on the desolate Celtic Sea.

And he'd found help. He'd survived. He'd helped Caius survive.

"We'll be in your corner," said Chance. "You have our confidence, and our support. Though, be warned—our support will likely feel less like aid and more like challenge."

Never, but in the company of his own brothers, had Swift known such camaraderie.

Chance and Cynfael's support, daunting as it sounded, Swift could welcome.

Despite that they clearly wouldn't carry him, it seemed just as certain that they'd never abandon him.

And their faith in him was sustenance. Through it, Swift saw in clarity what moving forward looked like.

"I've been royally knocked down," said Swift.

Cynfael rested his hand on Swift's shoulder.

"My heart is still stinging from Ash's deceit," said Swift. "And I understand how much work is ahead of me. Work I'll have to manage on a strength I don't feel that I have."

Cynfael and Chance said nothing. They just watched him, their presence seeming the best they could contribute to ease Swift's unrest.

"There always will be pain," said Swift.

Cynfael tightened his hold on Swift's shoulder. "Yes."

"Pain and rough seas," said Swift.

"There's no escaping those," said Chance.

"I might fail, I know." Swift pushed to leaning against his elbows. "Perhaps, even, failure is likely for someone who's been through what I have." He met their eyes. "But I know that this is the path I must trek."

Cynfael said, in Old Norse, "Valor is the gateway to destiny."

Swift relaxed into the sound of the saying, into the thunderous feel of Old Norse, its cadence like rain.

Chance caught Cynfael's gaze.

In Old Norse, he said, "So be it."

40

Swift, following Caius and Brooke, carried the last of their supplies to the dock, to the waiting yacht, piloted by Elias and, in his lap, Oliver.

Wind sheering the top of the water in Coracle Bay made visible a force that Swift could not see.

He watched the waves kick and roll beneath a strong northerly wind driving sea currents that would carry them back to Devonshire; wind wrapping the Earth, twisting on in the cosmos; wind summoning storms, driving mists, clearing skies, filling sails. Wind that would press him along the pathways he'd choose.

The wind's force, its constancy, rang of the connectivity to which Cynfael and Chance seemed so attuned. Those bonds, nebulous yet somehow tangible in the friendship Swift received from them—it seemed a whisper of the invisible current of destiny, the creation of his legacy—though he knew little of his destination and so few steps of the way.

How wondrously Cynfael and Chance spoke of destiny, and how closely they appeared to know Swift by what they claimed to have foreseen.

They were all at once the most profound enigmas Swift had

ever encountered, and the closest and most trusted friends he could imagine.

Why their paths had interconnected with Swift's and what destiny awaited them all—these questions, he was anxious to explore.

And what other bonds might Swift forge, connecting him yet more strongly to his legacy? What might tie him to the ancients who'd dreamed up the lore of the Star of Atlantis, who'd shaped the meaning of the Celtic star, of its seven profound points?

As much of a sense of home Cynfael and Chance lent, their friendship struck more as a gateway than the end of a journey.

Caius stood beside Swift on the bow as Elias and Oliver coasted the yacht over the great waves.

The rise and slip of the boat was an exhilarating rush, despite the terrible power it kept—power Swift could feel in the marrow of his bones, in the cadence of his dashing heart.

This cold wind striking, Swift discovered he could endure. He welcomed the sense of drive in it, and all the more because Caius was resting his warm hand on Swift's shoulder.

On this day, all Swift knew was that strong forces, strong purposes, bound him to strive for a legacy that could possibly be his—the privilege of reading medicine beneath Dr. Jairo Keats.

And where else might these winds carry him?

THE END

ALSO BY TRICIA D. WAGNER

WHAT MANNER OF LEGENDS MIGHT DARKNESS CONCEAL?

"SUN CHILD OF THE MOOR IS A WELL-WRITTEN, BEAUTIFULLY POETIC, FANTASTICAL TALE, EXPERTLY BLENDING MAGIC WITH REALITY. SYLPHIC FOLKLORE IS UNIQUE TO THIS BOOK AND HOLDS THE POWER OF BELIEVABILITY THANKS TO WAGNER'S MASTERFUL WRITING. THE FAMILIAL INTERACTIONS ARE REMINISCENT OF A WRINKLE IN TIME, MAKING IT A DELIGHTFULLY IMMERSIVE TALE OF LOVE AND PERSONAL GROWTH, WELL SUITED TO YOUNG AND ADULT READERS WHO ENJOY EXPLORING THE WORLD'S UNLIMITED POSSIBILITIES THROUGH A MAGICAL LENS."
- **MARY R. LANNI, MLIS,** *REEDSY DISCOVERY*

"SUN CHILD OF THE MOOR, WITH ITS LIVELY, ENGAGING ACTION WILL ENCOURAGE DISCUSSION AND DEBATE IN READER CIRCLES ABOUT THE CONSEQUENCES OF SPECIAL ABILITIES AND THE CONTRAST BETWEEN IMAGINATION AND REALITY, MAKING THIS BOOK A TOP RECOMMENDATION ABOVE MANY OTHER ACTION-PACKED FANTASIES."
- **D. DONOVAN, SENIOR REVIEWER,** *MIDWEST BOOK REVIEW*

READ THE STAR OF ATLANTIS SERIES!

THE STRIDER AND THE REGULUS, THE STAR OF ATLANTIS & THE SHEPHERD OF THE STARS

A STARRY-EYED BOY.
A CRYPTIC MAP. A MYTHICAL TREASURE.
WHAT PERILS AWAIT IN THE CHASING OF DREAMS?

"WAGNER HAS A BEAUTIFUL AND POETIC WRITING STYLE WHICH SERVES TO ENHANCE THE DESCRIPTIVE DETAIL SHE PROVIDES TO HER NOVELS. THIS GIVES HER BOOKS A WHIMSICAL AND OTHERWORLDLY QUALITY THAT SUPPORTS THE FANTASTICAL ELEMENTS WITHIN THEM. READERS WHO APPRECIATE THOUGHTFUL NARRATIVES THAT FOCUS ON THE HUMAN CONDITION WITHIN THE CONTEXT OF CHARMING AND MEMORABLE STORIES WILL QUICKLY FALL FOR THIS SERIES AND ITS IMMERSIVE QUALITY. THE MEDICAL AND SCIENTIFIC ELEMENTS FOUND WITHIN THIS BOOK HELP READERS PUZZLE OUT THE QUESTION OF WHAT IS TRUE IN SWIFT'S WORLD ALONGSIDE THE LEGEND AND LORE. THIS IS A SATISFYING SERIES THAT WILL SPEAK TO YOUNG ADULT READERS AND ADULTS ALIKE."
- MARY R. LANNI, MLIS, *REEDSY DISCOVERY*

"AS SWIFT LIVES UP TO HIS NAME AND HIS FAMILY LEGACY, YOUNG ADULTS RECEIVE A FAST-PACED FANTASY THAT WILL APPEAL NOT JUST ON THE ADVENTURE OR FANTASY LEVELS, BUT IN MATTERS OF THE HEART AS THE YOUNG STRUGGLE FOR INDEPENDENCE AND ACTION IN THE FACE OF PARENTAL RESTRICTIONS. TRICIA D. WAGNER'S ATTENTION TO PAIRING PSYCHOLOGICAL STRUGGLE WITH THE ADVENTURE OF FINDING A PROMISED TREASURE CREATES A STORY THAT PULLS ON THE EMOTIONS OF YOUNG READERS AS IT SATISFIES THEIR DESIRE FOR ACTION AND ADVENTURE."
- D. DONOVAN, SENIOR REVIEWER, *MIDWEST BOOK REVIEW*

FREE EBOOK

Night Swiftly Falling
by Tricia D. Wagner

Eight-year-old Swift is lost in dreams of sea
legends and pirate adventures, until an
encounter with the deadly power of the
ocean shocks him into reality.
Swift struggles to hang onto his childhood
fantasies, but his new understanding of the
fragile nature of life and friendships
threatens to swamp his hope.
Under the guidance of his older brother,
Caius, Swift must learn to brave the challenging waves of change without losing
himself to their destruction.

To get your FREE eBook, visit -
Night Swiftly Falling

ABOUT THE AUTHOR

Tricia D. Wagner is an award-winning novelist, poet, and short story writer. She grew up in Amarillo, Texas, chasing storms, riding stallions, sojourning through painted canyons, disappearing into floating mesas under starry skies.

She now lives in Rockford, Illinois (though the truth is, she's a citizen of a dozen fictional countries). Tricia works in research and lives day to day wonderstruck but luckily can feel her way about this terrifying, beautiful Earth through writing.

Tricia has pieces published in the *Write City Magazine*, *Chicago Newa*, *Word of Art 3D*, *Literary Yard*, and *Midwest Review*.

To learn more about Tricia, sign up for her readers' club, and hear about upcoming releases, visit:

www.TriciaWagner.com

AUTHOR'S NOTE

I love connecting with readers and writers. If you're interested in stories, then you're a kindred spirit to me, and I have lots more in store for you. To quote another kindred spirit in writing, Jedi Master Stephen King:

"Writing is magic, as much as the water of life as any other art. The water is free. So drink. Drink and be filled up."

If you're interested not only in stories, but in story creation, visit my website and sign up to receive a FREE **'Story Kickoff Character Worksheet.'**

I designed this tool for that first moment of getting our feet wet at the brink of a story.

To get your free worksheet, visit:
www.TriciaWagner.com